S0-BJV-516

NIGHT OF THE FURIES

◆ ◆

ALSO BY DAVID ANGSTEN

DARK GOLD

NIGHT OF THE FURIES

◆ ◆

DAVID ANGSTEN

THOMAS DUNNE BOOKS
ST. MARTIN'S PRESS NEW YORK

This is a work of fiction. All of the characters, organizations, and events portrayed in this novel are either products of the author's imagination or are used fictitiously.

THOMAS DUNNE BOOKS.
An imprint of St. Martin's Press.

www.thomasdunnebooks.com
www.stmartins.com

Book design by Jonathan Bennett

Library of Congress Cataloging-in-Publication Data

Angsten, David.
Night of the furies / David Angsten.—1st ed.
p. cm.
ISBN-13: 978-0-312-37370-2 (alk. paper)
ISBN-10: 0-312-37370-8 (alk. paper)
1. Erinyes (Greek mythology)—Fiction. 2. Americans—Mexico—Fiction. 3. Cults—Greece—Fiction. I. Title.
PS3601.N5545N54 2008
813'.6—dc22 2008024876

First Edition: October 2008

10 9 8 7 6 5 4 3 2 1

To my true love, Joanna—
last of the Eumenides

AUTHOR'S NOTE AND ACKNOWLEDGMENTS

IN THE eleventh book of Homer's *Odyssey,* the wandering hero Odysseus sets sail on a voyage to the Underworld, the ghostly land of the dead. He travels into a realm of perpetual fog and darkness to seek counsel from the spirit of Tiresias, the famous sightless prophet of Thebes, whose truth-telling wisdom will help guide Odysseus home.

This dark voyage of Homer's hero is known as the *Nekyia,* the "night-sea journey." The Swiss psychologist Carl Jung saw the *Nekyia* symbolically as a journey into the unconscious—the source of the creative and instinctual forces of life.

The unlikely hero of my novel *Dark Gold* made a voyage along the Mexican coast that was very much like a *Nekyia.* Miraculously, Jack survived, and—like the lost Odysseus—he's heading off again on yet another fateful voyage. If you'd like to sail along with him, just continue tacking through these breaking waves of text, and you'll soon find yourself on the wine-dark Aegran in pursuit of the elusive Aphrodite.

A warning from the author—I've been on this trip before. It's not for the faint of heart. The ocean's edge is unexplored, the divine winds must be trusted, and it's always an uncertainty whether you'll make it back with the goods.

Fortunately, we sail with an experienced and highly competent crew. My astute editor, Peter Wolverton, is a helmsman keen on keeping the ship from sailing too close to the wind. Up in the swaying crow's nest, his agile assistant, Elizabeth Byrne, gives fair shout of distant shores and fast-approaching ships. Keeping us wittily entertained on deck is my literary management team at AEI: the Renaissance Man and gumbo chef, Ken Atchity, a wonderfully wise companion and guide; his vivacious and talented partner, Chi-Li Wong, who prepares stupendous feasts in the galley; and the ship's armorer, Zen master Michael Kuciak, solemnly keeping the afternoon watch.

Who's the pretty lass up in the rigging? It's the sharp-eyed reader, Jennifer Minar, mending a tear in a topsail. Abaft are buff sailor boys Larry Tracy and Ted Dietlin, busily swabbing the deck. Screenwriter Debrah Neal is plugging holes in the hull, while novelist Roy Freirich squints up through the growing fog to chart a course by the stars.

Hauled up from the oars below, the beautiful galley slave Joanna, captured daughter of a goddess of the wind, cups her hand to the captain's ear and whispers hints of changes.

Bon voyage, dear reader. Your vessel is made of paper, but her keel is sound and swift. You will not be required to go aloft, and you won't be crammed into a bunk down in steerage; you will be ensconced in your own well-appointed stateroom, with a bright brass lamp, a goose-down bed, and a splendid view of the sea.

. . . At least until we run aground on the cloud-wrapped shores of Hades.

The darkness is well suited to devotion.

—*Euripides,* THE BACCHAE

I

EROS

◆ ◆

1

OUR DESCENT down the cliffs began around midnight. Light from the hidden moon stretched across the plain below and reached the Gulf of Corinth where it set the sea aglow. The view had been expansive and exhilarating in daylight; now it seemed treacherous and eerie. The dark wall of the mountain loomed ominously above us and dropped off steeply into shadows deep below.

We peered down warily into the abyss.

"Why in the hell are we doing this?" I said.

The paralyzing view made Phoebe philosophical. "We don't always know why we do what we do."

My genius of a brother sounded positively cheerful. "I think it's the Fates that have brought us here," he said. "We have no choice in the matter."

He started down the precarious path, hugging the steep wall of stone. For a moment, Phoebe and I watched him. "Sometimes I think Dan really believes that stuff," I said.

"He can believe it or not," Phoebe said. "The truth is we're free to do as we like."

She bravely followed him down the precipice.

I called after her: "Somebody said your worse troubles begin when you're free to do as you like!"

The two of them were fading into the darkness below. I don't know why, but I followed them.

IF IT really was the Fates that had brought us to this mountain, it was Dan who had done all the planning. He'd decided his experiment at Delphi should begin with a covert midnight skinny dip, what his girlfriend Phoebe suggestively described as our "nocturnal lustration." This was to be a ritual bath in the sacred Castalian Spring, the same spring used for purification by the Delphic Oracles of antiquity.

The spring was hidden beneath towering cliffs on the slope of Mount Parnassus. The cliffs formed the dramatic backdrop to the Sanctuary of Apollo, the cluster of ancient ruins where the Oracle had practiced her mysterious art for a thousand years. Breathing fumes that arose from a crevice in the earth, the priestess, known as the Pythia, would fall into a trance of possession and give voice to the transcendent thoughts of Apollo, the all-knowing god of the sun.

Today, bathing in the spring is forbidden, and the Temple of Apollo where the Oracle divined has also been deemed off limits. Dan therefore determined that our only chance to perform a proper augury was to sneak into the sanctuary late at night when we'd have the spring and the temple to ourselves. And so we had taken to the heights of Mount Parnassus, hiking all day up the sunny slopes, climbing as far as the Cave of Pan before returning at sundown to the lofty cliffs, where we awaited the cover of darkness.

Dan now demanded we descend without our flashlights, even

though we carried them in our bags. We'd used them in the cave we explored that afternoon. Its enormous cavern had been a favorite site for the worship of Dionysus, Apollo's half brother, the Greek god of intoxication and sexual revelry. Stalagmite pillars rose from its floor, looking like monstrous phalli. Dan had explained that once a year on a winter's night, the young women of ancient Delphi would make this same long trek up the mountain in the company of a single male—a youth dressed as Dionysus. In chilly mountain air, carrying torches, beating drums, playing flutes, and singing wildly, the women followed the youth up the cliffs all the way to the infamous cave. There they were said to be possessed by the god and indulged in an orgiastic frenzy.

As we made our way down the perilous cliff, this story replayed in my imagination. I began to speculate about our bath.

Phoebe Auerbach was a liberated Dutch girl who wouldn't be constrained by the usual inhibitions. Born in conservative Delft, she had been raised in freewheeling Amsterdam, and endlessly educated in America and Europe. She was currently on break from an excavation at a goddess site in Crete. In a postcard he had sent me while visiting the island, Dan had revealed that he met the young archeologist on what he called a naturist beach. He noted that despite their nudity, her behavior had been oddly formal. When Dan casually introduced himself, Phoebe offered him her hand—not for him to shake, he said, but, like a prince, to kiss.

The twisty route down the slope of the cliff demanded my constant attention, but still I couldn't seem to stop myself from envisioning Phoebe at the spring.

We're free to do as we like . . .

She was twenty-four years old, the same age as me, and four years younger than Dan. She was slim and sprightly, with an athletic figure, and boyish blond hair even shorter than my own. Her large eyes were an icy blue, the tops of her cheeks were freckled, and her mouth had a beguiling little curl at the corners as if always on the brink of a grin. Her laugh, which was loud, came easily and often, and made her seem even younger than she looked. She had a slight overbite that plumped her upper lip, and she spoke with a noticeable slurring of her r's—they sounded more like w's—an appealing wrinkle of accent in her otherwise "pewfect" English.

In his postcard, Dan had described her as "brilliant." While this may well have been true, my impression of her so far brought other words to mind: flighty, flirtatious, beguiling, brash. She had a lightning mind that kept us always on alert, and a tongue she couldn't seem to keep in check.

Phoebe followed Dan down the zigzagging path; I followed closely behind her. When she turned and caught me staring at her "pewfect" derrière, I tripped and nearly tumbled on top of her.

"Whoa!" she cried. She laughed and held me steady.

Dan called up from below. "You okay?"

"Fine!" Phoebe shouted.

Then she turned to me. "Jack's just having trouble keeping his eyes on the path."

"Sorry," I said.

Her face looked luminous in the starlight. "Well, don't be too sorry."

Dan was climbing back up to us. Phoebe went down to meet him. "Your brother and I were just dancing," she said.

"Which of you stumbled? Jack?"

I walked down to join them. "Your girlfriend saved my life."

He peered at me inquisitively.

"*What?*" I said.

Phoebe giggled.

"You feeling distracted? Unusual thoughts intruding? Images? Voices?"

I stole a glance at Phoebe. "Nothing unusual. Why?"

"We're getting close to the sanctuary," he said. He peered down the steep rock wall. "Hiking down this cliff at night—like shaving with a razor in the dark. It focuses your awareness. Puts you in the proper state of mind."

"You mean, like, terrified?"

"No," he said. "Receptive. By holding your attention, it frees the unconscious. Leaves you more . . . susceptible."

Phoebe glanced at me. "Susceptible to what?"

Dan squinted at the night sky. "Can't say to what exactly. We'll have to wait and see."

"Susceptible to falling," I said.

Phoebe laughed. She stretched up on her toes and gave Dan a kiss, watching me from the corner of her eye. "I'm not sure that Jack's in the proper state of mind."

We cautiously resumed our descent. "You're the Oracle," I said. "Dan's the desperate supplicant. I'm nothing more than an observer—my state of mind is irrelevant."

"Don't be so sure about that," Dan said. "Remember your quantum physics. The problem of Schrödinger's cat. There are no observers, only participants. The presence of your consciousness will influence the event."

Phoebe glanced over her shoulder at me. "I think it's already having an influence."

"Careful," I said. "You're a priestess, remember?"

She laughed. "And you are—what? Schrödinger's cat?"

"Jack has a vital role to play: your interlocutor. The Recorder of the Oracle."

I snorted. "The priestess needs a priest?"

"*High* priest." Phoebe giggled. She was growing giddy with exhaustion.

Dan was undeterred. He had spent the last two years studying ancient Greek religion and had become completely obsessed with the sacred rites and myths. "This path we're walking on is called the *Kakí Skála*—the Evil Stairway. Know why?"

"Because fools like us were forced to climb down it in the dark?"

"No," he said. "Because those guilty of sacrilege were thrown off it to their deaths."

Phoebe and I looked at each other. I don't know why, but we laughed.

◆ ◆

THE CASTALIAN Spring lay at the bottom of a lush ravine under steep cliffs that blocked out the moonlight. Just as Dan had predicted, the place was completely deserted. He said there was only one nightwatchman who guarded the holy sites, and he usually stayed in the gatehouse down the road, sipping his bottle of retsina. The sacred spring was fairly secluded; Dan was more worried about getting caught at the far more visible temple. Nevertheless, he warned, we'd need to stay alert, or we'd end up making our appeal to Apollo from the confines of the Delphi jail.

We climbed over a site fence and walked up the path to a rise of stone steps that led to a rock-hewn pool. It lay at the base of the cliff's rock wall, which was carved with several shadowy, hollowed-out niches. The spring, we discovered, was barely a trickle of water. The stone pool was not more than a couple feet deep, definitely not large enough for the group dip I'd imagined.

Dan removed his backpack. "It's running low," he said. "They siphon off the water for the town."

Modern Delphi lay a mile down the road and was geared entirely to the tourists. Even though we were staying in a hotel there ourselves, I found this vulgar theft of theirs insulting. "Talk about a sacrilege!"

The three of us stared at the cold, black water. It made a trickling sound.

Dan informed Phoebe that washing her hair was as far as she needed to go.

I felt simultaneously relieved and disappointed.

"Are you sure that's enough?" she asked.

"It's more than adequate," he said. "Only people who had killed someone were required to take a full bath."

He looked at me as he said this. The implication was clear.

Two years earlier, on a boat off the Mexican coast, I had encountered a deadly sea creature and a couple of drug-running pirates. A number of violent deaths had occurred. Although I thought of my role in the matter as one of self-defense, several people had been wasted, some of them my friends, and all of them largely on account of me.

From the way Phoebe was avoiding my gaze, it was clear she'd been told the story.

Dan unzipped his backpack. "I think I've got a swimsuit," he said, "if you don't want to go in naked." He pulled out a pair of sun-bleached surfer trunks.

I gave him a dirty look.

So this was how it was going to be. They were going to wash their hands of the matter and watch while I took a bath. I suddenly began to wonder if Dan's promise of a skinny dip had been nothing more than a crass enticement to lure me into his plan. I suspected even Phoebe had been in on it.

"How do you know *she* hasn't killed anyone?"

"*Jack!*" She placed the back of her hands on her hips in the classic pose of outrage.

"I know because I already asked," Dan said.

Judging from the glare Phoebe aimed at him, it appeared that he actually had. She huffily glanced back and forth between us. "People are nicer where I come from!"

"So you're not going in," I said to Dan accusingly.

"No," he said. "But with her help, I'm going to shave my head."

"You're *what*?" Phoebe had apparently not been let in on this little part of the program.

"It's important to make a sacrifice," he said. "The Greeks usually slaughtered a goat. Others left votive offerings in those niches in the wall. My offering is my hair." As we watched him produce various items from his pack—scissors, towel, shaving cream, razor—it became clear he meant to do exactly what he said.

I didn't get the connection. "Goat? Hair?"

"A possession of personal value. I don't care about goats, but I very much like my hair."

"I like it, too," Phoebe said wistfully.

He'd been wearing it down to his shoulders for as long as I could remember. "I don't understand," I said.

"*Do ut des*—'I give that you may give.'" He was setting up his barber's chair, a collapsible aluminum tripod stool with a triangular nylon seat.

I didn't want to get into which "you" he was referring to—Phoebe? Apollo? The cosmos? My brother liked to call himself a "spiritual atheist." He didn't believe in God or the supernatural, but he did believe in a version of what the Greeks had called the *Logos,* the fundamental, transcendent "mind" behind nature. Contact with this extradimensional intelligence could be obtained in various ways—drumming, chanting, praying, fasting, meditation, ritual, sexual abstinence, sexual indulgence, extreme physical ordeals—but none of these methods of inducing ecstatic trance was as ancient and effective as the use of psychoactive plants. Mushrooms, peyote, *ayahuasca,* DMT. Dan was a firm believer in the spiritual utility of hallucinogens. It was in fact the subject of his doctoral dissertation.

Phoebe was having trouble picturing her boyfriend as a baldy. "So it's kind of like bartering, then—your hair is some sort of payment for prophecy?"

"It's not a negotiation, Phoebe. It's an encounter with the divine." He continued rummaging through his backpack. "Socrates said true prophecy required the complete loss of human control, the total abandonment of the individual self to a higher, transcendent power."

Maybe the look of the black water was giving her cold feet. "I don't know," she said. "This is all beginning to feel a little crazy."

"It *is* a little crazy," he said. "That's the essence of ancient Mystery religion. It goes beyond understanding. Beyond the rational mind. The first Oracles were simple peasant girls from Delphi, virgins recruited by the priests. Divination doesn't require intellectual understanding. The less you think about it, the better off you'll be."

"How do I not think about it?" she asked.

"Keep it simple and follow the protocol: We cleanse ourselves in the spring. We make the sacrifice. Then we go to the Temple of Apollo and seek the advice of the god."

"Leave your brains behind?" I said.

"Leave your skepticism. Free yourself from doubt. Enter the temple with a pure heart. The process only works if you approach it with sincerity." He glanced up from his unpacking. "Suspend your disbelief, Jack. Think that might be possible?"

"You've given me plenty of practice," I said.

"Good," he said, and once again held up the swimsuit. "Want this?"

I stood tall. "Absolutely not. I'm going in with complete sincerity."

THINGS WERE not working out the way I had imagined, a fact that was true of my life to that point. I had dropped out of graduate school after only one semester, and ended up teaching English to immigrants for nearly a year and a half. Then I took off to travel the world again, to pick up on the journey that had been curtailed in Mexico, only this time I was going it alone.

It was isolation and seclusion I sought, with time to read and reflect, so the first few months were spent in Tahiti, in a rented shack on the island of Moorea. When the boundaries of the tiny island began to feel constraining, I moved on to bigger islands—Fiji, New Zealand, the continent of Australia. Finally, having depleted my cash, I moved to Tokyo, where I taught English to Japanese businessmen for a six-month stretch, a job I had set up before I left the States. When that was through I traveled again, first to Thailand, then to India, then to Istanbul, and finally into Europe.

I had turned into a version of the wandering soul my brother used to be. Now he was firmly ensconced in the academic world, working on his doctoral dissertation, and I was leading the life of the vagabond, roaming the world on my own.

I was staying at a cheap little *pensione* in Rome and working as a freelance tour guide, when out of the blue I got a call from Dan. Our mother back in Hinsdale had given him my number, and when he asked me if I'd like to come and visit him in Athens, I suspected it was she who put him up to it. She who had once been so worried about Dan was now more concerned about me. It was I, after all, who had lost my friends, and who seemed to have lost my way.

PHOEBE WAS behind me, cutting off Dan's long blond locks and collecting them into a pile. I tried not to think of her watching me. She hadn't said a word when I'd taken off my clothes. Perhaps a guy's nudity was nothing unusual for a "naturist" like herself. It had been slightly humiliating to undress in front of them while they remained fully clothed, but the boldness of the act seemed to feed on itself; it infused me with defiant vigor.

All that disappeared as I stepped out into the water. The mountain spring was freezing—fed no doubt by melting snows high up on Parnassus. It sucked the breath right out of me. My bare feet and ankles turned immediately to ice. My penis shriveled to nothing. I shuddered. In the hot sun, this spring would be cool and refreshing; now it was excruciating torture.

I carefully advanced across the slippery stone that formed the spring's shallow basin. My arms were held straight out from my sides, and my head was bent to watch what my feet were doing, like the old Greek we had watched dancing alone in an empty *taverna* in Athens.

That dance was sincere, I thought. The essence of sincerity.

Leave your skepticism . . . Suspend your disbelief.

When I reached the deepest part of the spring—it leveled off at my knees—I bit the bullet and slowly lowered my body into the water.

The pain was greater than I thought I could bear. It commanded my entire attention. I lay back slowly until my ears went underwater. My mind seemed to be screaming. My body felt on fire.

I was convinced I would pass out.

Yet something was happening behind the pain: a whispered voice emerging. My voice. Reciting a rhyme. Words amid the screaming:

Let this wash away my sins,
Purify my heart.
Give my life a new beginning,
Show me where to start.

I don't know where this ditty came from. The longing of my soul? The inspiration of Apollo? When the words went away, there was nothing but the cold. I was floating on my back in the water. The hollow niches in the wall above me looked like howling mouths. My arms and legs were spread out stiff, my breath was barely moving. I lay there staring through the crack of the gorge to the swath of stars in the sky. The cold and the stars were a single thing, there was no break between them. They were all a part of the frozen scream I seemed to be locked inside of.

Everything had suddenly stopped.

At that moment, fused with the cold, something jolted me.

A pair of hands grabbed my wrists. Others grabbed my ankles. Fingers clenched around my neck and yanked me under—

Terrified, I jerked upright, spurting a mouthful of water. For a moment I couldn't see.

Choking, dizzy, I quickly scanned around me. There was no one else in the spring.

Dan and Phoebe were still on the rocks, she still shearing his hair.

"You all right?" Phoebe asked. Her voice sounded far away—water in my ears. The two of them were staring.

I stood cautiously, searching the water around me. My heart was still banging in my chest. "There was someone . . . something in the water," I said. My head was spinning.

Dan brushed aside Phoebe's hands and rose up from his stool. "Someone?" he asked.

I stood naked in the middle of the spring, dripping wet, shivering, my hands clasped over my privates. "Yeah . . . they . . . they grabbed me."

Dan's eyes scanned the water.

Phoebe laughed. "Naiads," she said.

Dan moved closer, staring at the spring.

I asked him, "What are Naiads?"

He looked at me as I rubbed my wrists. "Water nymphs," he said.

"What, they live in the spring?"

Again Phoebe laughed. "They live in your imagination!"

I looked at my wrists. There weren't any marks. "Scared the hell out of me," I said. I realized I was angry. My trembling body felt strangely warm.

Dan searched my eyes. He didn't seem to like what he saw.

"You'd better come out of the water," he said.

2

EVEN AFTER I had dried off and climbed back into my clothes, the chill I had felt stayed with me. So did the feeling of that inexplicable grip. As I prepared to shave off the remainder of Dan's hair, I noticed that my hands were still trembling.

"How can they be in my imagination if I'd never even heard of them before?"

"I don't know," Dan said. He was sitting on his tripod, immobile as the Buddha.

I drew the razor across his lathered scalp, leaving a track of skin. "I know it's ridiculous," I said. "But it really felt like something grabbed me."

Dan didn't say anything. Just sat there like a rock.

He was watching Phoebe as she stepped up to the water. The Pythia had decided it was time for her "lustration."

She had borrowed Dan's towel, and she placed it, folded, under her knees as she knelt at the edge of the spring. She was wearing khaki shorts and a sleeveless denim shirt, but had taken off her hiking boots and set them on the rocks, and she tucked her bare feet underneath her. Then she removed the watch from her wrist and, twisting slightly in her kneeling position, strapped it to a belt loop at her hip.

As she did this, she glanced at us. A perfectly innocent glance, I suppose, but it struck me as utterly seductive.

I cleared my throat. "You say these Naiads are the offspring of a god. That makes them some kind of spirits, right? Just another loony Greek myth."

"A very old myth," Dan said. "Much older than the Greeks. Springs have always had their resident divinities."

This was certainly understandable, I thought. Cold, thirst-quenching, life-giving water sprouting like a miracle from the dry, rocky earth—what god-fearing goatherd wouldn't see that as divine?

I cut another track down Dan's soapy scalp. Somewhere an owl softly hooted.

With her arms propped at the water's edge, Phoebe lowered her face toward the surface of the spring. She took a short drink, noisily sucking the water. Then she raised her dripping face and for a long moment stared unblinking at the pond.

I stopped what I was doing. Dan remained silent. Had she seen something there, hidden in the spring, or was she caught by her own reflection? We watched her and waited, and neither of us spoke. There was something magical about her, kneeling by this primeval pool in the dark. Her pale arms and face, ghostly in the starlight, reflected on the undulating mirror of the pond. An aura of stillness surrounded her. Along with the unceasing trickle of the spring, we could hear the sporadic flutter of wings echo off the rocky walls above us. The place was suffused with an atmosphere of timelessness, with Phoebe the beating heart of it, as if she were some living token of its past.

At last she cupped her hands and splashed water into her hair. She did this until it was sopping wet. Then she paused again, staring at the water. Her snowy mop, now slicked to her scalp, tapered to a forelock that dripped into the pond. She remained in that position for another long moment, staring again into the water.

Perhaps she too was struggling to suspend her disbelief. Dan had not told me what her superstitions were, or even if she had any. Until now I had assumed she was another godless European. She had been dismissive of my little episode with the "Naiads" and seemed free of any piousness or reverence. In the few days I had known her, the only thing she showed any serious interest in were the physical remains of the distant past: temples, statues, ruins. She was a trained archeologist, after all; she knew as well as anyone the transience of beliefs.

As I continued denuding Dan's head, another rhyme came to me unbidden. This time I spoke it out loud:

> *Abode of gods, whose shrines no longer burn.*
> *Even gods must yield—religions take their turn.*

I remembered this from a book I had found in Dan's Athens apartment. "Who did that come from?" I asked him.

"Byron," he said. "Funny you should bring him up."

"Why?"

"Because he took the plunge in this very same spring. Poets have been coming here at least since Roman times. They believe the waters inspire the Muse."

"Really," I said. "I think I'm beginning to believe it my—"

Something suddenly flew out of the darkness, winging past us. Instinctively, we ducked, and I felt a flutter of air at my ear.

As quick as it came it was gone.

"What the hell was that?"

Dan didn't answer. The two of us scanned the treetops, then searched the ominous cliffs. I thought of the owl heard earlier, but this had been fast and furious. Even Dan had been startled.

Although the moon was hidden by the high canyon walls, its cold light shone on the upper cliffs, and between them the sky was awash with stars. Against this pale backdrop, I began to pick out flitting black flecks, like broken bits of black sky whirling through the air.

There must have been a hundred of them.

"Bats," Dan said at last.

"Yeah," I said. "A whole swarm of them."

"I wonder what it means," Dan said.

Everything had to have a meaning with him. "It means you're going batty," I said. My neck hurt from staring at the sky for so long. I looked down at the razor I was holding in my hand. A three-bladed disposable that Dan had kept too long. In the mix of foam and hair that had collected on the blades, I noticed a swirl of something darker.

Blood.

"Shit. I think I cut your scalp."

It was a small cut, fortunately, on a bony bump at the back of his head, but still it bled like crazy. I pressed my palm against it.

Dan had been prepared for this inevitability. While continuing to stare stonily at the pond, he slipped two fingers into his shirt pocket and pulled out a Band-Aid for me.

I carefully applied it to the cut. When I finished, I picked up the razor again and glanced out toward the pond.

Phoebe had vanished.

"What happened?"

I glanced around us. The pines stood silent. The cliffs lay bare. There was no sign of her anywhere in the darkness of the ravine. I stepped away from Dan and moved closer to the spring. Her shorts and denim shirt lay piled beside her boots at the water's edge. Moving closer, I glimpsed the milky satin of her panties in the pile.

I stopped. The black water in the pool was undulating.

Behind me, Dan remained seated, watching silently.

I stared into the water and began to discern her body under the surface. She was lying on her back, still as stone. Her eyes were open.

"Phoebe!"

I was about to jump into the spring when her face emerged from the water. She took in a deep breath, filling her lungs. Her eyes regained focus, and when she saw me standing there, she sat up with a splash.

"Are you all right?" I asked.

She nodded rapidly, but didn't speak. She seemed both calm and excited. Her hair was dripping into her face, and water gleamed on her skin. I noticed the pretty peaks of her breasts were erect with jutting nipples. When she saw how embarrassed seeing her made me, she crossed her arms demurely.

I glanced back at Dan. He seemed to be patiently waiting for me to finish his ridiculous haircut.

"You must be freezing," I said to Phoebe.

Again she nodded, yes. I was unused to her silence. It seemed the appalling cold of the spring had taken away her tongue.

I picked the towel up off the rocks and held it out to her. She didn't reach to take it, and I realized, after an awkward moment, she was waiting for me to leave.

I set the towel beside the pond and headed back to Dan.

His eyes were on me as I approached. I tried to avoid his gaze. "That girl is as crazy as you are," I said.

"Crazier," he replied. While I had been staring at flying bats and tending his bleeding cut, he must have been watching his girl undress and enter the frigid water.

I picked up the razorblade and resumed my task.

"Be careful," he warned as I set to work on the second half of his head.

Phoebe was climbing out of the water, lifting the towel to her face.

"No problem," I assured him, though my hands were beginning to shake.

She turned her naked backside to us and dried herself in front. The momentary glimpse I took was branded on my brain.

Dan had not said a word.

I focused again on the shaving. *Nice and easy,* I told myself, dragging the razor across his scalp. *Slow and steady. Breathe.*

From the corner of my eye I saw Phoebe bend to towel her luscious legs. Even the Buddha beneath my blade appeared to grow more tense. Again I stole a glance.

She will never leave my mind, I thought. *Never leave my mind.*

"Jack?" My brother was losing patience.

"Right," I said. I went back to the shaving and did not peek again.

PHOEBE WALKED up, fully dressed, drying her hair with the towel. When she laid eyes on Dan's shaved head, her expression seemed torn between disgust and disbelief. "You look like a boiled egg," she said.

I took it as an insult to my delicate work, having carefully removed every whisker. "I thought people were *nicer* where you come from."

Dan rose up, palming his naked scalp. "Are we feeling purified, Phoebe?"

"I don't know how I feel," she said, hugging herself. Her toweled hair stuck out in all directions, like she'd just pulled her finger out of a socket.

I held up my plastic razor. "You think maybe going bald would help?"

She no longer seemed in the mood for a laugh. Instead, she asked Dan a question. "Why do they call it the Castalian Spring?"

Dan was gathering up his shorn blond locks. "It's named after the nymph, Castalia," he said. "The story goes that when Apollo pursued her, she dove into the spring and disappeared."

Phoebe stared sadly at the water. "It's like the story of Daphne, then."

"Very similar," Dan said, heading around the pond.

"Another nymph?" I asked.

"Apollo's true love," Phoebe said.

We watched Dan place his offering of hair into one of the hollowed-out niches.

"He have any better luck with her?" I asked.

"No," Phoebe said. "Daphne ran away, too, and—"

Dan turned from the limestone wall with a look of alarm on his face.

"What is it?" I asked.

His index finger went to his lips. The two of us stared at him in silence. He was listening for something.

Bats fluttered overhead. The spring continued its gurgling. For the first time I noticed, back in the trees, the pulsing drone of cicadas.

Then we heard a man's loud voice. Something shouted in Greek. It seemed to have come from the path to the road.

Dan came splashing around the rim of the pond. "*Hurry!*" he whispered.

We quickly gathered our belongings. Dan stuffed his barber tools back into his pack and grabbed his tripod stool. We climbed over the site fence and ran off to hide among the pines.

Again we heard the man's voice, shouting a word or a name. As we settled into a hiding place amid thick brush and boulders, we heard the cry of another voice. It sounded even closer and distressingly like a scream.

Phoebe looked to Dan and me. The scream had come from a woman.

We waited.

Within seconds, we heard footsteps racing up the path. I inched up to peek over the boulders and find a view through the trees. The steps grew closer, and suddenly a dark-haired woman appeared, racing up the ravine.

The three of us rose up furtively to see her fleeing past. She was fleshy and ungraceful, and wore a simple summer dress that seemed to flow behind her. Indeed, it appeared that the dress was torn—one of her shoulder straps had ripped, and she clutched the drooping top to her chest as she hurried along the path. She came to a stop at the site fence and turned to glance behind her.

Her skin was a morbid white, but her face was flush with fear, her mouth and eyes stretched open.

Phoebe glanced anxiously at Dan and me.

Now we heard the man's footsteps pounding up the path. Lumbering far more slowly. We ducked the moment he appeared. He was older than the woman, grossly overweight, and was sweating and breathing heavily. He held a liquor bottle in his hand. He wore a cap, and the kind of uniform I had seen on park officials. Without Dan even saying so, I knew this was the nightwatchman he had earlier warned us about.

When he saw that the woman had stopped at the fence, he paused to catch his breath. "Kassandra!" he growled angrily. He pulled off his cap and wiped his brow, cursing in exasperated Greek. Then he started after her again.

The woman kicked off her sandals and began to scuttle over the fence. The fat man grabbed the hem of her dress as she dropped to the other side. The dress ripped and the woman shrieked.

Phoebe stood up. Dan grabbed her arm. She shot him an angry look.

"Wait!" he whispered.

The woman ran up the steps to the spring, her torn dress trailing behind her. The guard clambered awkwardly over the fence and tumbled to the ground. His bottle shattered on a rock. He cursed loudly and roughly in Greek as he picked himself up and went after her, leaving behind his upturned cap.

The two of them disappeared from view.

Phoebe was still standing. She jerked her arm from Dan. *"We've got to do something!"* she whispered.

Again the woman screamed. It echoed through the canyon. Then the guard hollered and we heard a splash.

Phoebe started toward them. Dan held firm to her arm. She looked at him as if he were crazy.

"Phoebe—wait!"

For what? I thought.

I charged forward, moving out from the trees.

"Jack!"

I ignored him and continued on, marching toward the spring.

Apparently it didn't occur to me the guard might have a gun. That he might be willing to kill us all to keep his crime a secret.

I was nearly to the fence when I heard the woman's shriek, followed by a thunderous splash.

And then . . . she laughed.

I stopped dead in my tracks. I was standing in the open on the path, frozen in confusion. I could hear the woman giggling now, and the guard's voice softly chuckling.

Dan called in a whisper, *"Jack!"*

He was standing several yards behind me, strapping on his backpack. Phoebe stood beside him.

I looked back toward the spring. We could hear their coddling voices now, murmuring to each other. Then I heard the woman moan. The moaning slowly grew louder.

I turned to join Dan and Phoebe, and we hightailed out of the Castalian Spring.

3

THE SANCTUARY of Apollo lay just up the road on the slope of Mount Parnassus. With the satyric nightwatchman now amorously engaged, we assumed that—for a while, at least—we'd have the place to ourselves. Nevertheless, in case another guard happened to be on duty at the entrance, we took a more roundabout route, abandoning the road and hiking through the pines to enter from the base of the cliffs.

The moon had risen over the mountain, casting shadows on the stone-studded slope and piercing the darkness of the woods. Dan had reconnoitered the area the previous day, and he now adroitly led us in a complicated route that crisscrossed up the mountain to the boundary of the site. There we were forced to climb another fence, but after that the way was fairly easy. An ancient road called the Sacred Way wound like a serpent through the sanctuary, and even in the shadowy moonlight our destination was clearly visible. The rising pillars of the Temple of Apollo stood out boldly amid the ruins.

In ancient times, the sanctuary had been crowded with towering bronze and marble statues given in tribute to Apollo, and with treasury buildings of the Greek city-states, where sacred vessels and documents and smaller votive gifts were kept. A theatre was built into the mountainside, and a stadium and a Temple of Athena stood nearby. The place had been the richly thriving, spiritual heart of Greece, where once a month a crush of visitors came to seek the counsel of the sun god.

All of that was gone now; only stones were left. Cut-stone blocks methodically excavated and piled back into place. Most were heavy construction blocks—foundation stones, pediments, retaining walls, steps. The rest had either been plundered by history or carted off to museums. This left the sanctuary bereft of life and a challenge to one's imagination. Only one small building had been fully reassembled—the Treasury of the Athenians—but its roof was missing, its foundation had been rebuilt, and the two white columns at the entry, like a pair of false front teeth, were obvious modern replacements. Even the Theatre of Dionysus, once a boisterous bowl of laughter and tears, was now a corroded, silent shell as somber as a cemetery.

I had walked these dead ruins in daylight. Now, in darkness, the ruins came alive. The rough texture of age and decay seemed to feed on the light of the moon, transforming its reflection into a phosphorescent glow. The great stones appeared more ethereal than rock; there was something magical about them. It was as if the secret souls of the stones, forced into hiding by Apollo's piercing eye, were liberated by the night, enlivening the landscape with a ghostly strangeness, a kind of vibrant gloom.

This was nowhere more apparent than at the Temple of Apollo. Like the other buildings, for the most part only the foundation remained, but this one was far larger and more intact than all the rest. An even more striking feature, however, clearly set the temple apart and made it the focal point of the sanctuary. Six stone columns had been carefully re-erected and stood above a stone ramp at the temple's front end. Their effect was mightily impressive. On the dizzying slope of the sanctuary, where fallen blocks of stone and rubble hugged the terraced ground, these massive pillars stood defiantly upright, confident and graceful, as if proclaiming to all the world their divine right to exist. The low moon cast them in blooming yellow sidelight and painted blue shadow, and they gave a sense of depth and space against the starry night.

The three of us stood in awe before them.

"They're beautiful," I said, though the word didn't come near to describing their strangeness.

"Ruins are always more enchanting at night," Phoebe said.

Dan appeared more possessed than enchanted. He put his hand to a glowing column, feeling the rough stone with his fingertips as if it were the limb of a girl.

"It's the light of Dionysus," he said, his voice barely a whisper.

I wasn't sure I heard him right. "Dionysus?"

He withdrew his hand and turned to me. "Apollo was the god of the sun; Dionysus ruled the night. The truth is, both gods shared this temple."

He stood back to take in the entrance. "The front of the temple faces east," he said. "It welcomed the rising sun, when light poured in through the open doors and shone on the golden statue of Apollo. The facade was inscribed with well-known quotations from the sages of ancient Greece, like 'Know thyself' and 'Nothing in excess.' Apollo was the lord of light and clarity, order and understanding."

Dan stepped through the columns and looked toward the opposite end of the temple. "The west end faced the setting sun. That side was dedicated to Dionysus and welcomed the coming of the night."

"I thought Dionysus was the god of the grape," I said. "Lord of drunken orgies. How could Apollo share the temple with *him*?"

Phoebe said, "It was only in the late phase of Greek culture that Dionysus was made into the god of wine and revelry. He was originally much darker, more irrational and strange. The god of ecstasy and madness."

"All the more reason," I said. "One god's all about light and order, the other one's dark and chaotic."

"The two were half brothers," Dan said. "Two sides of the Greek coin. Dionysus was Apollo's alter ego, a kind of shadow self. Apollo reigned at Delphi from the spring through the fall, but Dionysus ruled in the winter."

"Then why didn't his cult celebrate here?" I asked. "Why did they hike in the freezing cold to a cave way up on Parnassus?"

"The Greeks were never really comfortable with Dionysus," Phoebe said. "He arrived late to the Greek pantheon, coming up from the south, from island cultures rooted in the Mother Goddess cult. He was exotic, bisexual, irrational, dangerous. The sexual chaos he unleashed in his initiates—usually women—made the patriarchy nervous."

I joined Dan beneath the pillars. Before us, a broad, three-tiered foundation of blue-gray limestone extended back some two hundred feet along the terraced slope. Many of its paving blocks had been fitted into place, but there were long, deep, empty gaps exposing levels of the substructure and patches of the underlying ground. These gaps and varying levels made the whole reassembly appear haphazard, as if it were an unfinished stone-block puzzle, an abandoned plaything of the gods.

It was over these intermittent, uneven stones that the three of us now carefully walked. I felt there was something sacrilegious in our trespassing. Not only were we breaking local laws, we were treading over consecrated ground.

I tried to imagine the marble floor the way it once must have been: bare, polished, gleaming, a serene setting for the statue of Apollo.

Dan described it very differently. "It was cluttered with a horde of objects. Gifts and tributes left in honor of the god: shields from victorious soldiers; figureheads of captured ships; the sashes and bands of triumphant athletes. Chariot wheels hung from the ceiling. Weapons were propped against the walls. The floor was littered with statues, lyres, wine bowls, caldrons—you probably could barely walk through here."

"No wonder the place was plundered," I said.

"It was burned by Thracian invaders in 88 BC, and two years later sacked by the Romans."

"It looks like they didn't even leave all the stones."

"Actually, the Romans later restored it," Phoebe said. "The building wasn't dismantled until the Middle Ages. They wanted the valuable metal clamps that held the column drums and building blocks in place. That's what happened to most ancient buildings in Greece."

At the edge of a large, deep gap in the floor, Dan came to a reverent stop. "This is it," he said.

We had been looking for the basement chamber called the *adyton,* the room where the Oracle had communed with the god. It lay more than halfway back on the downhill side of the temple: a small, recessed compartment, sunk several feet into the temple floor.

We stood over it, gaping down at the shadowy space. The cut limestone blocks had the bluish look of ice. Tufts of grass and wildflowers peeked out from the dark; I could smell their sweet fragrance. The chamber, though only a few feet deep, was too deep for the moonlight; half fell into shadow, and the lowest part looked black and fathomless, like the entrance into a chasm.

I found this illusion mildly disturbing, but Dan's eyes roved over the mysterious space as if he had been looking for it all of his life.

This was the holy of holies. The inner sanctum. The most legendary sacred spot in all of ancient Greece. *Adyton* meant "inaccessible." Even the petitioners of Apollo—having traveled for weeks over hundreds of miles and climbed to these heights on Parnassus—even they were not allowed into this space. They knew about it only by its reputation: it held the source of the Oracle's power.

"I can't believe we're here," Dan said. "I can't believe we're *actually here.*"

"Believe it," Phoebe said.

Dan looked at us. "You know those famous quotations I told you were engraved on the temple's entrance?"

"'Know thyself,'" I said.

" 'Nothing in excess,' " Phoebe said.

"There were others. My favorite was the simplest. It consisted of a single letter. The Greek letter epsilon."

"It looks like the English letter E," Phoebe said, looking at me as if this explained everything.

"And . . . E means what?" I asked.

"Is," Dan said.

"Is?"

"Is."

"What does 'is' mean?"

"It means: 'You *are.*' "

I glanced at Phoebe. I wanted to laugh. But Phoebe was staring down into the dark with a look of total seriousness.

So . . . I didn't laugh. Instead, I thought about the epsilon.

E. Is.

I *am.*

The simple words reminded me of something. How I had almost died in Mexico. How afterward I had felt more alive than I had ever felt before. More *conscious* of being alive. And aware that every single thing around me—stones, grass, wind, trees—everything was equally alive and *present.* Existing here and now.

Is.

This awareness—so obvious, so subtle—seemed the most powerful and precious thing in the world. Yet somehow also the easiest to forget.

"I think I know why they put it there," I said. "I think it was a reminder."

Dan nodded. He seemed very much in the moment himself, gazing down into the chamber. "*Is* a reminder," he said.

He took off his pack and set it on a stone block. Then he unstrapped his tripod chair and carried it down into the *adyton.* He unfolded the legs of the tripod and took a seat in the center of the chamber.

He remained sitting there for a long moment, just staring at the wall in front of him.

I glanced at Phoebe. She looked at me and gave a little shrug.

I gave a shrug back. Then I scanned the sanctuary, looking for the nightwatchman. I wondered how long we had before that drunk showed up again.

Phoebe began walking along the edge of the foundation, examining the layout of the blocks. Her frazzled blond hair seemed to magnify in the moonlight; it glowed even brighter than the stones. As she stepped nimbly from block to block, I noticed a remarkable quickness about her, a graceful, limber lightness. Like one of Apollo's fleeting nymphs.

I joined her. "So," I said. "Do you believe in Naiads?"

"Of course not," she said. She continued studying the stones.

"Then what do you think grabbed me back there?"

"In the spring?"

"Yeah."

"Nothing," she said.

"Nothing?"

She looked at me, directly. "Nothing but your own fear."

"How do you mean?"

"You've heard of post-traumatic stress?"

"Yeah . . ."

"Dan told me you almost drowned in Mexico. He said you nearly died."

I nodded, recalling the horror of the water rising around me.

"You don't get over that easily," she said. "That kind of fear can stay with you, live inside your body, physically. I think what you experienced in that freezing pool was some sort of flashback drowning. Your extremities were turning numb, the muscles were tightening. The sensation might well have felt like somebody actually grabbing you."

It was true I'd had nightmares of drowning since, but still I wasn't quite convinced.

"Ask yourself," she said. "Do *you* believe in Naiads?"

I actually had to think about it. "No," I said finally. "I don't."

Phoebe turned her attention back to the puzzle of the blocks.

I glanced over at the *adyton.* Dan was still meditating. Only the top of his bald head was visible, as if he had sunk into the floor.

"Look at these stones," Phoebe said. She pointed down a row of blocks that stopped at the chamber's edge. "The location of the *adyton* breaks the normal rules of temple symmetry. It sits way off to the side and interrupts the interior colonnade that normally would have run right through it."

I tried to see what she was talking about, but it wasn't clear to me, at least in the dark. "So what does it mean?" I asked.

"The normal function of a Greek temple is to provide a sanctum for the statue of a god. But here the inner sanctum is placed to the side and recessed into the floor. It clearly seems designed to accommodate some feature of the terrain."

"The crevice, you mean?"

"Precisely."

Dan had told me about the crevice, days before in Athens, when persuading me to join him and Phoebe. The chamber, he said, had been set directly over a natural, preexisting cleft in the earth. This crevice was the reason the temple had been built here, on this precarious slope so high up on the mountain. It was in fact the reason the Sanctuary of Apollo—and probably the town of Delphi itself—existed here at all.

Centuries before the Greeks arrived with their god of reason in tow, this cleft on the slope of Mount Parnassus had been a source of mystery and awe. Herders in the vicinity had noticed their goats suddenly falling asleep or leaping in a frenzy. When the goatherds approached, they too would be affected. They would smell a honeyed, perfumelike odor and fall into a mystical trance. Some saw visions. Others became delirious. Many would rave incoherently, as if they were possessed.

Fumes from deep in the earth had found their way up through the serpentine fissure and floated out into the air. Sweet-smelling, intoxicating, these mysterious vapors came to be seen as the breath of Gaia, Mother Earth, or wisps of the *pneuma,* the vaporous souls of the gods. Breathing them became a way to commune with the transcendent. Shrines were eventually built on the site, and a local virgin recruited to play the passive role of the conduit, the mouthpiece of the divine.

The Oracle had been born.

I glanced back at Dan, who was still absorbed in his meditation. In the moonlight, his bald head glowed like a light bulb.

Phoebe noticed it, too. "He's reaching enlightenment," she said.

I laughed. "Maybe the vapors are working."

"No," she said. "Not anymore."

The cleft in the earth, the opening to Gaia, had vanished long ago, most likely as a result of the frequent earthquakes that shook this unstable region. A French team excavating the site in 1893 found no telltale crevice, and for the next hundred years, most archeologists dismissed the "vapor theory" as nothing more than a myth. But the theory was verified in 2003, when a team of scientists published their discovery that two seismic fault lines intersected directly beneath the Temple of Apollo, and that the faults were riddled with ventlike fissures. In crust deposits on the chamber's foundation stones, they found traces of an intoxicating gas called ethylene. Their evidence showed that ethylene and other hydrocarbon gases had traveled up to the surface via bubbling springs and vapors from bituminous limestone beds deep inside the earth.

Whether it was the sweet breath of Gaia or Apollo's narcotic *pneuma,* apparently the stories of the intoxicating fumes were true.

This discovery had ignited my brother's curiosity. He immediately began making plans to put the vapor theory to the test—and not just anywhere, but in the very same spot where the Oracle for a thousand years had gotten high with her god. The ethylene wasn't a problem, he said. That could be supplied. All that was required was a proper question, a question of suitable significance.

It was several years before that question finally presented itself. Dan refused to tell us what it was, saying he didn't want to screw up the protocol.

I asked Phoebe if she had any idea.

"No," she said. "But we're about to find out." She nodded toward the *adyton.*

Dan was climbing out of the chamber. He waved to us to join him.

"How was your med?" Phoebe asked.

"Wonderful," he said. The look on his face reminded me of how Phoebe had looked when she arose from the spring—somehow both strangely calm and excited. He glanced behind him, down the Sacred Way. "We'd better get on with it," he said. "You guys ready? Jack?"

I shrugged.

"Phoebe?"

She was patting her hair into place as if preparing for a date. "Ready as I'll ever be."

"Okay," he said. "Let's do it."

4

DAN PULLED from his pack a small, cylindrical metal tank with a pressure gauge under the valve at the top. From her pack, Phoebe withdrew a tightly wound coil of plastic tubing. Dan connected the tubing to the tank.

"No lighters, no matches, not even a flashlight," he said. "Nothing that might cause a spark."

Until the 1970s, ethylene had been widely used as a surgical anesthetic. Its tendency to explode, however, had brought its use to a stop.

Dan carried the tank back across the foundation stones, past the luminous columns, and down the entry ramp to the ground in front of the temple. There he set the tank down, lodging it snugly in place. This would be his base of operation, well beyond the range of the fumes. He wanted to be sure one of us stayed sober in case things got out of hand.

He walked back up the ramp toward us, unrolling the plastic

tubing behind him. It stretched out in a springy spiral over the broad foundation, and when he reached us, he asked me to hold the remaining coil while he climbed down into the chamber. From there, he took the tubing and stretched it down to the center of the floor, where he lodged the open end in the crack between two blocks.

He set the tripod seat directly over it. "The Pythia sat on a three-legged tripod, something like this, only made of bronze. The tripod was placed directly over the crevice, so the fumes would envelope the priestess."

Phoebe glanced at me, caught my eye, held it for a moment. That one brief look spoke volumes. *Please pay attention, Jack. You have to take care of me. Your brother, you know, is insane.*

She climbed down into the chamber. Dan took her hand and led her to the tripod. She paused there and gave him a look similar to the one she'd given me, as if trying to remember why on earth she'd allowed herself to trust him.

Finally, she sat on her tripod throne. Dutiful Queen of the Nymphs.

Dan crouched down and checked the tube, made sure it wasn't kinked and the upturned end was open. Then he gently held her hands and spoke to her softly. "I'm going to start out very slow," he said. "Just breathe normally. Gradually I'll increase the level of the gas. It shouldn't take more than a couple of minutes to begin to have an effect. Jack will keep an eye on you. You'll experience a slight loss of physical sensation, then a mild euphoria—it's very pleasant, really. As you know, I've tried it myself, and I assure you it's completely benign."

Phoebe nodded silently.

Dan's words may have been comforting, but I knew they weren't entirely true. Back at his apartment in Athens, I had read the writings of the ancient authors who reported on the Pythia's trance. While most described her as mellow and passive, many accounts told of her unpredictability, from wailing in rapture to flat-out fainting—and the occasional violent frenzy.

Dan rose to his feet and climbed out of the chamber. As he

picked up his pack, he nodded for me to follow him. We passed through the columns and walked down the ramp to the waiting ethylene tank.

Dan put down his bag. "Okay," he said. "I'll be right here. If anything starts to go wrong, let me know and I'll stop the gas. The effects wear off very quickly."

I suddenly felt unprepared. "How will I know if it's going wrong? How will I know she's all right?"

"You'll know," he said. "Just pay attention to her breathing. Give her three minutes before you ask the question. And don't get too close to the *adyton.* The fumes will be heavily concentrated there. You've got to try to keep a clear head."

Suddenly his job looked easy. "Why don't you deal with her, and I'll do this?"

"No," he said sternly. "The supplicant is never witness to the trance. That's the role of the priest. My unconscious wishes could influence her reply."

"Priest?"

"Relax. What you have to do is very simple. Just ask her the question and write down her reply. Write down everything she says. Here." He unzipped a pocket of his pack and pulled out a pencil and a small notebook.

I took it from him. "How will I know when to ask her the question?"

"Just wait until she's in her trance."

"How will I know that?"

"You'll know. The gas works fast. It should take just a couple of minutes."

I looked back down the Sacred Way toward the entrance to the sanctuary. Dan glanced back there, too. All we could see in the darkness were the glowing, ghostly ruins.

"I'll keep an eye out for the guard," he said. "Try not to worry about him; he's not going anywhere. Besides, he's too fat to catch us."

"Hope you're right." I peered across the temple floor to the *ady-*

ton. Phoebe wasn't visible from where we were standing—she sat too low in the chamber. It really would be up to me to make sure she was safe.

I looked Dan in the eye. "You sure you know what you're doing?"

"Of course not," he said. "That's the whole point."

I rolled my eyes, then turned and headed back toward Phoebe.

"Jack?"

I turned. Dan was holding up a small, folded piece of paper. "Forgetting something?"

"Oh." I walked back and reached to take it from him.

Dan pulled it away. "Do not read it until you read it to her."

"Part of the protocol?"

"The *divine* protocol."

I slipped the folded paper into the notebook and headed back to Phoebe.

For some reason, the sanctuary seemed quieter all of a sudden. Walking across the foundation, I heard no cicadas, no fluttering bats, no owls hooting, nothing but the sound of my own careful steps. We were completely alone on this slope of Mount Parnassus, and I couldn't stop thinking about how very dangerous our little experiment could be.

Ethylene was a potent anesthetic. According to Dan, even a mere whiff of the gas could induce a numbing euphoria. Heavier doses produced total insensibility to pain. Unlike narcotics, however, ethylene worked its magic without causing drowsiness or even dulling consciousness. Under its influence, a person remained alert and aloof in a state of disembodied bliss. Afterward, there were few, if any, side effects—perhaps slight nausea or headache—and little or nothing of the experience would be remembered.

Anesthesiologists occasionally reported confused, combative, even violent behavior, but the bigger danger was that ethylene gas in high concentrations could reduce the amount of oxygen in the air, leading to a total loss of consciousness. Indeed, the ancients told of several Oracles, perhaps overcome by an excess of fumes, who died in the midst of their rapture.

Phoebe had been informed of these perils and yet still had volunteered. I wasn't sure whether it was her own curiosity or her affection for Dan that enticed her. Who knows why people do what they do? She may have volunteered on a whim.

"You sure you want to go through with this, Phoebe?" I was standing on the ledge of the *adyton.* In the slanted moonlight her head was all I could see, floating below me in a pool of darkness.

She raised her eyes to mine. "If some hayseed peasant virgin could do it, why the heck shouldn't I?"

With these bold words, my concern for her vanished. "Okay, Miss Pythia. Prepare for liftoff." I waved to Dan.

Dan waved back in acknowledgment. Then I saw him crouch down to turn the valve on the tank. I set the bevel on my wristwatch.

Seconds passed. No hiss. No fog. No telltale odor.

Thirty seconds. Still nothing. Phoebe remained completely immobile.

A minute. She seemed to sway slightly as she took in a deep breath.

At a minute twenty seconds, the odor finally reached me. It smelled like ripe fruit or wilting flowers.

"You okay, Phoebe?" I backed up a bit.

"Fine," she said faintly.

The sweet odor grew more intense. I pulled up the neck of my T-shirt and tried to breathe through the cloth.

Phoebe's head was moving now, swaying very gently, as if to the tune of some internal melody.

I checked my watch: Two minutes had passed. One more to go.

The smell of the ethylene came through my shirt. I couldn't help breathing it, and began to fear it might be too strong, especially down in the chamber.

"You okay?"

Phoebe moaned. A soft moan, barely audible, with a tone of complete relaxation. I took it as a yes and waited.

The minute hand crawled around the dial of my watch. It seemed to be taking forever, and gave me the strange sensation that I was slipping into a dream. As happens when you stare at anything for long, the watch began to look unfamiliar, as if I had never seen it before. The dial was black, the numerals white. I noticed tiny sparks of light streaking across the crystal. I held my wrist steady and focused on the lights, and realized they were stars reflecting on the glass. The stars appeared quite clear and close, as if they had somehow been captured.

Phoebe moaned again.

I peered down at her blond head floating in the darkness. "You okay?"

She looked up at me with her mouth hanging open. "I think I'm turning into a tree!"

Am I supposed to write that down? I didn't even ask Dan's question—did I? I glanced at the notebook in my hand, still unopened.

Phoebe started laughing. "I can't help it—my brain made me do it!" She kept on laughing to the point of convulsion, and soon she was bent over laughing so hard that no sound escaped from her mouth.

I peered back through the pillars toward Dan, hoping he'd offer some help.

He didn't budge. His alabaster head looked like some lifeless part of the ruins.

Phoebe's laughter finally faded, and she looked at me again, her eyes now filled with pity, or maybe disappointment. "Nothing lasts forever."

"No," I said, speaking through my shirt. "Thank God for that."

She smiled. My anxiety suddenly dissipated. I felt extremely relaxed.

Phoebe seemed to acknowledge this. "You know I know it's a dream."

I lowered the shirt from my face. The sweet odor of a thousand flowers filled my empty body. There was nothing to fear anymore.

Phoebe was talking to the wall. "All the same the belly knows! All the way down to your toes!" Again she reeled with laughter.

I checked my watch and was shocked: Five full minutes had passed!

Quickly I opened my little notebook—and the folded paper dropped out and disappeared into the *adyton.*

"Bring your pillow!" Phoebe cried.

Peering into the darkness, I couldn't see the paper. I set my little notebook down carefully on the ledge. To filter the heady fumes, I stripped off my T-shirt, rolled it up halfway, and tied it across my face like a mask. Then I started down into the chamber.

My body felt slightly numb, my airy limbs tingly and strange. I seemed to move too slowly, as if I'd lost my will. Lowering down, my foot slipped. I fell in a dream to the floor of the chamber, and felt my finger break.

No—it was only the pencil.

On my hands and knees in the pit of the *adyton,* I searched for the paper and the broken stub. The darkness felt like a tactile substance, my fingers roaming through it—bare stone, tufts of grass, invisible, fragile flowers. Phoebe sat with her back to me, her voice softly moaning, her blond head like the moon. The pungent scent of ethylene fumes filled the inky space.

The pencil stub suddenly appeared out of nowhere, a tiny broken yellow shaft buried in the blackness. I reached to take it, and noticed something tucked between my outstretched fingers: the folded piece of paper. Somehow it had found its way back into my hand.

It was time to ask the Pythia Dan's secret question.

I gathered all my strength of will and forced myself to stand. My head emerged from the pit, and I took in the open expanse of the temple stretching out around me. The pillars were etched in moonlight, but I couldn't see beyond them from my lowly point of view. Dan was out of sight.

No matter, I thought. *The task at hand is mine—I, the noble priest of the Oracle.*

Phoebe sat before me, slumped in the tripod seat, her head tilted forward with her chin on her chest. I noticed her hair was still damp, and saw between the furrowed locks the white skin of her scalp. The nape of her neck looked livid, too, with a dark mole under her collar. She seemed to be breathing normally.

I lifted her face to the moonlight. Her eyes slowly opened, and when she saw me staring down, she sighed, softly moaning.

"It's getting hard to be someone," she said.

No longer did I have trouble understanding what she meant. I nodded in agreement. "It all works out," I assured her. Her pupils were widely dilated, a vast black hole in a halo of blue. She didn't blink, and her gaping eyes seemed to capture mine, the way I had captured the stars on my watch, so close and clear though a billion miles away. If you stare at anything long enough . . . Her live, liquid eyes now looked beautiful and strange: internal, perfect organs so nakedly exposed, like tiny selves in embryo revealed beneath their lids. These eyeballs stared at mine the same way mine stared at hers. It seemed a kind of miracle, that these living worlds of matter could reach across the void of space and somehow make connection, confirming our existence like reflections in a mirror.

E. Is. I am. We are.

Phoebe was falling deep into her trance. I could see it coming over her like an overwhelming thought, her attention turning inward, her eyelids drifting shut. She remained still and silent, face tilted to the moon. Standing bare-chested in my T-shirt mask, I loomed over her like some predatory bandit.

I pulled the mask down off my face and unfolded Dan's piece of paper. He had handwritten a single question in pencil. I read the question aloud to the Pythia:

How can I find the secret of the Eleusinian Mysteries?

The question was completely foreign to me. I had no idea what it meant.

Phoebe did not respond at first. She remained in her silence with her eyes still closed. I wondered if she had heard me all right, or whether she could hear me at all. It was perfectly quiet in the chamber, and I had only been a foot or two away when I spoke, but the trance she was in seemed impenetrable; nothing at all registered on her face. Her breathing, I noticed, remained steady and calm.

I pulled the mask back up over my face and waited.

How much time passed, I couldn't say. I was more than a little under the influence myself, and a dreamlike euphoria still filled me. So much so that I didn't even notice when she finally opened her eyes. I just suddenly realized she was staring at me.

The stare seemed to reach deep inside me. After a long and unnerving silence, words came out of her mouth, spoken in a voice I had never heard her use before—sexless, guttural, emotionless.

"Aphrodite leads the way to Dionysus," she said. "Dionysus leads the way to Eleusis."

I grabbed the notepad and scribbled down her words: *Aphrodite leads the way to Dionysus. Dionysus leads the way to Eleusis.* Then I looked back at her and waited for more.

Nothing came. Her eyes closed and she fell back into silence.

I looked at the words I had written on the page. I knew Aphrodite was the goddess of love, Dionysus lord of ecstasy and madness. But the words meant nothing more to me than had Dan's mysterious question.

What were the Eleusinian Mysteries? I seemed to have heard of them somewhere before, but couldn't remember.

Once again Phoebe's eyes opened. They focused sharply on mine. Never had they looked so alert and alight, filled with the living fire of consciousness. Her face seemed to glow like the marble in the moonlight, and she appeared more beautiful than I'd ever seen her before. Her lips, moist and slightly parted, were plump and shapely. The skin of her face was taut and flawless, framed by the damp-curled locks of her hair. The freckles on her cheeks had faded, washed away by the eerie light, but her fine dark lashes clearly outlined her eyes, and her brows looked brushed and elegant.

I heard the whispered echo of her voice in my head: *Aphrodite leads the way to Dionysus.*

Phoebe slowly reached up and pulled down my mask. Her eyes seemed to soften as they fell to my lips.

"Jack . . ."

She tugged on the T-shirt looped around my neck, pulling my face closer to hers. She held me there a moment, only inches away.

"Phoebe," I whispered.

Her eyes again found their way into mine, and she saw in them the same desire that I was seeing in hers, a desire that was more like a craving or compulsion, a mania that had suddenly possessed us. As much as it might be a betrayal to my brother, as much as I might be taking advantage of her state, I realized that making love to Phoebe was all I had really wanted from the moment I had met her.

She gently pulled me closer and brought her mouth to mine. She paused there with our lips barely touching.

Aphrodite leads the way . . .

I kissed her.

Softly at first, then . . . hungrily. Our mouths devouring each other.

I felt the soft stroke of her tongue and parted my teeth to take her. The wet flesh slid between my lips, teased my tongue, and retreated. Then her lips parted generously. Her fingers grazed my naked back. My hands took hold of her hair. When I tugged her head back and kissed her throat, she moaned and murmured my name.

Then, with a sudden jerk of her head, Phoebe went cold and silent.

I pulled away. Something had come over her. She was staring off blankly, her face upturned to a sky full of stars.

. . . the way to Dionysus.

"Phoebe?"

She slowly turned her face to me. Her eyes, which appeared to have been focused on some deeply buried thought, gradually sharpened and fixed on my face. Her head jerked again with a sudden spasm, and a look of horror came over her, as if her mind had just unearthed some long-forgotten terror.

Her voice cracked with fright. *"Oh my God,"* she whispered. *"Oh my God!"*

"What is it? What's wrong?"

She reached out to me, unable to speak. Fear strangling her words.

"Phoebe—"

She seemed unable to breathe. I moved to try to help her, but I was growing dizzy, overcome by the fumes, and once again I felt myself slipping into a dream. Everything seemed unreal.

Her hands pushed at me, batting me away. *"No!"* she cried. *"No!"*

I tried to calm her, to hold her arms, to carry her out of the chamber, but she fought me off frantically.

"Phoebe—I'm here—you're safe—"

She was up from the stool now, backing away, fighting off invisible attackers. Her cries of terror frightened me.

"Dan!" I shouted. "Help!"

The Pythia had descended into a frenzy, a shrieking and violent hysteria. I grabbed hold of her thrashing arms and forced her against the wall. She kicked and twisted and squirmed. She was screaming out, over and over, words I could not understand.

"Phoebe!" My brother suddenly appeared at my side. He helped me hold her down.

Phoebe looked back and forth between us, peering in fear at our faces.

"We've got to get her out of these fumes," Dan said.

The two of us readied to move her, but Phoebe had finally stopped screaming and appeared to be settling down. The sweet odor was dissipating. Dan had shut off the gas.

"You're all right," he assured her, feigning calm. "Everything's okay now."

"No," she whispered, shaking her head. And then she whispered the same words she had until now been screaming. The words I had not understood.

"The Furies are coming," she said.

Her eyes deliriously rolled to the sky. We held her as she fainted.

5

SOMEWHERE DOWN on the road below, police lights were flashing. We could see them reflecting on the cliffs.

"They must have heard her screaming," I said.

Dan was returning with his backpack. Phoebe lay slumped beside the rim of the *adyton,* slowly coming to. I picked up her pack and started to wind up the plastic tubing.

"Leave it," Dan said. "The tank, too. We've got to get out of here fast." Together we lifted Phoebe, slung her arms over our shoulders, and headed for the trees.

We hid outside the sanctuary, in a ravine near the base of the cliffs, waiting for the lights to go away and our Pythia to recover. The police, to our surprise, departed only minutes after they had arrived, without even bothering to inspect the grounds. We watched their flashing lights pass along the road to Delphi, apparently in a vain attempt to scare off any intruders.

As Dan had promised, the effects of the ethylene wore off

quickly. Phoebe was left with mild nausea, a slight headache, and no memory at all of her experience. Given our betrayal of my brother, I took her amnesia as a welcome relief.

By the time we completed the trek back to our hotel in Delphi, it was after four in the morning. We'd been awake for nearly twenty-four hours. Much of that time we'd been hiking Mount Parnassus, an exhausting undertaking in its own right, but add to it our ice-cold dips in the spring and the episode of madness in the temple, and you're left with one ragged little trio. Dan and Phoebe trudged like zombies to their room off the courtyard, and I clumped upstairs to my single above the street.

I slept profoundly, without the slightest hint of a dream. Around noon, I awoke to the growl of tourist buses hauling into town, brakes hissing as they rolled to a stop and disgorged their chattering cargo. These behemoths had just completed their three-hour journey from Athens, reminding me that we'd be making the return trip later that afternoon. Then, following a day or two at Dan's place, Phoebe would be leaving us, heading back to Crete.

I lay there in bed awhile, pondering this unpalatable prospect, while watching sunlight reflections on the ceiling and listening to the polyphony of voices from below. French, German, English, Greek. And something else I couldn't place. Swedish, Danish, Dutch?

It occurred to me that I'd never heard Phoebe speak her native tongue. I wondered now what it sounded like, especially coming from her. *I'll have to ask her to speak it,* I thought. *Maybe she could teach me a phrase or two. How do I say, "Kiss me," in Dutch? How do I ask, "Will you sleep with me?" Maybe we could make Dutch our own private language. Maybe the two of us could openly converse without Dan ever having a clue.*

Maybe.

I climbed out of bed. Immediately, I noticed a manila envelope had been slipped under my door. Dan had scribbled on it: *Meet you at the* taverna. Inside, I found the first three pages of the introduction to his doctoral dissertation. He'd been working on it for nearly a year now, but for some reason had not deigned to share it with me. Its title, *In Search of the* Kykeon, told me nothing, but a glance at the heading to the introduction made clear why he had decided to show it to me now.

I sat down at once to read it.

The Eleusinian Mysteries

Beginning around 1500 BCE and lasting for nearly 2,000 years, a great annual autumn festival was celebrated in Greece on the slope of a rocky hill by the ancient seaside city of Eleusis. Legend held that at this site an earth goddess named Demeter was reunited with her daughter, Persephone, who had been abducted into the Underworld by its lord and ruler, Hades. Persephone was allowed to rejoin her mother, but only for eight months out of the year, a bargain that resulted in the seasonal fecundity of the earth, the cycle that governed the growing of crops and the perennial blessings of Nature.

Around this myth of birth, death, and rebirth, a formalized ritual gradually developed that became known as the Mysteries of Eleusis. In essence, these secret initiation ceremonies involved the imbibing of a mysterious elixir and the display of hidden "holy things," leading to a profound experience of spiritual revelation.

The Mysteries celebrating Demeter and her daughter became the preeminent religious festival of Athens. Each year it attracted upwards of 30,000 people from all over the Greek world—men, women, young and old, from all classes, even slaves. All the great men of Athens participated, from Socrates and Plato to Pericles and Aeschylus. At least three Roman emperors—Augustus, Hadrian, and Marcus Aurelius—became initiates. Despite its longevity and vast renown, the essential elements of the Mysteries—the drink taken, the sacred objects displayed, and the nature of the revelation experienced—were never allowed to be divulged by anyone, under penalty of death. Hence, to this day, the secrets of the Mysteries remain unknown and are the source of unending speculation.

What is known is derived from ancient texts and the accounts of early Christian writers. They describe a week-long series of rituals that climaxed in a great pilgrimage from Athens. From Demeter's shrine at the base of the Acropolis, a vast procession of *mystai* carried off the secret "holy things" along the fourteen-mile road to Eleusis. To shield them from the eyes of the uninitiated, the sacred objects were carried in round baskets, called *kistai,* tied with purple ribbons. The celebrants, wearing garlands of myrtle, danced, sang, and shouted with joy as they followed the leader of the procession, a young male representing Persephone's son, Dionysus, the notorious god of revelry and madness.

At night, under torchlight, the procession finally reached Eleusis, and a special offering was made to Demeter. A day of fasting followed, and in the evening the *mystai* assembled in the *Telestrion,* or Hall of Initiation, a huge temple capable of holding several thousand worshippers. Here the fast was broken with the drinking of the special mixture known as the *kykeon.* Although it is reputed to have been a blend of barley and herbs, the ingredients of this mysterious infusion have never been definitively determined. What is known, however, is that following the imbibing of the *kykeon,* the "holy things" were at last revealed, and a deeply transformative, utterly awe-inspiring experience took place.

"Blessed is the man among mortals on earth who has seen these things," wrote Homer. The historian Plutarch described a great light "beheld in fear and silence." Aristotle explained that it was not any instruction the initiates received, but rather the intensity of the experience that gave to the Mysteries their remarkable power. The great dramatist Aeschylus was nearly lynched for attempting to portray the experience in a play, thus breaking his vow of secrecy. The Greek poet Pindar described the initiation as a vision of life beyond death: "Happy is he who, having seen these rites, goes below the hollow earth, for he knows the end of life and he knows its god-sent beginning."

Perhaps the greatest testament to the spiritual power of the Mysteries is the fact of their remarkable endurance. For nearly 2,000 years, from deep in Greece's archaic past, throughout the period of classical antiquity, even centuries into the Christian era, everyone who was anyone took part in these rites, and carried away with them the astonishing experience of an encounter they would never forget.

I found Dan and Phoebe out on the back terrace of the Taverna Vakchos, the same restaurant we had shared a late dinner in the day we arrived. That night, it had been packed with college kids who were staying in the fully booked hostel next door. Now, it was crowded with older French tourists, fresh off the coach parked out front, and I wondered how Dan had finagled a table with such a spectacular view.

The two of them were clearly finished eating and had been waiting there for a while. Dan was smoking a fat Hugo and typing away on his laptop. Phoebe sat sipping a cold Greek frappé from a straw while gazing out vaguely over the vast plain below.

I was pleased to see her brighten as I joined them.

"How are you feeling?" I asked.

"I'm good," she said. "Wonderful, actually. Slept like the dead."

"Me, too," I said. Our eyes lingered a moment, so long that I began to wonder if her memory might have improved.

Dan took the cigar out of his mouth. "Hate that expression—'slept like the dead.'" He looked at me. "What did you think of the paper?"

"What do I think? I think you're nuts."

"Why?"

I started to answer, when the waiter appeared.

"Uh, coffee, please. And a menu?" As he headed off, I pretended to call after him: "And would you bring me a cup of *kykeon,* please?"

Phoebe laughed.

Dan corrected my pronunciation. "It's *KEE-kee-on,*" he said.

"Whatever. Here's what I don't understand. Over fifteen hundred years have passed. If nobody's figured out what the stuff was, what makes you think you can do it?"

Dan shrugged. "Talent, experience, persistence? And failing all that . . ." He nodded toward the small notebook lying on the table. "There's always divine intervention."

I turned the notebook toward me and read my scribbles aloud. "Aphrodite leads the way to Dionysus. Dionysus leads the way to Eleusis."

"It's *i-LOO-sis,*" Dan corrected.

"Whatever. Do you remember saying this, Phoebe?"

Her lips were pursed around the tip of her straw. She shook her head.

"Do you remember anything that happened?"

She withdrew the straw and paused a moment, gazing off. "The last thing I remember . . . was you asking if I was okay." She touched my hand. "Thanks," she said. "I'm sorry I got out of control."

Again her eyes seemed to linger.

"My pleasure," I said. "I mean . . . No problem."

She smiled warmly. Her eyes were like pools.

Dan looked back and forth between us. Phoebe withdrew her hand.

"So . . ." I said. "Have you guys figured out what it means?"

Dan and Phoebe exchanged a bitter glance.

"I'd like to know what *you* think," Dan said.

"Well," I ventured, "according to your dissertation, Dionysus—or some young guy in the role of Dionysus—led the procession to Eleusis. So we know what that line is referring to."

Dan nodded. "Agreed. So what about the first line?"

"It's obvious—" Phoebe began.

Dan cut her off. "—I'm asking Jack."

"But he—"

"—Please, Phoebe. Just let him answer." The two of them eyed each other sharply, then turned to look at me.

"I don't know," I said. "Isn't Aphrodite the goddess of love?"

"And sexual desire," Dan added.

"Love," Phoebe insisted. "Aphrodite is the goddess of love."

"Jack?"

"Uh . . . I don't know . . . I suppose it could mean any number of—"

Phoebe interrupted. "It means you've got to fall in love, dummy—"

"Phoebe, will you *please*?"

They glared at each other across the table. Phoebe went back to her straw.

I was so caught up in the tension between them I hadn't even noticed the waiter. A coffee and a menu lay in front of me. He was awaiting my order.

"Uh . . . You know, I'm starving. Do you think I can get, like, a big stack of pancakes?"

Dan said, "We're in Greece, Jack. Not Wisconsin." He looked at the waiter. "Bring him a double order of *tiganites,* please. With *petimezi* if you don't have syrup."

The waiter took my menu and departed.

We sat there in silence a moment. I sipped my coffee, eyeing Dan and Phoebe through wisps of steam. I wasn't exactly sure what was going on between them. All I knew was it had to do with sex, so I thought I better try to change the subject.

"So what the hell are Furies?" I asked Phoebe.

"They're spirits of vengeance," she said. "That's really all I know."

"Do you remember seeing them?"

She shook her head. "No."

"The Greeks called them *Erinyes,*" Dan said. " 'Those who walk in darkness.' They took the form of women, with snakes in their hair and blood in their eyes. They were clad in flowing gowns, and carried an ax or a torch in their hands. It was the Romans who gave them the name 'Furies,' from the Latin word *furor.* They drove their victims insane."

"Who were their victims?" I asked.

"Criminals, murderers. Mostly they avenged the shedding of a parent's blood. Nothing escaped their sharp eyes. They pursued the guilty with speed and fury, allowing them no rest."

"So what do they have to do with the Eleusinian Mysteries?"

"Nothing that I know of," Dan said. "But they were attendants of Hades and Persephone, and lived with them in the Underworld. Some consider the Furies to be the dark side of Persephone."

"Hell hath no fury like a woman scorned," Phoebe said.

"I think I prefer Aphrodite," I said.

Dan sat back in his chair. "Aphrodite is actually related to the Furies. Gaia, goddess of earth, married Uranus, god of the sky, and their offspring were the Titans. The youngest of these, Cronus, castrated his father and threw his severed testicles into the sea. The drops of blood that fell on the earth gave rise to the Furies. And the genitals formed the foam of the sea, out of which arose Aphrodite."

"What a lovely story," Phoebe said. She noisily sucked up the dregs of her drink.

"Sex and murder," Dan said. "Oldest story in the world."

Phoebe teased the tip of the straw with her tongue. "Aphrodite and the Furies—they're rather like sisters, then, aren't they?"

"Sounds like a rock band," I said. I was growing impatient with all this incestuous mythology. "What do you think you saw last night, Phoebe? What made you so afraid?"

She shrugged, pushed her coffee away. "It may be I just have a guilty conscience," she said. "That's really what the Furies are about, aren't they? Those 'sharp eyes' pursuing you, driving you mad?"

"What could you have done to be so guilty?" I asked.

Again she shrugged, eyeing me. "There's always something, isn't there?"

I couldn't bring myself to deny it. I glanced at Dan. "What do *you* think it was?"

"I think it was probably just an overdose," he said. "A violent reaction from too much of the gas."

The waiter brought my "pancakes." These were crispy little fried puffs of dough, with some sort of grape juice syrup on the side. The very sight of them saddened me. In my recent months of travel, it happened with increasing frequency that my hunger provoked sharp pangs of homesickness. Foreign food seemed unable to assuage it.

"What about the 'Holy Things'?" I asked. "You must have some idea what they were."

"There's a lot of speculation," Dan said. "The Greek archeologist Mylonas thought it was bits and pieces of a Mycenean palace shrine that survived in Eleusis through the Dark Ages of Greece."

"Bits and pieces—like what?"

"No one knows. Some Victorian classicists assumed it must have included a phallus or a female sexual symbol."

I thought of Sigmund Freud with all that primitive art on his desk.

"How predictable," Phoebe said. "A bunch of priggish males turning the mystical wellspring of the ancient world into a peep show."

"Some of the ancient writers hint that it was nothing more than shafts of wheat or a handful of seeds—symbols of the goddess of grain and agriculture, Demeter."

"Awesome," I said. "Shafts of wheat."

"A profound revelation!" Phoebe exclaimed.

We laughed.

Dan didn't find it amusing. "It might not have mattered what the 'holy things' were," he said. "It was more about how they were seen, the state of mind of the beholder."

"As in 'stoned'?" Phoebe said scornfully. She didn't share Dan's enthusiasm for psychedelic drugs.

"In the right state of mind," he said, "any object can become a vehicle for transcendence. You can look at an ordinary rock and see it vibrate with *being.*"

Being. Is-ness. I thought of my wristwatch, how strange it had looked in the starlight. And Phoebe's eyes, so alive and mysterious. Was that only because of the gas I'd inhaled?

"What do you think the *kykeon* was?" I asked.

"It sure as hell wasn't barley tea," Dan said.

"You think it might have been ethylene vapors?"

"Unlikely," he said. "That kind of geological phenomenon is rare. Those gas vents were unique to Delphi."

"So what then? *Stropharia*?" This was Dan's favorite hallucinogen—*Stropharia cubensis,* the magic mushroom.

"The first to suggest that *kykeon* was hallucinogenic was the famous English scholar Robert Graves. He believed the *kykeon* was a psilocybin mushroom, probably baked into sacramental cakes."

"I doubt it," Phoebe said. "Eleusis was a harvest festival, and barley was grown nearby on the Rarian Plain. The elixir may not have been barley soup, but surely the grain had something to do with it."

"That's what the researcher Gordon Wasson thought," Dan said. "There's a fungus that infects edible grains. It produces ergot, which contains alkaloids that affect circulation and neurotransmission in the brain. Albert Hoffman, a Swiss chemist, worked with Wasson researching these psychoactive alkaloids and found they were precursors to LSD."

"Wow," I said. "So the Greeks were dropping acid in 1500 BC."

"Not exactly. Wasson and Hoffman believed the *kykeon* was a potion derived from infected barley, a specially formulated ergotized beer."

"I thought the Greeks were wine drinkers," I said.

"Beer is as old as bread," Dan said. "Xenophon called it barley wine, but—"

He had glimpsed someone across the room. "Excuse me a second," he said.

Phoebe and I watched him walk through the restaurant toward a woman who had appeared at the door. She was a plumpish Greek, with unruly black hair, a pasty complexion, and heavily made-up eyes. Her dress seemed far too tight for her weight. She acted a little self-conscious, but smiled in relief when she saw Dan approach.

He brusquely led her out the door.

I glanced at Phoebe. "Who the hell was that?"

"I can't be certain," she said. "But it appears your brother is wrangling with a whore." She nodded toward the window. "Look."

Outside, across a lane of parked cars, Dan brought the woman to a stop at the curb. She appeared distraught and anxious, talking a blue streak while Dan tried to calm her. It wasn't until he reached for his wallet that she finally settled down. Then, after counting the cash he gave her, she argued again until he handed her more. Apparently it was enough to make her happy: she left him with a kiss on the cheek.

"It's her," Phoebe said. "Last night. The spring."

"Yeah," I said. "Kassandra."

We watched her saunter away up the street, hips banging.

Seconds later, Dan was back at the table. He seemed preoccupied and upset, and took his seat in silence, until he finally noticed the two of us staring. "What?"

"You could have told us," Phoebe said.

"An unnecessary distraction," he growled. "I needed you to focus on preparing for the rite."

"Guess it didn't work out like you planned," I said.

"All she was supposed to do was distract him. I'd no idea she had such a flare for the dramatic."

"How much did it *cost* you?" Phoebe asked.

"More than I bargained for," he griped.

"The torn dress?"

"Yes. But money's not the half of it. Those flashing lights last night?"

"Yeah?"

"An ambulance. Our wheezing nightwatchman is in the hospital—she gave the letch a goddamn heart attack!"

6

BEFORE SHE left for Crete, Phoebe spent a day with us in Athens. Over a breakfast of oily eggs in Dan's cluttered apartment, we had a brief discussion about what we ought to do. Phoebe wanted to shop, saying she needed to buy good-bye gifts for Dan and me, and to find something Greek to send her father for his birthday. I wanted to head up to the woods on Mount Hymettus, which looked to me like the only place to escape the city's smog. Dan, however, persuaded us there were more important places to visit, ones he hoped might help us solve the puzzle of Phoebe's prophecy.

We had already been to the Acropolis together before we had headed to Delphi, but Dan now dragged us back again to find the Sanctuary of Aphrodite and Eros. It was not located atop the plateau, where the Parthenon and all the other famous ruins stood, but down on the side of the northern slope, where several primitive shrines were nestled among the steep cliffs and pathways.

From below the Acropolis, Dan led us up to a path along the cliffs. As we walked beneath the rocky walls, he told us about an obscure nocturnal fertility rite called the *Arrephoria.*

"Every year, four young girls were selected from noble families to be the servants of Athena, the goddess of Athens. They were a sort of Greek precursor to the Roman Vestal Virgins. The annual fertility rite involved carrying baskets on their heads, through an underground passageway and down a secret stairway to the Sanctuary of Aphrodite and Eros. Once there, they traded the secret contents of their baskets for other contents, which they brought back up to the Temple of Athena. No one knows exactly what it was they carried."

"What do you think it was?" I asked.

"I've always thought it must have been some kind of aphrodisiac."

"Oh, please," Phoebe said disparagingly.

"Why not?" he said. "Ritual sex was an integral part of the cult of Aphrodite. A female slave of the temple was called a *hierodule,* a sacred servant. At Aphrodite's temple in Corinth, there were more than a thousand of these women. People in the cult practiced the rite of *hieros gamos,* the 'holy wedding,' ritual intercourse with a god through coupling with another human. They believed it could induce a profound religious experience. It's the basic premise of the orgy. By dissolving bodies and boundaries, you dissolve all personal identification and take the plunge into matter."

The "plunge into matter" was a favorite phrase of Dan's. It described the state of mind he always seemed to be after: escaping the prison of the individual ego, merging with the boundless mind of nature.

"Americans have a phrase for that, too," I said. "It's called 'fucking your brains out.' "

"It's called a male fantasy," Phoebe said. "Ritual prostitution was nothing more than that—prostitution. There were plenty of brothels in the ancient world, but they were usually kept separate from the temples. In Athens, Solon established laws for prostitution, and he forbade procuring at the temple."

Dan and Phoebe argued over this for a while, two know-it-alls going at it. I finally interrupted.

"You think this aphrodisiac—assuming that's what it was—you think it might have been the *kykeon*?"

"Actually, I hadn't thought of it until Phoebe made her prophecy."

"Aphrodite leads the way to Dionysus. So you're thinking . . . orgy?"

"The Bacchanalian orgy. Dionysus is the god of dissolution. He was known as the Liberator. He freed you from yourself into ecstasy or madness."

We continued this discussion as we passed several shallow caves—one of which Dan said belonged to Apollo—and the cut-stone entrance to an ancient spring. A short ways beyond that we arrived at what Dan called "Aphrodite in the Gardens."

Though now mostly dry and rocky, there was a kind of garden-like feeling about the spot—an appropriately seductive enchantment. There was no temple or shrine, but simply a hollow in the side of the cliff, with massive boulders, clumps of ivy, and a spattering of tiny scarlet poppies. The rock walls held at least a dozen neatly carved niches like the ones we had seen at the Castalian Spring. According to Dan, they had once held votive candles and tiny figurines.

"For the common people, these rustic sanctuaries on the slope were more personal places of worship than the great monuments up on top."

After much searching of the rock walls, Phoebe finally located an inscription in ancient Greek. Tracing the letters with her fingertips, she announced that they spelled "Aphrodite."

Dan was peering through his binoculars toward the bottom of the slope. I asked him what he was looking for.

"I wanted to see how far this is from the Eleusinion—Athens' shrine to Demeter." He nodded toward some ruins far below beyond the trees. "During the course of the year, the 'holy things' were kept there, until they were carried in the procession to Eleusis."

"So the stuff they carried off from there might have been the same stuff the girls carried here?"

"It's possible," Dan said. "The girls might have carried down one of the 'holy things,' or perhaps an ingredient of the *kykeon.*"

"I don't see any path down there from here."

Phoebe looked askance at me. "Sixteen centuries have passed, Jack. Do you really imagine the path would still exist?"

Know-it-all.

Dan pointed out the Agora, the ancient city center, now a park-like stretch of ruins. "It's only a part of the ancient city," he said. "Much of it still lies there, under the Plaka." He nodded toward the oldest neighborhood in Athens, crowded with shops and *tavernas.*

"That's where I'd like to do my shopping," Phoebe said.

"We'll go there for lunch," Dan said. "For now, we go to the National Museum."

It was at this point that Phoebe started calling Dan "the Tyrant."

WE SPENT two long hours at the National Archeological Museum. Phoebe seemed particularly engaged with an eight-thousand-year-old marble figurine of a wide-hipped woman from Sparta. She described similarities and differences with goddess figures from Minoan Crete.

Across the courtyard in another gallery, Dan stood us before a fifth-century BC relief sculpture of Demeter and Persephone from Eleusis. It showed Demeter handing an ear of grain to a youthful male named Triptolemus, though Dan insisted it was actually Dionysus.

"The so-called experts have it wrong," he said. "They're still trying to exclude the unsavory Dionysus. At Eleusis, Dionysus was considered the son of Persephone, born to her in the Underworld. He was androgynous, halfway between two sexes and caught between two worlds. The Dionysian cults and the Eleusinian Mysteries were the last remnants of Minoan Goddess culture that survived into patriarchal Greece."

He took us up to the first floor to look at ancient pottery. One black vase showed the figure of a woman with snakes in her hands and her head cast back. He called it a perfect portrait of possession.

"It's physically accurate," he said. "That kind of jerking head movement is common. We saw it in Phoebe the other night."

"What's with the snakes?" I asked.

"Symbol of Dionysus. A living snake is a vehicle of the god. It added to the excitement of the Dionysian ritual—the sexual union of the god with the initiate. Ever heard of those snake-handlers in the mountains of Kentucky? It's part of their religious service. 'They shall take up serpents.' They go into an ecstatic dance, then pull rattlesnakes out of boxes and pass them all around."

Like the devil in the Garden of Eden, Dan led us down to another gallery where we contemplated a variety of classical nudes. Eventually, we found ourselves standing before the shapely sculpture of a naked Aphrodite, dated to 100 BC. Eros, the winged cherub, fluttered just over her shoulder, while standing beside her was the goat-god Pan, doing his best to seduce her. Pan had horns, an ugly face, and the hooves and legs of a goat. The lovely Aphrodite held a sandal in her hand, threatening to give the pest a swat. There could be little doubt what the sculpture was about—a point Dan drilled home with Phoebe.

"You still think Aphrodite is about love and not sex?"

"Of course I do," she said. "This only proves it. You can see for yourself, she's fighting him off. It's Pan that embodies the sexual impulse, the base and beastly side of man. Aphrodite epitomizes the power of love, the harmony and order of nature, all that is noble and beautiful."

"Hard to believe she's so above it all," he said. "Just look at the grin on her face."

"She's amused," Phoebe said. "Aloof and amused."

"You mean she takes pleasure in torturing him?"

"He doesn't look tortured to me," she said. "He's just doing what animals do."

They went on like this, back and forth, until finally I told them I'd kill them both if we didn't get out of the museum.

We had lunch in the Plaka. Afterward, in a souvenir shop, Phoebe bought Dan and me going-away gifts. From a shelf lined with Greek gods, she selected for Dan a small plastic statue of a very sexy Aphrodite. For me, who'd been complaining about the lack of a lamp by my mattress in Dan's apartment, she chose a Cupid candle, a fat little cherub with a wick sprouting from his head. Half an hour later, in a shop in a neighborhood closer to the Agora, Phoebe found a string of amber-colored worry beads to send as a present to her father. "It's perfect," she said. "He's always worrying about me."

Over this endless hour of shopping, the Tyrant had been prodding us to accompany him to Eleusis. Phoebe wanted to take the trip by taxi, given that the sky was darkening with clouds, but Dan insisted the ride was too expensive, so we ended up going by bus. By the time we reached the coast, a drizzle had begun. This proved only a hint of the coming disappointment.

After the description of Eleusis I had read in Dan's paper, I expected a Greek version of heaven on earth, a broad expanse of green pasture upon which mystical temples stood. Instead, we found the hideous industrial sprawl of the modern city of Elefsina. We passed belching petrochemical, steel, and cement works before finally reaching Demeter's Sanctuary, what had once been the glorious endpoint of the Sacred Road from Athens.

Dan had conveniently failed to warn us about the hellish setting. He also didn't mention there was nothing much to see. A vast graveyard of scattered marble from successive layers of history, the ruins at Eleusis were complex and confusing. The site lacked Delphi's spectacular landscape, and none of its structures had been much reassembled, so there was little sense of the layout or focus. Together with the horror of surrounding smokestacks and the smell of fumes from refineries, the place exuded an atmosphere of desolation and despair.

Did I mention that it was raining? None of us had brought umbrellas along, and now we wandered this bewildering city of the dead while a steady drizzle descended. Only a couple of hippie tourists remained at the site, and they appeared to be leaving. It felt as if we had arrived in the quiet that follows a funeral.

The first thing we passed of any note was an ancient water well, neatly capped with tightly fitted polygonal stones. Dan told us it was the Well of the Maidens, where, according to the *Hymn of Demeter,* the goddess stopped to weep in her long search for her daughter. We stood there in dutiful silence, staring down grimly at the open black hole, but by this point we were soaking wet, and neither Phoebe nor I could muster the interest to ask Dan a single question.

From there he led us to what he said was the Great Telestrion, the Hall of Initiation and the Mysteries, the windowless auditorium into which countless thousands had come to witness a miracle in the darkness. All that remained of the structure now was a large open stone square with scattered remnants of pedestals and partially restored tiers of seats that once had bordered the interior. We stood on this open space for a while, squinting into the rain, trying to imagine what might have occurred there three thousand years in the past.

We failed. No vision of an Aphrodite or a dancing Dionysus emerged from the grim stones around us. No recipe for *kykeon* thundered from the sky.

I wondered what Dan had expected. Why had he dragged us here? Why was he so obsessed with these Mysteries, dead for so many centuries? Probably dead for good reason, I thought. Most likely there was nothing more to them than the nothing we now saw in front of us. The secret at its center was a parlor trick, a stone phallus or a shaft of wheat, revealed in a brilliant beam from the sun, something the gullible Greeks, drunk on barley beer, might have swallowed in their stupor as a vision of their god.

People will believe in anything.

We followed Dan like idiots, shuffling through the rain, as he led us toward a cavern in the side of a granite hill. This, he explained, was the Plutonion, the entrance to the Underworld, ruled by the god of the shades, Hades. The ancients imagined it was through this cavern that the dark god had dragged Persephone, carrying her down into the realm of the dead to be his bride and queen. So began the myth that led to the Mysteries.

We entered the dry mouth of the cavern, glad to get out of the rain. Although one corner recessed into the dark, the cave itself was shallow and seemed an unlikely entrance to hell. The hippie picnickers had left bits of trash behind—an empty bottle of Roditis, the discarded husk of some blood red fruit, and the paper wrapper from a loaf of bread—but beyond this the cave had nothing to offer other than a roof to the rain.

We turned our backs to the flinty walls and stared out over the ruins.

"What now, Tyrant?" Phoebe grumbled.

Dan didn't have an answer. Our day-long search had come to an end—a literal and dispiriting dead end. Phoebe's cryptic prophecy remained a puzzling riddle, as remote as Persephone in the Underworld.

I glanced back at the garbage on the ground. "Maybe we should have brought along some bread and wine. Had ourselves a picnic."

"Bread and wine," Phoebe said. "Demeter and Dionysus"—she turned and looked down at the red piece of fruit—"and Persephone." She squatted to examine it, poking it with her finger. "Dan. Look."

He crouched beside her. "It's a pomegranate," he said.

I bent down between them and saw the mush of red seeds. "So what about it?"

"Whoever had this picnic had some knowledge of the myth," Phoebe said.

Dan stood up and explained. "It was a rule of the Fates that if anyone consumed food or drink in the Underworld, they were doomed to spend eternity there. When Zeus commanded Hades to release Persephone, Hades tricked her into eating four pomegranate seeds. That's why she had to stay in the Underworld four months out of the year."

"That's not the way I heard it," Phoebe said. "There was no trick involved. The pomegranate is a symbol of love, and for Hades it was a gift of love, which Persephone gladly accepted. She had come to love her husband as much as he loved her. She may have returned to her mother every spring, but she always came back to Hades."

"True love?" I said.

"Very much so," she said.

Dan disagreed. "Hades *abducted* her," he said. "A blatant crime of passion. He *stole* her virginity. *That's* the meaning of the pomegranate. Crush the pink husk and out pours the red seed. The allusion couldn't be clearer. That's why it's traditional at Greek weddings to crush a pomegranate under your heel."

"A patriarchal tradition," Phoebe said. "You talk the talk about partnership, but you're clearly a dominator at heart."

"I'm just calling it what it is, Phoebe."

"You're calling it the way you see it," she said. "And you see everything in terms of sex. It's juvenile."

"People always put down as juvenile what they've tried to suppress in themselves. But you can't ignore the most basic fact of life. You can't hide from the obvious truth."

"The myth of Demeter and Persephone has nothing to do with sex. It's about the pure and tender love of a mother for her daughter. *That's* the obvious truth."

"It's about the fecundity of nature," he insisted. "Why does she go back to Hades? Love, pomegranates? Who the hell cares? The point is she goes back *to sleep with him*!"

Phoebe and I stared at Dan. Even he seemed surprised by his own loss of temper. He strode off into the rain.

We watched him cross the deserted ruins, heading back toward the entrance. Phoebe stood motionless beside me. Whatever it was that had been going on between them had apparently just come to a head.

She glanced at me uneasily. "I'm sorry," she said.

"Hey, it's okay . . ."

We stared out at the rain. I forced myself to wait for her to speak.

Finally she did. "There's a reason he chose me as the Oracle," she said. She looked directly at me. "It's not just because I'm his girlfriend."

I looked back at her for a long moment, trying to understand. All this talk about sex—or the lack of it. "You mean . . ."

She nodded. "Yeah."

I continued staring at her. I think my mouth was open.

"No," she said. "I'm not gay."

I swallowed. "So, you and Dan . . ."

"No. Never."

I looked at the ground, then looked back at her. "Just Dan, or . . . ?"

"No one. Ever."

She turned and peered back out at the rain. I looked out there, too.

"The line about Aphrodite," I said.

"He thought it meant we should—finally . . ."

I looked at her. She seemed to be struggling with the idea.

"It's ridiculous," she said. "How could making love with me have anything to do with the *kykeon*?"

I shrugged. "I don't think it does," I said. "So, what did you tell him?"

She looked at her fingers a moment and picked at the ridge of a nail. "I told him what I've always told him: I'll only give myself to the man who truly loves me."

I folded my arms, then unfolded them. "You don't think it's him?"

She shook her head. "I don't know," she said.

"How will you know?"

"I'll know."

"True love?"

"True love."

We stood there for a while before she said we should go. The rain felt somehow warmer as we entered it again, crossing through the maze of ruins, heading back to Dan. I couldn't stop thinking about what she had said, how wrong I had been about her. Her hair was soaked as we walked through the rain, and I thought again about the dip in the spring, the look I had seen in her eyes that night, the kiss we had shared in the *adyton.* I wanted so badly to tell her what happened, but knew it could only be trouble. And they already had enough of that between them.

THE THREE of us barely said a word on the long ride back to Athens. The traffic in the rain was a misery. We were each left to our own passing thoughts, as remote and inaccessible as the passing signs, an alphabet soup of Greek.

Phoebe didn't sleep in Dan's bed that night. She slept on the couch across from the kitchen. I was so close I could hear her breathing from my ratty little mattress on the floor. At one point, I thought I might have heard her crying, but that was very likely just a dream. I woke up from a number of dreams that night, and Phoebe was at the heart of every one of them.

She left early to catch a bus the next morning. The bus would take her to the metro station, the metro would take her to the port of Piraeus, and from there she'd take a ferry on to Crete. Dan walked with her to the bus stop. I stayed back at his apartment, drinking the bitter coffee he had brewed, staring out his iron-barred kitchen window, wondering if I would ever see her again. I don't know how they said their good-bye, whether they promised to get together again, but I decided that I wouldn't ask Dan about it and that I had to stop thinking about her.

Dan spent the next week buried in books at the university library, searching for the meaning of the oracle. He started looking into chemical correlates of Aphrodite, from ancient Greek aphrodisiacs to the brain functioning of people in love.

One night he came home with a copy of an Italian research study that examined levels of the neurotransmitter serotonin in people who had recently fallen in love. The study showed a drop in serotonin levels similar to patients with obsessive-compulsive disorder. He said love also triggers the dopamine system, which is linked to psychosis and schizophrenia. In addition, it activates regions of the brain associated with risk taking and rage.

"Sounds like a mental illness," I said.

"It's more like a drug addiction. It shuts down the rational part of the mind."

"Yeah," I said. "It drives you crazy." The two of us nodded sagely.

While Dan made his daily excursions to the library, I wandered the meandering streets of Athens. Before our trip, the city had felt vibrant and intriguing; now it seemed ghostly and gray. The life had gone out of it, or gone out of me. I felt most at home in the ruins.

The day before I was to leave for Rome, I hiked the north slope of the Acropolis and found again the Sanctuary of Aphrodite and Eros. I had brought along the Cupid candle Phoebe had given me, and now I placed it neatly into a niche in the rock and lit the white wick with a match. The air was very still and the flame burned perfectly. I stood back to admire the offering, the mischievous god of love in the dead rock wall, his cherub head flickering with life.

Abode of gods, whose shrines no longer burn . . .

For a moment I tried to conjure up the memory of Phoebe, but all that came into my head were details—the delicate spattering of freckles on her cheeks, her towel-dried hair radiating like a freak, the mole I had noticed on the back of her neck, the way she had picked at her fingernail. The memory of her standing in the nude by the spring—an image I was sure would never leave me—had lately begun to fade from overuse, like a photograph too often exposed to the sun. The searing blaze of my desire had abated; all that was left now was the sentiment of longing, glowing like a cinder in my heart.

I opened my eyes to the flickering candle. *It will burn itself out eventually,* I thought. *Or succumb to the next passing breeze.*

Even gods must yield.

As I turned and started walking off, I noticed a glint of color in the achromatic wall. It was very near the place where Aphrodite's name was etched, the letters Phoebe had traced with her fingers.

I moved closer. A smile came to my face.

It was Dan's sexy, plastic Aphrodite.

Something about it was different. On the shelf in the souvenir shop, in the chorus line of deities from the Greek pantheon, the figurine had looked like a Vegas showgirl. Here, however, set high up in a niche in the wall of this ancient garden, the goddess of love and beauty looked divine. It may have been the angle, or the late light, or the state of mind I was in, but the statuette seemed almost alive.

For a moment, I allowed that Aphrodite might be real. Not a living, breathing goddess, but something more than a metaphor, or a symbol of romantic love. Aphrodite was a force that took possession of the soul. She was like all the gods as the Greeks thought of them: an energy that suddenly inhabits the heart, that lifts you out of the ordinary, out of the tired routine of existence and into a torrent of emotion. The sudden infatuation, the convulsive burst of laughter, the frenzy of a homicidal rage. The gods were a power that came from above and rattled the cage of our bones.

To feel the pangs of love was to be possessed by the goddess of love. To assuage the pain of love, then, one must appease this goddess. Dan's little offering, I had to assume, had been made with Phoebe in mind. An appeal to bring her back to him or to break her stubborn chastity. Of course, it might also have been a simple wish to solve his dissertation. Maybe it was all of these; I really didn't know. I couldn't even say what I was doing there myself. I didn't want to come between Dan and Phoebe, but I couldn't seem to let go of her, either.

Dan had said Aphrodite was the oldest of the Fates, those mythical weavers of destiny. If that were true, then perhaps our offerings were a gesture to fate—a bow in acquiescence, a humble plea for guidance.

Sometimes that's all you can do.

When I got back to the apartment that night, I made no mention of what I had seen or where I had been. Dan had returned from the library looking as glum as ever. His research seemed to be going nowhere, and Phoebe weighed on his mind. Dispirited, the two of us went out for our farewell dinner, more from a sense of family obligation than brotherly camaraderie.

We ate down the street at my favorite *taverna*—a small, warm place where I'd had my first meal in Athens, the dinner where Dan had introduced me to Phoebe. That night, we had all shared a delicious beef and rabbit *stifado,* a stew the proprietor had assured us was a classic of Greek cuisine. We proceeded to get very drunk on Roditis and gabbed until two in the morning. When everyone else had left and all the chairs were up, we watched the old Greek owner dance alone in the middle of the empty room. Dan called it the *hasapiko,* the "butcher's dance."

I remembered it like it was yesterday.

Greeks dine late in the evening, and on this final night we arrived so early there were no other patrons in the place. The old Greek did his best to be welcoming, but he seemed to sense our gloom. When he found out I was leaving in the morning, he walked off wordlessly, filled a carafe with red wine from a cask against the wall, returned and poured us both a glass, and set the carafe on the table.

"Gift of Dionysus," he said, then headed off to cook our meal, what would be my final *stifado.*

Dan raised his glass. "To the gods," he said.

I raised mine. "Amen."

At the very instant our glasses clinked, Dan's cell phone rang. Both of us thought immediately it must be a call from Phoebe. We were wrong. The call was from Dionysus.

7

BASRI PASHA was an old roommate of Dan's. In his undergrad days at the University of Chicago, the two of them had shared a graystone two-flat with an older female law student from southern Illinois, and a Chinese-American physics major moonlighting as a waiter in Chinatown. Basri was the youngest son of a wealthy shipping family from Istanbul. He had been sent to America by his father to obtain a first-class business education, with the idea of grooming him for senior management in their Miami or Long Beach office.

Basri, however, had other ideas. Though his family was not particularly religious, he had been raised in a Muslim country and felt constrained by its moral strictures. He also had a devilish streak. Confronted with the freedom America presented, he was soon applying the business skills he learned to nefarious and licentious purposes. He imported marijuana from a cousin in Miami and sold it in the South Side clubs. His clients began calling him the "Istanbul Express." For a while he became a kind of campus pimp, connecting a couple hookers he had met in the Checker Board Lounge with nerdy foreign students who could never get a date. The parties at his Hyde Park apartment were legendary. He hired live bands and exotic dancers, ran a cash bar, and charged an entry fee. He created a hash hookah lounge in the basement, the infamous Den of Iniquity. Although he pissed off the neighbors and had to pay off the cops, he always managed to have a good time and seemed to come out on top.

So it came as a surprise when, two months into his third year, "the Pasha" left the university suddenly to return to Istanbul. Dan found out later his cousin had been busted and the Chicago connection uncovered by the Feds. Dan didn't see him again until the following June, when Basri invited him to work over the summer as a dive tour guide on Key Largo, a boating operation connected to his family. The two of them worked together for months, reviving his cousin's lost business.

In the years since then they had kept in touch with each other, but it wasn't until Dan moved to Greece in pursuit of his doctorate that he started seeing Basri more often. The shipping magnate's wayward son had finally found a role in the family business, one for which he was eminently suitable. He had been given command of a fabulous yacht with a staff of six and the run of the entire Mediterranean. His job: the entertainment and lobbying of EU bureaucrats, port authority officials, and municipal politicians. "Twisting arms with a velvet glove" is the way he put it, though Dan described it as nothing short of bribery.

When he called during our farewell dinner in Athens, Basri was crossing the Aegean Sea with some Greek girls he had met in Istanbul. He told Dan they were heading to some Pan-Hellenic Greek Women Something-or-Other, and would be picking up their friends on the island of Mykonos, the libertine, sex-and-sandals capital of Greece. The friends they were meeting were all women, too, he said—too many women for one man; he felt obliged to share them. When Dan mentioned he was having dinner with his brother, Basri insisted he bring me along. We could join them for some partying on Mykonos. The two of us could stay on his yacht.

As Dan hung up, he stared at me, dumbfounded.

"What is it?" I asked.

"The answer to the oracle," he said.

BEFORE LEAVING Rome, I'd been freelancing as a tour guide, a gig I had started entirely on my own as a way to earn a few dollars. I had begun by hanging out on St. Peter's Square, offering free tours of the Vatican to English-speaking sightseers. The *Blue Guide* provided my expertise, but I soon came to add little flourishes of my own—Michelangelo sleeping with his boots on, or the story of the crazy Hungarian who took a hammer to the *Pietà,* or the reason the remains of St. Peter's corpse didn't include his feet. After a couple hours of these tantalizing tidbits, my spellbound patrons, steeped in Catholic guilt, felt obliged to pay me something—or to hire me for my far superior Roman Forum tour.

I did well enough to be noticed, and eventually I was offered a staff position with the Renaissance Tours organization—a job I had accepted and was planning to begin when I made my return from Athens.

This was the reason for my hesitation now, a hesitation Dan thought absurd.

"Yes, babysitting tourists in the Vatican. What a rare opportunity. That kind of offer may never come again."

I also wasn't wild about getting on a boat. As I now reminded my brother, I had very nearly drowned on one. And for this trip there'd be two boats to board: first the ferry to Mykonos, then Basri Pasha's yacht.

"A yacht full of girls, as I understand it," he said. "Could be very dangerous indeed."

It amazed me how quickly he had forgotten about Phoebe. Perhaps she'd been right about Dan all along: he truly was preoccupied with sex. Then again I could hardly blame him. If the girl I'd been in love with for the last eight months had held out as long as Phoebe had, I'd be eager for some Mykonos revelry, too.

He finally lost his patience. "Aphrodite leads the way to Dionysus," he said. "This offer has *got* to be connected to the prophecy. You know it is. You can feel it, can't you? Come on, admit it."

It was clear he wanted to forget about Phoebe, at least for a while. There were plenty of other fish in the Aegean. The fact was, I wanted to forget about her, too. Despite all you hear about falling in love, in truth it's a mindless misery. It's infantilizing and delusive. You're either giddy with infatuation or consumed by a jealous rage. You turn into an incredibly boring person. You can't think of anything else.

"Sorry," I said. "What were you saying?"

MYKONOS IS a short trip from the mainland—or so they tell you. Never trust the Greek sense of time. With all those centuries of history behind them, a few hours lost here or there mean nothing.

The bus from Athens arrived half an hour late at the port of Rafina. We ended up waiting a couple hours more for the ferry to depart. The delay was never explained, and our fellow Greek travelers simply shrugged it off as routine. Even the crossing took longer than usual—because of the wind, they said.

We passed along the coastlines of two large islands, both of them craggy and pleasantly green, before spotting the brown and barren hump of Mykonos, floating like a walnut on the sea. Dan had described it as the most popular party island in the Aegean, but from a distance it looked dry and desolate. Even as we approached the sparkling harbor of Mykonos Town, its whitewashed stucco seemed a long way off from the dark dens of decadence I'd imagined.

The village was a dazzling pile of white sugar cubes clustered around the bright blue bowl of the harbor. Our ferry docked with slow precision on the arm of the concrete jetty. We disembarked and moved with the shuffling herd of passengers past a line of local people hawking their hotels. Dan made a deal with one to store our backpacks for the day. Taking only what we needed, we headed for the beach. We wouldn't be meeting Basri until late that evening.

A bus took us across the island to a place on the sea called Platys Yialos. From there we hopped a boat to Paradise Beach, Dan's favorite hangout. By the time we arrived, I was woozy with fatigue and wanted nothing more than sleep. I kicked off my sandals and stretched out my towel; in seconds, I was totally out of it.

An hour or so later, I awoke in a sweat. Dan was standing naked at the edge of the water, talking to two girls who were topless.

I glanced around me. A lot of people were wearing swimsuits, but a lot of people were not. At least half the girls had shed their tops and many of the men were naked. An older woman sleeping on a rented lounge chair was wearing nothing at all. She had to be well over two hundred pounds. She lay sprawled belly-down with her fleshy arms dangling and the massive dimply boulders of her buttocks exposed. Beside her was a small naked boy with a plastic shovel, doggedly digging a pit in the sand.

Dan hadn't told me that Paradise was a nudist beach, something you'd think he might have mentioned. Maybe he simply assumed I knew.

I stripped off my T-shirt and stretched my arms, feeling the rays of the sun. Music pounded from the nearby bar, and all the flesh around me seemed to glisten in the heat. Following a sudden impulse, I stripped off my shorts and underwear and headed across the sand toward the water.

Stepping nude through a maze of naked and seminaked bodies, I felt the same sort of invigorating freedom I had felt at the start of my dip in the spring. There's a boldness and daring to nudity, a defiant denial of shame. It taps into something the pagans knew well and proudly celebrated—the sensual power of the human body. By reveling in the purely physical, they reached toward something spiritual. The exhilaration of nudity lifted them closer to the divine.

I strode boldly past Dan and the girls and dove out into the water. The sea felt cool and vibrant, and seemed to intensify the sense of elation. After the unrelenting music from the bar, the silence underwater was a pleasure. I swam along the bottom and my penis stroked the sand. Saltwater worked its bitter way into my eyes. I leaped up through the waves like a dolphin.

Dan and the two girls were watching. He said something to them and they laughed. The larger of the two girls, a scraggly blonde, had a flabby set of jugs and a head too small for her body. The other one was prettier but skinny, almost gaunt, her thin arms folded tightly, as if against the cold.

There's a grotesque variety of human shapes, a fact made glaringly apparent when bodies are no longer hidden in clothes. Lately, I'd been required to gaze at a lot of classical nudes, statues of athletic males and shapely female torsos. Phoebe said the ancient Greeks invented the art of the nude, turning the human body into an object of perfection. Youthful males were sculpted in the image of Apollo, while the female nude was an Aphrodite, dubbed by the Romans "Venus." The ancient Greeks set the original standard, embodying in their subtle stone the ideal proportions of beauty. Twenty-five centuries later, we still measure ourselves against those stones. And measure our fellows against them, too.

As my eyes now wandered over the variety of figures lounging and loitering on the beach, they seemed to hone in on those closest to perfection. *What is it, finally, that draws one person to another?* The lives of a thousand offspring might be traced to a single glance.

The girl who held my eyes now was stepping lazily through the surf, gazing down at the frothy water, seemingly lost in herself. She was wearing a bikini with sailor stripes and the emblem of an anchor embroidered on the cups. Her hair was a rich black, cut to her shoulders, and tangled from drying in the wind. Her mouth was slightly open, and her downcast eyes were dark. She looked like a sated panther, moving with a kind of languid grace, dragging her toes through the water. Something about her—maybe the strength of her profile, or the whiteness of her skin, or the way she peered with quiet intentness at the strangers parading around her—told me she was different from the rest, that this was not the sort of place she came to very often. There was an air of youthful innocence about her, but an air intriguingly tinged with darkness, a sort of sensual contentment. I found the very sight of her arousing.

"Bro!"

Dan was plowing toward me, his belly parting the waves.

"What's up?" I said. I remained submerged, with only my head protruding.

"Ready for a drink?" he said. "I told them we'd buy the first round."

The girls stood where he had left them, chatting with each other and glancing out our way. The bar on the beach was rocking.

"You go ahead," I said. "I'll be there in a minute."

"Something wrong?"

"I'm fine," I said. "Just got a . . . little problem."

A grin spread across his face. "Oh," he said. "And who gave you that little problem?" He looked back toward the beach.

The girl I'd been watching was gone.

"Aphrodite," I said.

THE TWO girls were from Dubrovnik and spoke a primitive English. Shortly after Dan bought them beers, their fat-necked Yugoslav boyfriends showed up and whisked them both away. Dan and I smoked some Nepalese hash, then drank beers and ouzo while watching bikini-clad women dance on a platform by the bar. I kept an eye out for Aphrodite, but didn't see her again.

Eventually, we caught a bus back to Mykonos Town. We were supposed to meet Basri at midnight, less than an hour away. I would have liked a hot shower and a place to change my clothes, but had to settle for a splash bath in a public restroom along with the other vagabond beach bums.

Just as Dan had predicted, the town of Mykonos came alive at night. No autos were allowed on the streets, so everybody walked. The twisting, slate-paved lanes and alleyways were jammed. Dan navigated the crowded corridors and seemed to know where he was going. I followed with no regard to direction, having given up any pretense of learning my way around.

The hash had left us hungry and parched. Stopping briefly at a little café, we ordered falafel and beer. We ate standing up at a counter by the open window. A white cat slept peaceably on the windowsill, oblivious to a thousand passersby.

"Schrödinger's cat," Dan joked. "Is it dead or alive?"

"Overdose," I said. "Too much observation."

"Too much *Nepeta cataria.*"

Dan had written a hundred-page paper on the pharmacology of *Nepeta,* the catnip plant, a particular interest of his. "When I was in the Yucatán," he said, "I met a girl who smoked *Nepeta* mixed with *Damiana.* She claimed *Damiana* leaves were used by the Maya and the Aztecs as an aphrodisiac."

"Did it work?" I asked.

"Never did a thing for me. She said it helped with her menstrual—"

"There she is!" I stared out the window.

"Who?"

"The woman from the beach."

She was walking down the street with several other women, all young, attractive, dark-haired Greeks. They were dressed up—more so than most of the female tourists—and they had an air of self-possessed elegance about them. They did not chatter with one another but strode along in silence, taking little interest in the people they passed, and paying no heed at all to the many men who stopped in the street and stared.

"Which one?" Dan asked.

"Green dress—with the pearls." Her hair was pinned up in back, revealing a long neck adorned with a double loop of pearls. The low, strapped, draping dress revealed a shapely figure, and the hemline stopped well above her knees, exposing ivory thighs. On her feet were sandals of an ancient design, laced with thongs that continued halfway up the calf and tied there; I had seen them before on Greek statues.

"Knockout," Dan said. We craned our necks out the window as the bevy of beauties disappeared in the flowing stream of the crowd. "I bet they're going the same place we're going."

After paying the bill, we followed the street in the same direction until we came to the Skandinavian Bar. This was supposedly the hottest club in Mykonos, at least according to Basri. The building itself took up an entire block and consisted of several rooms, with an upstairs disco, two full bars, and a large, open-air lounge.

It was shortly after midnight and the party was in full swing. It took us twenty minutes waiting in line just to make our way into the disco. People stood shoulder-to-shoulder, and the pulsing beat was so loud that I couldn't hear anything else, not even Dan shouting in my ear.

"Whatever," I answered with a shrug.

We wiggled our way to the bar. The air was smoky and humid, the strobes were flashing brightly, and all the tanned and sunburned flesh glistened with a feverish sheen. Under the spinning mirror ball, the whole place seemed to be moving. A drag queen who looked like a Teamster in a blond wig swung crazily around a dance pole. She'd apparently been hired to discourage inhibition, and the partiers seemed eager to oblige.

There was no raised platform here; women who wanted attention danced directly on the bar. Looming above us, a brunette wearing sunglasses expertly coiled her midriff while holding a lit cigarette. A Latin-looking woman loosened her blouse, sharing her brassiere with the loudly appreciative room. An overweight Tina Turner displayed her magnificent endowments as she bent to toss her black mane over the upturned faces of admirers.

How many beers had I drunk this day? More than I had drunk in the past two weeks. Still, I took hold of the ice-cold bottle that Dan now passed back from the bar. Again he shouted something to me, words I couldn't hear. We sipped the beers and settled in to watch the girls perform. Nothing much happened until a stocky guy in shorts climbed up on the bar and started dancing with Tina Turner. The guy looked vaguely Middle Eastern, with a broad smile, an appealing face, and eyes that sparkled like the devil's.

Dan turned around and shouted something to me. Then he turned back and, to my astonishment, hopped up onto the bar himself. He started dancing on the other side of the big black woman, now sandwiched between the two guys. They performed a three-way bump-and-grind, with Tina deploying her hips to the hilt. The stocky guy suddenly ripped open his shirt and exposed his hairy chest and beer gut. This brought catcalls from the men in the room and raucous cheers from the women. The guy turned to Tina, egging her on, but she wasn't buying into the bargain.

I gaped as Dan yanked off his Hawaiian shirt and whirled it over his head. The crowd was howling. Then both guys went down on one knee and held out their pleading arms toward Tina.

Finally, Tina popped her top.

The bar went bonkers. The stocky guy reached around her fabulous boobs and gave Dan a smacking high-five.

That's when I realized the guy was Basri.

8

FROM OUT of the thick crowd at the bar, the Istanbul Express emerged, shirt unbuttoned, face in a sweat, carrying a bottle of ouzo and a tall, slim glass of ice. He walked right by me, and as I started to shout hello, he nodded for me to follow.

Dan was just behind him. He was carrying two more tall glasses with ice, and he handed them to me so he could button up his shirt.

"How'd you like the show?" he shouted.

"Should take it on the road," I said.

We tried to keep up with Basri, who was plowing ahead through the backslapping crowd. He led us outside and downstairs to a patio that was also jammed with people, but the music was not as loud. Two young Greek women were waiting for him. They were sitting on stools at a tall, round table, their bare legs crossed beneath their dresses, smoking sweet-smelling clove cigarettes in a slow and extravagant manner. Basri kissed each girl on the cheek, then set his glass down next to theirs and splashed each one with ouzo.

He turned to Dan and me and filled our glasses to the brink. "So, the brother that almost died. Mexico is dangerous, yes? Glad you live long enough to meet." He smiled brightly as he held up his glass. "*Ya sus!*"

"*Ya sus!*" we replied.

As we tapped our brimming glasses, liquor spilled on the table.

"The Greeks say spilling is a good omen," Basri said.

"A libation to the gods," Dan added.

We sipped our drinks.

Basri cast an eye on Dan. "So, your friend, the blonde—she leave you for somebody rich?"

"Worse than that, Basri. She left me to go dig ditches in Crete."

He slammed the bottle down. "*Always* you are having this problem. The girls you find, they are not real women, they are not wanting a man. They are wanting always *something* else. The digging, the grad school, this thing, that. Barbara—remember? Two years with us in that house. You always were wanting to sleep with her, but she had no time for you—no! She must study 'the Law.' Always 'the Law.' The Law was you could never fuck her, my friend!" He laughed. "Just like that Frenchie in the Keys, what's her name . . ."

I'd been waiting for Basri to introduce his friends, but he ignored them and went on talking. It didn't seem to bother the women. Disengaged, languorous, they barely gave Dan and me more than a glance as their eyes roamed over the tables. How long had they been with Basri? How old were they? Twenty, twenty-five? The two women looked so similar they may very well have been sisters. Their faces were classically Greek, with strong cheekbones, long noses, thick black brows, and penetrating eyes. One had a beauty mark above the corner of her mouth; the other wore a blue silk neck scarf. As Basri babbled on, they tilted their squinting faces as they dramatically dragged on their cigs. It was as if, for thousands of years, they'd been listening in silence to the bluster of men and were inured to their egotistic ramblings.

"I'm Jack, by the way. This is my brother, Dan."

"Oh, of course," Basri said as the girls reached out limply to shake my waiting hand. "Marina. And Irene. These beauties I met three days ago. Club in Istanbul—Shahmeran—heard of it? *Fantastic.* Very hot now." He turned to the women. "Where is everyone?"

"Dancing," said Marina, the one with the scarf. "The others will join us later."

"They have many friends," Basri said. He raised an eyebrow to Dan. "I am no more a lonely man." He laughed infectiously, peering into our eyes.

I asked the women, "What's your organization?"

"The Pan-Hellenic Women's Chorus," Marina said. They gazed at us impassively.

Basri said, astonished: "Can you believe? They sing hymns in church—like nuns!"

"Byzantine hymns?" Dan asked.

"And ancient music," she said.

"Really?" Dan asked, perking up. "Do you sing the ancient dithyrambs?"

"On occasion," she said.

Dan turned to me, elated. "The wild hymns to Dionysus!" He looked at the women. "I didn't think anyone performed them anymore."

Irene fixed her steady gaze on him. "The West has grown weak," she said. "We need to rediscover our pagan roots."

"*Abso-fucking-lutely!*" Dan said.

"Dionysus!" Basri cried, rising from the table. "Lord of the dance! Come, come!" He took the girls by the wrists and dragged them laughing into the crowd.

Dan and I hurried to follow them. "Wait," I said, and dashed back to grab the bottle of ouzo. When I turned round, I found they had vanished.

I plowed in after them.

THE TECH-TRANCE music in the disco formed a pulsing ocean of sound. As I pressed my way through the crush of dancers, the sound seemed to be physically connected with my body, as if it were amplifying the beat of blood vessels or the coursing of neurons through my brain.

The lingering effects of the hashish had been exacerbated by the drinking. It appeared to slow my visual perception with a kind of ocular echo, a lagging, wraithlike repetition trailing every move. Dark-haired, dark-skinned dancers seemed to multiply before me. Women from every nation in Europe glided by like ghosts. The women wore shorts that revealed their thongs, and filmy summer blouses you could see through. Stars from the mirror ball swept across their faces, and the brilliant flash of the strobe lights seemed to scatter their limbs through time.

In the middle of this fool's paradise, I came to a sudden stop. I was standing before a beautiful woman in an emerald dress and pearls—the panther from the beach! She was dancing with the Greek girls with whom I'd seen her walking.

For a moment I just stood there, gaping. Her dancing displayed the same catlike grace that had guided her limbs through the water. Sensuous, yet self-contained; aware, yet focused inward. She danced as if the music were only played for her, as if everyone around her was imagined. In that moment she appeared to be the center of the world.

My body began to respond to her in the same way it responded to the music: it felt compelled to move. I turned to find a place to leave the bottle I was holding. A tall, handsome, gray-haired man reached out to take it from my hand. The man appeared oddly out of place. I smiled in thanks, then turned away and danced toward the woman. My eyes were drawn down to her thighs, which glowed in the flash of the strobe lights. The straps of her sandals were laced tight around her calves. Her hair, neatly pinned in back, was falling loose in errant strands, softly caressing her neck. Her white pearls seemed to burn in the dark, and the glistening skin over her delicate clavicles gleamed with a tactile vividness. The square cut of her emerald dress revealed the tops of her breasts, which jostled and shifted with the movement of her arms as her hands traced the flow of the music.

Gradually, my presence seemed to draw her out; I could see her awareness emerging. More than once, her amber eyes drifted up to mine. The slightest hint of a smile flit across her face.

I moved closer.

Soon we were dancing face-to-face, her eyes gazing openly at mine. This gaze of hers was not a woman's knowing look of lust, nor did it betray any timidity or fear; it had a kind of innocence about it. For a woman who so readily provoked a man's desire, she seemed remarkably unaware of her power, as if she had never made use of it before, as if it were something new.

We stopped dancing.

I leaned in and shouted, "What's your name?"

She moved her face very close to mine. "Damiana," she said.

Did I hear her correctly—Damiana? I was about to ask her to repeat it when Basri suddenly appeared behind her, laid his hands on her shoulders, and kissed her boldly on the neck. She turned to him and smiled. He was with Dan and another group of girls, including Irene and Marina. Damiana and her friends seemed to know them all, but she hadn't realized I was with them. Altogether now there were nearly twenty girls clustered around us. I decided they must have all been part of the organization, the Pan-Hellenic Women's Chorus. With their simple elegance and classical beauty, they seemed a notch above the other women in the room, as if they had just stepped off some European cruise that had drifted in from a previous century.

Basri commandeered a bartender's tray arrayed with shots of ouzo. The glasses were quickly dispersed, and although we couldn't hear the jolly yachtsman make his toast, we all downed our drinks in unison. Then a track kicked in with a hammering beat, and we fell to dancing again.

I noticed the women wore similar sandals to the ones I had seen on Damiana. All of them danced with her same lack of self-consciousness, a primitive yet graceful abandon. They were not mimicking the latest street craze, or the dancing of the tourists around them. Their gyrations seemed to bode forth from deep inside themselves, from some primal but cultivated core, as if from a tradition all their own.

There was something very beautiful about it, and something a little bit frightening. An uncontrolled fervor, the body expressing impulses that completely escaped the mind. I found it fascinating, and could not take my eyes away from whoever was dancing before me.

We must have gone on for an hour or two. At some point we found ourselves out in the night, walking in a loose procession down a crowded street. Basri led us like a drunken Pied Piper. Other women from the chorus joined in our walk as we made our way down to the harbor. Men we passed studied the women like a parade of exotic animals.

Somewhere along the way, I introduced Dan to Damiana.

"*Damiana?*" he said.

"Yeah," I said. "Can you believe it?" I explained to her that we had just been talking about a Central American plant named *Damiana* when we saw her pass by on the street.

"It's another synchronicity," Dan said. "A meaningful coincidence."

"In Greece, it is not an unusual name," she said.

"Does the name have any meaning?" Dan asked.

Damiana fingered the pearls at her throat. "It means . . . tame. And . . . friend. A true friend."

"It's definitely synchronicity," Dan said. "It may portend something significant."

Damiana grew quiet, as if disturbed by the thought. "It is only a name," she said. She moved away and joined the rest of the women.

Dan and I glanced at each other and shrugged.

At the harbor, we split off to pick up our packs, and then met the group back at the dock.

Basri had bribed the harbor officials to allow him to tie up his yacht at the jetty. I saw him now pressing bills into the palms of various dockhands and guards as we passed through the gate and walked out to his boat. They seemed both amused and envious at the sight of us: three young men and a gorgeous troupe of women traipsing tipsily down the quay to climb aboard the largest power yacht in the harbor. Most of the men knew Basri by name and didn't seem surprised by the company he kept.

"Mr. Pasha, you need my help tonight, yes?"

"Mr. Pasha, too many women, they going to sink your boat!"

"Mr. Pasha, take me with you—please!"

Dan and I, in a boozy haze of lust, watched as Basri helped each woman climb aboard his boat.

"Aphrodite leads the way to Dionysus," Dan said groggily.

"You can say that again." The future—at least for tonight and perhaps the next few days—looked positively scrumptious. A ten-to-one ratio of females to males. The possibilities boggled the mind.

"You must not come with us," a voice whispered.

We turned to find Damiana standing behind us. "The two of you should leave, quickly," she said.

"*Why?*" Dan asked.

She glanced up anxiously toward Basri. He was offering his hand to a red-haired woman, guiding her onto the boat. "It is not safe," she said.

Dan scoffed, "What do you mean, not safe?"

Her gaze was unsteady, and her lower lip trembled slightly. She was clearly inebriated, but her fear seemed sober and genuine. "I am afraid for your lives."

Her eyes moved back and forth between us. Then she pushed past us and hurried aboard the boat, slipping by the others in line.

For a moment I flashed on Phoebe, screaming in the pit of the *adyton.*

"Dan?"

"What?"

"You still think this is a good idea?"

His eyes were glued to the line of women still filing onto the yacht. "You think we have any choice in the matter?" He continued staring at the women. "We're in the hands of the Fates," he said.

I started to disagree with him, to repeat what Phoebe had once said to me, but somehow the words never came. *Dan's wish has come true,* I thought, recalling his plastic Aphrodite in the niche.

I turned to watch the last girl climb aboard the yacht. It would be no exaggeration to say the woman looked divine. As she took hold of Basri's outstretched hand, she glanced back at us and smiled.

I don't know why, but we followed her.

9

BASRI'S MOTOR yacht was enormous, but I was too drunk to be properly impressed. I could barely see the end of the thing as we staggered aboard in the dark. The glossy black aluminum hull reflected the lights of the harbor, while the sleek upper floors were a ghostly white, their windows darkly tinted, with the muted glow of the interior lights silhouetting the women inside.

Basri immediately put on some music and told us to help ourselves to the bar. Then he went into the pilothouse to take the yacht to a mooring in the harbor.

At the granite-top bar in the expansive living room, Dan and I concocted martinis. Women flitted past, chattering in Greek. Although we offered, we couldn't seem to entice them to join us for a drink. They appeared to be preparing for something as they scurried off with bags and clothes to particular rooms on the yacht.

Dockhands shouted, and the boat cast off. It barely felt like we were moving.

Drinks in hand, Dan and I entered the pilothouse. Basri was there, working the wheel, maneuvering the yacht through the harbor. Although intently focused on the task at hand, he appeared to be entirely relaxed. I wondered aloud how he could handle the colossal boat after all the drinking we'd done; I'd have had trouble navigating to the bathroom.

Basri laughed. "It's only a problem if you're stoned," he said, glancing pointedly at Dan.

"I told you that wasn't my fault," Dan said.

"You've piloted this boat?" I asked.

"Once," Dan said. Apparently he'd had a little accident. Dan stepped to the window and peered down at the forward deck. "Where's your crew?" he asked.

"On leave. I pick them up Thursday in Cyprus. There I do battle with the European Commission. 'Til then, I am on my own. The way I like it. Total freedom."

We watched him as he studied monitors, pulled levers, searched the water, spun the wheel. Talking all the while. "Make yourself at home, my friends. Tonight we party like sultans." He turned conspiratorial. "These women—you see them? They are like Greek women used to be. Not like your blonde with her statues. I promise you, we are having a *fantastic* night. Know what I am saying? Like nothing you ever seen."

"Where are they from?" Dan asked.

"An island very near to here. Ogygia."

It sounded like "geisha" with an O.

"Never heard of it," Dan said.

"Greece has thousands of islands. No one knows them all."

Dan and I stepped outside onto the tapered bow, passing between a small Zodiac dinghy and a Kawasaki jet ski tied down to the deck. As the bow spun out over the bay, the view of the sparkling harbor made me dizzy. "Too much ouzo," I said.

"Me, too," Dan said. "Thank God for the martinis."

The boat cruised away from the lights of the harbor. In seconds, the water looked black and foreboding. I fought off a tremor of fear.

We went back inside. On the deck below Dan showed me the vast and plushy hookah room, where Basri claimed his "business" was conducted. Opening the door to his luxurious master suite, we stumbled upon a dozen women in various states of undress.

We stood in the doorway, gaping. Discarded clothes lay scattered on the floor. Apparently, the ladies were changing into more suitable party attire. No one took any notice of us; they continued undressing as if we were housemaids come to turn down their beds.

I silently closed the door.

We climbed the spiral staircase to the highest deck on the yacht—the "flying bridge," Dan called it. Town lights glistened in the distance, and stars shone bright overhead. The piped-in Middle Eastern music rose like a cobra through the air. The deck held a slew of empty lounge chairs, another full bar, and a steaming, bubbling hot tub.

"Fantastic," I whispered. "This I cannot believe."

Dan said, "You're starting to talk like Basri."

"No," I said. "Look."

Three women were emerging from behind the mists of the tub. Shimmering light from the bubbling water played against their faces. They were dressed in diaphanous nightgowns—sheer, fluted, ivory sheets fastened with a clasp at the shoulder. The women reminded me of a painting I had seen, a Botticelli, I think, in Florence. As we walked forward to meet them, I was trying to remember the name of the painting, or what the three women in the picture were called, so I could say something clever to these three women now. But when we finally came close enough to speak, I saw that beneath their gauzy gowns, these women were very, very naked.

It stunned me into silence.

Dan's eyes roved up the tallest of the three. "Is that a chiton you're wearing?"

I choked off a laugh. It was the lamest pickup line I'd ever heard him use.

The woman merely nodded in response. She was slender and

shapely, with long, straight, rust-colored hair. The hair helped cover her breasts in the see-through gown, but it didn't reach as far as the patch between her legs. Even drunk I felt embarrassed, but couldn't seem to resist taking a bit too long of a peek.

She grinned at me. Her dark eyes glimmered. I sensed something vaguely unsettling about her.

"Ancient Greek tunic," Dan explained. "Looks like the classic design." He seemed to be genuinely fascinated.

Despite the fact she was nearly naked, the woman seemed completely unabashed. "They are made of the finest Greek cotton," she said, "on the island where I was born."

"Ogygia?" Dan asked.

Again she nodded.

I looked to the other two girls. "Is that where you're from, too?"

They stared at me blankly.

"They don't speak English," the tall woman said.

"Oh. Well—I'm Jack. This is Dan. What are your names?"

"I am afraid you will not remember our names," she said.

"Try me," I said.

"I am Thalia," she said. She nodded toward the girl beside her. "This is Aglaia. And she is Euphrosyne."

She was probably right about the names, but the girls themselves would be hard to forget. Both were gorgeous. Aglaia had rosy cheeks and curly black hair. She looked considerably younger than Thalia, maybe twenty-two or -three, but she had a more voluptuous body. The other young girl, who giggled when her name was spoken, had a flawless complexion, and dark-lined eyes with a mischievous flare.

"Looks like we're going to have a toga party," I said. "And I thought they only had sororities in America."

"A gift of the Greeks," Thalia said.

"Like the Trojan horse?" I asked.

She grinned her thin-lipped grin. "We are women, not warriors."

"You won't get any argument about that," I said.

"What will *you* wear?" Thalia asked.

I wasn't sure I heard her right. "What will we *wear*?"

"Tonight. The orgy."

Dan and I exchanged a look. I gulped.

Dan said, "We'll wear whatever you tell us to wear."

She looked to see if I were in agreement.

"Whatever," I said with a shrug. "When in Greece . . ."

"Do what the Greeks do," she said.

She moved closer to me and reached out her hand to take my martini. I gave it to her. She took a sip and swallowed. Then, with her long, painted fingernails, she picked the olive out of the glass. She held it up before my mouth. "Open," she said.

I did. She pressed the olive into my mouth. I chewed.

"Kiss," she said, leaning in.

I stopped chewing. She kissed me. I could taste the martini on her lips. She pulled away, then handed back the glass.

I stared at her, dumbly, the masticated olive in my open mouth.

"Kiss," she said to Dan. She was standing before him, waiting.

Dan glanced at me with a look that betrayed nothing. He stepped forward and took her in his arms. Bending her back, he kissed her like there was no tomorrow.

I glanced at the other girls. They were watching the kiss, entranced.

Dan and Thalia finally came up for air. She staggered back, staring at him. She wiped the back of her hand across her mouth. Her eyes fastened on his with a kind of animal intensity.

She moved back toward him. I wondered if she was going to kiss him again.

She slapped him hard across the face.

The blow threw his head to the side. Dan was stunned. He turned back, angry, glaring at her.

Thalia stared at him defiantly. Then she reached up gently to caress his reddened cheek. Dan was breathing rapidly. Their eyes were locked on each other. She dragged her fingers down his throat and laid her palm on his chest. This seemed to have a calming effect.

She took his hand in hers, then turned and led him away.

We watched as they headed down the spiral staircase. I turned to the girls in confusion. "What the hell was *that* about?"

They looked at me, uncomprehending.

I gulped down the rest of my martini. "I think I need another drink," I said.

The black-haired girl took the glass from my hand and carefully set it down on the bar. Then she took hold of my empty hand, and the mischievous girl took the other. They led me off to the staircase. I was trying to remember their names.

THE BEDROOMS were three floors down. As the girls led me into one of them, I noticed Thalia closing the door to the one across the hall. The look on her face gave me a chill. Behind her I saw a dim figure standing alone in the dark.

"Dan?"

Thalia grinned as the door swung shut.

The girls gently towed me into the room and sat me on the edge of the bed. I tried to calm my pounding heart. *Why was I so anxious? Certainly Dan could handle himself. And so can I,* I thought. *What danger could these women be?*

"I'm from Chicago," I said. "I've never been to an orgy before. How does it work exactly?"

The girls didn't respond. The one with the mischievous eyes dimmed the lights and turned up the Middle Eastern music. A brassy, pipsqueak horn was weaving a weird, snaky tune.

The other, voluptuous girl approached and stood directly before me. I peered through the milky gown at her breasts, squeezed together in the vice of her arms as she reached to unbutton my shirt. Her softly molded shoulders gleamed with the luster of moonlit marble. The woman's wavy black hair, loosely but artfully arranged, dangled in delicate coils to her cheeks. As she focused on the task at hand, her mouth opened in concentration, revealing behind her cherry lips the brilliant white of her teeth.

She removed my shirt.

A pair of hands encircled my neck. I felt a ripple of fear. The girl with the dark-lined eyes had crawled onto the bed behind me. Her hands now slid to my shoulders, and she gently pulled me down on the mattress.

Looking at her face, upside down, I tried to make sense of her expression. Was it a smile or a frown? Before I could decide, she lifted her nightgown over my face and got up on her knees above me, offering a startling view of her crotch. Just as quickly she pulled it away, the gown retreating across my face, again revealing her frowning smile.

I suddenly remembered her name. "Euphrosyne!"

As if in reward, she rose up on her knees again and gave me another glimpse.

Meanwhile, the black-haired girl had removed my pants and was now stripping off my boxers. She tossed them aside and knelt at my feet. Slowly she spread my knees, and her hands moved up my thighs.

"Aglaia!"

Once again the chiton fluttered over me as the generous Euphrosyne proffered another glimpse. This time I saw her breasts as well, bobbing beneath the gown.

The fear I had felt turned into excitement. A shudder of desire went through me. I was now lying with my feet on the floor, naked and supine on the bed, with little Miss Mischievous flashing her wares, Miss Voluptuous tickling my thighs.

If their intention had been to arouse me, there was growing evidence of success.

Euphrosyne lowered her face and kissed me. Her tongue pressed into my mouth. My tongue went into hers. An upside-down French kiss, bizarrely erotic, like discovering a strange new orifice.

In the midst of this kiss, Aglaia took hold of me. I nearly exploded in her hands.

Euphrosyne finished kissing me and once again wafted her chiton. This time I couldn't resist—her sweet buns had been beckoning: I reached to take hold of her hips.

With a giggle, she wriggled free of my grasp. I sat up and reached for Aglaia.

Aglaia pulled back with a shriek. A playful look on her face.

I reached again for Euphrosyne. She skittered across the bed. I rolled over and scrambled after her. She barely escaped my clutches.

Aglaia knocked off the light switch. Suddenly I couldn't see a thing. And all I could hear was the snaky music, that writhing, feverish horn.

I climbed off the bed and groped through the dark. The airy brush of fleeting fabric sent me lunging after it. I banged into a dresser. The girls giggled merrily. Heading toward the sound of their voices, reaching into the dark, I stumbled back into the bed. The girls went scrambling across it. I crawled after them, but again they managed to escape my grasp, filling the air with their shrieks.

I heard the door across the hall bang open. Thalia let out a scream of delight as she raced off into the hallway. I heard Dan go thumping after her. Then our door flew open suddenly, and the two girls fled from the room.

I climbed off the bed and looked down the hall. They were spiraling up the staircase. As quickly as I could, I pulled on my jeans and went after them.

10

I WAS still zipping my pants as I pounded up the stairs—a dangerous operation under the circumstances—so I paused for a moment when I reached the next floor to finish without causing any damage. When I looked up, I saw Dan standing in his boxers and a roomful of women staring at us.

The lights were off, and the room was dimly lit with candles. At least thirty women were standing in the shadows, each of them wearing a chiton. Euphrosyne and Aglaia, flush from their flight, were finding a place among them. Dan was standing a few steps in front of me, without his pants or shirt. His boxers could not quite contain his excitement; his hands were covering his crotch.

"I . . . uh . . . must be in the wrong room," he said. He started to turn away.

"Danny Boy, is that you?"

It was Basri's voice. The women parted, revealing the Pasha, reclining on a plushy couch. Two girls in chitons lounged beside him. He too was wearing his boxers, along with an open shirt, revealing again the bulging gut he had displayed to great acclaim at the club. One hand rested on the thigh of a woman, the other held a martini glass by the stem.

Thalia was standing behind him.

Basri took note of Dan's predicament. "Well, you look plenty warmed up, my friend. How about Jack? Ready to begin?"

I gulped, and nodded.

"Come on in—don't be shy!"

We meekly entered the room. Dan had told me this was Basri's famous hookah lounge, an upscale version of the Den of Iniquity from his university days. It was a large, luxuriously upholstered space, lined with Persian carpets, velvet drapes, plush satin pillows, and silk futons, with yet another bar in one corner of the room, and in another, a giant Turkish hookah pipe.

Basri, looking like an overfed satyr, struggled to extract himself from the couch. "I think we're all assembled then. Let's get on with it, shall we?"

Someone turned off the music. The women dispersed themselves around the room, gradually arraying into a circle. Dan and I joined them, taking places near Basri. Being half undressed made us feel ill at ease, but the women paid no mind. They remained aloof in their elegant chitons, like classical feminine figures circling the bowl of an ancient vase.

A small, athletic-looking woman, with a shaved head and round, black-rimmed eyeglasses, began blowing a tune on a simple reed flute. Thalia sang to the melody in Greek. Her voice was high-pitched and lovely, but the tune was oddly archaic and meandering, like an ancient aria or a medieval hymn. Soon the other women were joining in the song, adding atonal textures and rhythmical refrains.

"It's a dithyramb," Dan whispered. "A call for Dionysus."

As we listened, my eyes wandered through the candlelit room, taking note of familiar faces: Thalia with her long, rust red hair; Marina minus her scarf; Irene with her cover-girl beauty mark. Euphrosyne and Aglaia, directly across, seemed totally focused on the singing. With their upraised faces and closed eyelids, they looked like a sculpted pair of angels.

The beautiful Damiana stood two down from Dan; I had to lean forward to see her. She appeared even comelier in her diaphanous chiton than she had in her green dress and pearls. Once again lost in her own inner world, she did not return my gaze but stared straight ahead, as if singing to some invisible being.

I wondered again why she had warned us to leave. A creeping uneasiness came over me. The air felt suddenly cold.

From the flickering shadows behind the women a striking figure emerged. He wore an elaborate purple robe and a large, menacing mask. The mask was made of bronze or brass, with dark, gaping eyes and a hollow, smiling mouth.

I knew at once it was Dionysus—the "god" the women had been calling for. The gold-embroidered robe looked like the vestment of a priest. I assumed it was a man, but he seemed to walk with a female's grace, as if he were floating on air. Wavy, dark silver hair rimmed his gleaming mask. His glinting eyes were hidden in darkness.

Following behind this androgynous Dionysus were two young women carrying ritual vessels. One held a heavy amphora, a long, vaselike ceramic jug with two curving handles at the top. I had seen several like it at the museum in Athens. The second girl carried a dazzling silver drinking cup, cast with two faces back-to-back, and wide looping handles that rose above the rim.

The girls followed Dionysus into the center of the circle.

Around them the women began to sing a chant, hauntingly low and repetitive. The masked Dionysus took the silver drinking vessel, and the girls raised the heavy amphora. Tilting it to the cup, a darkly gleaming wine poured forth. The girls stood solemnly behind Dionysus as he raised the brimming cup to the gods.

The women continued their low, moaning chant. Dionysus carried the vessel to Thalia and ceremoniously handed it to her. Thalia bowed her head, then raised the drink to her lips and sipped.

Once. Twice. Three times.

Dionysus took the cup to the next woman in the circle, and she repeated the drinking ritual—once, twice, three times. He passed the cup to Marina, then Irene, and continuously on around the room, each woman taking the three requisite sips. When the cup ran dry, it was refilled from the amphora, then passed to the next in line. All the while the women sang the mysterious, moanlike chant.

Finally, the cup came to Dan. As he raised it to his lips, I could see clearly the two faces on the vessel, one of a man, the other of a woman. Dan solemnly imbibed. He seemed taken aback by the powerful taste and looked up in surprise at Dionysus.

The god remained impassive.

Dan glanced at me, then took his second sip. This one he savored, and the third he greedily gulped.

The cup was returned to Dionysus. The girls raised the heavy amphora and filled it up again. This time, I could clearly see the liquid pouring out. I had assumed that it must have been wine, but the color, I now noticed, was more purple than red. The fluid was frothy like milk or beer, yet it poured with a gleaming viscosity that resembled a syrup or oil.

Dionysus turned and offered me the cup. I took it by its high, looping handles and held it for a moment in front of me. The vessel was ancient and the metal heavy, but the faces were delicately tooled. Details had been artfully hammered in the silver, with gold filigree in the hair of the heads and inlaid ivory and glass for the eyes.

I looked at Dionysus' eyes, tiny glints of light in the black voids of the mask. The smile-frozen face seemed uncannily near, and at the same time strangely remote. Again I thought of Damiana telling us to leave, and of Phoebe's dire warning of the Furies.

These women, Furies? Impossible, I thought. Nymphs or goddesses maybe, but surely these nubile beauties were the opposite of Furies.

I took a sip of the mysterious drink. It seemed to explode in my mouth. A succession of sensations and flavors arose. At first it tasted harsh, then slightly sour, then, to my surprise, almost sweet. It tasted like bitter beer and honey. It had a granular, syrupy texture, but was bubbly and tart, almost sparkling. It sent a warm rush of steam through my body and all the way out through my limbs, and I felt a sudden surge of energy in my head, as if a torrent of bursting bubbles were coursing through my brain.

The drink was like nothing I had ever drunk before. Or like everything I had ever drunk all mixed up together.

The women continued chanting. Dionysus stared. All of them patiently waiting for me to take my second sip.

I raised the cup to my lips and drank. The metallic taste of the silver rim mixed with the scent inside the mug and the complex fusion of flavors. Again I felt the steamy rush, the effervescent jolt. It reminded me of my freezing dip in the spring. Everything seemed to stop.

Although the women continued their singing, a strange sort of silence came over me. I noticed the cold metal of the mug in my hands, the peculiar aftertaste of the drink in my mouth, the living eyes staring out from deep inside the mask—all suddenly vital and vividly present.

Dan was standing beside me, staring into the air. Beyond him, Damiana was chanting. She appeared to be under the same trance that had captured the rest of the circle, a trance induced by this drink in my hands.

It is not safe, she had warned. *I am afraid for your lives.*

My shadowed face stared back from the purplish pool of the drink. Slowly, I raised the cup for a sip. The liquid struck my lips, but I did not take it into my mouth, and only pretended to swallow. Two would be enough for me. I had already gone far enough; I needed some hope of returning.

I handed the cup back to Dionysus. Though his hands looked more like a man's than a woman's, he held the cup delicately in his fingertips, and he moved with the same sort of unhurried grace I had noticed in Damiana and the dancers.

He handed the bowl now to the woman beside me, and following her, to another and another. It felt like I was staring down a curving hall of mirrors, an endless cycle of ceremony.

I was falling deeper into the trance. Soon I was repeating aloud the words I had been hearing. Words chanted in an ancient tongue, strange and visceral-sounding.

It was Basri's turn at the well. He took it with less solemnity than pleasure, greedily gulping down his three. He would gladly have taken a fourth, it seemed, but the frozen face of Dionysus deterred him, and he dutifully handed the great cup back, the last of all to be sated.

Dionysus gave the vessel to the girls, and they carried it off with the amphora. The masked god moved into the center of the circle and gave a sharp clap of his hands. The chant ended abruptly.

Seconds later, music flowed into the room again, piped in over the speakers. It resembled the music playing earlier, with simple strings, pipes, and horns, only this was wilder, more percussive and primitive, with clashing cymbals and tambourines, and the thundering beat of drums.

The women began drifting out from the circle and swaying their bodies to the sound. Soon they were swirling around Dionysus like fluttering moths around a fire. Their movements were strangely stylized, yet remarkably rhythmic and quick, with strong strides and flowing arms, their ghostly nightgowns streaming.

Basri, Dan, and I stood mesmerized. The women were scented and beautiful, their supple torsos twirling past, eyes flashing lethal fire. Gradually we found ourselves drawn into their dance, wandering through the flow of bodies, touched and turned by caressing hands and swirling hair and fabric. Dionysus had mysteriously vanished; all that remained was this whirl of flesh, comely and swift, concealed by the thinnest of threads.

I caught glimpses of Dan and Basri, their eyes alight with excitement, their mouths stretched wide and eager. They looked like drunken lions in a rushing herd of deer.

Basri was the first to reach for a woman. She shrieked and fled away laughing. He turned to grab another, then another, and another, and soon the man was spinning in a whirl.

Dan was chasing Thalia. She easily slipped away. Another women grabbed his face and kissed him. When Dan tried to hold her, she broke away and ran. He chased her through a cacophony of shrieks.

My eyes roamed over the whirlwind of women, each looking eager and fiery and wild. The profusion of opportunity was astonishing. My heart pumped madly, my breathing escalated, and the hard-on in my jeans was nearly bursting. Never had I been so totally aroused; the excitement was nearly unbearable. I felt myself teetering on the edge of control, as if ready to embark on a rampage.

I grabbed the wrist of a passing woman. She turned, flushed and excited. There was a dare in her eyes, a defiance. A look clearly taunting me to take her. I reached to embrace her, but she quickly wriggled free, and springing off, instantly vanished. She was lost in the cloud of women swiftly flowing past—singing, laughing, shouting.

Euphrosyne suddenly appeared out of nowhere with that mischievous look in her eye. Her neck and shoulders looked sweet enough to bite. I moved toward her and she backed away. I lunged for her and she fled.

As I chased her through the throng of women, she squealed with glee, glancing back, hair flying loosely behind her. All I could think of was her lifting her chiton, teasing me with glimpses of her cunt. I wanted to catch her, and kiss her, and spank her, and fuck her. I wanted to overpower her completely.

Chasing after her, I ran smack into Dan. Sweaty, giddy, manic, he put a little scare in me: I thought it might be possible he'd actually lost his mind. He grabbed my face between his hands, peered into my eyes, and spoke with a burning intensity.

"Take it, Jack. The plunge. The plunge into fucking matter!"

He stared into my eyes and shook me, then threw me aside and went after a girl. She screamed as he tried to catch her.

A thrill went through me. *The plunge into matter. Total freedom of action in the physical world.*

Several dozen women were prancing around me, their bodies radiant and ready, offered up for pleasure on the altar of the earth. *What is there to hold me back? What could possibly stop me?* I saw with sudden clarity a view of total freedom. To live fully in the moment as an incarnated god. Able to do anything. To experience everything.

Aglaia glided into view. The Voluptuous One whose hands had nearly brought me to an end. Black curls, soft skin, exquisitely endowed. She moved among the bodies, prettily dancing past, her wary eyes watching like a fawn within the herd.

I moved slowly toward her.

She saw me coming immediately and tried to slip away. I sprang. She gasped and ran. Screams erupted from the women in my path as I went tearing after her.

This one I would not let go. This one I would fuck.

I tripped over Basri and crashed to the floor. He was naked on his hands and knees, clutching at the chiton of a woman trying to crawl away. Another woman, big as a blimp, was riding on his back. Her chiton hung off her shoulders, exposing massive breasts. A third woman slapped his bare ass red.

More were going after him, piling on in a frenzy.

I got up and looked for Aglaia. She was standing across the room, hiding behind some women still caught up in the dance. I went directly for her, calling out her name. It was drowned in the music and the voices of the women, hollering and laughing as they whirled around the room. Dan was on the floor, a woman naked under him, her arms around his head. It was Thalia—she was howling, with a half-crazed look on her face. Another woman appeared, threw up her chiton, and sat down on Dan's naked bottom.

Aglaia ran off behind the dancing women. I went after her again, obsessed with the hunt, intent on this particular woman. Not for any rational reason. There was no thinking at all. I was no longer even conscious of myself. All that remained was the impulse, the pursuit and indulgence of lust.

Finally, I caught her in a corner of the room. She crouched like a wrestler, awaiting my attack. I launched myself like a leopard. She lunged to escape, but I grabbed hold of a wrist and pulled her toward me. The excitement in her eyes was electric. Her other hand swept through the air and struck me in the face, like the slap Dan had taken from Thalia. I grabbed hold of the hand and twisted it, forcing it up behind her back, pressing her against the wall.

My cheek was smarting. I was surprised that I liked it. The anger it provoked made me want her even more.

She was breathing hard and struggling to free herself. With my left hand I ripped the chiton from her shoulder, the metal clasp flinging to the floor. Her back was exposed all the way to her hip. I ran my hand over her body. Her skin was damp with perspiration, and she smelled of the same scent I'd noticed in the bedroom, a bright scent of flowers and a musky scent of earth, as if she'd been rolling in a meadow. Her hip flared out to her dimpled derrière, which I felt with my hand and the inside of my wrist, my fingers probing underneath her.

I pressed my lips to her shoulder blade, and nosed beneath her black curls to the gentle curve of her neck. There I bit her softly, holding a fold of her skin in my teeth. As my fingers found their way inside her, she moaned and relaxed in her struggle against me. I released the bite of flesh and loosened my grip on her wrist. She turned, slowly twisting around, and lifted her arm up over me, releasing a breast from her half-open gown.

I kissed her throat. Her chest heaved beneath me, and again the scent of wildflowers wafted from her skin. My hand could not encompass her breast as I lifted it to my mouth. It tasted of salt and powder. A wavy black curtain of hair draped me as I feasted. Her fat, engorged nipple endured the onslaught of my tongue.

Euphrosyne was suddenly behind me. She reached her arms around me and started unzipping my pants. Her chest swelled against my back, her breathing warmed my neck. She reached into my jeans and took hold of me. I was as stiff as a randy satyr. She held it like she owned it while giggling in my ear.

I dragged the chiton off Aglaia's shoulder. The gown dropped to her waist. She struggled to free herself and push me back as I pressed in tight upon her. When she turned her face aside, I kissed her pulsing temple and nibbled at her ear. Her arms slid over my shoulders, and she hugged my face to her breasts.

Euphrosyne's arms were still wrapped around me, her hands still clamped on my cock. She treated it like her toy. My pants had fallen to my ankles, and she ran her bare foot up and down my leg, stroking her thigh against me.

Over the throb of the music, I heard Basri groan, and a woman's voice called out in Greek a word or a phrase like a song. Aglaia turned and kissed me. She touched her tongue to mine. Euphrosyne finally released her grip, and together with Aglaia, the two of them tugged me away from the wall and down with the bodies on the floor. I caught in the writhing mass of flesh a glimpse of Dan, his bullet head locked between a woman's thighs. Farther off, Basri was riding atop the big woman who had earlier been riding on him. His face was buried in the crotch of another standing with her legs open before him. Women were climbing over one another, trying to get their hands on his body.

Half a dozen women joined Aglaia and Euphrosyne as they kissed and caressed and sucked me on the floor. Irene's chiton was half torn off; Marina was totally naked. An elegant-looking woman hiked up her gown and lowered herself to my face. I clawed at her with my tongue and she pulled herself away. Then another came and did the same. Then another. And another. They drove me into a frenzy of rampaging lust.

I went after them like a madman. We wrestled into a writhing mass. Women scratched and slapped and bit me. I licked and fingered and felt and fucked. Thrusting deeper into the frenzy, I rammed my way into rapture, burrowing into their flesh. My body ignited in a blaze of sensation. Thought was entirely obliterated. It seemed I could no longer see—only hear, smell, taste, touch. Everything blurred in a violent flux. I lost all sense of separation, of being bound in a single sheath of skin. In that explosion of consciousness, I vanished into a devouring maelstrom of matter: eyeballs, buttocks, bellies, breasts, lips, tongues, teeth—

The last thing I saw before losing myself was the beautiful face of Damiana. This stranger who had captured my eye on the beach, this dancer who had moved like a panther, was approaching naked on her hands and knees.

Her teeth were tinged with blood.

II

THANATOS

◆ ◆

11

WAS I *unconscious or sleeping?*

I seemed to be floating on an Olympian cloud. My eyes couldn't focus on the whiteness. My temples throbbed. My limbs ached. My mouth felt dry and cottony.

As I rose up painfully onto my knees, I saw I'd been lying on a polar bear rug. The rug was stained with blood.

I was naked. There were scratches and bite marks all over my body. Many of the tears in the skin still bled. My scalp felt oddly tender, and my penis was raw and sore. My shoulders and knees and elbows ached. When I noticed a similar aching tension in my fingers, I realized I was clutching something tightly in my fist.

I opened my hand. A bloody little stick of flesh lay on my palm.

Short and thick as the butt of a cigar, it was creased and curved, with a round, tapered tip. Wiping the blood away revealed a wrinkled knuckle and a broad thumbnail.

From the size, it appeared to be a man's thumb. It had been

ripped from the joint where it joined to the hand. The red root of torn flesh covered the metacarpal, from which severed blood vessels hung like scarlet threads.

I stared at it, stunned, for what must have been a full minute, trying to figure out whose hand it belonged to, and how it had been torn off, and *why. Did I do it myself?* I had no memory of it. Certainly tearing off somebody's thumb is a thing you wouldn't easily forget. I wondered how it was even possible. It must have taken great strength. *Why would I ever do such a thing? Why would anybody?*

The nail, I noticed, was bitten back, which made me think it was Dan's—he bit his nails obsessively. Basri may have done the same, of course. The thumb might even have belonged to a woman—at least one of them had been large enough to have had a thumb this big.

I stood up and looked around the empty room. *Where has everyone gone?* I had no idea how long I'd been out. It appeared to be early dawn. Somber gray light from an undraped window fell across the carpeted floor, revealing more scattered bloodstains. Basri's shirt lay draped across the couch, his torn boxers crumpled on an Oriental rug. Dan's boxers dangled from the bar. There was no sign of a single chiton, or any other clothes from the women. I noticed my jeans lying in the corner, the same corner where I had captured Aglaia, pinning her body against the wall.

What have I done? Our playful sexual encounter had come dangerously close to rape. She seemed to have lured me into it, then deliberately resisted, which only increased my desire. I tried to remember what had happened after that. The bodies writhing around me. The women's sexual assault. My final, explosive rampage.

And Damiana. Crawling toward me with blood in her mouth.

What the hell happened? What was in that drink?

My head was throbbing. I found it hard to focus or make sense of anything. Still holding the thumb in my hand, I started toward the corner to pick up my jeans and stepped into a pool of blood saturating the carpet. Jumping back, I stamped a bold red footprint on the rug.

The sight of the footprint frightened me.

Someone had clearly been murdered. Most likely it was the same person whose thumb I held in my hand. It suddenly seemed quite possible that I had taken part in the murder. Given my state of mind at the time, I certainly couldn't prove that I hadn't.

I rubbed the sole of my foot on the carpet, trying to smear the footprint out and wipe the blood from my skin. Something sticky came off with the blood. I crouched down for a closer look and probed it with my finger.

It was a clump of human hair, torn out from the roots.

In the dim light, with all the blood, I couldn't tell its color. I wiped my finger clean on the rug. Then I went over and pulled on my jeans. As I zipped up, I noticed on the wall nearby a large handprint in blood.

Again I felt a shiver of fright. I moved closer to examine the print. All five fingers had left an impression. The hand had rested on the wall, then slid down leaving a bloody smear. I looked at my hands. The left was clean, but the right hand that held the severed thumb was stained red with blood. I dropped the thumb to the floor. Then I raised my bloody hand to the bloody print on the wall.

It fit perfectly.

I shuddered. In a panic, I backed away, then turned and ran from the room.

ON THE floor above, the main saloon was empty. I went up front to the pilothouse and found it empty, too. Through the windows I could see the lights of the harbor. The eastern horizon glowed faintly, the sky was overcast and gray, the water dark and silvery.

I left the pilothouse and ran up the stairs to the flying bridge, the top deck where Dan and I had met the three women. There was no one up there, either. Most of the deck was open to the sky, which seemed to be pressing down overhead, an unbroken mass of heavy clouds. A cool breeze ruffled my hair. The hot tub bubbled noisily.

My martini glass sat on the bar where Aglaia had placed it. Other than that, there was no sign anyone had been on the deck.

As I started back to the stairs, I glanced at the horizon and noticed there was something strange about Mykonos. The ships in the bay had all turned into fishing boats. White stucco houses stood piled above the shore, but the island appeared to have changed shape during the night. A mountain now loomed above the town.

The island was not Mykonos. We had traveled away from it during the night, and arrived here, at this strange harbor, while I'd been passed out down below.

Where am I? And where has everyone gone?

I remembered having seen a dinghy on the yacht. The size of it had impressed me. I hurried to the back of the top deck and peered out over the rail. The dinghy was gone. The spot where it had been tied up, three floors down at the stern, was empty.

The women, Dan, Basri—someone had taken it to shore.

I scrambled down the staircase again and searched every floor, every room of the yacht, calling out for Dan and Basri. There were ten bedrooms in all, including a small one behind the engine room and another behind the pilothouse. Every one of them was empty. I found no trace of the women at all; their bags and dresses had vanished. Dan's pack and mine remained exactly where we had left them. I checked for our passports and wallets. Nothing appeared to be missing, not even the cash. Clearly, this wasn't a robbery. The master bedroom closets were filled with Basri's clothes, and in the bathroom, his razor, toothbrush, and contact lens case lay where he'd left them on the counter. Obviously he hadn't packed before taking leave of the ship.

I gulped down some aspirin from his medicine cabinet. My frightened face stared back from the mirror.

I was the only one left on a boat where a murder had been committed. I may have had a part in that murder. My brother might well be dead. If I were the only one found on the boat—literally with blood on my hands—I'd be the prime suspect.

I had to get off the yacht as quickly as I could. Before I could even consider going to the police, I had to locate Dan and find out what happened. Only then would I know what to do.

The Zodiac tender and the jet ski were still tied down on the forward deck. I decided I should take the tender; the jet ski would draw too much attention. For the same reason I decided to avoid the harbor and come ashore farther up the island. I scanned the shoreline and picked a spot—a white gravel beach beyond the fringe of the town. At this early hour it looked deserted.

THE LEADEN sky lightened at the horizon as the sun began its climb. It cast the island's mountain in a peculiarly colored light, a strange mix of rosy dawn and ugly, yellow dusk. As I steered the Zodiac toward the shore, I glanced back at the yacht, anchored out in the bay. The black hull gleamed like midnight, but the white walls of the upper decks reflected the odd, orange light. It looked like a bloody ghost ship.

My Zodiac was the only boat moving on the water. The tiny outboard droned across the silent bay like a zipper, leaving a minor wake behind that nudged the fishing boats. Of the few figures I could make out on shore, no one seemed to pay me any mind. A fisherman stretched nets out on the dock. A storekeeper swept his sidewalk. A boy climbed onto his bike.

When I passed beyond the arm of the harbor, I saw there was no one on the white gravel beach. Just a neat row of upturned hulls, hauled up onto the shore. Beyond their bows was a low stone wall, and beyond that a rocky incline to a road that led into town. An old stone building flanked by cypress trees looked abandoned. Alongside the trees a steep, stone staircase led up the incline to the road.

I gave the outboard one last shot, then cut the engine, lifted the prop, and coasted onto the beach. I donned my backpack and hauled the Zodiac up onto the shore. The yellow craft stuck out from the row of wooden boats, but I didn't know what else to do with it.

The boy on his bicycle was pedaling up the road. He glanced at me briefly and waved. I found it somehow reassuring, and headed for the stairs.

The square stone building behind the cypresses appeared to be abandoned. Greek graffiti in blue letters were fading on the building's facade: έλευθερία. As I walked past, I peered through the trees into the dark archways and the glassless windows above them. I didn't see anyone.

At the top of the stairs, I had a view of the harbor and down the street into town. The street was cobbled, and most of the houses were built of stone and sealed in stucco. Rising from the sea of red-tiled roofs was the large golden dome of a church. Far off I spotted a stout woman waddling down the street, a broad, shallow basket propped against her hip, her head wrapped in a raven black scarf. The streets looked as twisty and narrow as those in Mykonos and covered the crowded hillside. Eventually the houses gave way to the mountain, which peaked somewhere beyond my view.

Below, the harbor was coming alive. Fishermen in captain's caps were busy on the dock, and a group of people were assembling around a boat at the edge of the water. I assumed they were buying fish, but no fish or cash was changing hands, and the crowd seemed agitated. With a jolt of panic I realized the boat was Basri's dinghy.

I raced down into the town, but it took me several exasperating minutes to find my way to the beach. One street gradually turned and narrowed, ending in a cul-de-sac. Another initially promising lane led me back up the hill. Finally, I spotted a young Greek couple descending a narrow staircase. I slipped past them and hurried to the bottom, which let out onto the esplanade, a flagstone walkway bordering the waterfront. Just beyond it lay the gravel beach, with Basri's dinghy and the gathering crowd.

The boat had been beached, but half of it was still in the water. As I approached, I saw that several of the onlookers were tourists or vacationers, either Greek or European; I didn't hear a word of English. Most of those gathered appeared to live in the village: fishermen with bristled, wind-blasted faces, and shopkeepers whose sharp eyes showed serious concern. I worked my way through the crowd to get a closer look. One or two people gave me scrutinizing looks, but most seemed to assume I was a tourist.

All at once the crowd stopped their chattering and turned to look behind them.

A policeman, led by a small, anxious-looking man in a suit jacket, had stepped off the esplanade and was heading across the strand.

I squeezed between two large barefoot fishermen and peered over the side of the boat. I froze in horror. Inside lay Dan's naked corpse, curled in the fetal position. His flesh had been badly bitten and scarred, and his arms appeared to be wrapped around a wrinkled ball of blood.

A memory flashed into my head—a woman shrieking madly—

Someone pulled me back as the policeman made his way through the crowd. I was so stunned, I couldn't speak—and I wasn't sure that I should. I gaped in silence as the cop brushed past. He was a burly, bearded man, with a cigarette in his mouth. He looked fatigued and slovenly in his hastily donned uniform, and he had a drooping gray mustache and long, disheveled hair. Silent, grimacing, he stared at Dan's body a moment, then tossed his cigarette to the sand and climbed up into the boat.

After taking a closer look at his face, he slapped Dan several times on the cheek.

I pushed closer, my heart racing.

Dan stirred.

He was unconscious, not dead. A murmur rumbled through the crowd.

I was so relieved, I nearly shouted. For a second I debated whether to lay claim to him and to reveal to the cop who I was. I started moving toward him, thinking that if I told the policeman everything that happened, if I explained to him that—

The cop lifted from Dan's arms the object they were holding. It was wrapped in Dan's Hawaiian shirt, saturated in blood. He set the thing down on the seat. Then he gingerly pulled back the bloody cloth.

I gasped.

Inside was Basri's head.

The crowd exclaimed, stepping back in revulsion, then immediately moving forward to take a closer look. The cop growled orders for us to move away, but everyone, including me, ignored him. We peered over and between one another, angling for a glimpse at the horror.

The cop grumbled to himself. Searching the bottom of the boat, he reached down under where Dan was lying and pulled up a strange-looking ax.

Another exclamation erupted from the crowd.

It was a double-headed hatchet, each blade facing in the opposite direction. It appeared to be very old and made of bronze, with an intricate design in the metal, and a long, slender, almost delicate handle. The ax looked as much like a work of art as an actual tool or weapon.

The blades glistened with blood.

Dan lifted his lolling head, trying to rouse himself. His sleepy eyes struggled with the scene unfolding around him: the bloody head on the seat, the ax in the policeman's hands, the crowd of leery onlookers. It was hard to tell how awake he was, how much he was understanding. I still felt groggy myself; had I drunk all three sips like he had, I'd still have been unconscious on the yacht.

The crowd murmured among themselves, and although I couldn't understand the words they were saying, I had no doubt one of them was "murder." The yacht was clearly visible out in the harbor, and they all seemed to be eyeing it now. Several men headed off toward their boats. The cop shouted for them to stop, and they turned to argue with him. Presumably he didn't want the evidence disturbed. I thought of my bloody handprint. But I had taken my wallet and passport with me, along with Dan's and Basri's. It wouldn't be so easy for them to find out who we were.

Finally the policeman prevailed and the men joined in to lift Dan from the boat. He was barely able to stand. His naked body, scratched and bloodied, made me think of Jesus. Like an aging

Mary Magdelene, an old Greek woman offered her apron to wrap around his waist. This made him look both tragic and ridiculous. The burly cop pulled Dan's arm over his shoulders and started into the crowd. There must have been upwards of forty people now gathered at the shore, a mixture of tourists and townies. We parted to make way as they walked him off the beach.

As they passed by, Dan caught sight of me. He was groggy but still conscious enough to hold me in his gaze. Following his initial recognition, there came a look of warning and a slight shaking of his head. *No,* he seemed to be saying. *You must keep yourself out of this.*

When I looked up, I saw the cop was eyeing me as well. Fearing he might notice some family resemblance, I nonchalantly turned away and slid back into the crowd. If he was suspicious of me, he didn't show it. He continued on, walking with Dan, without once looking back.

Although most of the tourists remained on the beach, much of the town crowd followed them. I trailed behind at a distance, far enough not to be noticed. They walked several long, winding, uphill blocks to what must have been the police station, though the only thing to identify it as such were the security bars on the high-set window and the blue-and-white squad car parked out front. Although a few men went inside with Dan and the cop, most remained out on the street, talking in hushed voices and lighting cigarettes.

I watched them with increasing anxiety, trying to decide what to do. I wanted desperately to talk to Dan, to find out if he knew what had happened. But there was no way I could see him now without turning myself in. We might both be indicted for the murder.

A dog barked from a window nearby. A voice called out to shush it. Shutters opened above me, and a woman shook out a dust rag and peered down curiously.

The dog continued barking, and the men down the street began looking my way. One of them crushed out his cigarette, staring at me intently.

I turned away casually and ambled down an alley. As I rounded the corner, I ran.

BACK DOWN on the esplanade, I ducked into a café. The place was nearly empty. Two local men at a table in the back were sipping Turkish coffee from tiny cups and smacking checkers on a backgammon board. I took a seat at a small table in the front beside a young, backpacking couple. When the short, balding proprietor appeared, I asked him for a bottle of water and a coffee.

The man noticed my hands were shaking. He looked at me for a moment. Although he appeared to understand English, I was afraid to ask him any questions that might arouse more suspicion. I waited until he went back to the kitchen, then turned to the two backpackers.

"Excuse me," I said, speaking in nearly a whisper. "Can you tell me what island this is?"

The boy was lanky, with acne scars and ruffled hair. The girl, a blonde, reminded me a little of Phoebe. She exchanged a look with her boyfriend, then turned to me in confusion. "I'm sorry? What you are asking?"

"This island we're on—what is it called?"

Now she looked genuinely curious. "Ogygia," she said.

It was the only answer that could have made any sense. "How did you get here?" I asked.

"The ferry," the boy said. "From Páros."

"When does it come again, do you know?"

"We board tomorrow morning," he said. It turned out they were students from the University of Heidelberg. They said this was the only town on Ogygia; the rest of the island was olive groves, vineyards, and pastureland, all on the slopes of the mountain. They were planning a hike that morning. "We are told on the cliffs is a monastery," the boy said. "And higher up are caves."

They asked if I was American, and if I had heard about the

naked man in the boat and the decapitation. When I told them I had seen the policeman take him, they began to ask me questions.

The proprietor came to collect their bill.

"I really don't know any more than you do," I told them.

The bald man glanced at me again before he headed back to the kitchen.

I noticed the dinghy had been pulled up onto the beach. Several locals had gathered beside it, undoubtedly pointing out bloodstains and recounting the morning's tale. Out in the harbor, a few fishing boats had anchored near the yacht, but I didn't see anyone boarding it.

As the German couple left the café, I spotted the policeman marching onto the wharf with his entourage of citizens. He climbed into what I assumed was the police boat, a white-hulled fiberglass cruiser that looked at least forty years old. They helped him unlash the boat from the dock, and the cop was soon rumbling out over the water on his way to investigate the yacht.

My heart was hammering. *Don't panic,* I thought. *I've got to keep cool and figure this out.*

I tried to imagine what the cop would make of the bloody mess on the boat. Would he assume it had all been done by Dan? The women had left no trace of themselves. I wondered what had happened to the rest of Basri's body. Had it been tossed overboard? Why had Dan made a prize of his head? Why had I been holding his thumb? That had not been chopped off, but torn out by the root.

How could this nightmare have happened?

Basri had been murdered. My brother was in jail. I was a fugitive, possibly a killer. A policeman was heading to the scene of the crime. Eventually, he'd find the Zodiac and begin a search for me. If I was captured, Dan and I could easily be put away for life.

I didn't have much time. I couldn't talk to Dan without the risk of getting caught. I had to locate the women and find out what had happened. But I didn't speak any Greek, and I didn't know a soul on the island, no one in the country who could help me.

No one. *Except . . .*

12

DAN HAD left his cell phone in his backpack; I had grabbed it along with his wallet and passport before I left the yacht. Now I began digging for it in the bottom of my pack. I found it and turned it on. The number was listed in his directory, but when I tried to call, the screen read "No network available." The island was off the grid.

I considered asking the café proprietor if I could use his phone, but I feared I had already aroused his suspicions, and I didn't want to risk being overheard. After paying my bill and picking up some change, I headed for the square with the old-fashioned phone booth I'd passed on the way to the waterfront.

The clouds were dispersing, the sun was breaking out, and the streets of Ogygia were awakening. I hustled up a lane past tourist shops just opening their doors. A father and his two little boys walked by me, wearing only their swimsuits. A bent old Greek lugged an enormous basket of bread on his back. Another man peddled past on a three-wheeled cargo bike. There were no autos on the flagstone streets; it felt like a medieval city.

I almost got lost again looking for the square. The many twisting alleys were bewildering. Arching passageways, steep stone stairs, high walls shrouded with ivy. Eventually I came into the treeless plaza, where an outdoor market had been set up and was thriving. I headed directly for the phone booth.

My hands were still shaking as I fumbled with the coins. I plugged them in and dialed and waited as it rang.

And rang. *Answer,* I prayed. *Please be home. Please, please—*

"Yásou—".

"Phoebe?"

She continued speaking in Greek.

"Phoebe—it's me, Jack."

It wasn't until I heard the *beep* that I realized I was talking to a machine. I quickly blurted out a stumbling message about Dan and I being in serious trouble, that we needed her help, that we were on an island called Ogygia, that she could reach it on the ferry from Páros, and to please come as quickly as she could. I told her I'd look for her on the ferry in the morning.

I hung up.

An empty silence filled the booth. My call seemed desperate and pathetic. *Why get Phoebe involved in this nightmare? How could she possibly help?*

I stared out at the old women shopping in the square. They looked like black-cloaked dwarves. A wave of nausea came over me. A sickening feeling of dread.

We're in the hands of the Fates, Dan had said.

I pushed out of the booth and took a deep breath. The air smelled of fish and the smoky odor of game. I drifted into the square.

The round stone fountain was bone-dry and lifeless, with nervous pigeons perched on the pillar at its center, and two old women resting on its rim. A sleeping dog nearby looked dead. Walking past it, a man led a mule to a beehive oven, where his wife began unloading the animal's massive bundle of sticks, fuel for roasting the chicken and rabbit skewered inside the fire. Smoke from the oven hung in the air and lent to the confined space of the square a gloomy illusion of distance.

Peering through this smoky haze, my eyes fixed suddenly on a woman across the way. Something about her looked familiar. Although much younger than the other local women, she was dressed even more conservatively, with a black head scarf and a long black skirt that gave her the appearance of a nun. I moved closer to get a better view. A grizzled merchant half her height was selling her a few dolmades. It wasn't until she started to walk away that I finally realized who she was.

Damiana.

My heart soared. Even though I couldn't quite see her face, I was certain it had to be her. The black scarf couldn't hide her satiny curls, and she had the same graceful, languorous gait I had so longingly admired on the beach. She briefly perused the other stalls—holding up a glimmering cluster of grapes, smelling a bundle of lilacs, picking through bins of almonds and chestnuts—before finally purchasing a handful of dates and what looked like a child's toy, a small bird carved in wood that dangled from a string.

I moved closer, my pulse pounding hard. I was tempted to walk right up and tap her on the shoulder, but suddenly I feared she might reveal who I was and possibly make some kind of scene. So I hid among the buyers and waited. When she finally left the square and headed up a street, I followed surreptitiously behind, hoping to find out what I could before confronting her.

The street was fortunately a popular route. Both tourists and locals were walking it, and I could easily blend into the crowd. Damiana nibbled a date as she climbed the curving road. When she encountered a flight of steps, she lifted her skirt off her ankles, and I noticed she wore the same long-laced sandals she had worn the previous night.

More than once a passing Greek tipped his hat in respect. Although she appeared to acknowledge them, she never once stopped to talk.

Toward the top of the hill, she turned abruptly and entered a narrow alley. I waited at the street until she vanished around a turn, then cautiously followed in after her.

The walls of the alley were two and three floors high, with several flying buttresses arching overhead. I followed the sound of her steps on the cobblestones. At one point the lane narrowed to the width of my shoulders, and an arched top covered it like a tunnel. At the end a skinny cat waited to get a glimpse of me, then suddenly fled as I approached. The lane jogged sharply, straightened, then turned back again. I heard a splash of water tossed from a pail, and seconds later, as a door closed, I stepped over the resulting puddle. The sound of footsteps suddenly faded away, and as I rounded the final bend, I saw that Damiana had exited into the street.

I hurried after her.

The street bordered a large square, at the end of which stood a great Byzantine church. A rickety bus rumbled past, spewing a noxious fog. I watched Damiana cross to the church and enter through large wooden doors at the side.

The basilica dominated the leafy square and looked quite striking from afar. A large golden dome with slender, arched windows capped one end; a belfry tower rose from the other. Between them, smaller conical domes sprouted from its red-tiled roofs. Attached to the church was another stone building, built in a later century but designed in a similar style. I thought it must have been a school or a rectory, though it appeared to be no longer inhabited.

Only a few tourists occupied the square, along with a middle-aged Greek woman walking a dachshund, and a nun in a full, flowing habit floating away down the street.

The bell in the tower rang out. I figured it must have been the call to mass. The tourists, who had been snapping pictures of the church, suddenly gathered up and filed inside.

I crossed the street and followed in after them.

◆ ◆

It took a moment for my eyes to adjust. There were very few windows in the thick stone walls, and the interior was dim and smoky. I stepped slowly forward into the open nave of the church. A few dark figures sat alone in the pews, and a group of tourists were gathered in a corner, off to the side of the central dome. A woman's voice among them reverberated softly.

I sensed a kind a palpable stillness in the air, and paused to gaze at the ceiling.

The bright wash of morning sunshine squeezed through the narrow windows high up in the dome, casting angled beams of light against the upper walls. These walls were covered with elaborate mosaics, glimmering scenes of Christ and the saints, which bathed the dusky space below in an eerie luminescence. An odor of mold and stale incense permeated the damp air and added to the tactile sense of tranquility, the seemingly touchable silence.

I approached the crowd of tourists who had gathered around their guide. It was her voice I'd been hearing, and as I got closer, I realized she was speaking perfect English. When I wandered around to the back of the group and turned to look at her face, I saw it was Damiana.

". . . some of the finest mosaics in all of Greece," she was saying. "Several were damaged in the earthquake of 1881, but—"

She stopped when she spotted me, long enough for her audience to wonder who I was. All of them turned to look at me. After a moment, Damiana recovered and carried on with her spiel.

"—much of the damage has been repaired. The church was built in the thirteenth century, when the island was a part of the Byzantine Empire. Late in the fourteenth century, the Venetians took control, and following them, the Ottomans, who ruled over all of Greece for three hundred and fifty years. They whitewashed many of the frescoes, intending to obliterate them, but it actually helped to preserve them. If you look at the wall behind you, you can see the Nativity scene, which has been partially restored . . ."

She continued, trying her best to ignore me while leading the group along. Apparently, she was employed by the church as a docent. She seemed to know everything about the building. She spoke at length about its architecture, and the design and construction of the dome. Her knowledge of the many mosaics was impressive. She described the scenes depicted and the techniques of the craftsmen, pointing out subtle details in the intricate designs.

I grew impatient. "What was there?" I asked obnoxiously, pointing to a bare spot in the Betrayal in the Garden. An apostle was leaning toward Jesus, and most of his head was missing.

"Earthquake damage," she said flatly. "Couldn't be repaired."

"Yes, I can see that," I said. "But what is it that's missing?"

She seemed reluctant to answer. "It's . . . the Kiss of Judas," she said.

"That's what I thought. A shame it hasn't been fixed. I see Peter lopping off the soldier's ear—that's in perfect condition."

The tourists eyed me. I knew I was being ridiculous, but it felt good to vent my anger. Damiana looked at me without responding, then went on with her talk.

When she finished with the mosaics, we moved into the narthex, the vast entry hall, with tall pillars supporting its soaring conical domes. This, too, was filled with mosaics, and the floor was intricately patterned with marble. Beyond it was the belltower, which had been added after the earthquake, and to the side off the apse was a passage to the building next door.

This building was not a school or a rectory, as I'd thought, but an infirmary, built to care for the sick during the rule of the Venetians. She took us down into an operating room she said was used to care for those wounded during the Greek revolt in 1822, which led to an Ottoman slaughter, and again in the Second World War, when Ogygians resisted the Nazi occupation. They finally closed the O.R down after the civil war that followed. "The last few decades," she said, "have left the island in peace."

After hearing this tumultuous history, I doubted the Ogygians would enjoy their peace for long.

I waited while she wrapped up her talk and answered the

tourists' questions. Then, when the last of them had left, I asked her some questions of my own.

"What happened last night?"

"I'm sorry," she said. "I don't know what you're talking about."

"You *what*?"

She turned and walked away.

I followed her. "Last night. On the boat. You were there."

"I've never seen you before," she said.

I grabbed her arm. "Never *seen* me before? You've seen me, all right. And I've seen you. And you weren't exactly wearing that . . . burqa a you're wearing now."

"Let go of me," she said.

"Tell me who you are. Tell me what the hell is going on."

"Let go of me or I'll scream."

She was looking directly at me. I stared back at her. I had no doubt she would do what she said. But still I was unwilling to relent.

Damiana turned her face away. I waited for her scream.

"Begging your pardon?" An elderly gentleman and his wife were standing just inside the door. The man held his hat to his chest. He hesitated a moment, then asked in the kindliest voice, "We are wondering, *Signorina* . . . when is next you are talking?"

I released Damiana's arm. She glanced at me, then straightened her sleeve and answered. "The next tour is at noon."

"*Grazie,*" the Italian said, bowing his head slightly. He took his wife's arm, and they slowly shuffled out the door.

Damiana turned to me.

I looked her straight in the eye. "Basri is dead. My brother is in jail."

"I cannot help you," she said.

"You can tell me what happened. You can tell me *why.*"

She shook her head, staring vaguely. "No. No one can understand this."

"Please," I said. "I have to understand."

She looked away.

"Who were those women?" I asked.

She looked back at me. "I warned you once. I will tell you again: *Leave this island while you can.*"

It seemed she felt genuine concern for my safety. "My brother is in jail," I said. "They think he killed Basri."

"It is too late for him. You must save yourself."

"From *whom*?"

She looked at me with something like pity in her eyes.

"They will kill you," she said.

HER WARNING reverberated in my mind like some gnawing, demonic echo. *They will kill you.*

Who were these women, these choirgirls, these whores of Dionysus?

When Damiana refused to tell me any more, I left the church in a huff and started searching through the town. There had been over thirty women on that boat; I was bound to run into one of them. I checked in shops and cafés. I walked the waterfront. I hiked out to the public beach, climbed the streets into the hills, and hung out in the squares. Scanning everyone I passed, I never glimpsed a single face I recognized from the boat. Where were these Aphrodites who had lured us into murder? I searched their twisting streets in vain. Repeatedly I found myself lost in their labyrinth, with Damiana's baleful warning rattling through my head.

They will kill you.

In the late afternoon I returned to the church and waited for Damiana to leave. The sun had dropped behind the mountain, and a soft, dusky light had descended on the square. The last group of tourists gradually straggled out the entrance, and moments later Damiana emerged, locking the great doors behind her.

She didn't head back the way she had come, but crossed the lane behind the church and climbed a cobbled street. I followed at a safe distance, not wanting to be observed. At the top of the hill, she turned and continued down a narrow lane that wound along the hillside. She stopped at a very old stone building that turned out to be a school. I had missed it in my ramblings. Children were pouring out the doors, and one of them, a young boy, ran to grab her hand.

Damiana offered him a gift: the toy carved bird she had purchased in the square. The boy seemed delighted. He dangled the bird from the string and spun it before his face. They walked on together. The boy was probably six years old; too old to have been her son. I decided he must be her brother.

This proved true when they finally reached their house and their mother came out to greet them. I watched from a distance, behind a row of trees. The house was a modest, whitewashed cube like others all around it. Out front was an old, round-fendered pickup truck, its hood raised, with a man bent over the engine. When the boy came running up and wrapped himself around the man's leg, the old guy surfaced, and the boy showed off his little carved bird. Damiana gave her father a peck on the cheek, then turned to walk back inside with her mom. The boy went charging in after them, and the father went back to his tinkering.

After a moment I turned away and headed back down the street. I felt completely exhausted, and I could not even begin to make sense of what I'd seen.

THAT NIGHT I checked into the *Argonauta,* a small hotel with a WELCOME sign I had noticed earlier in the day. It turned out the aged proprietor didn't speak any English; she communicated by pantomime while mumbling to herself in Greek. The room I was given on the second floor was small, clean, and spare; its single window, which overlooked the street, offered a narrow view of the harbor.

My intention was to rest for a while before continuing my search, but once I laid down, I fell fast asleep and didn't wake until late in the night, when I heard two women talking. I lay there awhile, drowsily listening. The voices seemed to come from the floor below. When I heard the front door to the hotel shut, I got up and went to the window. A shrouded figure veiled in black moved off down the street. I watched as it disappeared into the dark.

13

THE FERRY from Páros was half an hour late. I waited anxiously on the waterfront, doing my best to blend into the crowd. All down the esplanade, tourists were perusing the market stalls and stopping into the *tavernas* and open-air cafés. Though life appeared to have returned to normal, I noticed occasional lingering stares, and nervous parents keeping a close watch on their children. Dan's bloody dinghy had been hauled away during the night, but Basri's yacht was now moored at the wharf, right alongside the police boat. I wondered if the Zodiac remained where I had left it. Just as I was considering hiking over there to see, a booming horn sounded, and the ferry entered the bay.

Praying that Phoebe would be on it, I headed down toward the dock.

Tourists waiting to leave the island were lined up there with their baggage. I noticed the two Heidelberg students standing among them, along with several tourists I'd seen in the church, and the well-dressed, elderly Italian couple.

Suddenly I saw the police car nosing out onto the esplanade. It rolled to the foot of the wharf and stopped.

I turned quickly away, ducking into a newsstand. Pretending to examine the baffling Greek papers, I watched the overweight, slovenly policeman huffily extract himself from his car.

The ferry plowed its way toward the dock.

The cop strolled over to the line of tourists waiting to depart. He stopped to exchange some friendly words with the elderly Italians, and appeared to answer a question from the blond German girl. He wasn't checking passports or questioning anybody; it seemed he simply wanted to find out who was waiting in line.

The ferry tied up and began disgorging tourists. A white-haired man I took to be the ferryboat's skipper walked over and offered a cigarette to the cop. Soon they were both hidden behind the disembarking passengers, and I ventured out from the newsstand, hoping I might spot Phoebe.

The arriving visitors looked as varied as those in line to leave, though most appeared to be Greek families and younger couples on holiday. I noticed one man traveling alone. He carried a shotgun cradled in his arm and a game bag slung over his shoulder. Trim and fit in his seventies or eighties, with a handsome, cleanshaven face and wavy gray hair under his seafaring cap, he strode swiftly down the dock, passing the slow-moving tourists. I turned to watch as he hiked up the road. Somehow he seemed familiar, but I was sure I could not have known him. He was obviously a hunter who came here often; he appeared to know exactly where he was heading in the hills.

Many of the tourists were now passing me, rolling their bags down the esplanade. I anxiously searched the faces for Phoebe. The crowd on the dock was thinning, and the cop had reappeared. I saw him shake the hand of the skipper and head back toward his car.

Afraid I might be noticed, I quickly turned away.

"Jack!"

I looked back. At first I didn't recognize her. Her hair was tucked under a red beret, and her eyes were hidden behind rhinestone sunglasses. She had on redder lipstick than I'd seen her wear before, and a tightly wrapped silk scarf was tied around her neck. She wore calf-length khakis, a white cotton blouse, and a windbreaker. Her cheeks looked rosy from the sun and the wind, and when she took off her shades, her blue eyes dazzled.

"Phoebe."

She kissed me, then had to rub the lipstick off my cheek. "You look worried, sweetie. Where's Dan?"

I started to tell her, then stopped. The cop was standing at his car, peering down the esplanade.

"What's happened?" she asked.

I threw her pack over my shoulder and took hold of her hand. "Come on," I said. "I'll tell you all about it."

WE TOOK a table near the back of a bar where I thought we wouldn't be noticed. Phoebe ordered a frappé and something for us to eat. Then she folded her arms together and leaned back into her seat.

"Well?"

I told her everything. The whole story, starting with the phone call from Basri on my last night in Athens, all the way through to waking up on the yacht with his thumb in my hand, and Dan getting hauled off by the cop. I told her about the mysterious drink on the boat, and yes, I told her about the orgy. I probably told her more than she really wanted to know. It just came pouring out. I'd been puzzling over it for twenty-four hours; when I finally had someone to talk to, I couldn't seem to stop.

Finally I told her about Damiana, how I had followed her to the church and confronted her, and how she was unwilling to tell me what she knew.

Phoebe asked if I'd been to see Dan.

"Not yet," I said. "I'm afraid to. My prints are all over that boat.

That's part of the reason I called you. To talk to him, find out what he knows."

Phoebe looked worried. "That girl . . ."

"Damiana?"

"You say you saw blood *in her mouth?*"

"Yes."

She stared at me a second. "Let me see your wounds."

I glanced around at the other tables. Nobody seemed to be paying us any mind. I pulled up my sleeve and showed her a bite on my arm. It was sore to the touch, and I feared it might be infected. Lifting my shirt, I pointed out another on the side of my hip. I pulled up my leg, and showed her a bite on the inside of my thigh.

"There's more—on my backside. I—"

"It's all right," she said. "What about your joints—elbows, knees, fingers—you feel much pain there?"

"Yes," I said, astonished. "They've been aching ever since I woke up on the yacht."

"You don't remember anything beyond what you've told me? Anything more that happened that night?"

"No," I said. "Just . . ."

"What? What is it?"

I shrugged. "My dreams. Last night. I think things were coming back to me."

"Like what?"

A creepy, cold tingle went through me. "Things I'm not sure I want to remember."

Phoebe was watching me carefully. *She knows something,* I thought. Something about what happened. "How did you feel," she asked, "when you finally took the plunge?"

"How did I feel?" This was something I clearly remembered. "Fantastic," I said. "Like nothing I'd ever experienced. I was overcome with this intense excitement. I felt totally . . . completely . . ."

"Ecstatic?" Phoebe said.

"Yes," I said. "Exactly."

"The word comes from the ancient Greek *ekstasis,* meaning 'to stand outside yourself.' To *lose* yourself. It's the ultimate goal of the *orgia.*"

"I was so absorbed in it . . . I lost myself completely. It's why I can't remember."

"The Greeks would say you *were* absorbed—*consumed* by Dionysus. Consumed with your exuberance. 'Enthusiasm' comes from another Greek word: *enthousiasmos,* meaning 'inside the god.' You were completely possessed."

I *had* felt possessed, in a way. Enthusiastic, certainly. Faced with a roomful of willing females dressed in diaphanous nightgowns, what young heterosexual male wouldn't be enthusiastic?

"I know they got us excited," I said. "And maybe I went a little crazy, but . . . I'm not sure I'm ready to believe in a god who's been dead for two thousand years."

"Of course not," Phoebe said. "But it might give us some insight into who these women are and what they believe."

"Who do you think they are?"

"I'm not sure," she said. "But given their dress, the ritual, the orgy, I assume they're a revival of a Dionysian cult."

"You've heard of this before?"

"Not exactly. There are pagan groups in Athens, and in Europe and America, too. But they worship peacefully, and they're generally not secretive. They're denounced by the Greek Orthodox Church, but they openly proclaim their right to practice the ancient rituals. This group, this 'Pan-Hellenic Chorus'? Obviously, they're different."

"Maybe they're not an organization," I said. "Maybe they just came together to commit this murder."

"Why do you say that?"

"Because it's the only way to explain it. Look: everyone took three sips of that drink. Everyone but me—I took only two. That's why I woke up earlier than Dan."

"So?"

"So I don't think I was supposed to. I think I was supposed to be out of it on that boat—just like Dan was on shore. He was left there for the police to find—with Basri's head in his arms. Once he was in custody, they knew the cops would come out to the yacht and find me. If I hadn't woken up and left when I did, they *would* have found me. I'd have been caught at the scene of the murder and hauled into jail with Dan."

"So you think you were set up."

"The women murdered Basri. They wanted Dan and me to take the blame."

Phoebe didn't seem to be entirely convinced.

"How else do you make any sense of it?" I asked.

"It may have just resulted from the ritual," she said.

"You mean the orgy?"

"The orgy was only the beginning. The female worshippers of Dionysus were called Maenads, 'the raving ones.' They drove themselves into a kind of madness, a wild, contagious frenzy. Nothing was forbidden. In their ecstasy they would tear some animal apart with their bare hands and eat it raw. On some islands—Chios, Tenedos—there was a tradition of human sacrifice, the killing of a young man representing the god."

I pushed away the plate of lamb I'd been working on. Suddenly I wasn't so hungry.

Phoebe continued. "Euripides' most famous tragedy was about Dionysus. It's called *The Bacchae.* Dionysus was also known as Bacchus, and *Bacchae,* or *Bacchantes,* was another name for the Maenads. The play is about a king who disapproves of the cult and outlaws the worship of Dionysus. But he's so curious to see the women in their frenzy that Dionysus, in disguise, lures him out into the mountains to spy on them from a treetop. When the roving *Bacchae* find him, they pull him down and tear him to pieces. The king's own mother partakes in the frenzy, blind to the fact it's her son they're destroying."

"Tear him to pieces?"

"It was called *sparagmos,* tearing the victim limb from limb, and *omophagia,* the eating of the raw flesh of the dismembered body."

I shook my head in disbelief. "I don't understand."

"For the Maenads, it was a way to worship the god in human form. The intent was to contact and commune with the divine. To be possessed, and in turn to possess the god. To be made literally full of the god."

"By tearing a man apart and *eating* him?"

"To be like the god, you must eat the god. And you must eat him quick and raw, while the blood is still flowing. The blood is life. It's the only way to add his life to yours."

"This is the twenty-first century," I said. "Nobody could possibly believe that anymore."

"You were raised Catholic. *Eucharist* is another Greek word. The sacrament of communion is a symbolic remnant of human sacrifice. Celebrants eat the 'body' of Christ and drink his 'blood' as wine."

Transubstantiation—I remembered that strange idea, and I'd believed in it, too. But I couldn't imagine believing in this. "There's got to be another reason," I said. "If it was simply a religious frenzy, they would have killed Dan and me, too."

"I think you did get caught in their frenzy. But their intended victim was Basri."

"Why him?"

"I don't know," she said. "There were a number of traditions in ancient Greece of selecting victims for sacrifice. He could be a temple slave, or a captured warrior, or a condemned criminal. In some traditions, the king himself was chosen. For days or weeks, sometimes for an entire year, the anointed victim would be wined and dined and offered every pleasure, until on the final day he was sacrificed."

As incredible as it sounded, it seemed to fit with what had occurred. Basri had been seduced by the women in Istanbul. For days they indulged him, sexually and otherwise, then lured him to meet the rest of the group in Mykonos. Finally, at the peak of a frenetic orgy, they tore him apart and cut off his head. Dan and I may have been set up to take the blame, but there was little doubt that Basri was the chosen one.

I marveled at Phoebe's insight. "You really *do* know it all," I said. "Where do you *get* this stuff?"

"My work in Crete. Some believe the Dionysian cults descended from the Minoan civilization that preceded the ancient Greeks. That double-headed ax you described? It's called a *labrys.* The Minoans considered it a sacred instrument. The ancient palace at Knossos on Crete is called the Hall of the Double Ax. In the Goddess culture of the Minoans, priestesses used the *labrys* in sacrificial ceremonies. There's some indications of human sacrifice among the Minoans as well."

We talked awhile longer, trying to figure it out. Phoebe believed the killing had been irrational and religious. I thought that it must have been a calculated murder although, for the life of me, I couldn't tell her why. Either way we both agreed on the danger we were in. I had witnessed a murder and had managed to escape; Phoebe had arrived to help find the truth, a truth they might be willing to kill us to protect.

She insisted I come with her to visit Dan and talk to the police. "You have to tell them everything you know," she said. "Tell them exactly what happened."

I said I couldn't, not yet. "I'm afraid I'll be locked up like Dan. While I still have a chance, I need to find out why this happened, and prove that we weren't alone on that boat."

Phoebe wanted to know what she should tell the policeman. How had she found out about Dan?

"Tell him the truth," I said. "I'm sure they've noticed the Zodiac by now; he probably knows I'm here. Tell him you received a call from me, but you don't know where I am. You came to see Dan."

We left the café, and I led Phoebe to the hotel to drop off her bag in my room. I was relieved that the old woman who had checked me in was nowhere to be seen, and the hotel appeared to be vacant; the guests were apparently exploring the town or sunning themselves on the beaches. We climbed the stairs to my room.

The window and shutters were open, and sunlight shone on the bed and the wall. Phoebe pulled off her red beret and fluffed her hair with her fingers. Then she sat down on the edge of the bed to change her shoes for sandals. "Give me a second," she said, and went to freshen up in the bathroom.

I waited at the window to keep an eye on the street. I knew it wouldn't be long before the cop would be coming for me. I had to find Damiana and talk to her again. She was my only link to the women on the boat; she had to be persuaded to help me.

Gazing down over the street, I remembered the woman I'd seen the night before, gliding off mysteriously, as if she were part of a dream.

"Okay, I'm ready." Phoebe stepped out of the bathroom. She looked the opposite of that black figure I'd seen, and not at all a dream. I felt a sudden welling of affection, and was very glad to be with her. "I never told you," I said, "but thank you for coming."

"I was glad you called," she said. She stood there, looking at me. Her eyes were deep blue diamonds.

We headed for the police station. I tried to take a back route to keep us out of view. We ended up in an alley that gradually tapered and became so narrow we could barely make it through. I told Phoebe the maze of streets was even more bewildering than on Mykonos. "I think they *want* you to get lost," I said.

She said there was some truth to that idea. "People have been living on these islands for thousands of years. They often fell victim to invaders and pirates, who raided and looted the towns. The layout of the streets was designed to baffle them. A band of strangers swarming into town would soon get confused or trapped in dead ends, while the inhabitants concealed themselves on the rooftops and tried to pick them off."

I was reminded of Damiana's tour and her story of the island's long history. When we finally came within sight of the police station, I told Phoebe that while she went in to see Dan, I'd pay another visit to the church. We agreed to meet up later, back at the hotel.

Phoebe hugged me tightly. I realized suddenly just how scared both of us were. "Promise me you'll be careful," she said. "We don't really know what we're dealing with."

"I've got to try to find out," I said.

Once again, as I entered the church, I was struck by its remarkable stillness. The shadowy air seemed hazy and cool, undisturbed by the beams of sunlight slanting down from the dome. It appeared the church was completely empty, and the quiet seemed to confirm it. I listened for a moment until I heard a woman's voice, and what sounded like the closing of a door. The sound had come from what Damiana had called the narthex, the main entrance hall at the opposite end from the dome.

I started toward it. My steps echoed off the fresco-covered walls, whose painted saints stood mutely staring, watching me pass like an intruder. Halfway down the narthex, I noticed a passage through the wall that led to a parallel hallway. I poked my head in and heard the murmur of a conversation coming from behind a closed door.

One of the voices sounded like Damiana's, but it was the other woman doing most of the talking, all of it in Greek. I decided to wait until their meeting was finished, and moved back into the narthex. At the end of it was a bright, square room with high-set, latticed windows. As I walked into it, I realized it was the base of the belfry tower. A crisscrossing staircase led up from the side. A velvet rope hung across it.

It may have been simple curiosity that led me to unhook the rope and wander up the stairs, but I suspect it had more to do with the fact that it was forbidden. I wanted to see what I hadn't been shown; I wanted to know Damiana's secret.

The staircase was extremely narrow and twisted back and forth. It opened into a dimly lit second-floor room with a single round window in each of its four walls. The room appeared at first to be empty, but as I stepped out onto the creaking wooden floor and peered into the dimness, I saw a thousand dark eyes staring back at me.

A chill shot through me. I froze.

From floor to ceiling, the walls were lined with glass bookcases, and each shelf was neatly stacked with rows of human skulls.

What had I stumbled upon? Some secret ossuary? The skulls seemed to be on display, yet the room had been clearly roped off.

I moved closer to examine them. The pale skulls were old and dry. Without flesh and features, they all looked remarkably similar: gaping eye sockets, triangular nasal slot, tawny yellow color. All the lower jaws were missing. Some of the skulls appeared so small I figured they had to be children's.

I began to notice that many skulls had signs of injuries. On one, I saw a jagged hole above an eye socket. Another had a large piece missing from the top, as if it had been smashed with a club. Many had straight-edged cut wounds, as if from a knife or a sword or—quite possibly, I thought—an ax.

With a shudder I flashed on the image of Dan holding Basri's head.

I backed out of the room to the stairwell. Voices were coming from inside the church, visitors arriving for the tour. Glancing up the stairwell, I saw it led to a trapdoor and figured it must be to the belfry. On impulse, I headed up the stairs.

The trapdoor opened out into an airy chamber, with a balustrade around the perimeter, and pillars supporting the dome of the roof, beneath which the great bell hung. The open, arched windows revealed a stunning panorama. The mountain loomed high on one side, and the blue Aegean stretched out on the other, with the town lying neatly in between. After the dusty dimness of the dreary vault of bones, the view from this breezy tower made me dizzy.

Gazing out over the village, my eyes fell on the square below, with its green clusters of trees and its splashing central fountain. A pair of tourists crossed the square and headed toward the church. At the same moment they entered the door, a woman in black emerged.

My eyes immediately clung to her. It was the same cloaked woman I had seen the night before from the window of my hotel room. In fact, I now remembered, I had seen this same nun cross the square the morning I had followed Damiana. *Was she the one just meeting with her now?*

I raced down the zigzag staircase. From the windowed room at the base of the tower, I hurried through the church to the exit. Tourists stood scattered around the interior, and I glimpsed Damiana gathering them together. She turned and stared as I rushed out through the door.

I jogged into the middle of the square and scanned around for the woman. The fountain bubbled noisily. Three old men on a bench beside it, thumbing worry beads. A soccer ball rolled by me, chased by two young boys.

Finally, I spotted the nun.

She was crossing to a bus stop at the corner of the street. Moving swiftly, her long black robe flowed in rippling folds behind her. Her head was veiled in black as well, and her hands were tucked in her gown. She joined two other local women waiting at the corner, and just as she arrived, the small blue bus appeared.

I hurried after her. An unshaven man in a threadbare suit jacket tipsily stepped off the bus, then the nun and the two women climbed on board.

The door was just closing as I hastened in behind them. The driver, a potbellied Greek with elfish eyebrows and wire-rim spectacles, gave me a second glance and grumbled to himself. The bus was filled to capacity with local people, not a tourist's face among them. They eyed me suspiciously as I made my way down the aisle.

A stocky workman in overalls offered the nun his seat. As she turned to take it, she revealed for the first time her shroud-encircled face.

I gaped in utter amazement.

14

THE BUS rumbled up the street. I was so shocked I stood there in the aisle, frozen in place, openly staring down at her. When she looked up, she recognized me and instantly turned her face away. She refused to look at me again.

I remembered well the last time I had seen her. Lying naked on the floor under Dan's thrusting hips, a look of madness on her face, howling with pain or pleasure. I remembered her standing before the masked Dionysus, the first to be offered his drink. And I remembered her initial appearance on the yacht, the tall, slender body and long red hair, leading the trio of seductresses, kissing me brazenly on the mouth and rewarding Dan's kiss with a slap in the face.

"Thalia."

She continued staring toward the window of the bus.

I spoke louder. "Thalia."

Still she ignored me.

"You see, I remember your name," I said.

I wanted to rip the phony veil off her head. Give her a slap to remind her. I knew she would refuse to tell me the truth, just like Damiana. Who were these crazy women who had lured us into a murder?

"Thalia!"

Slowly she turned her face to me and leveled an icy stare. "I am Mother Melissa Capetanos, abbess of the Monastery of the Panaghia."

Everyone around us was looking at me. The man who had given up his seat for her suddenly got into my face. He pushed me angrily toward the rear of the bus, barking gruffly in Greek. I couldn't understand a word he was saying, but I certainly got the idea. I was a crazy Americano hassling an innocent nun.

I put up my hands and moved back. "All right, all right," I said.

People moved away from me, allowing me plenty of space. As I stood in the aisle toward the back, I could feel their wary glances. The bus climbed to the edge of town, stopping twice to disgorge passengers without taking any more on. Seats soon began opening up, and when there were no more people standing, I sat down several rows behind Thalia.

She never once looked back. The bus rode high along the base of the mountain, giving us a view of the sea. On a lofty plateau of vineyards, the driver stopped for two fieldworkers waiting at the side of the road. Before they got on, several men got off, including the gruff fellow who had "defended" Mother Melissa. He cast a threatening glance my way as he descended from the bus. After all his glaring looks, it was a relief to see him go.

The bus turned inland and climbed up higher. We passed a boy on a bike, struggling up the slope—the same kid who had waved to me at the beach the day before. Above us, the mountain seemed to recede into the sky, its peak never visible. The landscape grew rocky and rugged, with scattered patches of pines and lots of low-lying shrubs. We passed several working windmills, their white-canvassed wheels turning slowly in the breeze. At the edge of a grove of trees, I spotted a man in a sports jacket with a rifle slung over his arm. He stood watching the bus go by, and I realized it was the gentleman hunter who'd arrived at the dock that morning. The old man must have been one heck of a hiker.

The road climbed a saddleback ridge, then dropped into a wooded ravine. On one side, a high stone promontory jutted out over the trees. Atop this flat-topped pinnacle of rock stood a castlelike cluster of buildings. With its medieval stone walls and multidomed church, I knew it must be the monastery the German students had mentioned.

The bus wound its way along the wall of the ravine toward the mountainside entrance to the citadel. Through the trees, the blue ocean sparkled in the distance, with the white town piled like sea foam on the shore. The monastery reigned above it all in supreme isolation. Set on its towering column of stone, it looked improbable, yet perfectly appropriate, like a crown on the head of a king. The walls, damaged and crumbling, they appeared to be as old as the mountain itself, as if they had been carved from the rock.

The bus slowed to a stop before an arched doorway with a wrought-iron gate, the only visible entry through the wall. Thalia rose from her seat and walked to the front. She was the only passenger to exit.

When I jumped up and followed after her, no one tried to stop me. Only old men and a few women remained, and the potbellied driver seemed oblivious. I turned at the door and asked him when the bus would be returning.

His eyes looked huge in his spectacles. "No today."

"Not at all? You mean there's no bus back to town?"

He nodded toward the monastery. "Is no open. No tourist."

I glanced out the door. Thalia was walking briskly to the gate. There were no tour buses, no parked cars, no one else around. I hesitated. It was miles back to town. I had to meet up with Phoebe. But I couldn't let Thalia go after following her all this way.

The passengers were all staring at me. The driver drummed his fingers on the wheel.

"Thanks," I said, and stepped off the bus.

Thalia had unlocked the gate and was slipping inside. The bus pulled away as I hurried toward her. "Wait!" I shouted.

She closed and locked the latch. As I reached the gate, she backed away. I shouted through the bars. "I have to talk to you!"

"I have nothing to say. You should not have followed me."

"Basri's dead," I said. "My brother's in jail. You've got to tell the police what happened."

"What happened is past. It cannot be undone." She turned to walk away.

"Wait!" I shouted.

She ignored me and kept walking. I rattled the gate, then shouted again, "I'll tell the police what you did! I'll tell them you killed Basri!"

She stopped. Turned. Faced me for a moment. Then she walked back toward me, stopping just out of reach.

For a moment she simply stared at me. In the glaring sunlight, her eyes looked pale gray, the pupils shrunk to pinpoints. Not a single strand of red hair showed beneath her veil. Her mouth was pulled tight and slightly open in threat, and tiny beads of sweat had formed on the ridge of her upper lip.

It was Thalia's face, but she looked like a different woman.

"Why did you kill him?" I asked.

Her eyes didn't blink. "You can ask yourself the same question."

A moment passed in silence. "No," I said. "I didn't . . . I had nothing to do with it."

"Then why haven't you gone to the police?"

I started to answer, but hesitated. Her eyes pierced mine like needles.

"If you start walking now," she said, "you will make it back before dark. You must leave this island before they arrest you. You must never come back here again."

I was incredulous. "I can't leave without my brother!"

"You must. It is too late for him."

She said this as if she thought I actually could accept it. As if it were a simple statement of fact. There was nothing I could do for Dan. I could only try to save myself.

"Who are you?" I asked. *"What is this place?"*

"I am Mother Melissa Capetanos, abbess of the Monastery of the Panaghia." She gave me one final look, then turned and walked away.

I stood there in disbelief. *Does she really believe she can be rid of me so easily?* A brass bell hung to the side of the gate. I grabbed the rope hanging from the clapper and yanked. The clang rang out across the courtyard and echoed off the mountain wall behind me. She ignored it and walked on. I rang the bell again.

"I'll go to the U.S. Embassy!" I shouted. "I'll tell them what you did!"

She disappeared through an archway across the flagstoned yard. There was no one else around. I struggled with the lock, but couldn't open the gate. I shook the bars in frustration.

She had been right about going to the police. And going to the embassy in Athens was absurd. Unless I had evidence against her, I had no way to prove she had been on the yacht. If I did go to the authorities, it was far more likely I'd be incriminated along with my brother Dan. She, after all, was the abbess of a monastery; I was a vagabond American. Who would Greek officials be more likely to believe?

I had to find out who she was. I had to find out their secret.

I stepped back. The iron gate had to be twelve feet high and was closed off by the arching wall above it. To the right, the wall abutted the craggy mountainside, impossible to scale without ropes and climbing gear. To the left, the pinnacle dropped off steeply. I moved as far as I could along the wall and peered down over the edge. The green bottom of the dizzying ravine was visible far below.

The gray-and-black sandstone rock was pockmarked with holes and indentations. Scattered gnarly bushes clung tenaciously into cracks. I couldn't see ahead around the curving wall of the monastery, but I knew the best views would be overlooking the valley, so I figured there was bound to be a window somewhere. Without really giving it too much thought, I found myself edging out onto the rock, moving alongside the base of the wall.

At first it was surprisingly easy. There were plenty of cracks and footholds in the porous rock, and the base of the wall formed a ledge I could grip. I moved along slowly and methodically. Then, about twenty feet out, I made the mistake of looking down. There was nothing but air for a thousand feet. The rock curved gradually inward under me. The sight seemed to suck the air out of my lungs, and an icy tingle clawed at my gut.

I didn't look down there again. I focused instead on what was in front of me: where to put my hand, what would make a foothold, where the hell I was going.

I passed beneath a couple windows too far up to reach. At one point I came to a cavelike indentation with a ledge that was flat enough to stand on. After resting there a minute, I continued on around the face of the cliff until finally I saw something promising. Water was trickling down the rock and dripping off into the air. It was coming from a rectangular hole in the base of the monastery wall. I climbed over to it and discovered it was an open storm drain, large enough for me to fit through.

I crawled in.

The tunnel was wet and slimy and dark. At first I couldn't see, but as my eyes adjusted, I discerned a distant ray of daylight. I crawled along the drain horizontally for what must have been twenty yards. When I reached the light, I saw it was coming from an opening above; the sky could be seen through an iron grate. I listened for a minute and didn't hear any voices, only the cawing of crows. When I reached up and tried to move the grate, I discovered it was embedded in the stone.

I slammed the palms of my hands against it. It wouldn't budge. I slammed it again to no avail. Then I noticed my hands were bleeding.

At least I thought they were; both were covered in blood. But when I examined them in the light, I saw no cuts or abrasions.

Suddenly I realized the blood had come from the water coursing through the drain.

I'd been crawling through a river of water and blood. Apparently it was coming from farther up the line—which meant there had to be another opening.

The passage narrowed as I moved on ahead, forcing me to squirm on my belly. I strained to see into the inky blackness. My clothes grew sopping wet. I heard the plash of skittering rats.

Finally, I reached another opening. The pipeline continued on, but was far too narrow to crawl through. Dim light showed through the grate above; this was an interior space. I listened for a full minute. The only sound was the trickle of water coming down the drain line.

This time when I tried the grate, it jiggled in its slot. When I struck it with the palm of my hand, it popped loose onto the floor. I stuck my head through the opening and peered out into the room.

Pale daylight shone through the iron grate of a window. It fell on stacks of wooden crates and cardboard boxes, and on shelves holding packages of foodstuffs, glass jars, and bottles. Wine barrels were stacked in a pyramid against the wall. Near them lay piled rows of bulging burlap sacks. One corner of the room was heaped with firewood; in another corner a massive barrel stood on end.

I climbed out of the hole and replaced the grate over the drain. The cellar floor looked perfectly dry. Obviously it wasn't the source of the trickling water and the blood; that must have been coming from farther up the line. As I glanced around, I noticed a muffled, suckling sound. A black cat was lying on a spilled sack of flour, nursing a litter of kittens. The fur of the kittens had turned white from the powder, and the mother was busily licking them clean.

Footsteps descended the stone stairwell. I glanced around frantically, looking for somewhere to hide. Across the room in the corner stood a large, upright wooden barrel. I hid behind it as the door creaked open.

First I heard light footsteps, then the murmur of a woman's voice, cooing sweetly in Greek. I slowly peered out over the barrel and saw a figure in black—another veiled nun—crouching over the litter. She picked up one of the kittens and cradled it against her chest. At this point she was standing in the light from the window, and I could see her face quite clearly. She was young and pretty, with a beauty mark on her cheek.

I recognized her immediately. She had been at the table with Basri when we'd had our first drink at the club. Marina wore the blue scarf. This woman was Irene.

She set down the kitten, then stood and brushed the white flour from her chest. She glanced up at the window a moment, then crossed the room and moved aside something on the shelf. Under it she found a pack of clove cigarettes and a box of matches. She hastily lit up a cig, glancing again at the window. She took a deep drag.

I noticed bloody water from my sopping shoes had left wet footprints behind. They passed close by where the girl was standing. I slid back down behind the barrel, careful not to make a sound. The water was forming a puddle beneath me and moving out onto the floor.

The girl exhaled noisily. Again, I peered at her over the barrel.

She was staring down at the footprints, a puzzled look on her face. Her eyes started following them across the room.

I ducked down and held my breath. The woman started toward me. I wondered if I could jump her and keep her from screaming.

A shadow suddenly passed by the window, accompanied by the sound of footsteps. I watched Irene quickly put out her cigarette and stuff the pack back into her hiding place. She waved her hands in a futile attempt to disperse the lingering smoke.

A woman's voice called down from the top of the stairs. Irene called back in Greek, then hurried to the pile of firewood and gathered up a bundle. She carried the wood across to the door and hastily left the cellar.

I listened as the irate voice outside scolded her in Greek. It continued reprimanding as the two of them walked away.

Alone again, I stepped out from behind the barrel and waited until the voices had vanished. Then I opened the door and crept up the stairs.

THE STAIRWELL let out onto a stone-paved alleyway between two buildings. One appeared to be a church or chapel, with arched windows of leaded glass. The other was the building from whose cellar I'd just emerged. I peeked through one of its ground-floor windows and saw it was the refectory—the monastery dining hall—with a long wooden table and high-backed chairs. The room was empty, but through a doorway beyond it was the kitchen, from which I could hear voices and the clatter of pots and pans.

I crept down the alleyway, ducked under the kitchen window, then crossed to the chapel. It was a small building of rough stone and looked to be very old. I peered through a window and could see no one inside. There was only the single entrance in front, set within a carved-stone archway. The coffered door showed traces of pale blue in the wood grain, but looked as if it hadn't been painted in decades. I gently pushed it open.

Inside, it was silent and dark. Dim light showed through the rippled glass, but the end with the altar had no windows at all and lay completely in shadow. There were no pews, only the cold stone floor, and the walls held no paintings or tapestries. Candles were perched on floor stands by the door, and several more stood beside the altar.

I walked across the room to the massive block of stone. A large picture sat on this primitive altar, a Byzantine oil painting on a panel of wood, mounted within a massive, elaborately carved frame. The image was an iconic portrait of the Madonna and Child, set on a brilliant gold background. The Virgin had large almond eyes and a small mouth, and the baby Jesus looked like a tiny grown man.

The mounting of the picture seemed peculiar. I noticed the panel was not fully attached to the frame, but seemed to float inside it, held in place by metal tabs at the top and bottom, and by tiny wooden doll rods at the middle on either side. The tabs had left scrape marks on the edges of the painting. Curious, I slid the tabs from their slots. The picture immediately swiveled loose, and with a little nudge, the painting flipped, top over bottom, to reveal another painting on the back side of the panel.

I was astonished.

The painting was much older and in far worse condition, yet it looked immediately familiar. It pictured two women standing on either side of a youthful male, with one of the women handing something to the boy. It took me a moment to realize this was the same subject we had seen in the relief sculpture at the National Archeological Museum. The sculpture had come from Eleusis, and the women were the goddess Demeter and her daughter, Persephone. Demeter was handing an ear of grain to the boy, whom Dan had insisted was Persephone's son—none other than the god Dionysus.

I stared at it, intrigued. The painting, with its great age, looked mysterious and strange. A relic of the pagan past; but what did it mean exactly? I wondered if I could somehow use it to make our case to the police.

Finally, I turned away from the altar and started back to the door. For the first time I noticed there were small objects floating above me, difficult to see in the dark. I paused and peered up at them. They hung from the ceiling on long loops of string, and appeared to be some sort of ornaments.

I moved directly under one. It consisted of a small, round wheel with spokes, with something hanging inside it. As my eyes adjusted to the dark, I saw that what was tied to the spokes was a small dead bird.

"What the hell?"

Dozens of these macabre birds hung down from the ceiling. There was something weirdly unnerving about the way their dead heads dangled.

The icon on the altar was too big to carry off, but this little curiosity was certainly not. I jumped up, grabbed a wheel, and snapped it loose from the ceiling. The wheel was made of vinelike twigs braided into a tightly woven circle. Four spokes formed a cross, at the center of which the bird was attached. The bird had a long neck and a large, oddly shaped head, with a speckled pattern on its wings and chest. It looked like a small woodpecker. I wrapped the loop of string around it and stuffed it gingerly into my pocket.

Outside, there was no one in sight, but I could hear the sound of women singing. I crept down the alleyway toward the sound and came to an open courtyard.

In a rock-rimmed circle at the center stood a magnificent, long-needled pine tree. Pinecones littered the shaded ground around it, and the broad expanse of stone pavement was overgrown with grass. The square was framed by a colonnaded cloister—or at least by what was left of it; whole sections of the walkway had long ago collapsed, perhaps from an earthquake or fire. Across the way, a white-stoned church, blackened with age, shimmered like a mirage in the hazy sunlight. The church was the source of the women's singing.

No doubt it was the so-called Pan-Hellenic Women's Chorus. The hymn they sang sounded medieval, but like their chanting on the yacht, it had the same vibrant passion, as if the women's very souls were bound up with their song.

A bell rang out. The same brass bell I had rung at the monastery gate. I listened. It clanged again. Someone wanted in.

I left the courtyard and hurried toward the sound. It seemed to have come from farther up the alleyway on the other side of the buildings. I stuck close to the walls and shadows, trying to keep out of sight. The sound of the women's chorus gradually faded away behind me. I could see a column of thick smoke rising from a chimney. This, I thought, was where Irene must have been taking the firewood.

I cut through a narrow passageway that stunk of cat urine. It ran between what looked like a large dormitory building and a single floor lavatory set alongside it, from which a puddle of water had leaked. The passage, as I'd guessed, opened into the entry courtyard.

I got there in time to see a nun walking toward the gate. She was a large woman, and she wore an apron with her sleeves rolled up; I immediately assumed she was the monastery's cook.

The boy I'd seen on the bicycle was waiting outside the gate. The two exchanged greetings, and the nun opened the gate to let the boy in. He rolled his bike inside and set it against the wall. Then he pulled from the handlebar basket a package wrapped in butcher's paper. He carried it as she turned and led him back the way she had come.

I wondered if this was how the nuns had their meat delivered. It was doubtful they'd be capable of hunting or preparing wild game; they must have relied on local hunters, or purchased their meat from butchers in town. This bicyclist was no doubt the delivery boy.

As the two of them crossed the yard, I recognized the nun. She was the big woman from the yacht, the one with the massive breasts and thighs I had seen straddling Basri. She and the boy vanished through a passage in the wall. The moment they were out of sight, I snuck along the wall to follow them. When I reached the passage, they were exiting its opposite end. I hurried after them, but when I got to the other end, the two had vanished again.

I was standing at the edge of a long, narrow, overgrown courtyard. The buildings that bordered it were built of crumbling and decaying stone, and appeared to be abandoned. One looked like another dormitory, its windows black and vacant. A second appeared to be the ruins of a chapel that looked as if it had been bombed. Across from it was the building with the chimney from which the smoke was rising.

I cautiously made my way toward it.

The stone walls seemed blackened with age and were thickly covered with ivy. It was a hexagonal structure, with the chimney rising from the center. I had toured a monastery in the Italian Alps, and remembered it had what they called a calefactory, or warming house, that looked very much like this. But here we were in the middle of the day, with winter a long way off. These nuns were apparently using it to cook.

I crept around the building, looking for the entrance. When I found it, I noticed the boy in the grass nearby, playing with a spotted gray-and-white cat. He was dangling a string in front of it—presumably the same string that had wrapped the butcher's package. The cat was going crazy with the teasing, and the boy seemed completely preoccupied. I made my way toward the door.

Just then, the big nun emerged from inside, and I flung myself against the wall. She was carrying a wooden bucket of water, and I noticed for the first time that her apron was smudged with blood. She set the bucket down by the boy, dipped a ladle into the water, and offered him a drink. He thirstily gulped it down. Then he gave her back the ladle and she dipped it once again. As she handed him this second drink, I slipped inside the door.

A gagging stench filled the air. I could barely breathe. Except for the fire, the room was completely dark. The building had no windows. I stood near the door with my back against the wall, waiting for my eyes to adjust. The crackling fire blazed in an open hearth in the center of the room. Two nuns with their backs to me were tending it with pokers. They, too, wore aprons, and had their sleeves rolled up. I edged along the wall and crouched down behind a pile of kindling to hide in the flickering shadows.

A huge black kettle was boiling on the fire. Large hunks of bone and meat lay on a table beside it. The boy's package, partially unwrapped, lay on the table, too, along with another bucket of water and a pair of iron tongs.

When one of the nuns turned to the table, I saw that it was Irene. She grabbed the tongs and, with the help of the other nun, who was prodding her poker into the pot, pulled out a long flank of boiled meat and carried it over to the table. She dropped it there, steaming, then clamped a raw and bloody piece from the uncooked pile, carried it back over, and plunked it into the pot.

The other nun went to the table and ladled cold water onto the boiled meat, sending a sizzle of steam into the air. *Is this woman Marina?* It was hard for me to tell. Her head was wrapped tightly in the black scarf, and I couldn't get a look at her face.

The water she poured spilled off the table and splashed to the floor, where it flowed through an iron-grate drain. This, I realized, was where the bloody water was coming from in the drain line I had crawled through.

Using a meat cleaver and her bare hands, the nun stripped the cooked meat off the large bone and flung the meat into the fire.

My eyes stayed with the bone. I had thought at first it must have been the femur of a cow. Then I thought, with revulsion, it might have belonged to a horse, given its thickness and considerable length. Finally, as Irene picked it up in her iron tongs and carried it back to the pot, I began to think it may have come from another creature entirely.

She dropped the femur into the boiling water.

The fat nun came back inside with the bucket and set it down roughly on the table. Then she pulled open the butcher paper and lifted out the bicycle boy's hand-delivered prize.

I slowly rose to my feet, staring in astonishment.

She was holding Basri's head.

15

I WAS so stunned by what I had seen, I froze and stood there, gaping. As she dropped the rotting head into the pot, the big nun turned and spotted me. She shouted something loudly in Greek, and the other women suddenly wheeled in fright.

Marina held up the bloody cleaver in her hand. Irene raised her poker like a club. The fat lady yanked out a log from the fire and came at me like a thundering ogre.

I ran.

Right out past the kid with the cat. Across the open courtyard. I tripped on a broken flagstone and fell, sliding on my hands and knees. Irene came down with her iron poker. I rolled aside and it clanged to the stone. Marina took a swipe with her cleaver. I dodged it, got up, and ran.

The women were shouting at the top of their lungs. A bell started tolling loudly. For a second, I didn't know where to go—everything looked the same: black buildings, gaping windows, a maze of passageways. The fat lady slugged me in the head with her log. A burning ember caught in my ear. As I screamed and shook it out and went stumbling away, the iron poker stuck me in the ribs. I angrily grabbed ahold of it and yanked Irene to the ground. The two other women came charging toward me, and I swung the poker at them. The big nun grabbed it in her meaty claw and snapped it out of my hand.

I tried to grab it back, but the cleaver came flying through the air at my head, and I quickly whirled to avoid it. Irene, on the ground, grabbed hold of my ankles. I tumbled and crashed to the stone.

When I looked up, I saw the boy running off, heading into a passage. I rolled as again the poker came down, chipping the stone by my head. As I started up, Marina struck my neck with the stick, then tried to jam it into my throat. I grabbed it and held off the glowing tip, then shoved it aside and again rolled away.

I took off after the boy.

He had gone into the same passage I'd followed him through earlier. The one that led to the entry. I raced full bore through that passageway now, desperate to catch up to him. As I emerged from the other end, I saw nuns pouring out of doorways and passages, spurred by the tolling of the bell. The boy was heading through the gateway with his bike, and I reached him just as it was closing.

"Sorry, kid—I owe you one." I grabbed the bike away from him and took off down the road. He didn't even try to come after me. As I glided along the edge of the mountain, I glanced back and saw the nuns crowding at the gate.

I don't know why, but I waved.

IT TOOK me less than an hour to make my way back to town. Most of the road was downhill, and for much of it I simply coasted. This proved to be a blessing, for I was in too much pain to exert myself. My hands and knees were smarting from the tumbles I'd taken, the side of my face still burned, and two of my ribs were so painfully sore I feared they might be broken. In spite of all this—or because of it—I felt lucky to have escaped alive.

As I rode the bike through town, I noticed that I seemed to be attracting many stares. Several people stopped to gape as I passed. When I entered the lobby of the Argonauta, the old Greek landlady gasped. It wasn't until I was up in my room that I saw what had drawn their attention. A bloody phantom stared back from the mirror. My face and throat had been blackened and burned, my knees and palms were raw, and my shirt and shorts were soiled with blood from my crawl through the monastery drain.

I was so shocked by this appalling apparition that I didn't even notice Phoebe's message at first—a small pink Post-it on the middle of the mirror. *Gone to look for you at the church,* it said in a neat, feminine script. Obviously she had grown tired of waiting and figured something must have gone wrong.

I suddenly noticed an odd, animal odor. After searching a bit, and finding that the smell seemed to follow me around the room, I realized it was coming from my pocket.

The dead bird.

I'd forgotten all about it. The wicker wheel was scrunched, and the bird's wings and feet and head had all been compacted together. I carefully unfolded the disgusting little thing, then slipped it into a Ziploc bag I found inside my backpack.

Evidence for the defense.

I washed up in the sink, cleaned my wounds, decided that my ribs were probably *not* broken, and quickly threw on fresh clothes.

Then I took the kid's bike and raced up to the church.

For some reason—maybe the late hour of the afternoon—the square was full of children playing. Watching them from the bench near the fountain were the three old men, twirling and clattering their worry beads.

Inside the church, Damiana appeared to be at the tail end of her tour, heading into the infirmary with half a dozen people. I didn't see Phoebe among them, and after searching through the interior, went to look for her outside. Walking around to the side door, I found her at the curved wall of the main apse, examining the church's foundation.

"Jack! You were gone so long—"

"Are you all right?"

"Yes," she said.

"How about Dan? Is he okay?"

"They're moving him to the mainland tomorrow. He's going to be arraigned at the courthouse in Athens."

Time was running out. I had a lot of questions for her, but knew they had to wait. "We've got to get Damiana to help us," I said. I looked over her shoulder at the wall of the church. "What were you doing out here?"

"I was going crazy waiting, and I started looking at these foundation blocks." She pointed to markings on the stone she'd been examining. "This one appears to be a grave slab from the Roman era. Christian churches were frequently built over ancient sacred sites—often using the very same stones."

I started to tell her about the painting I'd seen, but she suddenly noticed the burn on the side of my face. "Jack!"

"It's nothing," I said.

"What happened?"

"Some nun whacked me with a burning stick."

"What?"

"That's what *I* say. It was worse than Catholic grammar school." I took her hand. "C'mon, we've got to talk to Damiana."

THE TOUR was ending as we came into the church. Damiana was in a conversation with two well-dressed Greek women, a mother and daughter, but when she saw us coming down the aisle, she excused herself and started toward her office.

"Damiana!"

She kept walking.

We followed her into the narthex through the forest of marble columns. "I've been to the monastery," I shouted, my voice echoing. "I talked to Thalia . . ."

Damiana stopped. She didn't turn around. We walked up and stood behind her.

". . . or do you call her Mother Melissa?"

She lowered her head in silence.

Phoebe looked at me. "What are you saying?"

"The Greek Chorus Girls. Turns out they live in a monastery up on the mountain."

Phoebe was astonished. "They're *nuns*?"

"Yeah. And that's not the half of it. Tell her, Damiana."

Finally, she turned to face us. She hadn't seen Phoebe before. After looking her over, she turned her gaze on me. "If you talked to the Mother," she said, "then there is nothing for me to tell you."

"Oh yes there is," I said. "And I think you know what it is."

She stared back at me without blinking.

Phoebe was growing anxious. "Jack—"

"Tell us, Damiana. Tell us where the bones come from. All those skulls you're collecting in the attic."

Phoebe thought I was losing it. "What are you talking about?"

"Up in the tower, under the belfry. There's a room full of skulls and bones. Thousands of them." I watched Damiana's face as I spoke. Her expression revealed nothing.

I turned to Phoebe. "It's a collection of their murder victims. Basri was only their latest."

"How do you know?" Phoebe asked.

"'Cause I saw his corpse at the monastery." I looked at Damiana. "The nuns were boiling the body parts to separate the bones."

"My God!"

"You're the one who told me about the Maenads, Phoebe. Well, take a good look. Here's one in the flesh."

The two of us stared at Damiana. Her eyes looked sad and fatigued, as if she were suffering under the burden of her silence. Slowly, she shook her head. A gesture of futility. It seemed she couldn't begin to try to make us understand. "I'm sorry," she said. "I have tried to warn you."

"You can do more than that," I said. "You can tell us what you know."

"This I cannot do," she said.

"Then we'll tell the police," I said.

"Yes. Of course. But then you must leave at once."

"Why?" Phoebe asked.

Damiana's voice was flat and fatalistic. "If you stay on the island, you will not survive the night."

Phoebe and I exchanged a glance.

I looked at Damiana. "I can't leave here without my brother."

She heard the emotion in my voice; it seemed to tug at her heart. I remembered she had a brother, too.

"Please," Phoebe pleaded. "I beg you."

Damiana glanced between us. For a moment she seemed to hesitate.

A telephone rang, startling us. She waited until it rang again, then went into her office to answer it.

Phoebe and I waited and listened. We heard her speak some words in Greek.

"I think it's her father," Phoebe said. "Something's wrong . . ."

The call was brief. She emerged pulling on a black shawl. Her face was grim. "I am told the police are ordering all visitors to leave the island immediately," she said. "A ferry has been ordered to the harbor."

"Why?" I asked.

"The nuns at Panaghia. They reported that a man broke into the monastery and attempted to kill them."

"What?"

"They gave the police your description."

Phoebe looked distraught. "Jack . . ."

My mind was racing. *Of course—I've been an idiot! Who wouldn't believe the nuns? The mad head-chopper is still on the loose! The police will be looking for me at the harbor. Checking every passenger. If we stay, we'll be the only foreigners left, with nowhere on the island to hide.*

Phoebe was having the same thoughts. "What should we do?"

I looked at her. I thought of Dan. What he had said about the Fates. "I don't think we have any choice," I said.

I turned to Damiana. "We're going to the police. Will you help us?"

She backed away. "I'm sorry," she said. "I cannot. There is no one here who can help you." She clutched her shawl tightly around her and hurried out of the church.

OUTSIDE, THE children had all abandoned the square and taken their voices with them. An unnatural silence ensued. All you could hear was the weep of the fountain and the piercing cry of a bird. The air seemed as still as the air in the church, and even the light was peculiar: the sun had slipped behind the mountain and left the town in a luminous shade.

Walking through this strange dusk, we made our way to the jail. I asked Phoebe what she'd found out from the police.

"Believe it or not, they apparently don't have much crime here," she said. "There's only one cop on the island. His name is Vassilos. Andreas Vassilos."

"I've seen him," I said. "He looks like a drunk."

"I don't think he'll be sympathetic. He just wants to pass the problem along to the authorities in Athens. Make the whole thing go away."

"I suppose Ogygia is no different than most Greek islands," I said. "It survives on tourism. Murder is bad for business."

Up ahead an older couple was leaving a small hotel. Other tourists, bags in hand, were heading toward the harbor.

A Greek family—father, young mother, little boy—dragged their suitcases hurriedly past us down the street. The wheels rumbled loudly. When the boy slowed to stare at us, his mother grabbed his hand and pulled him along, eyeing me warily.

For a second I remembered the thumb clenched in my fist, and my bloody handprint on the wall. I asked Phoebe if Dan had remembered anything about the killing.

"No," she said. "He can't begin to comprehend what happened. He's terribly distraught about Basri. But he seems remarkably unconcerned with the situation he's in. I tried to make him face the facts. He's going to be charged with murder. Instead, he's obsessed with the mysterious drink. Says he's never had anything like it—and as you know, he's tried *everything*."

"Does he think it's the *kykeon*?"

"He says it fits with the prophecy. Your 'Aphrodites' led you to Dionysus, and Dionysus led you to . . . well, something like the ecstasy of Eleusis."

We finally reached the police station. The light had faded and the street was empty. Even the squad car was gone.

I tried the door and found it locked. No one answered my knock.

"He's left" Phoebe said. "Must be down at the wharf."

That meant Dan was alone inside. Sitting in his cell. I banged on the door with my fist.

"Jack. It's no use."

The single narrow horizontal window was high up on the wall and encased in iron bars. Too high to reach or to see inside. I called out for Dan.

No answer.

A ferry horn sounded from the harbor.

"We've got to find Vassilos," I said.

We continued down the street, then turned and descended the twisting route that led to the waterfront. The closer we came to it, the more people we encountered: bellhops pushing luggage carts; street vendors hawking last-chance souvenirs; tourists, families, children, couples—all of them dragging suitcases or carrying bags, and looking harried and scared and upset. The anxiety in the air was palpable. The news had quickly spread. A man had been decapitated. Nuns had been attacked. The killer was on the loose. The island had finally become so dangerous it had to be evacuated.

A decrepit old taxi rolled past, the first I had seen on the island. It was jammed to the brim with passengers, and baggage was tied to the roof. The driver honked to part the growing crowd making its way to the wharf.

At last we came out onto the esplanade. Phoebe kept her grip on me as the jostling crowd grew thick. A couple hundred people were converging from the streets. Everyone was heading toward the dock.

The air seemed darker near the water. Gulls circled and squawked overhead, adding to the cacophony of voices. Out at the pier was a large ferryboat with a great black funnel, and a second boat, a hydrofoil, with a crosslike radar tower. The huge ships made Basri's yacht, secured nearby, look like a rowboat.

I nearly tripped on a little girl. She was searching the ground for something she'd dropped. Her mother was fighting the flow of the crowd, trying to retrieve her. Phoebe took the girl's hand and helped her to her mom. I spotted what the girl was looking for and picked it up off the ground—a small, tightly twisted circle of twigs. Tied inside it was a tiny, carved-wood bird.

I stared at it in my hand. My mind racing back. It was the same trinket I'd seen Damiana give to her brother—a toy version of the dead bird wheels hanging in the chapel.

I waded through the crowd to the girl. "What do you call this?" I asked.

She grabbed it out of my hands and clutched it to her chest. Her mother glared at me suspiciously and pulled the girl away. She spat out words I didn't understand, then dragged her daughter off into the crowd.

I watched them go.

Phoebe was waiting for me just up ahead, where the crowd jammed together at the entry gate. Two ferryboat officers were checking people through. Tourists were fumbling for their passports or IDs, which had to be inspected and approved.

"There's Vassilos," Phoebe said, as I caught up with her.

Standing off to the side with the ferryboat captain was the

bearded and bedraggled policeman. He looked slightly less slovenly than the last time I had seen him, as if the urgency of the evacuation had somehow sobered him up. His wrinkly blue uniform shirt was tucked into his pants, which only seemed to emphasize the enormity of his gut. His policeman's cap was tilted back on his head, and his hair flowed out from beneath it, reaching over his collar to the epaulets of his shirt. Despite this disheveled demeanor, he had a prideful air about him, staring aloofly over the crowd with a calm and noble authority. I had to wonder how he might react to what I was about to tell him.

"Here goes nothing," I said.

As I started away, Phoebe stopped me. "Wait."

I turned to her. She looked at me a moment and held my arm. "I'm afraid. What if . . . ?" Her blue eyes searched into mine.

I hugged her in my arms. "It's all right," I said. That afternoon, she had pleaded with me to go to the police; now she was having second thoughts. Following the nuns' accusation, I could be charged with breaking and entering, assault, perhaps even murder. But I had already made up my mind. Or the Fates had made it up for me.

"We have to tell them the truth," I said. "It's really all we can do."

She knew that I was right, and when she lifted her glistening eyes, they seemed to give me courage.

I turned and headed for the cop.

The ferryboat captain was talking to Vassilos, who stood with a cigarette in his hand, watching the people walk by. I figured he was looking for someone based on the nuns' description, and when his eyes finally landed on me, they did not move away. He watched me walk up through the crowd until I was standing before him.

The ship captain stopped talking, and the two of them stared at me, waiting for me to speak.

"You're looking for the wrong person," I said.

The policeman glanced at the ship captain, then looked back at me. "And how do you know this?"

"Because I'm the one you're looking for, and I'm not the one you want."

Vassilos's bloodshot eyes peered from beneath his drooping brows. His voice was soft and gravelly. "It was not you who break into the monastery?"

"I did. But I swear I never tried to hurt anyone."

"Of course." He turned his head slightly and studied me for a moment. "I have seen you before," he said.

I nodded. "Yesterday. On the beach. The American you found in the boat is my brother."

"Yes. His friend, the girl, she tell me this." He peered suspiciously down his hawklike nose. "Why did you not come to me before?"

"I had to find out what happened on the yacht."

"And did you find?"

"Yes."

He continued looking at me for a moment, then turned to the captain and spoke to him in Greek. The captain gave me a scrutinizing look, then tipped his cap to Vassilos and headed back to his ship.

Vassilos stepped up, took my wrist, and clapped a handcuff around it. He pulled my arm behind my back to attach the other wrist.

"I just turned myself in," I said. "Do you really think I'm going to run away?"

"No," he said, grinding his cigarette under his foot. "But then—I would not think you would rape a nun, either."

"What?"

16

Dan and I shared the little concrete cell. Apparently, it was the only jail in Ogygia. A square, windowless room with two cots, a single toilet, and no sink—Dan still hadn't cleaned the dried blood off his body. Vassilos had given him a pair of orange drawstring pants and a matching shirt with the number "11" stenciled on the back; they looked like E.R. scrubs. While I kept sitting down and standing up and pacing the little room, Dan stood with his hands propped against the metal door, peering out the wire-mesh window. With his shaved head, bare feet, and bloodstained arms, he looked like a convict in a Tarantino movie.

"You break the law, the worst they do is take away your freedom." After two days alone in the stir, Dan couldn't seem to stop talking. "Like Mommy forcing you to go to your room. In Europe, even if you've murdered someone, all they can inflict is a time-out. It might be a long time-out, but even that's unlikely."

"How do you suppose they'll feel about me having had my way with a nun?"

"If you're actually convicted of rape, you won't get more than a year or two."

This didn't sound all that reassuring. Dan had spent months behind bars in Colombia and Mexico; once for smuggling cannabis, and once for selling fake antiquities. He'd had plenty of practice with "time-outs." I'd never even seen the inside of a jail. "What do you expect them to do, Dan? Cut off your head? Cut off my balls?"

"There are countries that'll do that, you know. That's why when I travel in the Middle East—like when I tried to go to Saudi for the *hajj*—I always make sure—"

He stopped. Put his ear to the door. "He's off the phone."

"Finally."

"Phoebe's talking."

"Good."

"Not so good. They're arguing again."

I had already showed Vassilos the dead bird and told him about the barbecue at the monastery. He hadn't listened to me any more than he'd listened to Dan.

"The nuns of Panaghia?" He had been astonished, then delighted, to discover I was capable of making up such lies.

If I had seen bones and meat at the monastery, then it had to be the nun's cook preparing a beef *stifado.* He insisted that Basri's head had been delivered to the morgue. The chapel I had snuck into was occasionally used for Ogygian weddings; the bird in the wheel was a harmless charm, a traditional Greek talisman of love. And as far as the bone room in the tower of the church, everyone in Ogygia knew what that was: the bones were those of islanders killed in the Greek War of Liberation, the infamous Ogygian massacre of 1822. At one time it had been a part of Damiana's tour.

With my arguments thus deflated, and Dan and I now shut in jail, it was up to Phoebe to save us. She'd been out there for over an hour, trying to talk him into taking us to the monastery so that I could show him Basri's bones. It was the only chance we had of proving the nuns had committed the murder. But Vassilos had been busy with other matters, mostly to do with the tourist evacuation—irate phone calls, angry drop-ins, missing baggage, missing people, and arguments with hoteliers and merchants upset about losing business. I thought he must have begun to wonder if the evacuation was necessary, but the whole thing had gotten so far along that he couldn't call it off, and certainly not before verifying that Dan and I were the only murdering rapists on his otherwise peaceful island.

I showed Dan the Ziplocked bird and asked him if he'd ever seen one.

He sat down on the cot, extracted the bird in the wheel from the bag, and examined it gingerly in his fingers. "The bird is called an *iynx,*" he said, dangling it from the loop of string. "In English, it's known as a wryneck because of the way it twists its neck with sudden, crazy jerks."

"Vassilos said it was a symbol of love."

"That comes out of the myth. Iynx was a sorceress who offered Zeus a love potion. When he drank it and fell in love with a girl, his wife, Hera, took revenge by turning Iynx into a wryneck. 'Iynx' is where we get the word 'jinx.' "

"What's with the wheel?"

"That was Aphrodite's doing. Remember Jason and the Argonauts?"

"I remember the movie."

"Well, this part is not in the movie." Dan set the wheel on his lap and started twisting the loop of string. "To get the Golden Fleece, Jason needed to win over Medea—another beautiful sorceress. But how do you cast the spell of love on a sorceress? Aphrodite, being the goddess of love, had an idea and decided to help him. She fastened a wryneck inside a wheel and hung it from a string. Its jerking neck set the wheel spinning, and Jason used its hypnotic whirl to mesmerize Medea."

Dan raised the now tightly braided string and lifted the wheel off his lap. The string began unwinding, and the wheel with the bird spun in the air. "It's a symbol of possession," he said, watching it whirl. "The crazed twisting of the neck, the obsessive circular motion of the mind. These little wheels were said to have been hanging from the ceiling of the Temple of Apollo at Delphi."

I thought of Phoebe that night in the temple, and the ecstatic female figure on the museum vase. I'd noticed similar spasmodic movements with the girls during the orgy on the yacht.

Dan dropped the dead bird on my lap and went back to peer through the window.

"What's happening?" I asked.

"She's flirting with that son of a bitch."

Somehow this didn't surprise me. "Does it look like it's working?"

"No."

He turned away and paced the room.

"What do you think was in that stuff we drank? Do you think it might have been the *kykeon*?"

"I've been thinking about little else," Dan said. "I figure it must have been some sort of barley wine—I could taste the grain, along with a strong, almost bitter mint flavor, what I thought must have been pennyroyal. Pennyroyal is a mild hallucinogen, but if the drink was made from barley, it may fit into Wasson's ergot theory. Ergot is a fungus; in fact, it forms into tiny little mushrooms. *Claviceps purpurea* is the type that forms on barley, which may have been what gave the drink that weird, purplish color."

"Purple haze?"

"It's like I told you. *Claviceps* contains ergonovine. Ergonovine is a psychoactive lysergic acid amide, a precursor to LSD."

"But how do you explain the sexual arousal? I've never been so horny in my life."

"It's probably an aphrodisiac added to the wine. The ancient Greeks developed a bunch of these concoctions, called *satyrion,* after the mythical satyr. Dioscorides—the original pharmacologist—mentions a *satyrion* derived from an orchid. I've always thought it might be the same plant Theophrastus wrote about centuries earlier. It was sent to Greece from the king of India, and the slave who carried it boasted of making seventy consecutive 'sacrifices' to Aphrodite."

I'd always written off Dan's interest in aphrodisiacs as just another one of his cockamamie obsessions. Now, after what had happened on the yacht, screwing seventy consecutive times didn't strike me as all that unlikely.

But the orgy had gone well beyond the act of sex. "What about the violence? Those women literally tore Basri apart."

Dan began pacing the room. "I've been thinking about that," he said. "When Theophrastus wrote about the *satyrion,* he used the verb *existimi,* which means 'to excite, stimulate.' But the same verb also has the meaning 'to make someone go mad.' Which suggests it might create a chain reaction when combined with the ergonovine. Lysergic acid has a powerful effect on the neurotransmitter serotonin, which regulates things like mood, sexuality, anger, aggression, and is linked to obsessive-compulsive behavior. It also has effects on other transmitters, like dopamine and adrenalin. So depending on the mixture of the *kykeon,* it might trigger anything from a blissful euphoria to an uncontrolled adrenalin rage."

"You think there was too much ergot?"

"It's possible. The trick isn't just the mixture but the method of preparation. You've got to extract the psychoactive compounds and exclude the more toxic alkaloids. Nobody's been able to figure out how they did it. The original formula was kept by the priests of an ancient family, descended from the kings of Eleusis. It was held in secret under penalty of death and passed down from generation to generation for centuries. Then, almost overnight, it vanished. All the pagan cults, including Eleusis, were outlawed by the Roman emperor in AD 391."

"After what happened to us on the yacht," I said, "I can understand why they'd shut it all down."

"The ritual on the yacht was different," he said. "There was something sinister about it."

"What do you mean?"

"The *kykeon* is only a catalyst," he said. "Everything depends on the context and the setting—and most of all, the intent. At Eleusis, the intent was to experience a profound spiritual awakening. Everything was carefully arranged to channel the energy in that direction. Each initiate had a personal guide to accompany them through the ceremonies, and the *kykeon* was imbided in the strictly controlled environment of the Telestrion, following a tried-and-true ritual procedure, a sacred tradition developed over centuries."

Dan stopped pacing and faced me. "On this island, these women . . . We don't know what their intention was."

"I think their intention was murder," I said.

"You may be right," Dan said. "If we want to prove we're innocent, we've got to find out why."

ANOTHER HOUR passed before Phoebe finally gave up on Vassilos. It was nine o'clock at night and the three of us were starving. She talked him into allowing her to pick us up some gyros, then ate with us together in our pathetic little cell.

We puzzled over why the women would have murdered Basri. Dan wasn't aware that Basri had any enemies, and said his shady business dealings were a thing of the distant past. If the killing was purely religious, as Phoebe seemed to believe, I wondered how they had decided on this particular guy.

"It may have been a matter of fate," Dan said. "Wrong place at the wrong time. He did meet the women in a bar, after all—"

Keys rattled, and Vassilos opened the door.

He pointed to me and then to Phoebe. "You two will please come with me."

"Where are we going?" I asked.

"The monastery," he said.

We all exchanged a glance. "Why?" Phoebe asked.

"The morgue called," he said. "Someone has stolen the head."

17

We rode up to the monastery in the backseat of Vassilos's squad car. The car was a dilapidated clunker and a thorough mess inside, yet remarkably nimble on the winding mountain road. I took the car as a metaphor for Vassilos himself. He was an overweight slob with a drinking problem, but he had an alert mind and a certain charm about him, a graceful, almost delicate manner. His voice was delicate, too; coarsened from years of smoking, I assumed, but now refined to a gravelly whisper. I had to keep leaning forward to hear him.

"What did you say?" I asked.

"I am asking the lady if she mind the cigarette." It dangled unlit from his lips.

"No," Phoebe said. "I don't mind."

"Very kind," he said, flaring up his lighter. "I will lower the window."

The charm was focused solely on Phoebe; me he seemed to re-sent. Perhaps he thought it was impolite to have ravaged one of the nuns. He had once again clapped me in the steel handcuffs, though this time he had mercifully buckled them in front, which made it more comfortable to sit.

"If the circumstances were different," Phoebe said, "I imagine I would have liked this island." She was sitting beside me, gazing out her window at the shoreline far below. Cool night air breezed through the car and lightly ruffled her hair.

I wondered why Vassilos had brought her along. Obviously, he couldn't leave her alone at the jail with Dan, and I suppose he hoped to keep her out of trouble. But I couldn't help thinking there might be another reason; that any man—sheriff or not—who happened to cross paths with Phoebe was bound to develop something of a crush on her.

The road leveled off into a gently rolling stretch of vineyards. I remembered this was where the fieldworkers had gotten off the bus. "Do the islanders make their own wine?" I asked.

Vassilos turned and briefly glanced at me, as if he resented being asked to play the tour guide. When he answered, he spoke to the windshield. "The vineyards are owned by the monastery," he said. "The *monachai* make the wine."

I turned in confusion to Phoebe.

"The women monks," she said. "In the Eastern Orthodox Church, there's no real difference between a monastery for men and a monastery for women. But in English we still call the women monks nuns."

"So, these nun-monks—they make wine?"

"Apparently." She leaned to catch Vassilos in the rearview mirror. "How long has the monastery been here?" she asked.

"Was built in eleventh century," he said.

Phoebe waited in vain for him to elaborate. "Can you tell us any more about it? Why is it called *Panaghia*? It means 'the Virgin,' doesn't it? How did it come to be built here?"

He shrugged halfheartedly. "I can tell you, but . . . is only a story."

"I'd like to hear the story," she said. "It's what I do for a living—put together stories from the past."

"You are historian?" he said.

"Archeologist," she said.

"Then you know these stories—they are only myths."

"Often there is truth to a myth."

He scratched his scalp. "Yes," he said. "Sometimes . . . is true."

"Then you'll tell us?" She was smiling coyly into the rearview mirror, and I realized she was flirting with him again to try to get him to talk.

Vassilos was driving effortlessly, with only his thumb on the bottom of the wheel, as if he had ridden this route all his life. He glanced several times at Phoebe in the mirror. Finally, he began telling us the story of the monastery.

"Eleventh century—a thousand years ago, yes? The Eumolpidae, a very old and respected family, lived on this mountain. They have a daughter with a beautiful voice, and she is singing, always singing in praise of God. One day, she find an *ikon* buried up on the mountain. It is a statue of the Virgin Mother, the *Panaghia,* and the people of Ogygia, they believe it is a miracle. They go to the emperor, ask him to build a monastery and church at this place, the very place where the *ikon* was found." He turned and glanced at us. "That is how the Monastery of the Panaghia came to be."

"What happened to the girl?" Phoebe asked. "The daughter of the Eumolpidae."

"She join the monastery. And when she is older, she become the abbess. She was known as Mother Melitta."

I said behind my hand to Phoebe, "The original singing nun."

Vassilos overheard me and snapped, "The *monachai* are famous for their singing. They perform all over Europe."

Phoebe said, "Some of these monasteries are repositories of Byzantine music. They've managed to keep it alive for centuries. The chants are descended from the choral music of the ancient Greeks. Isn't that right, Mr. Vassilos?"

His gaze shifted again to the mirror. "So I am told, Miss. The sisters' singing is very beautiful."

"Yeah, very beautiful," I said. "On the yacht they sang a lovely little chant—just before they killed our friend."

Vassilos glared at me in the rearview mirror. The tires began crunching gravel on the shoulder, and he swerved back onto the road.

Phoebe shot me an angry look, then tried to calm him down. "It makes sense—your story about the girl from the aristocratic family. In Byzantine society, if a proper, educated woman had musical talent, the only place she'd be allowed to express it was in sacred music, in the nunneries and monasteries. They could be a kind of cultural retreat for women who didn't marry."

I looked at Phoebe like she'd gone insane. *Cultural retreat?* The monastery we were heading into was a brothel full of witches.

I'd begun to worry that the nuns knew we were coming. Certainly, they would have expected that I'd return with Vassilos. If so, they would have hidden away the remains of Basri's body. *What would I do if we couldn't find anything?* I might have no choice but to try to escape. Vassilos, I had noticed, carried a holstered gun. And he kept the keys to the squad car and the handcuffs clipped to a loop of his belt.

The road turned inland and climbed higher into the pines. Vassilos focused on the tightly curving route, winding through a tunnel of trees lit by the beam of his headlights. When we finally came over the saddleback ridge into the steep ravine, the view opened up, and we could once again see the far-off Aegean glistening in the moonlight, and harbor lights twinkling on the shore down below.

Up ahead on the gloomy tower of rock, the monastery came into view. The crumbling walls looked like ruins in the moonlight, and the structures and towers within it seemed dead. Only the central dome of the church looked to be fully intact; it gleamed like the skin of an onion.

I asked Vassilos what had happened to the place. "It looks like it's been through a war," I said.

"It's been through many wars," he said. "Worst of all was the *katastrofi.*"

"You mean the Greek revolution?" Phoebe asked.

"The Ottoman Empire ruled us for centuries. When the War of Liberation came, they decide to make our island an example. Their soldiers came into our streets and houses, slaughtered our men, women, children. Thousands they took as slaves. Many fled to the mountain, to take refuge in the monastery. The soldiers followed them. They dynamite the walls, set fire to the church, destroy the library, burn the convent, rape the nuns."

He glanced at me as he said this last bit. *No wonder he hates me,* I thought. I remembered the shelves full of skulls in the church tower. Testament to a massacre.

"*Why?*" Phoebe asked.

"The soldiers are looking to destroy the famous *ikon,* the statue of the Virgin. But the *monachai* hid it on the mountain. Most of them were killed, and no one has ever found the *ikon* since."

Phoebe and I glanced at each other.

"Do you think it's true?" Phoebe asked him. "Or just another myth?"

"You said yourself, Miss. Sometimes there is truth in the myth."

Vassilos drove the car to the entrance and parked near the monastery gate. The place looked dark and deserted. He and Phoebe got out of the car, and Phoebe came around to open my door and help me out. We followed after Vassilos as he headed up to the gate. The stone wall loomed ominously above us, blocking the light from the moon. The only sound was our footsteps on the gravel; the night was utterly silent.

Vassilos clanged the bell at the gate. The noise seemed to shatter the air. We waited. No one appeared. Again, Vassilos rang the bell. Still no one came. Phoebe and I pressed closer to the gate, peering into the darkness. The narrow plaza was empty.

Vassilos unclipped the key ring from his belt, shuffled through the keys, and plugged a long-stemmed skeleton into the lock. As he turned it, the gate creaked open.

We stepped into the shadowy courtyard. Cupping his hands around his mouth, Vassilos called out a greeting in Greek—"*Akousate!*" It hung in the air like the sound of the bell, answered by a deafening silence. The few windows facing the courtyard were lightless, and the corridors between the buildings were dark. There was something unsettling about the silence of the place, and I noticed Phoebe unconsciously moving closer to my side. She put her hand lightly on my arm.

"There's no one here," she whispered.

"Then why do I feel like we're being watched?"

Vassilos quietly moved ahead. We followed him into a dark corridor, and as I stepped across a puddle, I realized it was the same route I had walked through earlier in the day—the passage between the dormitory building and the one-floor lavatory. The moon was reflected in the puddle, and when I looked up to find it in the sky, I noticed something else: the roof of the lavatory was made of thatch.

I called to Vassilos. "Wait a minute."

He and Phoebe stopped and turned. I went to the entrance of the building and, struggling with my handcuffs, opened up the door.

It was dark inside, but not completely dark. Moonlight leaked through the slender sapling trunks spanning overhead. Still, it took a moment for my eyes to adjust. When they did, I saw it wasn't a lavatory at all, and I wondered where the hell I'd even gotten that idea. The long room was filled with aisle after aisle of narrow tables holding small potted plants. There were hundreds of them.

Phoebe and Vassilos entered behind me.

"It's some kind of greenhouse," I said.

Phoebe came up next to me. We took a closer look at the plants. They were all the same: between one and two feet tall, with thick, spiky leaves and elaborate, bizarrely shaped flowers.

"An orchid," Phoebe said. "But I couldn't begin to tell you what kind."

I leaned down and took a sniff; the flowers were sweetly pungent, and reminded me immediately of the women on the yacht, the wild, floral aroma that had scented their skin. A thrill went through me, a visceral memory of the excitement I had felt. The feeling sent me racing back to that night, to the overwhelming lust . . . and the bloodlust.

"What is it, Jack?" Phoebe was tilting her head to catch my eyes.

"Nothing," I said.

Nearby, on an open tabletop with a brass watering pitcher and a rusted pair of iron scissors, lay a pile of orchids with their flowers clipped off and their roots exposed. Phoebe picked one out from the pile and examined a pair of small, round tubers attached to the roots.

She held them up for me to see. "Remind you of anything?"

"Yeah, something very precious to me."

"The name 'orchid' comes from the ancient Greek *orkhis,* meaning 'testicle.' Dan told me they're named after a genus of orchids in ancient Greece that had twin roots resembling the human scrotum."

I looked at her skeptically. "Sounds like a desperate attempt to seduce you."

She grinned. "He never quits."

I asked her to put one of the cut plants into her rucksack to show to Dan. As she did so, Vassilos tried to stop her.

"This is private property," he said.

I held up the root and showed him the gonads. "See this? It's an aphrodisiac. What do you think the nuns would be doing with that?"

Suddenly he looked interested. "Aphrodisiac?"

I pointed to a pail full of the tubers on the floor. "A thousand nights of bliss," I said.

He backed off, and as we were leaving, I saw him slip a couple of the tubers into his hat.

◆ ◆

OUTSIDE, WE continued down the alley to the large cloistered courtyard with the giant pine tree in the middle and the church at the other end. "They were singing in there this afternoon," I said.

Now the square was silent and the church looked dark and empty.

"This way," I said, taking the lead from Vassilos. "I want to show you something." We proceeded along the ruins of the colonnaded walkway to the chapel I had visited earlier.

I led them inside. The interior was completely dark, and Vassilos didn't have a flashlight, but fortunately he did carry a lighter. Ignoring my handcuffs, I pulled a beeswax candle from a stand near the entrance. Vassilos lit it and we proceeded toward the altar. The dead birds hanging overhead drew a gaping stare from Phoebe.

I nudged her. "According to the Sheriff here, those are love charms. And this is a wedding chapel."

"How romantic," she said.

At the altar I lit a few more candles. Phoebe seemed intrigued with the massive block of stone and ran her hands over its surface. "It's very unusual," she said. "I've never seen a Byzantine altar quite like it."

"That's nothing," I said. "Get a load of this." There were enough candles lit now to illuminate the icon panel. I unfastened the swivel clamps and gave a little demonstration: Holy Virgin on one side; Demeter, Persephone, and Dionysus on the other.

Phoebe moved in for a closer look. The pagan painting was badly corroded; whole sections of the image had been abraded or burned, or had simply faded away. As she studied it, Phoebe grew intensely curious. "This is amazing," she said.

Vassilos airily dismissed her excitement. "It is not as you think. This is St. Demetra, the patron saint of agriculture. The people here have prayed to her for centuries."

"It's possible," Phoebe mused, as her eyes roved over the painting. "Many of the old gods and goddesses were replaced by Christian saints. It was a common way of bringing pagans into the Church.

Simply incorporate their deities. Like St. Brigid in Ireland—her traits were based on a Celtic goddess. But *this* . . . I don't know how . . ." She was so intensely focused on the painting she couldn't seem to finish her thought.

To me, the image was more than obvious. "Demeter, Demetra. What about the other woman? Persephone. And the boy Dionysus?"

Vassilos shrugged. "They are all saints," he said dismissively.

"I don't see any haloes."

Vassilos turned and gave me a look; he was clearly losing patience. "I see no halo on you, my friend. Why do you show me these things?"

"These are ancient pagan gods," I said. "These nuns are not what you think."

Phoebe closely studied the painting, running her fingers over the wood. She seemed to be struggling with something.

"What is it, Phoebe?"

She slowly drew back and stood upright. "I'm not sure," she said. "It's just that . . . This looks much older than the Byzantine era."

"You mean it's from the ancient Greeks?"

"The only paintings we have from the ancient Greeks are what they put on their pottery. They also made paintings on wood panels, but . . . we only know about them from their writings. None of the panels has survived. If this is an actual ancient Greek painting . . . it's the only one of its kind."

She looked at me, stunned. "It would be absolutely priceless."

The two of us turned to stare at the painting. Then I turned to Vassilos. "What do you make of that, Sheriff?"

He glanced at Phoebe, then glared at me. "This is not your Wild West, and I am not your 'Sheriff.' You say you can show me the head of your friend. Show me now. Where is it?"

Some people just can't appreciate art. "Right this way," I said, and headed for the door.

◆ ◆

In ancient Greece, *hubris* was a punishable offense. They even invented a goddess to deliver retribution: Nemesis, daughter of Night and Darkness.

I got lost trying to locate the calefactory. The buildings all looked different in the dark, and without the smoke from the chimney to guide me, I had trouble finding my way. Two wrong turns and a circling back to the starting point had Vassilos ready to strangle me; but eventually, more by accident than design, we found ourselves stepping into the overgrown courtyard where earlier that day I'd been attacked.

There wasn't a soul in sight, but again I felt we were being watched. I stood for a moment and listened. Except for the astounding vocal performance of a lone nightingale, the place was completely silent.

We crossed toward the hexagonal warming house. In the moonlight it looked even more funereal. A cat cried out from the shadows. The black chimney loomed against the starry night sky. I turned to see Phoebe lagging behind us, carefully scanning the ground. I wondered if she might be watching for rats.

Vassilos ambled along beside me. I pointed out to him the locations of my various terrors. "Here's where I tripped when they chased me. See the broken flagstone? And look! Here's the spot where one of them tried to kill me with the poker. You can see the chip in the stone." Vassilos looked, but he seemed to be merely tolerating me, an effort that made him more exasperated with every point I made.

"Jack—look at this."

Phoebe was crouched to the ground several yards behind us. As we walked over, she was pulling up some grass and weeds around a large, rectangular stone set amid the irregular pavement.

"These blocks are fitted tightly together, unlike the flagstones. They form a line, you see? Right across the courtyard." She walked along the row of rectangular blocks, moving forward toward the calefactory. "They appear to be limestone. I think they're foundation blocks."

She found more and continued tracing the outline of the foundation. I joined in with her, searching the grass-covered puzzle of stone. Even Vassilos seemed to take an interest, casually scanning the ground.

"It looks like the remains of an ancient temple," Phoebe said at last. She pointed to the original line she had found. "These blocks must have supported the wall of the *naos,* the inner sanctum that held the statue of the god. Look at how incredibly tight they're fitted. Ancient Greek architects were obsessed with perfectly fitting stones."

"What's this out here?" I pointed to a massive, square-shaped stone a couple yards away from the foundation line.

"It's a base stone for a column," Phoebe said. "The colonnade ran along the outside of the *naos,* right along here." She pointed down the line toward the calefactory. Then she paused for a moment, staring at the hexagonal building. "That's interesting," she said. She turned to Vassilos. "Which way is east, do you know?"

He glanced around and saw the dark mountain looming over the chapel behind him. He turned and pointed in the opposite direction, toward the calefactory. "There is east," he said.

"That's what I thought," Phoebe said. She walked to the end of the foundation line, just in front of the calefactory. "Here's where the front of the temple was. Most temples faced east, so the priest would be facing the direction of the rising sun when offerings were made to the gods."

Now Vassilos was losing patience. "And so what of this?" he steamed. "I am Greek—I hear this since I am a child!"

"Then you know that religious rites were held outside the temple, not inside as in churches. The sacrifices were burned on an altar that stood out in front of the temple."

We all turned and faced the calefactory with its towering central smokestack.

"The altar would have been right there," she said.

I was still trying to figure out just what this meant when a cat screeched behind us, and the three of us spun around to the sound of footsteps echoing across the courtyard.

The dark figure of a man was disappearing into an alleyway.

"Wait!" I shouted. I went running after him. It had to be the person who'd been watching us, I thought, the presence I'd felt since we'd arrived. With my hands still in cuffs, I couldn't run fast, but I loped across to the alley into which he'd disappeared.

Phoebe followed. Vassilos called after us, lumbering behind. I glanced back and saw he was unfastening his handgun.

The alley ran alongside the ruins of the chapel and led out into a tiny, open courtyard. No one was there. I ran to another narrow lane, but that was empty, too. At the end of it, I looked either way. No sign or sound of the man.

Phoebe appeared behind me.

"Not here!" I said.

She hurried to the other courtyard exit. I followed her, but it was only an archway; it ended at the edge of the cliff.

The two of us stared down the sheer wall of rock to the moonlit valley below.

The man had vanished.

"Who do you think it was?" Phoebe asked.

"I'm not sure," I said. "But I could take a guess."

The Sheriff's voice echoed from the courtyard behind us. We turned to see him enter the archway with his gun.

He looked out of breath. "You will not run from me again," he commanded.

"We weren't running from you," I said. "We were chasing that man. Do you have any idea who he was?"

Vassilos eyed me suspiciously. "I should ask you this question."

I traded a glance with Phoebe, then looked back at him. "My brother and I were the only other men on that boat. Except for the man in the mask."

"Yes. The Dionysus. So you have told me." He strapped his pistol back into his holster.

"Do any men live at this monastery?" Phoebe asked.

"No," he said. "Only the Sisters."

"Then don't you want to find that man?" I asked.

"Our island is small. I will find him. But first I will find if you are telling me the truth."

VASSILOS OPENED the door to the calefactory and plunged into an inky darkness. Phoebe and I tentatively followed him inside. The air was dry and smelled of a stale, tangy smoke. We peered into the darkness until Vassilos flared up his lighter and ignited a handful of straw. He threw some kindling onto the hearth and jammed the burning straw underneath it. In seconds, a fire was blazing.

He stepped back and glanced around. The pokers and tongs stood upright in a rusted iron rack. Beside them was a shovel, a broom, a mop, and a dustpan, all tidily arranged. A fresh stack of cut wood was neatly piled nearby. The big wooden table had been cleared off and scrubbed, and the water pail with its dangling ladle had been scooted underneath. On the other side of the hearth, sitting alone in the middle of the stone floor, was the giant cast-iron cooking pot, the one in which the fastidious nuns had boiled Basri's bones.

The three of us approached it. With a sinking feeling, I found myself eyeing—not the pot, which by now I knew had to be empty—but Vassilos's belt loop, where the ring full of lock-up keys jangled temptingly. I wanted to snatch them, run off, and steal his car. But I couldn't help noticing, clear over on the other side of his considerable waist, the policeman's handgun strapped in its holster. *Do I dare to go for the one, knowing he'd go for the other? Can I—wearing handcuffs—try to go for both? And if I do, and pull it off, could I really, actually, credibly point a pistol at a cop?*

This was going to be as close as I came to trying to escape. Vassilos was right—he was not a Sheriff, and this was not the Wild

West. As the big man rounded to face me, and Phoebe turned away, I suddenly felt as empty as the inside of the pot.

The nuns had pulled off a murder. Dan and I were screwed.

I BEGGED and pleaded with Vassilos all the way back to the squad. *"What about the man? Why not search the rest of the place? Where are all the nuns?"*

He was having none of it. The place was clearly empty. Apparently the Pan-Hellenic Chorus had left the island again.

Phoebe followed glumly behind us, lost in a maze of thought. The only way out, she must have assumed, was to find ourselves a lawyer.

When we reached the car, Vassilos opened the rear door and started to usher me in. I was still babbling, pleading my case, when suddenly he raised his hand to shush me.

He'd heard something. "Listen," he said.

Until then, the mountain had been deathly silent. The only sound we'd heard on the monastery grounds was the liquid song of the nightingale. Now, out of the silence, we heard a distant sprinkling of voices, tiny bits and pieces of sound floating through the air. Joyful cries and screeches. Shrill cackles and caterwauls. Wild shrieks and screams. Mixed in with this far-off clamor was a tiny tumult of pipes and drums and tambourines, and high-pitched voices singing.

"There!" Phoebe said, pointing up the mountain.

I turned and searched the vast, ominous darkness of the dome. Far up, on a shadowy bluff, was a winding procession of fiery torches and figures dressed in white.

"The Bacchae," Phoebe said.

18

ACCORDING TO Vassilos, it was called Mount Nysa, and it reached a summit of nearly three thousand feet. The monastery stood roughly halfway to the top. Driving up from the town, the lower slopes had been gradual and green, but hiking up from the monastery the terrain was rocky and steep, with deep fissures and gorges, and sheer cliffs and promontories jutting into the sky. Scaling it in the dark now reminded me of Parnassus, and what Dan had called *Kakí Skála,* the "Evil Stairway." There, of course, we had been descending into trouble; here we were eagerly climbing toward it.

Somehow, Vassilos had managed to find a footpath up the mountain. How he did this without a flashlight I couldn't begin to imagine; he either had better night vision than me, or he had climbed the route before. Then again, he may have simply stumbled onto the path. According to Phoebe, who'd done a lot of hiking in Greece, these twisting lanes up mountainsides were common all over the country.

"The trick," she said, "is to be able to distinguish between animal paths and human paths. If the path is full of goat tracks, it's likely to end up nowhere. But the man-made routes have been developed over millennia. Trial and error eventually settled the most favorable course from one place to another. They can usually be depended on to get you where you're going."

Where we were going appeared to be the summit of the mountain. We caught occasional glimpses of the ghostly *monachai,* but mostly the only trace of them was their song descending with the breeze, or the racket of their instruments, or their high-pitched squeals of delight. We tracked them the only way we could, by following the trusty path. It wound through scattered, windswept bushes that clung to cracks in the rock, and rose up narrow cliffside steps ascending like a stairway to heaven. The path had a feel of great age about it, as if indeed its well-worn stones had been trodden upon for centuries. Although the way was steep, the cleverly calculated switchbacks kept us climbing at a moderate grade.

Phoebe took the lead. The overweight Vassilos lagged behind, and I struggled along in my handcuffs. Following my repeated complaints, he finally agreed to remove them.

He unlocked them with a key from his jangling key ring. "If you try to run away," he said in his soft, gravelly voice, "I think it very possible you will fall." He glanced over the precipice and looked me in the eye.

Phoebe called to us. She was waiting up ahead.

I broke the stare with Vassilos and started up the path. He followed closely behind.

Phoebe had found something. It looked like some sort of woodland scepter, or primitive magic wand. She held it out to Vassilos. "Do you recognize it, Captain?"

Vassilos looked at it, but he did not take it from her, and simply nodded yes.

To me, it looked like a walking stick with a pineapple mounted at the top. Phoebe handed it to me. "It's a *thyrsus,*" she said. "The sacred wand of Dionysus."

The rigid stick had been neatly inserted into the base of a large, spiky pinecone, from which strands of ivy dangled.

"They're carried by the Maenads," Phoebe said. "The pinecone, I would guess, is from that big fir tree in the courtyard of the monastery. The pine tree, like the ivy, is sacred to Dionysus."

I noticed the stick was strong, and segmented like bamboo. The pinecone, wreathed in ivy, was heavy and solidly attached. With its sharply tipped seed scales, it resembled a medieval mace. "It looks like a weapon," I said.

"In the Euripides play, Dionysus calls the *thyrsus* his 'ivy-clad spear.' It has a phallic connotation: the shaft that ends in the head; the pinecone seed of the tree. It's a magical instrument of wildness and fertility."

She took it from me to marvel at again. "Until now," she said, "the only ones I've ever seen were painted on ancient vases."

Vassilos scanned the heights above. "We must hurry," he said. "I fear we are losing them."

In fact, their voices could no longer be heard.

WE CONTINUED our trek at a quickened pace, with Phoebe and her magic wand leading the way, and the fat policeman windily trudging behind me. Soon the fortresslike monastery was as far below us as the Maenads had once been above us, and eventually we emerged onto a cliff top. The summit still remained out of view, but in the dark at the base of a bluff above us, we could see the snaking trail of torches and the ghostly chitons of the Maenads.

We were closer to them than we'd ever been, but something was very different: The cavalcade was moving in an enigmatic silence.

As the wheezing Vassilos paused to catch his breath, Phoebe and I waited in the darkness and watched the muted procession. I suddenly noticed who was leading it. "Look," I said. "It's the boy!"

We couldn't see for sure from the distance, but I felt certain it was the boy with the bike. He carried a torch, and he looked to be half-naked.

"*Iacchos,*" Phoebe said. "It's where the name 'Bacchus' comes from. The youthful Dionysus."

I didn't care what they called him. "On top of everything else," I said, "maybe we can nail them for child abuse."

Vassilos was bent over, hands on his knees, sucking wind. He didn't have the energy to even stand up and look.

The women carried their magic *thyrses* like walking sticks. A few of those toward the front of the line appeared to have something perched on their heads. I asked Phoebe what she thought it was.

"Hard to tell from here," she said, "but I think they must be baskets. You remember the Caryatids, from the porch of the Erechtheion on the Acropolis?"

"Yes." There had been six sculpted figures holding up the roof, women with baskets mounted on their heads. After the Parthenon temple, it was probably the most photographed structure in Greece.

"The head baskets were used for carrying sacred objects," Phoebe said.

"Any idea what those objects might be?"

"In the Mystery religions, they were always kept secret."

Secrets. Mysteries. I thought of Dan's story of the virgins on the Acropolis, carrying mysterious objects down to the shrine of Aphrodite; and the "holy things" carried from Athens to Eleusis, not to be divulged under punishment of death. What was the point of all this secrecy and silence? It seemed to me the secret of the Mystery religions was to keep these damn secrets a mystery.

"Why do you suppose . . . ?"

I didn't finish my question. The boy with his torch had suddenly disappeared. The women who followed him were disappearing, too.

"I don't believe what I'm seeing," I said.

The nuns were becoming invisible. Vanishing into the night.

"It's almost like . . ." I turned to stare at Phoebe's wand.

"Magic?" she said. She looked to Vassilos. "What is going on up there?"

The decrepit cop, no longer wheezing, glumly lumbered past us. "They reach a cave," he grumbled.

"Oh," she said. "Of course." She turned to watch them a moment. Then she turned to me. "Try to remember, Jack: They *are* only human."

THE PATH headed off in a different direction from where the Maenads had been on the bluff. Vassilos said it eventually led to another well-known cave, frequented by tourists. To reach the cave the women went into, we'd have to leave the path and do some climbing. Vassilos led the way.

As it turned out, there was a meager path, of sorts. It was sporadic and meandering, but as Phoebe and I gradually got the hang of it, we passed our plodding police guide and ascended the slope fairly quickly.

Unfortunately, not quickly enough. By the time we reached the place where the nuns had vanished, they were nowhere to be seen or heard. We scanned the wall of the cliff and saw no portal in the stone.

"I'm sure it must have been here," Phoebe said. "They were halfway across the base of this ridge."

As we waited for Vassilos to catch up, the two of us searched for the entrance to the cave. We probed into crevices, peeked behind bushes, climbed over boulders and rocks, but we couldn't find the mouth that had swallowed the procession.

"We're either in the wrong place," I said, "or those pinecones really are magic."

Vassilos finally showed up and slumped down on a boulder. He looked completely exhausted and was gasping for breath. I assumed that he suffered from asthma, or that tobacco had ruined his lungs.

"Too much hard living?" I said.

He shrugged wearily. "Smoke, drink, eat, make love—this is living. How can a Greek give up living?"

Zorba in his golden years had turned into a wheezing wreck.

"Keep indulging yourself," Phoebe said, "and you'll give it up soon enough."

"Where's the cave?" I asked. "We've looked everywhere."

"Even in the daylight, the cave is hard to find."

"So it *is* here?" I said.

He nodded toward the cliff. "Behind."

I turned and looked at the steep slope of rock. "I don't see any cave."

"I don't either," Phoebe said.

Vassilos achingly rose from the boulder. Half of his shirttail hung out of his pants. "You are not looking right," he said. He lumbered forward and climbed a short way up the slope. In the dark it looked like a blank wall of rock, but with a simple side step, Vassilos disappeared.

"I'll be damned," I said. We scrambled up after him.

A billion years ago, a triangular section of rock had broken loose and separated from the granite wall behind it. This apparent act of a god had left an open crevice and the entry into a cave. Looking at it head-on, you couldn't see the gap. It was a perfect optical illusion and made the entrance virtually invisible.

"Captain?"

Phoebe's call was swallowed in the blackness of the hole. We cautiously stepped inside.

The air was cool and damp and smelled of goat; it was so dark we couldn't see a thing. I felt Phoebe touching my arm and took her hand in mine. In the quiet, I could hear her breathing.

She called out again for Vassilos. "Captain?"

His cigarette lighter clicked and a tiny flame erupted, illuminating his bearded profile. He searched the wall of the cave, casting a massive shadow behind him, until he found a niche that held a torch, a wrapped bundle of reeds. He picked it up and lit the end; it burst into a powerful blaze. Fueled by grease or animal fat that spat and sputtered as it burned, the torch released a sooty smoke and lit the entire chamber.

The cavern was surprisingly spacious. Its high ceiling was felted with spiderwebs and completely blackened with soot. No stalactites dangled down, and only one mound of rock rose up from the floor—a massive, round, flat-topped boulder. It appeared to have been chiseled into shape.

Phoebe went immediately toward it. "It looks like an altar," she said.

"It's the same kind of stone we saw in the chapel," I said. "Only this is round."

"It is from the time before the Greeks," Vassilos said. "These people live on the island many thousand years ago. They worship a goddess."

Phoebe was examining a relief carving in the stone, a worn and amorphous female figure.

"Could it be Demeter?" I asked.

"Possibly," she said. "Why?"

"She was the mother of Persephone. Who in turn was the mother of Dionysus." Now I suddenly felt like the know-it-all.

Phoebe seemed uncertain. "It might be a precursor of Demeter. It resembles figures from the older Goddess cultures of Crete and Asia Minor."

I turned to Vassilos, holding his torch. "How do you know about this place?"

He took off his cap and rubbed the sweat from his forehead. "I live on this island all my life," he said. "There is little I don't know about it."

"Apparently you don't spend much time up here, or you'd know these nuns are lunatics."

He smiled eerily. His hand slipped into his hat, and he pulled out the orchid bulbs he'd picked up at the monastery. "Maybe you are needing these," he said.

"What?"

"You see the Sisters coming here. You think they are making the orgy."

Now I thought Vassilos was losing it. He seemed to be slightly delirious from all the climbing we had done. Maybe the altitude had got to him. Or the noxious air in the cave. I wondered if he had some kind of condition. *"Are you all right?"* I asked.

The smile fell from his face. "I will find what is happening here." He headed off toward the back of the cavern.

Phoebe and I watched him carry his torch into a tunnel-like passage.

"He's crazy," I said.

Phoebe agreed. "There *is* something odd about him."

We stood watching the light recede, glanced at each other, then followed him.

WE HADN'T gone far before we began to hear the Maenads. Their music emerged from deep in the cave and grew louder the farther we went. First came the rhythmic booming of a drum, then the noise of flutes and pipes, and finally, weaving through it all, the cry of the women's chant.

Vassilos walked just ahead of us. We squinted into the smoke from his torch while trying to see out in front of him. The passage narrowed in places, but frequently opened into spacious caverns that reached beyond his light. Rock formations grew more bizarre the deeper we penetrated. Riblike ripples, stalactite spikes, stones that looked like teeth. The wrinkled walls grew damp and close, like mud-wet elephant hide. The rock ceiling pressed down upon us, then rose up like a cathedral. Massive, shadowy boulders dwarfed us. Our feet sank into sand.

My eyes kept returning to the burning torch. The flame was growing weaker and would eventually leave us in darkness.

"We go in much farther, we won't get out. That torch of yours won't last."

Vassilos ignored me. He seemed determined to find the nuns. More curious even than Phoebe and me.

The women's voices echoed past. Shouts, screams, laughter. Behind it all the constant rhythm, the beat of their reverberating chant.

We emerged into a broad, sloping space with a high, slanted ceiling. The women sounded louder and closer. Holding aloft his sputtering torch, Vassilos led us out into the chamber, and the walls came alive with our shadows.

He brought us to a halt, leveling his arm to stop us.

Torchlight flickered in passageways. Shouts and shrieks erupted.

"They're coming!" Phoebe whispered. Vassilos jammed his torch in the sand, plunging us into darkness.

Out from the passageways, wild Maenads emerged, torches blazing. They raced through the cavern, shrieking madly, hair flowing behind them. In the blur of flames and flowing chitons, they looked like phantoms streaming through the corridors of hell.

I reached for Phoebe and touched a wall of rock. She was gone. The Bacchae were pouring in from all directions. Vassilos had already hidden himself—I couldn't see him anywhere. I spotted Phoebe running with a Maenad on her trail. I ran after her and came face-to-face with a grimacing witch, her eyes burning with firelight. She screamed and leapt on top of me, burying her teeth in my neck. I tumbled with her to the ground and fell on her burning torch. Grabbing a fistful of hair, I hauled her head back and threw her off, then scrambled back up on my feet. The tail of my shirt was burning.

Other Maenads spotted me and filled the air with shrieks. I rolled to the ground to put out the fire. Then I grabbed the still-burning torch and fled into the nearest passageway. Gleeful shouts echoed behind me as I raced down a curving corridor. The passage finally opened into another cavern, and up ahead I saw the glow of torchlight and flickering shadows—the source of the chanting, the flutes, and the drum.

I jammed my fire into the sand and hid myself in a crevice.

Within seconds my pursuers ran past, giddy and panting, their gowns flowing as if in a dream, their flames sputtering noisily. A moment later another swarm blew by, a blur of fluttering fire and chitons.

Then they were gone, and all I could hear was the chant. I cautiously emerged from my hiding place.

Back the way I had come was darkness. Ahead I saw the glow of torches and heard the roar of the women's chant. I wondered which passageway Phoebe had taken, and whether or not she'd been caught. My torch was dead; I had no match to light it. Without it, I couldn't go back in the dark. The only way was forward, deeper into the cave.

As I crept along, I kept thinking of Phoebe. I feared she'd been attacked by the woman chasing her. She could easily have gotten lost in the dark; the cave seemed to have innumerable passages. And I wondered where Vassilos had fled to. He might have been afraid to use his gun, to aim it at the Sisters. Maybe he was hiding in the dark like me. Perhaps, I thought, he had grown too curious, too interested to witness their mysterious rites. Like the king in Euripides' play, he'd succumbed to his own fascination.

The witch had taken a bite of my neck. I wiped away the blood running down into my shirt. My back had been burned and was screaming with pain, and my knee had been bashed and was bleeding. I moved ahead cautiously toward the light and the noise, glancing nervously behind me. Hugging close to the wall, I approached the entrance and peered inside.

It opened to an enormous space, a seemingly limitless cavern. A fire burned at its center. Around it the Bacchantes were dancing. Many held snakes in their hands. Some held torches or *thryses* and chanted; others blew reed flutes and pipes. One strong woman pounded a large round drum. The cacophony in the cavern was deafening.

I slipped inside and crept along the wall until I reached an outcrop of rock. Fiery shadows danced around me. A haze of smoke filled the air. I crouched low behind the rock and peered through the whirl of Maenads.

In front of the fire was a massive stone altar, even larger than the one at the entrance. Behind it loomed a tall stone figure, the statue of an ancient goddess. She stood stiff-backed, draped in robes to her feet. The lower half of an arm was missing. Her triangular face and tightly twisted strands of hair were simple and stylized, almost primitive in appearance. The stone had decayed and the carving had weathered, smoothing out her facial features and blurring the vertical folds in her robe. This was not the luminous marble of a supple Aphrodite, but rough stone carved into a formalized pose, rigid and austere. There was something intimidating about it.

If the statue was the long-lost *Panaghia,* the *ikon* of the Virgin Mary, it was a very strange Mary indeed. And what she was presiding over was even more bizarre.

Several women behind the altar were unpacking woven baskets—the ones they had carried up so gracefully on their heads. These women, these living caryatids, were pulling out the treasured and mysterious "sacred objects" and piling them up neatly on the altar.

These "holy things," it turned out, were no surprise to me. Their selection seemed perfectly appropriate. They were simple, symbolic, and frightening. They were human, yet somehow something more than merely human. They were ordinary, yet exposed a glaring truth that made them extraordinary. They seemed to hold the secret of the mystery of life, a secret that can only be revealed in death.

They were bones—human bones.

Femurs. Scapulas. Tibias. Ribs.

I looked at them in wonder—and in fear. To use the religious term, I looked at them in *awe.* They might as well have been what the Bacchae believed: the physical remains of a god.

It was, of course, the skull that most captured my attention. The women placed it ceremoniously at the center of the altar. I was immediately convinced it was Basri's, that in fact all the bones on the altar were his.

They were merely the latest in a long line of offerings. Thousands more bones just like them were piled against the base of the altar. They looked as if they'd been piling up for centuries. Skulls, hip bones, clavicles, vertebrae—every human bone you could imagine.

Through the dancing whirl of the Maenads, I saw a pair of hands grasp the skull on the altar and raise it into the air like a Eucharist.

It was Dionysus. The epicene god. In his grinning mask and long purple robe, he towered over the whirlwind of revelers. Firelight reflected on the bronze of his mask, and the upraised skull seemed to glow above his head. With his round, gaping eyes and contorted black mouth, he looked like a gleeful deity of death.

He placed the consecrated skull back down on the altar. Then he began gently laying bones into the fire. A femur, a scapula, a tiny bone from the foot or hand. One of each type was put into the blaze, while another was added to the pile on the floor. He dropped the jawbone into the flames, but left the skull on the altar. One was offered to the fiery god, the other would be kept for posterity.

Curiously, behind him, the caryatids were pouring ashes from the fire back into their now empty baskets. Billowing clouds of fine powder were rising up into the air.

The Maenads, meanwhile, carried on their manic dance. Their chitons had been reduced to rags, and many of the women ran naked. They flung their hair as if struck by a wind, and tossed their heads back, exposing swollen, bulging throats. They whirled and shouted and laughed. One lifted a snake up over her face and fed it into her gown. Several of the women collapsed in a faint as they reached the limit of exhaustion.

I spotted the boy approaching the altar. He was wearing what looked like an animal skin, and he carried a double-bladed *labrys,* a bronze ax like the one found with Dan when his boat washed up on the beach. Behind him walked a woman with the amphora in her arms, the vessel that had held the *kykeon.* A second woman carried the twin-faced chalice. They joined Dionysus at the altar.

The masked god was performing the ash ritual there, reaching down to the edge of the fire to scoop ashes into his cupped hands and pour them into the baskets. He repeated this several times. Finally, he picked up a torch from the blaze and led his entourage into the crowd.

Bacchantes swirled around him like a cyclone around its center. It was obvious they'd already partaken of the drink. I wondered if Dionysus was leaving them.

Suddenly, I realized he was walking toward me.

I ducked behind the rock. For a moment I considered making a break for the passage. But something held me back. Something that bothered me. Something about Dionysus.

Slowly I rose up from my hiding place. He was leading his entourage directly to me, as if he had known all along I was there.

The dancing Bacchae followed him.

I stepped out from behind the rock and stood there waiting for them. My eyes zeroed in on the man in the mask.

I realized I knew who he was.

19

THE PIPES and drumming had come to a stop. The Maenads swarmed around me. There had to be fifty women, every age and size and shape. Strands of ivy hung from their hair. Their chitons were ripped and ragged. Their flesh was soiled with soot and ash, their faces tracked with tears. Many wielded pine-cone *thryses,* others held torches above their heads and rattled tambourines. They closed in, breathless, eyes and mouths agape. A volatile horde of hysterics.

I backed against the wall. My arms and legs were trembling. My heart climbed into my throat.

Insane little giggles erupted. Heads jerked like the jinxing bird.

Andreas Vassilos stepped forward and removed his metal mask. The policeman's long hair fell to his shoulders. On his face he had that strange look, the same as when he had offered me the aphrodisiac. An eerie grin, a hint of daring.

The two women filled the chalice with the purplish *kykeon* and carefully handed it to him. He gave them his torch and held the chalice out to me.

"The blood of Dionysus. In the name of the Lord of Liberation, I offer you . . . *your freedom.*"

My freedom?

I looked at the chalice, then at him. I knew that he had to be high on the stuff. He must have just imbibed it. His mouth was drawn, his teeth were bared. His eyes were black and glassy, with a flinty flicker of light from his torch. He looked eager, excited, infused with vigor. Ready for the plunge into matter.

Around me all the faces were filled with this look, this feverish anticipation. Tall Thalia with her long red hair, her eyes wide and fiery. Voluptuous Aglaia of the shiny black curls, her pearl chiton in tatters. The mischievous Euphrosyne, brazenly naked, looking keen and flushed. Marina, Irene, the women from the yacht—all the bloody Maenad sisters were here, all except—

"Please," said Vassilos, holding out the chalice, waiting for me to take it.

Again I looked at the inky fluid trembling in the cup. My legs were shaking. My heart was banging. Fear fluttered through me like a madly brewing storm.

The fever of the women was infectious. I felt the heat from their crackling torches, smelled the sweat of their skin. Their eyes, their flesh seemed to quiver. Lured by the animal intensity of their passion, I felt a strange impulse to give myself over, to throw my body to the wolves. There *was* a kind of freedom in the madness of it. A liberating desire for destruction.

This time it was I who'd be the stand-in for their god. The bread of their unholy communion.

My eyes turned to Vassilos. The aquiline nose. The red-veined eyes. The splotchy, sagging face. He had the look of an aging blueblood, a patrician who had fallen into decadence and decline.

Suddenly it came to me: I knew who he was. "You're descended from the family of that girl. The one that found the buried statue."

Vassilos drew back the chalice and slowly straightened his

spine. "The Eumolpidae," he said proudly. "My blood is the blood of ancient Greece. Descended from the kings of Eleusis."

All at once it fell into place. The Eumolpidae. The family that held the secret of the Eleusinian Mysteries. The priests who mixed the formula of the *kykeon.*

"How did you come to be here?" I asked.

"The Mysteries were outlawed by the Christian emperor. The family fled to this island. The island of our ancestors."

I looked over the panting faces of the Bacchantes. If Vassilos had actually descended from this family, it was likely that these women had descended from it, too. But why were they killing people?

"I don't understand," I said. "The Eleusinian Mysteries honored Demeter and Persephone. I was told they were a celebration of love. Your ritual . . . it's all about sex and death."

"We worship the son of Persephone, the Divine Child of the Underworld, the Lord of Liberation. It better suits our purposes."

"Your purposes? What purposes?"

I glanced at the women around me. They were slowly crowding closer.

"You're nothing but murderers," I said.

Vassilos silently grinned to himself, then lowered his eyes to the *kykeon.* "I offer you heaven," he said. "But you are not worthy."

With a gesture he summoned the boy, who promptly emerged from the crowd behind him. The boy was still draped in what looked to be the hide of a deer and carried the double-bladed *labrys.* Vassilos took the ax from him, exchanging it for the chalice.

The boy stepped back. Vassilos replaced the mask on his face. Then he held the ax out between his hands and lifted it into the air.

The drum began pounding, and the Maenads started toward me, their faces aglow in the firelight. Thalia, the Mother Abbess, was fervently leading the way.

I prepared to lunge through them and fight my way out. I decided to go directly at Thalia.

"Wait!"

It was Phoebe's voice. Coming from out of the crowd.

I spotted her weaving her way through the throng, carrying aloft her *thyrsus.* She emerged to stand beside me, holding the stick like a staff.

I stared at her in shock.

Phoebe had cast off her clothes and rucksack and was wearing her sandals and a white chiton. She had blended seamlessly into the crowd in order to hide herself.

Now she stood boldly before them. Her cheek was streaked with scratch marks, and her throat looked red and raw, as if it had been throttled. I noticed blood splattered on the shoulder of her gown, and wondered if she had injured her head.

She seemed unnaturally calm.

"I will drink the libation," she announced. "Blood of the Lord Dionysus."

Vassilos stared from behind his mask.

I watched her, stunned. "Phoebe?"

She glanced at me, her eyes fierce. She looked completely determined.

Vassilos stepped forward, ax in hand. He lifted his mask, and his head twisted slightly in doubt as he peered into Phoebe's eyes.

She stared back without flinching.

I shook my head in disbelief. *"Don't do it, Phoebe."*

She glared at me. *"I must."* Again she looked at Vassilos.

"To choose this course is wise," he said. He threw me a sideways glance. "It is better to come willing into heaven."

Again with a gesture he summoned the boy.

Impassive, angelic, the boy stepped forward and held out the chalice. Vassilos took it and offered it to Phoebe.

"Your freedom," he declared.

For a moment, she stared at the cup. Then she turned to me and held out the *thyrsus.*

I looked into her eyes. Hard as diamonds. It was obvious there was nothing I could say to change her mind. I thought about grabbing her arm and running, but how would I drag her out of the cave and fight off the horde of women? Reluctantly, I took the stick from her. Then I stood there, helplessly, a witness to the rite.

She reached for the cup with both hands. It seemed to me they were trembling. For the first time I thought she must be afraid. She took hold of the twin-faced chalice and held it under her gaze, peering in wonder at the brimming elixir. The inky purple liquid reflected the flames, and its strange light seemed to dance on her face, as if it were hypnotizing her.

Vassilos, the Bacchantes, all of us stood watching, waiting for the virgin Maenad to drink.

Phoebe raised the cup to her lips. Her eyelids fell closed as she slowly tilted the glinting chalice, filling her mouth with the *kykeon.*

She lowered the cup, and, staring forward, swallowed the elixir in a single gulp.

I thought of the way I had felt when I drank it: the explosion in the mouth, the complex fusion of flavors, the warm rush of steam through my limbs, the sudden surge of energy, the intense heightening of awareness. I watched as all these sensations now progressively passed through Phoebe. At first she seemed inwardly focused, as if following its flow through her body. Then, after a moment, her eyes lifted, and she looked at the silver chalice in her hands.

Glistening, ancient, beautiful.

She turned her gaze on Vassilos, then upon me, then at all the faces around her. Her eyes seemed to burn with sharpness and intensity. That total awareness of the physical world and a vision of unbounded possibility.

I was watching a transformation. From woman into Maenad. One more sip and she'd be right where I had been—beyond the point of return.

"Phoebe. Please."

She looked at me. Her eyes were fierce. She turned to the chalice and raised it to her lips. Again she took a drink of the elixir.

Vassilos watched her with a devil's delight. The smile of death on his face.

Until Phoebe suddenly leapt forward and spewed the fluid in his eyes.

Vassilos's hands shot to his face, and Phoebe went charging into him. They crashed together into the mass of women. Screams and shouts erupted.

I rushed in after them, but stopped as the Bacchae began suddenly backing away. It was Phoebe, emerging with the bronze ax, swinging it to fend them off. Vassilos lay blinded on the ground behind her, trying to clear his eyes. His neck had been cut and was bleeding, and his robe had been ripped aside, revealing his disheveled uniform underneath. Thalia quickly attended to him.

"Catch!" Phoebe tossed me something glinting, jangling. I grabbed it out of the air.

The Sheriff's key ring. She'd ripped it off his belt. I looked at her in amazement, then jammed the keys in my pocket.

The Maenads circled.

I joined with Phoebe, and we faced them back-to-back, I with the *thyrsus,* she with her ax.

Thalia was bent over Vassilos, her long hair hiding her face. She rose to her feet with a torch in her hand and turned to us in fury.

The Mother let loose with a blood-curdling scream.

The sound went through us like shrapnel. We stood there frozen, shuddering. Other Bacchantes joined in Thalia's cry, and the howl of their chorus grew louder and louder, resounding through the vast expanse of the cave, building to a deafening roar. Soon all were shrieking at the top of their lungs—a single, terrifying wail.

The sound brought my heart to a stop.

Thalia started toward us with her torch. Others fell in behind. Her mouth was drawn, her teeth bared, her face contorted with rage. She rose to her full height and lifted her arms, ready to pounce on Phoebe.

Phoebe let rip with a scream of her own. A primal, cringe-inducing screech. In a fit of madness, she swung her ax at the Maenad—a perfect, sweeping, horizontal arc razoring Thalia's gown.

Thalia's mouth went slack. She stumbled to a stop and stood gaping at her belly. A thin red line slowly seeped through her chiton. She touched her fingers into the blood, and dropped her torch to the ground. Her stunned gaze rose in confusion to Phoebe.

The Bacchae hesitated.

Phoebe raised her ax and peered into their faces. She had a lunatic look in her eyes.

"Back off, you bitches!" she hollered. "Get out of our *fucking* way!"

The Maenads cowered, momentarily confused. They glanced at Thalia, bent and bleeding, and at Vassilos lying on the ground.

I cautiously picked up Thalia's torch, then fell in beside Phoebe. Holding our *thyrsus* and ax at the ready, we started toward the passage I'd come in through.

Miraculously, as we moved toward them, the crowd of women parted. We walked slowly forward with our weapons raised, watching for the one who would attack. My torchlight fell on their faces in the dark. They looked fascinated and fearful and desirous all at once. A woman I'd seen earlier wildly tossing her head was staring at us now through the locks of her hair as if she were peering through a jungle. Irene stood gaping with a snake around her neck, its flicking tongue at her ear. Another familiar woman, strong-limbed but small, wore a thick crown of ivy on her shaved head, and on her body a fawn skin like the boy. She held a reed flute in her hand, and her face was streaked with ash. Aglaia emerged in the rags of her chiton, one breast dangling in the open like a fruit. She had a strange look on her face, and I wondered what she might be thinking, if she was even thinking at all.

A man's shout echoed through the cavern, and we turned to see Vassilos hobbling up behind us, rousing the Bacchae to join him. He was clutching his neck to keep it from bleeding. Thalia was walking beside him, holding her bleeding gut.

The Bacchae began to follow.

Phoebe and I took off. We burst past the remaining women in our way, and Phoebe started toward a low-ceilinged passage.

"This way!" I said, pulling her back toward the corridor I had entered from.

"No—here!" she insisted. She disappeared into the dark. Assuming she knew something I didn't know—and having no time to argue—I raced in after her.

The passage had a low, slanted ceiling that forced us to run in a crouch. I kept thinking it would open up, but it narrowed rather than widened. Eventually we were scurrying through a tunnel-like tube, twisty and tight as the gut of a snake and unnervingly claustrophobic. Soon we were crawling on our hands and knees. I figured this was why she'd insisted on this route—so Vassilos wouldn't be able to follow.

It seemed to have worked. I kept glancing behind us, but couldn't see anyone coming. Crawling with the torch in front of me, I had to stay far enough behind Phoebe so I wouldn't burn her feet. I had seen the blood on her shoulder; now I saw blood on her leg as well.

"Phoebe, what happened to you? Are you all right?"

She didn't answer.

"Phoebe?"

She kept crawling ahead as fast as she could. We crawled on for another twenty yards until the passage finally opened into a low-ceilinged cavern. It was different from any I'd been in before, a forest of spiky stalagmites that made it nearly impossible to move.

Phoebe took the torch from my hand and searched into a shadowy crevice to the side.

"What are you looking for?" I asked, following her in.

Again, she didn't answer.

"Phoebe, are you sure—?"

She stepped over something on the ground, and when I lowered the torch to see it, my heart leapt into my throat.

The white corpse of a naked woman lay stretched along the ground. She had short black hair, a narrow face, and long, spindly arms and legs. She lay twisted, half on her side and half on her back, with her head cast to the side, exposing beneath a wreath of ivy a wash of blood at her temple. The body appeared to have been dragged into the crevice and abandoned.

A foot away from her face lay the murder weapon—a rock, glistening with blood. The Maenad had been smashed in the head.

Phoebe's backpack lay where she'd left it, stashed at the rear of the crevice. Her clothes had been hastily stuffed into it. She slung the pack over her shoulder, then stepped back over the corpse to me.

For a moment she paused and looked into my eyes. Again, I noticed the splattered blood on the shoulder of her chiton.

"Are you all right?"

Her diamond eyes were hard to read. In the darkness and the firelight, they had a strange sparkle to them. It could have been a glimmer of guilt or fear, but it seemed to have a touch of madness.

She moved past me without saying a word.

I followed her.

She led us through the forest of rock, weaving this way and that. I quickly lost my sense of direction. Finally, we emerged into a large open space with a high, slanted ceiling, and I realized it was the same cavern where the pack of wild Maenads had attacked us.

It was clear to me now what had happened to Phoebe. She had fled into this forest of stalagmites, pursued by one of the crazies. She'd been attacked, strangled. In defense, she had grabbed a rock and struck the woman in the head.

The blow had killed her. The deed had probably occurred in the dark.

Phoebe must have heard the singing and the drums through the tunnel. She had changed into the woman's chiton and crawled through until she saw their light. There she had slipped unnoticed into the group. When she saw that I was about to be attacked, she had acted decisively to save me.

"Phoebe. Wait."

We were crossing the cavern, heading for the exit. She stopped and turned to me.

"Why did you drink it?" I asked. "Why did you actually drink the *kykeon*?"

Her eyes had that look, that strange, burning glimmer. "Because I knew I was going to need it," she said.

"*Need* it?"

She nodded. "Yes."

Of course, I thought. Especially after what had just happened. That killing may have been her first, but very likely it would not be her last. Not if she wanted to get off the island alive.

I peered into her fiery eyes. *Courage is a kind of madness,* I thought.

Shouts reverberated through the cavern, and firelight lit up the darkness behind her.

"This way!" I whispered, grabbing her wrist.

WE RAN off into the passage. This time we couldn't extinguish our torch—we needed its light to escape. Phoebe held it above her head and quickly took the lead. Wearing only her tight-laced sandals, she somehow nimbly navigated the winding, rocky terrain. I followed in her shadow, and several times I tripped, but the Olympian torch-bearing marathon runner never seemed to miss a single step. *It must be the* kykeon, I thought. The remarkable acuity it lent to the senses. I had often noticed a preternatural athleticism with Phoebe; now she seemed the very incarnation of a sprite.

We could hear the women racing through the cavern far behind us. Shrieks of joy and laughter, as if they were taking great pleasure in the chase. They, too, were high on the *kykeon,* and far more potently than Phoebe. At least three drinks to her one. Given the level of hysteria, I wondered if they might have imbibed even more. They had danced themselves into rags. The drug must have touched off an adrenalin boost. How else could they sustain such intensity?

We came out into another cavern and ran along the wall until we picked up the passage again. This had to be the final stretch, I thought. We'd been through several caverns now; the exit would be close.

A figure suddenly swept past me in the dark. Swift, silent, animal-like. With a scream she leapt onto Phoebe, and they tumbled hard to the ground. Phoebe's torch went flying, and the *labrys* clattered on the rocks. I could hear the two women fighting in the dark, and grabbed the torch to find them.

They passed through the torchlight, locked together, a twisted coil of animal hide, chiton, and naked flesh. The girl in the deerskin with the shaved head had wrapped herself around Phoebe's back and was biting her ear. I dropped my *thyrsus* and the torch, yanked back the woman's head, and locked my arm around her throat. With a jerk, I wrenched her from Phoebe. The woman and I stumbled back. She elbowed me and twisted free, then swung around and swiftly punted.

The kick to my groin completely stunned me. Everything in my body seemed to stop. I folded over on top of the pain, and her sandled heel flew up again and struck me in the face. The blow knocked me back, bursting open my lip. As I landed on the ground, I saw Phoebe raise the pinecone *thyrsus* and swing it like a baseball bat.

She bashed the freak in the head. The *thyrsus* cracked in half. The woman spun and landed on the torch, plunging us again into darkness.

"Jack?"

I felt Phoebe's hand on me. "Are you all right?" she whispered as she helped me to my feet. The pain in my groin made me nauseous.

The girl was stirring. We could hear her moan.

Phoebe was searching the ground in the dark. She found the backpack and handed it to me, but we couldn't find the *labrys.*

"We've got to move," I said.

Shouts and squeals reverberated through the tunnel. We could see the distant glow of the approaching Maenad horde.

The two of us turned from the glow of the torches to face an impenetrable darkness. "We can't outrun them in the dark," she said. "How will we defend ourselves?"

I glanced back again at the advancing mass of Maenads. They

would easily overwhelm us. "I don't know," I said. I took her hand and began to move forward through the dark, my mind in a race with fear.

"Look!" Phoebe whispered.

Far ahead in the blackness of the passage, a light had suddenly appeared. Not the flickering light of a torch, but something steady and strong, like a flashlight or a lantern.

We continued moving toward it. Slow at first, then faster. The light silhouetted boulders and rocks and helped us make our way. We were nearly at a run when we finally came within reach of it.

Suddenly, the light disappeared.

We slowed to a stop at the point where it had vanished. "What happened?" Phoebe asked. We were standing in total darkness again.

Behind us the horde of Maenads were advancing. We could see their torchlight clearly now, a tiny matchstick army in the dark.

We turned to face forward again, and realized we were standing at the entrance to yet another spacious cavern. As my eyes adjusted, I made out the silhouette of the round, flat-topped altar and beyond it a pale triangle of moonlight.

"The entrance!" I said, and grabbed Phoebe's arm.

She was staring off to the side. Something had caught her attention. I peered into the dark and saw the figure of a man backing into a crevice.

"Who are you?" Phoebe whispered.

The figure receded into the shadows. Not a word came out of the dark.

I glanced back at the closing horde. "C'mon!" I said. "Hurry!"

We flew like the proverbial bats out of hell.

III

ELEUTHERIA

◆ ◆

20

PHOEBE AND I pounded down the cliff in the dark. The Bacchae followed some distance behind, shouting and chanting erratically, their meandering torches ablaze on the slope. Our lack of a torch should have slowed our descent—we had nothing but the moon for light—but somehow Phoebe's heightened instincts kept us on the path.

When we reached a level stretch over yet another cliff, we paused to catch our breath. Below us the rock wall dropped off steeply, and the monastery hovered like an island in the dark.

Phoebe looked manic. The side of her head was covered in blood. The bite to her ear had torn the cartilage, and blood had run down her neck to her shoulder and saturated her gown. The abrasion on her leg was bleeding, too, but she didn't seem to pay it any mind.

I figured it was the *kykeon.* Like the ethylene at Delphi, it had an analgesic effect.

"We've got to stop your bleeding," I said. "Isn't there a bandage in your pack?"

Her panting face was wild and fiery, caught in the adrenalin rush. "No time," she said. "They catch up to us, they'll throw us off these rocks." She took off again down the path.

After this brief moment's rest, Phoebe moved faster. Even following her footsteps, I had trouble keeping up. Her nimble feet seemed to dance over the stones, her ivory gown flowing behind her. The shimmering view of this fleet-footed fairy, and the constant zigzagging back and forth, began to induce a kind of ambulatory trance, and I felt a peculiar detachment. The danger of the Maenads was real enough, and the threat of a misstep was vivid, but somehow the winding race to escape had begun to feel like a spiraling dream, a descent into some mythical realm, a land of cruel gods and their playthings.

I kept my eyes on Phoebe. Her hair, the nape of her neck, the stain of blood on her shoulder, the repetitive flash of her scurrying feet. Her body, glimpsed through the moonlit chiton, appeared both angelic and vulnerable. Though she flew down the mountain like some airy woodland nymph, she was mortal and frighteningly fragile. I realized I would do anything to keep her from getting hurt.

Anything.

WHEN WE finally spilled out onto the road, it came as a kind of shock. The sudden horizontal flatness and solidity. The utter stillness and quiet. Up the way the monastery stood mutely in the dark. Before it, the car sat waiting, its rear door still hanging open, just the way we'd left it.

The shouts and screams of the Bacchae had stopped. The mountain had fallen into silence.

We scanned the cliffs as we hurried to the car. Not a single torch could be seen. "Where the hell are they?" I wondered.

Phoebe said nothing. She climbed into the backseat through the open door, slammed the door shut, rolled up the window, and pounded down the lock.

I threw the backpack onto the passenger seat and got in behind the wheel. Phoebe immediately locked my door and all the other doors in the car. She was panting with fear. She grabbed the backpack and pulled it into the backseat.

I fumbled with the ring of keys until I found the car key. Inserting it into the ignition, I couldn't get it to turn. *Is it the wrong key? Maybe it's for a different car. But didn't I see him put it on the ring?*

I couldn't seem to focus on what I was doing because I couldn't stop glancing out the window. The darkness had enveloped us. The light was on inside the car, and all I could see was our reflections.

The key wouldn't budge. I checked to make sure the car was in park. I put my foot on the brake. Finally, by turning the wheel a bit, the key suddenly turned, and the engine groaned to life.

Phoebe buckled her seatbelt. *Why did she sit in the back?*

I flipped what I thought was the headlight switch. The wipers started sweeping, scratching dry glass. I shut them off and tried another. The interior light went out. I jumped when I saw something moving in the dark, but it turned out to be Phoebe's reflection—she was opening her backpack. I tried the next switch.

The road all the way to the gate lit up. I didn't see anyone around us.

The lane was too narrow to turn the car without backing up to the shoulder. I shifted into reverse and threw my elbow over the seat to look out the rear window.

Phoebe was digging through the pockets of her pack.

"You okay?" I asked. Her silence was disturbing.

Intent on her search, she didn't seem to hear. I backed up to the wall of rock. Then looked down to shift. Accidentally, I over-shifted and dropped it into second. I moved it into drive, then looked back up at the road.

The headlamps shone across the empty tarmac and out into the sky.

"I think we've got them beat," I said.

I turned the wheel and sped off down the road. On one side the cliff wall rose up steeply; the other side dropped into forest. Ahead, the road curved gently, gradually revealing itself.

I locked my seatbelt. Straightened my back. Adjusted the rearview mirror.

"There they are!" I said. Phoebe turned to look.

Ghosts were straggling out onto the road behind us. They looked zombielike and ragged. All their torches were out. They disappeared as we sped around the bend.

"They must be exhausted," I said. "They can't possibly keep up that intensity."

In truth, I wasn't so sure. Phoebe still looked manic. She had gone back to digging in her bag. *Obsessive-compulsive behavior,* I thought. *Another effect of the drug.* I kept glancing at the rearview mirror, trying to catch a glimpse of her, hoping to calm her down.

I smiled reassuringly. "It's like you said. They *are* only human."

Still absorbed with her backpack, she either didn't hear me or simply didn't care.

"What is it you're looking for?" I finally asked. The road was dropping down the saddle into the spread of pinewoods.

Again I thought she didn't hear me. "Phoebe?"

Finally, she found what she was looking for and held it up to show me.

A corkscrew. The folding kind that waiters use.

"We going to have some wine?" I asked.

Phoebe wasn't smiling. She was opening the foil cutter, the short-bladed knife in the corkscrew.

What in the fuck is she doing?

"Phoebe . . . ?" For a second, I couldn't get any words out. "I . . . don't think you'll need that," I said. "Let's wait and have champagne."

She stared ahead blankly at the windshield, repetitively flicking the blade with her thumb.

I watched her in the rearview mirror. "Phoebe?"

"The Furies are coming," she said.

"What?"

"The Furies are coming." Her voice was flat and strange. Like the voice that came out of her at Delphi.

"Phoebe. Try to remember: You've taken the *kykeon.* You need to maintain—"

"The Furies are coming! The Furies are coming! The Furies are coming!"

She was shouting, her face blanching in terror. I turned to put my hand on her to try to calm her down. She batted it away.

At the same instant I heard a crack and a thud and a bump of the tires, and I saw out the back window the heap of a body lying on the road.

I whipped around. The windshield was cracked. Women were running directly at the car. Instinctively, I slammed the brakes and yanked hard on the wheel. The car skidded and the tail spun out, sweeping toward a woman in a ragged chiton.

Thwump!

I tried to turn the wheel. Something shattered the passenger window. The car flew off the road and into the ravine. Grass, boulders, trees. We were bouncing so hard I couldn't see. Then we took a flip into weightlessness. One . . . Two . . .

Just before we struck the tree, I heard Phoebe scream.

"Jack!"

TAKE THE plunge into matter, bro'."

Dan? Is that you?

Everything had suddenly come to a stop. I was lying on my back in the Castalian Spring, naked in the freezing water. Beyond the rim of the canyon above, stars burned like distant torches. The hollows in the cliff looked like the gaping eyes of the god.

Fingers crept around my neck. I seemed unable to move. Hands gripping my wrists and ankles hauled me down into darkness.

Somewhere, a woman was screaming.

I CHOKED and sputtered back to consciousness. The car horn was wailing. The window was shattered. Chips of glass glimmered like diamonds.

White arms were reaching for my hair and my throat. A small, clenched hand was stabbing the arms with the blade of the corkscrew knife.

People are nicer where I come from.

My eyes drifted shut.

THE PRESENCE of your consciousness will influence the event."

Dan again.

We were following him down the Evil Stairway. Phoebe glanced over her shoulder at me. "I think it's already having an influence," she said.

Dan grabbed my face between his hands and peered into my eyes like a laser. "Take the plunge, Jack! The plunge into fucking matter!"

I AWOKE to a field of diamonds. They came into focus on the ceiling of the car. Plopped in their midst was a large mossy rock that apparently had crashed through the window.

My head was bent against the ceiling. Bits of glass were stuck to my cheek. The seatbelt cut across my shoulder like a knife. Phoebe's backpack lay on the ceiling beside the rock, but Phoebe was no longer in the car.

Shouts and grunts and shrieks were emerging from somewhere

nearby in the dark. I smelled the stench of burning oil rising from the engine block.

The car lay upside down. It had landed against the trunk of a fallen fir tree. The massive, rotting log blocked off all exit from my side of the car. On the other side, both windows had been smashed, and the rear door was open.

Peering out that door into the dark, I saw a squirming heap of Maenads clinging upside down to the earth like bees on a hanging hive. Phoebe had been dragged out and was being attacked. I could hear her muffled screams from the pile.

Reaching down into the seat, I managed to press the seatbelt release, and my body crumpled against the ceiling. My head was bleeding, my shoulder was hurt, but miraculously nothing felt broken. I wormed my way across to the rear passenger door, and as I moved past the boulder and the backpack, I realized I was looking at a weapon.

Alone, the rock would be too unwieldy to handle; effective for a single smash, but useless against the mob. But if I put it *inside* the pack, I could hold the pack by the handle at the top and swing it at the Maenads like a club. Phoebe's clothes would soften the blow, so I could knock them away without killing them.

I opened the pack, rolled the big rock into it, closed it up, and slid out of the car. My head swam dizzily as I stood upright. Blood dripped into my eye. I wiped it away with the back of my hand, taking little chunks of glass with it. Then I grabbed the pack by the handle and started across the slope.

The Bacchae were so immersed in their madness they didn't even see me at first. There were fifteen, maybe twenty women, all piled in a writhing heap, with Phoebe buried under them. These women seemed younger and more energetic than the ones I'd seen in the rearview mirror. They groaned and shrieked and tore at one another as they burrowed their way into the mountain of flesh. Their ivory chitons were ripped and ragged, and many of the women were naked, the mass of their bodies like a single organism—alive, voracious, devouring.

I felt the welling of a primal rage. A scream erupted from me, a howl that echoed out over the ravine. Several women looked up from the pile; some even backed away, but most were so lost to hysteria they barely took any notice. I was charging across the slope as I howled, swinging the bag with the rock, and when a Maenad with a *thyrsus* came running at me, the blow from the bag sent her flying. More of them attacked me as I slammed into the pile. I swung the pack in a sweeping circle, and the rock struck their bodies with muffled thumps. Many began moving away, and I briefly caught a glimpse of Phoebe, bloodied and struggling in the middle of the heap.

Someone behind me grabbed hold of the bag. I turned to see red-haired Thalia with a look of rage on her face. Her gown in front was soaked in blood from the slice of Phoebe's ax. She pulled at the bag, and when I yanked back, the handle ripped. The bag tore open and the rock fell out. Thalia tossed the pack aside and came charging at me. We both tumbled back into the throbbing mass of flesh. Knees, breasts, buttocks, elbows, hair, hands, eyes. Women kept piling on, all of them biting and clawing me. They tore at my clothes and my skin. They pulled my limbs, twisting joints. I clenched my hands tight into fists to keep them from tearing off fingers.

Struggling to free myself, I came face-to-face with Phoebe. She was bloodied and weakened and desperate, but her eyes still burned with the madness of the drug. She was caught in their grip and fighting them off. We looked at each other for the briefest moment.

It was long enough—I knew at once I could not be stopped.

Something mysterious came over me. Entirely spontaneous and instinctive. It may have been from anger or my protectiveness toward Phoebe, or even from the primal fear of death. I felt a peculiar sensation in my limbs, and became conscious of a sudden flow of energy, as if fire and steam were being *breathed* into my chest.

I rose up like a tidal wave, taking bodies with me. With a roar I threw the women off, and yanked them away from Phoebe. Most came right back at me, and I fought them hand-to-hand.

This only seemed to increase their fury. They smashed me with their sticks and torches, and bit and clawed like animals. One came at me with the mossy rock, smashing it into my shoulder. Phoebe rose up and joined in the battle. We fought them back with total abandon, a rage to match their own. Finally, we crashed through the mob of women and fled toward the darkness of the woods.

Phoebe, with amazing alertness, grabbed her bag on the run.

THE STEEP ravine was thick with trees. Beams of moonlight slanted through, but the forest floor was dark. Shrieks shook the still air. The Maenads raced behind us. Glancing back, I caught their ghostly forms amid the pines.

Fueled by panic, Phoebe flitted down the slope; I ran just behind her. Her chiton, in tatters, clung to a single clasp. Blood streaked her skin. She'd lost one of her sandals. I could hear her breathless panting as she raced down through the trees.

We came out onto a grassy slope, a clearing in the woods. A circular pen made of pine boughs held half a dozen goats. The goats stirred and their bells clanged as the two of us darted past.

Immediately, we entered another wood, sparser than the last. Moonlight filtered through the trees; we could see and hear more clearly. Behind us, the goat bells jangled. Amid the shrieks of the women, we heard the shout of a man.

We slowed and looked back. In the pale light of the clearing, the Maenads came to a halt. For a moment the women seemed uncertain, peering into the trees. Several started running in another direction.

We raced on ahead.

Leaving the woods, we came into a swale of tall, yellow grass, what looked to me like wheat. Halfway across it, I grabbed Phoebe's arm.

"This way!" I whispered. We cut across the slope of the field, then ducked down into the grass. Lying on our bellies, we were totally concealed.

We waited.

Both of us were out of breath, our blood pounding so hard it was pulsing in our ears. We peered out over the golden grass, back toward the edge of the woods. It remained dark and silent.

"Was it Vassilos?" Phoebe whispered.

"I don't think so," I said. "He's much too slow to have made it this far. Maybe the guy from the cave."

The moonlight gave the golden field a soft, velvet sheen. Phoebe pulled out a stalk of the grain. She examined the spike and tasted the seed. "Barley," she whispered.

I don't know how she knew it was barley. Maybe the Dutch girl had grown up on a farm. "For the *kykeon,* you think?"

"Barley was grown on the plains of Eleusis."

"I bet this land is owned by the monastery," I whispered. "They grow the grapes and the orchids. Why not grow the grain?"

We waited and watched. No one came out of the woods.

"Maybe they went after that guy," I said.

Phoebe was scanning the surrounding landscape. "Look!" she whispered.

In the distance, beside a stand of trees, was the dimly lit window of a farmhouse.

"Let's make a run for it," I said.

Phoebe clutched my arm to stop me. Once again we scanned the edge of the woods. Nothing could be seen in its darkness.

She looked at me and nodded. We got up and ran toward the house.

21

THE FARMHOUSE was two stories high and looked to be as old as the island. It was built of dark stone with whitewashed mortar; in the moonlight it looked like a spider's web. A single upstairs window glowed; the rest of the estate lay in darkness.

We crept through a copse of fig trees, past the stone wall of a melon patch, then alongside a dirt pen holding several pigs. A flock of sheep stood behind a fence in a field, and nearby was a pine bough corral with a mule. The animals stirred as we moved toward the house. Suddenly, a dog started barking.

Phoebe and I glanced behind us, expecting the Maenads to come streaming from the woods. But still no one appeared. We approached the front door of the house, and the wolfish dog edged toward us, growling.

A light appeared in a downstairs window, and a moment later the door swung open. A lanky man with a gray mustache peered into the yard and spotted us. He was wearing a robe, and a gas lantern dangled from his upraised hand. He looked curious and confused. Phoebe was standing in her torn and bloody chiton with her arms crossed to her shoulders, attempting to hide her nakedness. My shirt, too, had been ripped open and stained with blood. On an island that had seen its share of war, we must have looked like a couple of refugees stumbling out of the past.

The man called his dog. Immediately, it stopped growling and bounded back into the house. The man's young wife appeared at his side, also in a robe, her eyes flared with apprehension.

Again I scanned the woods for the Bacchae.

The man called out a question in Greek. Phoebe started to answer, trying to find the words in his language to explain the bizarre situation we were in. But before she could get a full sentence out, the resounding peel of a distant bell drifted out over the mountain.

A church bell.

At this late hour, in the stillness of the night, there could be little doubt of its meaning. It was not the perfunctory tolling of an hourly chime, but the strong, persistent sounding of an alarm. I realized at once it had to be coming from the monastery. The older nuns we'd seen in the rearview mirror must have gone back to send out a warning.

The man's wife immediately receded into the house, calling for her husband to join her. The man hesitated. Phoebe pleaded. Finally, he backed away and pushed the door shut.

We searched the darkness around us.

The front door opened again. With a sigh of relief we started toward it, but the farmer's wife was only releasing the dog. It came tearing across the yard at us. We turned and bolted for the woods.

We could hear the dog approaching behind us, its breathing raspy and eager. Our feet could not carry us fast enough. As we reached the trees, the giant hound leapt onto Phoebe. She screamed and tumbled to the ground. The hound overran her, then scrambled back to attack.

I raced to stop it as it went for Phoebe's throat. She threw up her arms to block it. Its teeth locked on her wrist.

Digging into the fur at its neck, I hauled back and pulled it off her.

Phoebe rolled away. The animal charged at me.

Before I could react, it was on me. The giant hound knocked me down. Teeth flashed before my face as I struggled to push it away.

Suddenly the animal yelped, a high-pitched squeal of pain. It released me and hobbled off, whimpering back toward the house.

Above me stood a man holding a long-bladed dagger. A rifle was slung from his shoulder. He offered me his hand.

In the distance, the bell continued tolling.

I took the man's hand, and he pulled me up. He was old and gray, but remarkably fit. He wore a seafarer's cap, and had a hunter's game bag strapped to his back. I recognized his face.

The man looked closely at my neck and saw it wasn't bleeding. "Luck is with you," he said. He spoke with a thick accent. His handsome face was deeply wrinkled, his black eyes glinting slits.

"I saw you yesterday," I said. "You came in on the ferry."

The man was warily scanning the field, on the watch for Bacchantes. I eyed the ornate dagger in his hand, its long blade dripping with blood.

Phoebe stepped beside me, holding her bleeding wrist. "Who are you?" she asked.

With the sharp blade of the knife, he cut a strip of cloth from the bottom of his shirt. "My name is Gurpinar," he said, slipping the blade back into his scabbard. "I am from Cypress." He gestured toward Phoebe's wrist.

Phoebe threw me a glance, then held her arm out to him. Two rows of canine teethmarks penetrated her skin.

The man quickly wrapped the wound. Still watching for the Bacchae. "You have lost someone," he said.

Again Phoebe glanced at me. "A friend was killed," she said.

"Those women murdered him," I said. "My brother is in jail."

The bell continued its unnerving toll. I searched the trees for the Maenads.

Gurpinar finished tying off the bandage. "Leave now, quickly. I lead the women away. You must get off the island, tell what you have seen."

"Why are you helping us?" Phoebe asked.

"I lose someone, too," he said.

"Here on Ogygia?" Phoebe asked.

"On Mykonos," he said.

Suddenly, I remembered seeing him before. Handing him my bottle of ouzo. "You were there!" I said. "In that bar on Mykonos!"

The man was peering across the field. "The bell calls," he whispered. "More and more are coming."

We turned to look toward the farm. Emerging from the house was the ghostly figure of the farmer's wife, draped in a white chiton. Other ghosts materialized in the dark woods around her. The young wife hurried to join them as they flew out over the fields.

The Bacchae were streaming toward us.

"Go," the man said. "Run!"

FOR NEARLY half an hour, Phoebe and I raced down the slopes of Mount Nysa. The tolling of the monastery bell finally ceased, but another, more distant bell could now be heard in its place. The sound was deep and resonant. When we came to the edge of a bluff and saw the town on the shore below, we realized it was coming from the tower of the church.

"Look at that," I said. Lights in the town were blinking off, the village gradually darkening. "The whole town is being warned about us. Everyone on the island must be locking up their doors."

"They're leaving us to be killed," Phoebe said. "We're the only outsiders left."

Except for the hunter, Gurpinar. They'd have to kill him, too, I thought, *to keep their cult a secret.* I wondered whose murder had brought him from Mykonos, and why he had followed us here. Whatever the reason, I was glad for his help. He seemed to have led the Bacchae astray and given us the chance to escape.

We descended through several pine tree woods, each one sparser than the one before. The slopes grew less steep and more open to view, with a maze of low, stacked-rock walls bordering cultivated fields. The moon was high overhead now, no longer blocked by the cliffs. Its gray light cast shadows across the landscape and bathed the rocks in a ruinlike gloom.

Climbing over the wall of a vineyard, we spotted what looked like a towering Maenad—a giant windmill set amid the rows. Mounted on a massive, whitewashed tower, the huge wheel stood perfectly still, its sails white and windless.

We were out of breath and near to exhaustion, but most of all we were thirsty. Hurrying to the tower in hopes of finding water, we arrived and walked around the base, looking for the entry.

The door was bolted shut.

Turning away in discouragement, my eyes fell on the round stone rim of a well, a few yards away from the tower. A metal bucket lay beside it, with a rope that tied to a beam across the top.

I immediately dropped the bucket into the well and heard it splash into water. When I hauled it up, it was nearly full. I dipped my hand in and took a taste. There was nothing peculiar about it, so the two of us cupped our hands in and greedily drank our fill.

Afterwards, I slid down to rest against the well. We had seen no Maenads from the time we'd fled the farm. Whatever had happened to them, it seemed for the moment we were safe.

Phoebe finished drinking and stared out over the vines, water dripping from her chin. Her eyes looked dark and fierce, still in the grip of the *kykeon.* Blood had caked on her neck and shoulder, her chiton hung in shreds, and cuts and bites covered her body. I noticed her raw bare foot was bleeding.

"Give me the med kit in your pack," I said.

She was still gazing at the moonlit vineyard.

"Phoebe?"

She looked at me, then she let the backpack slip from her shoulder and drop on the ground in front of me.

I searched through it and found the small plastic medical supply box. There wasn't much in it—cotton swabs, Band-Aids, an elastic bandage, a snakebite kit, poison ivy cream. I pulled out the Band-Aids and the bandage.

Phoebe wandered off between rows of the vines. She appeared to be checking out the grapes.

A sudden flapping of wings startled me. A shadowy bird fluttered to the tower.

I turned and dropped the bucket into the well and filled it again with water.

"Come here," I said to Phoebe as I hauled up the pail.

Phoebe walked back over to the well. She held a dark clump of grapes in her hand, and she was chewing a mouthful of them.

I smiled as I set the pail of water on the ground. "Cabernet? Or Pinot noir?"

She held out the grapes for me to try. I tore a couple off and popped them in my mouth. "They're juicy but they're not quite ripe," I said. I spit them out on the ground. "In fact, they're fucking bitter."

Phoebe seemed to think they were fine. She raised the clump above her face and gnawed off a dangling mouthful.

Grapes of Dionysus, I thought. I wondered if the *kykeon* had affected her sense of taste. Pain didn't seem to register; why should bitter grapes?

Now juice from the grapes was running down her chin. Her behavior was beginning to disturb me. "Phoebe," I said calmly, "if you're going to make it down this mountain, it's important we wrap that foot of yours." I reached out and gently took her hand. "Step over here," I said, guiding her toward the bucket. "We need to wash it first."

I kneeled down in front of her and took ahold of her ankle. She stared at me, still chewing, holding the clump of grapes in her hand. The moon, high behind her, left her face in shadow, but the luminous wings of the windmill fanned out above her head.

I lowered her foot into the bucket. The water filled with mud and blood. Gently, I massaged her toes and her heel, and the tender sole with its blisters and cuts, and the top of her foot where the skin had been torn, and all the way up her ankle. On her slender calf I noticed a garish gash where human teeth had broken the skin. I rinsed the wound with handfuls of water, lifting them up, one after another, running my palm up her leg. Her knee, poking out from a rent in her chiton, was scratched and abraded, and dirt had mixed into the blood in the skin. I cupped my hands together and lifted out prayerful offerings of water which I laid upon the knee like a blessing. Gradually the blood and dirt washed away, and the tender knee glistened wetly in the moonlight.

It looked like the knee of a goddess. I don't know why, but . . .

I kissed it.

Phoebe moaned. The hand clutching the clump of grapes lazily dropped to her hip. The juice of the grapes bled into her chiton, and I reached up to take them from her. But her fist tightened around the cluster; she did not want to release it. Dark skins and liquid squeezed through her fingers, and the black juice flowed down her leg.

I looked up at her face. She was staring down intently at the hand that held the grapes, now wet and running with their juice. Her mouth was open, and she seemed to have lost control of her breathing. Her eyes followed her dripping fist as it slipped the clutch of grapes through the rent in her chiton. She pressed the clump up between her legs, and mashed the grapes up against her. Her eyes rolled skyward and her lids fell shut. Rivulets of black juice ran down her thighs. She let out a deep-welling sigh.

The squished clump of grapeskins dropped to the ground. She lowered her eyes and stared at me. She took a firm grip of the slit in her chiton, and ripped it open up to her navel.

She held it there, open, allowing me to see.

I remained on my knees and stared. My eyes could not seem to sate themselves. Something inside me trembled. All I could hear was the sound of her breathing, and the throbbing pulse of my blood.

Phoebe dropped down on her knees before me. Her eyes seemed to burn with that Dionysian fire. The moon lit her hair like an aura. Her ragged chiton hung from only one shoulder, leaving the white marble of a breast unveiled. Her chest heaved with feverish breathing, and her wet lips, plump and open, revealed bright incisors tinged by the grapes.

She tore off the clasp holding the chiton, and the tattered gown dropped to her waist. Her glowing white body, so delicate and creamy, was blotted with blood from scratches and bites, and swollen and discolored with contusions. Her arms were bruised where the bitches had grabbed her, and her throat looked as if she'd been strangled. Still she seemed completely unaware of any pain; the sudden surge of lust had overwhelmed her.

She pressed her mouth to mine, and her tongue slipped through my lips. My eyes were inches from her blood-caked ear. I heard her breathing frantically, rasping through her nostrils. Her eyes were strangely flared and ravenous, filled with a Maenad-like greed. She ripped off my ragged shirt and tore my belt apart. Then she climbed right out of her gown and launched herself on top of me.

Her body felt warm and keenly alive. Her wet thighs slapped and slid over mine, and her small breasts quivered as she trembled. Again she lowered her mouth to my lips and slipped her tongue inside.

I'd been hard from the moment she'd touched me. Now, on my back, wedged between her slippery thighs, I stroked against her cunt.

The hell with Dan, I thought. *It's me she really wants.* As her body squirmed and shifted, I readied to throw her onto her back and bury myself inside her.

The windmill flared above me, eerily lit by the moon. In its stillness it looked like a clock that had stopped, freezing the moment in time. I suddenly became aware of myself, caught in the rapture of *enthousiasmos,* but remaining apart from it, too.

A haunting pair of yellow eyes peered down from the tower. An owl staring at us. It didn't make a sound.

I knew I could not go through with it. This was not love we were making. This was Aphrodite or an aphrodisiac, a chemical or a goddess or a Bacchus that possessed us. Phoebe was no longer herself. I was no longer Dan's brother. I knew I couldn't let this be our night to surrender. To give up what she'd held so close for so long. Or for me to give up what I knew I should not.

"Phoebe . . ." I hugged her tightly to make her still, and whispered into her ear. "Phoebe, wait."

She resisted and pulled me toward her and tried to kiss me again.

"Wait," I said. "We can't. Not now . . ."

I held her still until she stopped. Gradually, her frantic breathing slowed. The mania melted from her eyes. Her lids fell shut and she let out a cry, a sound like a mournful plea. All the fire and steam went out. She seemed to physically crumple, like the grapes she'd released from her grip. Slowly she turned her face away and rested her head on the ground.

For a long moment she was silent. She turned her body away. I heard her sniffle, and tears were flowing. When she finally spoke, it was in a whisper I could barely hear, as if she were talking to herself.

"I killed her," she murmured. "I killed that woman."

Her body seemed to curl in on itself, as if she were trying to shut out the world.

I wrapped myself around her. "You did what you had to do," I whispered. "You didn't have any choice."

She lay in my arms without speaking.

"Your clothes are in your pack," I said. "Let's get dressed and go down and get Dan."

She nodded sadly and wiped away her tears.

We pulled on our clothes in the dark. Neither of us spoke about what had just occurred. I wrapped Phoebe's foot with the bandage, then I wrapped the bandage with a strip from her chiton, tying it off at her ankle. We used Band-Aids to stop the bleeding from her ear and to close the other cuts on her body. The *kykeon* episode appeared to have passed, but still she seemed a little twitchy and distracted, as if she were hearing voices in her head. It reminded me uneasily of Delphi.

We took a final drink of water before we headed off. There was no sign of the Bacchae anywhere around us, and we didn't hear their screams or shouts. But ten minutes after we had left the vineyard, as we made our way down a grassy slope, we heard the resounding blast of a gun.

22

THE SOUND had come from farther down the mountain. It echoed out into the still night air. A second shot quickly followed the first, which gave us a bead on the direction—beyond a ridgeline of trees to our right. We hurried to the ridge and just beyond found a view over a shallow valley, but nothing could be seen in the darkness.

"You think it was him?" Phoebe asked.

"If it was, he may need our help."

We headed down into the valley.

Half an hour later, we found ourselves peering over the edge of another bluff, staring down at yet another upland pasture. This time, out on a golden, moonlit field, beside a dark tower and a black grove of trees, was a large, shimmering horde of Maenads. They seemed to be running about and playing in the field.

I found the scene incredible. "There must be at least a hundred down there! Where the hell are they coming from?"

"The women on the mountain," Phoebe said. "They're all joining in with the Bacchae."

"It looks like they're playing some kind of *game,*" I said.

They flew beneath the trees like a shifting flock of birds. It appeared they were throwing things and chasing one another for them. This went on for several minutes, with peals of laughter and howls of delight. Then, abruptly, with wild screams of joy, they all ran off, swarming down the grassy slope and vanishing into the woods.

"I hope they're not heading for town," I said.

In seconds they had disappeared entirely.

We descended from the bluff, and several minutes later we were crossing the field. Ancient, gnarled olive trees reached up toward the moon. The dark stone tower loomed before us. In the middle of the golden expanse, at the place where the women had been swarming, Phoebe stumbled on something.

"It's an amphora," she said. She lifted the handled vase and examined it. It was smaller than the one that held the *kykeon* in the cave, but the shape was exactly the same. Phoebe heard liquid sloshing inside and lowered her nose to the opening.

"Is it—?"

"Yes," she said, handing it to me. "I'm fairly certain it is."

I recognized the mint smell of the elixir.

We glanced around. The place had a creepy stillness. Several more amphorae lay scattered on the ground.

"They must have been refueling," Phoebe said. "Its effect has already begun to wear off of me. They want to sustain their mania."

"And I bet it was given to the Maenads that joined them—the women who live on the mountain. They'll all be mad for us now."

A weight of foreboding fell over us. The thick black trunks of the surrounding trees were pockmarked with holes like mouths.

Carrying the amphora, we started toward the tower. I had thought the tall structure was the remnant of a church, but Phoebe informed me it was a dovecot, a dwelling for carrier pigeons.

The tower was cylindrical and roofless, and the black-gray stone of its rounded wall was mossy and crumbling with decay. The entry door had long ago vanished, leaving nothing but a black, rectangular hole.

As I approached it, Phoebe held back. I noticed something glistening on the wall by the door.

"Jack . . . Please don't go in there."

I reached out and touched the glistening spot. The blood on the stone was still wet.

I turned to Phoebe. She was backing into the shadow of a large olive tree. "Let's please just leave this place," she said.

My curiosity could not be controlled. "Wait there," I said. I turned from her and cautiously entered the tower.

The sound of fluttering wings startled me. My eyes rose up in the blackness. Birds fled out the open top of the tower into the moonlit sky. They left the inky space below in a still, uncanny silence.

The dank air held an odor I recognized at once: acrid, coppery, copious blood.

Straining into the darkness, I noticed a pale, glowing light, high up in the wall to the side. I stepped toward it and immediately stumbled into something on the floor. As my eyes adjusted, I saw it was the body of a Maenad. Her ivory chiton was barely visible in the dark, but she lay so utterly still and silent I knew at once she was dead.

Waves of emotion rippled through me: fear, anger, disgust, and with a sad twinge of guilt, a feeling of relief.

I stepped over the body toward the glow in the wall. It turned out to be a small flashlight lying inside a square niche, just at a height where I could reach it. The batteries were low, and the beam was aimed at the side of the niche, blocking its feeble light. I took it in hand, and as I did the light flared wide, and I noticed another niche right beside it, stuffed with a canvas bag. Then I noticed that the entire wall—that the whole inside of the structure, in fact—was honeycombed with these niches, square indentations built into the stone that went all the way up the length of the tower. It looked like the inside of a gigantic beehive.

I aimed the flashlight at the dead Maenad. She lay on her back against the wall, just inside the entry. Her torso and her head were twisted to the side. At her chest the chiton was soaked in blood, released from the gaping wound just above her heart. With her face turned away, I couldn't see who she was, but I didn't want to move her to take a closer look. Knowing that the woman was dead was enough.

A rat passed through my light beam, skirting the edge of the floor. I followed it with my light for several feet, and suddenly I was staring at a man's severed arm.

It had been violently ripped out from the shoulder. Bloody muscle and ligaments hung ragged from the bone. The hairy forearm had been chewed on, and several fingers were missing from the pallid, wrinkled hand. The floor around it was covered with blood.

I felt suddenly lightheaded. Steadying myself at the wall, I slowly moved to the door for some air.

Phoebe was standing under the tree, hugging her arms, waiting. "Are you all right?"

It took me a second to gather my voice. "Yeah," I said. "One more minute."

I noticed that where my hand was resting, the stone had been recently blasted away. There were chunks of shattered rock on the floor.

I turned back inside and scanned the room with the light. The rest of the man's body was scattered over the floor, along with the bloodstained shreds of his clothes. A leg from the knee had been severed clean off with the blade of a knife or an ax. Portions of the calf muscle had been gnawed on. I spotted discarded fingers and a long fleshy ear. The pinecone of a broken *thyrsus* lay beside the rags of an empty chiton.

Near the center of the room, surrounded by the stubs of several burned-out torches, I came across the man's lank torso. It still had a leg and an arm attached, though much of the flesh was ripped open and bloody.

I aimed the light at his chest, and felt a sudden surge of vomit rising in my throat.

The man's ribs had been torn out. A hideous cavity of blood and guts remained.

I staggered back to the wall, and that's when I finally stumbled onto the man's severed head. It lay on its side at the edge of the floor, where it had rolled and settled in a pool of black blood. It, too, appeared to have been hacked off with several blows of an ax. The eyes and nose were missing, and blood ran over the leathery face, but when I saw the man's thick gray hair and the broken shotgun lying nearby, I knew at once who it was.

The hunter's gun had been smashed against the wall; the barrel was bent and the stock was shattered. Cartridges lay strewn across the floor. Among them sat the man's bloody seafaring cap.

The Maenads must have been chasing him. Perhaps he'd tried to hide or to rest in the tower. He'd shot the first one that came through the door, but by the time he took aim at the second, they'd gotten a grip on his gun, and the blast went into the wall. Then they'd piled on him like a swarm of killer bees.

Phoebe called to me. I started for the door. Then I remembered the canvas bag in the niche. I reached up and grabbed it. It was the hunter's game bag.

When I turned, I stumbled on another corpse, one I had not seen earlier. A young woman sheathed in a bloody chiton. Gurpinar's dagger had been thrust into her chest. Her eyes were frozen in horror. With sudden shock I recognized the face of the farmer's wife.

OUTSIDE, PHOEBE was crouched down under the tree, poking at something in the grass. "Look at this, Jack."

I walked over and aimed the feeble flashlight at the ground. It illuminated a gently curving, bloody white bone. There were strands of ligaments attached.

Phoebe looked incredulous. "It dropped out of the tree," she said.

I aimed the light up into the tree and after a moment's searching spotted two similar bones dangling from the branches. "It's what they were tossing around out here." I looked at Phoebe. "They're his ribs."

"*Gurpinar?*" Phoebe looked stricken. "He saved our lives."

"More than once," I said.

I handed her the flashlight and started searching through his bag. She aimed the beam into it as I dug inside the various compartments. I found shot cartridges, several tins of sardines, a small digital camera, a near-empty bottle of Loutraki water, and wrapped in the rags of a white chiton . . .

A human skull. Cleaned of flesh and boiled white.

I gaped at it. "I bet he took it from the altar in the cave," I said. "He must have gone in after they left."

Phoebe stared. "Do you think . . . ?"

"I don't know," I said. I lifted it before my eyes, trying to imagine Basri's face. "The bone does look pretty fresh."

A small sack tied with a string had been wrapped along with it. I set down the skull and opened it. The sack was filled with a black-gray powder. I handed it to Phoebe.

She gathered some in her fingers. "Ashes," she said. "From the sacrificial fire."

"I saw them filling the baskets with it. What do you suppose they wanted it for?"

"I'm not sure," Phoebe said. She dug her fingers in and found charred remnants of bones and cinders of wood. "They're the remains of an offering to a god. They're probably considered sacred. You and Dan were raised as Roman Catholics—you know about Ash Wednesday?"

"First day of Lent," I said. "The priest wipes ashes on your forehead."

"Those ashes are from the burned palm fronds that were used on Palm Sunday the previous year."

I recalled the words the priest would speak as he applied the ashes in the shape of a cross: "Remember you are dust, and to dust you shall return." It was intended to remind you of your ultimate fate and encourage you to repent for your sins.

"I wonder what Gurpinar wanted with them," Phoebe said.

"Evidence to show the police," I said. "Like that skull. I bet he took pictures with his camera, too."

In a zippered inside pocket I found the man's billfold and passport. The passport showed his picture and appeared to be from Cypress. The billfold held a newspaper clipping.

I unfolded it. The paper was yellowed and falling apart. The article displayed a black-and-white snapshot of Gurpinar standing with a much younger man. Both of them held shotguns and appeared to be on a hunting trip. The article was written in Greek. "What's this about?" I asked, handing it to Phoebe.

The print was faded and the flashlight was dim, so she had some trouble deciphering it. "This article is a year old," she said. "Apparently the young guy disappeared on a bird-hunting trip in the Aegean. He was traveling with his grandfather, Mantolu Gurpinar. The old man has been looking for the boy ever since."

"Does it say where he last saw him?"

Phoebe searched the article. "Mykonos," she said. She slowly translated: "Gurpinar reported that the boy went out to a nightclub for the evening and"—she raised her eyes to me—"he never came back."

"What day, what month was it?"

Phoebe scanned the page until she found it. "Oh my God." She looked at me again. "September eighteenth."

"A year ago yesterday. Same day of the year that Basri was taken."

"And the same time of year the Eleusinian Mysteries were celebrated."

"This man's grandson was another one of their sacrificial victims," I said. "The old man must have somehow traced him to Ogygia. But how did he know about the nuns? How did he know it would happen again?"

"No idea," Phoebe said. "But he must have come back to find out what goes on."

I looked up at the bones dangling from the tree. "Well, he found out, all right."

Phoebe pointed the beam of the light at my belt. "What's that?"

"Gurpinar's dagger," I said. I'd stuck the long blade under my belt like a sword.

Phoebe grimaced. "I hope you're not going to need it."

We put the camera into her backpack, along with Gurpinar's passport, his wallet, the skull, and the sack of ashes. We drank the water in the bottle, then filled it with the remaining *kykeon* from the amphora—a little evidence of our own, and a sample for Dan to analyze. While doing this, we debated whether the old man had figured out that Vassilos was in on the murder, and whether he'd planned on taking his case to the authorities in Athens. We had to start thinking about all that, too—how would we get anyone to believe us?—but first we had to get off the island.

"Let's hurry," I told Phoebe as I threw on the backpack. "We've got to beat Vassilos to the jail."

WE DESCENDED onto another plain of fallow fields. Eventually, we found ourselves hiking down a narrow lane flanked by loosely piled stone walls. This lane led to a dirt road that meandered down the mountain for a mile or so before reaching the highway, the main road that wound down the mountain to the village.

It was the middle of the night, and the black ribbon of road was silent and empty. We had not seen or heard the Bacchantes since they'd disappeared into the woods, which led us to hope they were staying on the mountain and not heading into the town. But we feared they were still on the prowl for us. As we hiked down the open highway, we kept our eyes peeled for their ghostly chitons and listened for their exuberant voices. At one point Phoebe thought she heard their cries, but it turned out to be a flock of geese flying past the moon overhead.

We passed several farmhouses scattered over the slopes. I wondered how many had disgorged their resident Maenads to join in the nocturnal hunt. The houses were dark and shuttered, and we did not attempt to approach them, but hugged to the shadows of the trees by the road. It was under one of these moonlit trees that Phoebe came to a sudden halt, staring down the slope of the mountain.

"Oh no!"

I searched the darkness below and quickly spotted the teeming horde. Like a flowing mist or a stream of white water, they cascaded down through a shallow ravine and out over the variegated fields. Even at a distance, their excitement was palpable. Their gleeful voices rang through the stillness of the air, and their flowing gowns, in countless numbers, shimmered like the scales of a snake.

"They *are* heading for town," I said. "They know that's where we're going."

"They'll beat us to the jail," Phoebe said anxiously.

She'd been walking more slowly, and now I noticed why: the strip of cloth I'd wrapped around her foot had worn into shreds. I could see blood seeping through the remains of the bandage.

"I've got another strip of cloth in the pack," I said. "We better wrap that foot, or you're never going to make it."

"There isn't time," Phoebe said.

I pulled off the pack. "There won't be time if you can't walk." In the bag I found the second strip I'd torn from her chiton. I crouched down and started wrapping her foot.

Phoebe steadied herself against the trunk of the tree. "They'll kill Dan," she said. "They'll tear him apart."

"Then we've got to catch up to them, somehow."

"How?" she said.

"I don't know."

"You don't know because there is no way."

I knew she was right, but didn't want to believe it. Not after seeing what they had done to the hunter. As I wound the cloth around her foot, I struggled to come up with a solution.

Nothing came to mind.

"Do you smell that?" Phoebe asked. She was looking up at the tree.

A soft, herbal scent hung in the air. "What is it?" I asked.

"Bay leaves. This is a laurel tree."

"Don't tell me that's a part of the *kykeon,* too."

"I doubt it," she said. "The laurel tree is sacred to Apollo."

"Oh. Good. The rational one. Ask him what to do when you can't find any rational way out of your problem."

Phoebe didn't respond. I continued wrapping her foot.

"Hear me, oh god of the silver bow . . ."

I looked up. Phoebe had spoken the words while gazing up at the tree. Now she began declaiming loudly in Greek.

"Phoibe, su men outo xaire, anax, ilamai de proseuxe . . ."

Her voice was formal and somber. I had no idea what the words meant, but the sounds had a kind of beauty to them, a guttural, archaic eloquence.

"What was *that*?" I asked when she finished. I was tying off the cloth at her ankle.

"Nothing," she said with a shrug.

I stood up. "Didn't sound like nothing. In fact, it sounded like a prayer."

Phoebe looked uncomfortable. "Couldn't hurt," she murmured.

I pulled on the backpack. "I didn't know you—"

"Jack—look!"

I turned. A pair of headlights was coming up the road.

"It's a truck!" Phoebe exclaimed.

It looked like an old pickup from the 1950s. Big round fenders and a fat, round cab. The shifting gears made a grinding noise as the truck struggled up the slope.

"Wait here," I said.

I trotted out onto the road. Phoebe ignored me and followed. We stood in the middle of the highway together, waving our arms as the vehicle approached.

It ground to a halt in front of us. I held up my hand to block the headlights, but still couldn't make out the figure at the wheel.

"Wait here," I said. Laying a hand on the hilt of my dagger, I warily walked to the driver's window.

Phoebe followed right behind me.

The window rolled down with a squeaking noise. I stared at the driver in shock.

"Damiana!"

"I've been looking for you," she said. "Hurry, there's not much time."

23

WE SUDDENLY found ourselves flying down the mountain in Damiana's truck. The truck belonged to her father, she said. She had taken it—against his will—after refusing to join the Maenads for the evening's Bacchanalia. Whether this unexpected turn of events was due to the influence of Apollo, I couldn't say for sure, but now we would reach the town in a matter of minutes—well before the Bacchae could beat us to the jail.

I should have expected a smirk from Phoebe, but she seemed to take the miracle completely for granted, as if they occurred every day of the week.

It was cramped and warm in the creaky little cab. Phoebe sat between Damiana at the wheel and me at the passenger window. I rolled the window halfway down and a breeze swirled around us. We all stared ahead at the road unwinding in the headlights.

"Why did you decide to help us?" Phoebe asked.

Damiana glanced at her, at the scratches on her neck and the crusted blood on her bandaged ear. Shame and guilt seemed to darken her face. "I couldn't . . . I couldn't let them kill you," she said. "Too many people will die."

"We just saw one of them," I said. "An old man, a grandfather. The Maenads tore him to pieces."

Damiana turned to me, ashen-faced, then stared ahead out the windshield. "Gurpinar. The Cypriot."

"You *knew* him?" I asked.

She glanced at me nervously. "He stopped at the church yesterday. He had been here . . . almost a year ago."

"Looking for his grandson?" Phoebe asked.

She nodded. "He asked me many questions then. About the monastery."

"Did you tell him?" I asked.

"No," she said. "But he knew. He recognized one of the Sisters. He had seen her on Mykonos."

"So he went to the police chief," Phoebe said.

"And Vassilos gave him the runaround," I said.

She peeked at us anxiously. She seemed reluctant to say any more.

"Why are they doing this?" I asked. "Why did they murder our friend?"

"Please," she said. "Please do not ask me these things." She watched the road descend through a grove of ancient olive trees. The pruned black branches looked twisted and tortured, as if they'd been forced into worshipping the sky. "I will help you and your brother," she said. "But you must promise to leave our island. Never come back here again."

Phoebe and I stared at her.

"I don't understand," I said. "How can you—"

A woman screamed.

Damiana slammed on the brakes. A stark naked woman was standing in the road. The truck swerved to miss her, and the headlamps turned their light into the trees, where a horde of howling Furies came pouring out of the dark.

Stones glanced off the hood. A large rock cracked the windshield. As the truck bounced wildly off the shoulder, I tried to roll up my window, but a pinecone *thyrsus* crashed through and struck the side of my head. The blow made me dizzy, and the broken *thyrsus* rattled to the floor.

A Maenad rolled across the hood and slammed against the glass. Her crazed eyes blazed with madness. Damiana jerked the wheel, and the woman tumbled away.

Another jumped on the running board. She tried to open my door. I jabbed her with the broken *thyrsus,* thrusting her into the mob.

The truck swerved back up onto the road. Maenads filled the headlights. Hands reached through my shattered window and scratched across my throat. Something cracked behind us. I turned to see a bronze ax slam against the glass. Bacchantes had climbed into the bed of the truck and were trying to break into the cab.

"Don't stop!" I shouted to Damiana. The truck had broken through the horde, but Bacchae were chasing behind us.

Again the ax blade glanced off the window. Three Furies were smashing at the glass. I climbed out onto the running board and raised my *thyrsus* at them.

"Stop!" I shouted.

One of them came at me with her *thyrsus.* The razor-seeded pinecone slashed my ear and implanted itself in my shoulder. I lost my footing on the sideboard and nearly slid off the speeding truck. My *thyrsus* dropped and clattered down the road. With my ankle dragging over the passing tarmac, I clutched to the rim of the window, cutting my fingers on the broken glass.

Again the woman whacked me with her *thyrsus.* This time I grabbed her stick and swung her off the truck. She tumbled away into the darkness.

Phoebe leaned out and hauled me up.

The Fury with the ax slammed the rear window, finally shattering the glass.

Phoebe screamed.

I launched myself into the bed of the truck. A woman came at my face with her teeth. I socked her square in the jaw. This stunned her long enough that I could knock her off the truck.

The other came at me with the ax. I dove as the blade swung down. It clanged against the metal floor. I crashed into the tailgate.

The woman wheeled on me in a rage, blowing hair lashing her face. Her chiton was a tattered and filthy rag. Her mouth was smeared with blood.

I stood and pulled Gurpinar's dagger from my belt. We rounded each other like gladiators. Suddenly I recognized the Fury's face.

"Euphrosyne!"

The one who had teased me with those glimpses on the yacht. Now she seemed barely human.

"I don't want to hurt you," I shouted.

She laughed her mad, high giggle. I slowly lifted my knife.

With a flash the ax swished through the air and caught the blade, knocking the dagger clean out of my hand. I stared at my open palm in amazement.

She came at me, howling, slashing wildly, blades slicing air. I fell back, pinned in the corner. She swung the ax up over her head—

Suddenly she stopped. Her mouth froze open in shock. She looked down at a growing stain darkening her side. Slowly, she turned around.

Phoebe stood before her, looking as stunned as Euphrosyne. She was holding the bloody dagger in her hand.

Euphrosyne raised the ax to strike her.

"No!" I dove and pushed her, and she tumbled from the truck. Her ghostly form receded into the darkness.

Damiana, driving on, shouted over her shoulder, "Are you okay?"

Phoebe had dropped to her knees. She was staring at the dagger in her hand.

"Yes," I shouted. I peered warily at the road behind us. "Keep driving till I tell you to stop."

I knelt on one knee in front of Phoebe. Her hair was blowing in the wind. She lifted her gaze from the dagger.

"They *are* Furies," she said.

She seemed badly shaken by the stabbing. "Yes," I assured her. "Of course they are."

"No. I mean . . . they're not Maenads."

She wasn't making sense. "Phoebe—"

"At Delphi, the oracle. It's bothered me, what I said—'the *Furies* are coming.' Furies, not Maenads."

"It doesn't make any difference," I said.

"It does," she said. "Maenads, the Bacchae, are worshippers of Dionysus. Furies, or *Erinyes,* are avenging spirits from the Underworld. They take the form of women and seek revenge for murder. Usually the murder of a parent."

"You're saying these women are *spirits*?"

"No. I'm saying you've been right all along. Basri's killing was more than a religious rite. It was a vengeful murder."

"But *why?*"

She held out the dagger. "Look," she said. "Look closely."

I took the bloody knife in my hands. The long silver blade was intricately engraved, and the convex handle was neatly wrapped with a ribbon of white leather, capped with a turban-shaped pommel. I'd hardly noticed before, but the weapon was really quite beautiful.

"It's a military dagger," Phoebe said."The kind that's awarded to officers."

I studied the elaborate engraving on the blade. It seemed to be purely decorative.

"Look," Phoebe said. She turned the handle of the dagger toward me and pointed to the silver cap on the pommel.

Cast into the metal was a crescent moon and star.

I stared at it for a long moment. Slowly at first, then suddenly, the whole bloody story of the island fell in place.

"Damiana!" I shouted. "Stop the truck!"

24

PHOEBE AND I scrambled back into our seats. Glass littered the inside of the cab. We were stopped at the edge of a darkly plowed field somewhere near the outskirts of town.

Damiana threw the truck into gear and headed back onto the road.

I turned to her. "Gurpinar was a *Turk,*" I said. "He must have been a military man. Either that or he's descended from one. And if I remember, Basri's family is descended from an admiral of the Turkish navy. That's why he was chosen, isn't it? Same as Gurpinar's grandson."

Damiana glanced at me, then held her eyes on the road.

Phoebe looked at her. "They're descendants of the Ottoman Turks," she said. "The army that committed the massacre in 1822."

"When did it take place?" I asked. "What month? What day?"

Damiana hesitated. "The massacre began on September eighteenth."

"The same day of the year Gurpinar's grandson disappeared," I said. "That's the reason he came back here now. He knew your history. He wanted to see if it would happen again, on the anniversary of the slaughter."

She continued silently staring ahead. The road was passing swiftly.

"Damiana," Phoebe said, "there's no reason to hold back any longer. This can't stay hidden anymore. You realize that, don't you?"

Ever so slightly, she nodded.

"Those women aren't Furies," Phoebe told her. "They're *murderers.*"

Damiana looked at her. Her eyes flitted back and forth between us, then she looked back at the road. She seemed to be struggling with something she knew could never be comprehended.

"On our island . . . we have always kept the old rites alive. The *monachai* . . . for centuries . . . they held them secret from the Church." She peered out from under her brow at the road. "When the Ottoman's burned the monastery, and massacred the monks and the people . . . the Bacchae went back to their primitive roots. They turned to human sacrifice to fulfill the need for revenge." She turned her gaze on Phoebe. "Ever since, once a year, they succumb to the spirits of the Furies."

Damiana seemed too civilized, too *rational* for this. *"How could you possibly join them?"* I asked.

She stared out vaguely into the darkness of the road. "My family's ancestors . . . they were tortured and butchered and raped in the massacre. Many of the girls were taken away . . . raised as Ottoman slaves." She paused, then turned to look at us. "Like my mother, and my grandmother, I was recruited to the monastery. The abbess there is strict. The life is harsh and repressive. Once a year it is relieved . . . with four days of indulgence . . . and the murder of a blood descendant of our enemy."

Phoebe and I stared at her. "Then . . . you've done this before," I said.

"No," she said. "You must believe me. This was the first year I took part in the rite."

I saw no reason to doubt her. She couldn't have been more than eighteen or nineteen years old.

"I know now it is evil," she said. "I know it is wrong. Wrong to murder a man for the sins of his ancestors. Wrong to carry on this grievance forever."

Phoebe laid her hand on Damiana's arm. "You must leave with us," she pleaded. "Help us bring an end to the killing."

Damiana seemed uncertain.

Phoebe turned to me to assure her. "We'll put an end to it, won't we, Jack?"

I looked at her, then at Damiana. This killing of Turks had been going on for nearly two centuries. The pagan cult itself had lasted for millennia, surviving the Romans, the barbarians, and the Christianization of Greece.

The chance we'd live to tell their story was looking rather dim.

"If you get us off this island," I said, "I promise you, we'll end it. But first we have to get my brother out of jail."

THE TOWN of Ogygia was quiet and dark; it was nearly three in the morning. As Damiana drove us down the narrow, winding streets, the rattle and rumble of the truck on the cobbles reverberated off the high stone walls and broke the slumbering silence. We peered out through the cracked windshield toward the farthest reach of the headlights, half expecting the Furies to appear. While Vassilos might still be somewhere on the mountain, we knew the women were fast approaching.

For now the streets were empty.

"The bells have tolled," Damiana said. "The women on the mountain are in thrall to the *Erinyes,* and the people have locked themselves indoors. If you venture out on a night of the Furies, you are more than likely to be killed."

A night of the Furies? No wonder they had rounded up the

tourists and shipped them off the island. If not they'd be left with a bloodbath, an international calamity with the media descending.

They'd cleared the island of everyone but the ones who knew their secret.

Damiana hurriedly navigated the maze of unlit streets.

"I'm lost," I said to Phoebe.

"Me, too," she replied.

"I'll drive you to the harbor," Damiana said, "after we pick up your brother." The plan was to steal away on Basri's yacht. Assuming we could find his keys at the station.

"You're coming with us, aren't you?" I asked.

Damiana didn't answer.

"You must," Phoebe said.

She glanced at us. "I, too, have a brother," she said. "My family has always lived on this island."

I remembered her picking up her little brother from school. "Aren't you afraid of what will happen if you stay?"

Again she didn't answer.

"You must come with us," Phoebe insisted.

Finally, we turned onto a street I recognized. The police station was halfway up the block. A light was on inside, the only visible light in the neighborhood. As Damiana pulled up in front, I flew from the truck and went to the door.

It was locked. I whipped out the keys and started inserting them, one by one. The ring held more than a dozen. Phoebe and Damiana waited behind me.

"Listen," Phoebe said. "It's them."

I paused. The street was deathly quiet, but drifting down out of the sky was the distant sound of the Furies, the same sprinkling of cries and screeches we'd first heard up on the mountain. These voices that initially had aroused our curiosity now instilled a horrible dread. I felt my stomach fluttering as I fumbled with the lock.

"What if the key's not on there?" Phoebe worried aloud.

I was down to the final few. "It's *got* to be one of these," I said.

The Furies grew louder and louder. I tried the fourth key. The third. I heard a distinct, high-pitched cackle I was certain I'd heard before. I tried the second-to-the-last key. Phoebe and Damiana kept their eyes on the end of the block. Finally, I plugged in the last key. This one had to be it.

It stuck and would not turn.

"Impossible!" I said, and forced it.

The key broke off in the lock.

"Fuck!"

The Furies' shouts were so loud now they seemed to fill the streets. We looked at each other in panic.

"You sure you didn't miss one?" Phoebe asked.

I tried to pry out the broken key. "Doesn't matter now," I said. "The goddamn lock is jammed!"

"Use the dagger," Phoebe said. "Try to pry it open."

Of course! I whipped out the knife and pressed the blade between the door and the jamb. Using it like a lever, I threw my weight against it.

The doorframe bulged and creaked. I pushed with all my strength.

Suddenly I crashed against the wall.

The blade had snapped. The dagger fell broken and useless to the ground.

The door remained locked.

Phoebe and I looked at each other in fear. All we could hear were the Furies.

Damiana turned and walked away.

"Where are you going?" Phoebe asked.

She flung open the driver's door. "Jail," she said.

We watched in confusion as she started up the truck. She threw it into gear and backed up. Then she shifted with a noisy grind, and suddenly the truck lurched toward us.

Phoebe and I jumped out of the way. Damiana accelerated, angling toward the door. With a loud crash, the truck slammed the frame. The corner of the bumper burst the door open. The truck's hood popped, and a geyser sprayed from the broken radiator.

The engine stalled.

I hurried over and pulled open Damiana's door. Phoebe was right behind me. Damiana lifted her head and turned to us. She'd broken her lip on the steering wheel.

"You all right?"

She nodded groggily and started climbing out. I helped her down. She looked shaken, but nothing seemed broken. She glanced toward the end of the street. We could hear their shouting distinctly.

"They're close," Phoebe said. "Hurry."

We clambered over the mangled bumper past the spewing steam. Inside, the large room was lit with a single overhead light. We all looked toward the jail door, where the whiskered face of my brother gazed from behind the wire-mesh window.

"Dan!" Phoebe called, rushing to the door.

He shouted through the glass. "It's about time!"

"Here," I said, tossing her the keys. "You're bound to have better luck than I did."

She immediately started trying them in the door.

I turned to Damiana. "We've got to find the keys to the yacht."

She headed to the closet. I went to Vassilos's desk.

It was overflowing with a mess of papers and tottering stacks of files. A small cup blackened with the dregs of Turkish coffee sat atop a magazine—*Rolling Stone*? There were several official-looking rubber stamps with Greek letters, and a fancy fountain pen that had been taken all apart.

I searched everything, throwing aside the papers and knocking away the piles. Then I ransacked the drawers. They were filled to the brim with junk. The bottom drawer was a veritable liquor cabinet, complete with shot glasses and tumblers. None of the drawers appeared to hold any keys.

Damiana was at a closet, searching jacket pockets. She turned to me and shook her head.

"What are you looking for?" Dan asked. He was standing outside the jail door with Phoebe, who apparently had found the right key. When I told him, he reached into his pants pocket and pulled out the set of keys.

"How did you get them?" I asked.

"His pen ran out of ink when he was questioning me. He went searching for the inkwell, and I swiped them off his desk."

"Let's go!" Phoebe said, moving toward the door. We followed her and started outside, stepping over a puddle of radiator fluid as we climbed around the bumper of the truck.

Phoebe abruptly halted. The Furies were approaching from the end of the street. Their voices rose at the sight of us, and the horde surged forward.

"Back inside!" Dan yelled. We followed him back through the entrance. "I heard him lock a door at the rear."

We raced after him down a short corridor, past a bathroom and a storage room to a door at the end of the hall. He unbolted the lock and peeked through, then stepped out into the alley.

We followed him as he paused there, trying to figure out which way to go.

"This way," Damiana said. She dashed off down the alley.

We all fell in, running after her.

"I thought she was one of them," Dan said.

"Not anymore," I said.

DAMIANA CLEARLY knew her way through the village. I remembered tailing her the day before, when she'd taken a winding alley as a shortcut to the church. Now she raced through the bewildering streets at a speed we could barely keep pace with. Given the deep darkness and the intricacy of the labyrinth, it was a wonder she didn't get lost—or that one of us didn't fall behind and disappear into the maze.

She seemed to be taking a route that would be difficult for the Furies to follow. We could hear their shouts and cheerful cackles drifting over the rooftops. It was impossible to tell where the mob was exactly, but one thing was certain: they were close. From the sound of their voices, coming from seemingly every direction, I assumed they had split up to find us. I half-expected to run across them at every turn we made.

When finally we emerged from a twisting alley onto the esplanade, we were all out of breath and panting. Damiana paused for a moment, and we looked down the shore and out along the wharf. The ferries were gone, and except for Basri's yacht, the dock was nearly empty. The boat and the whole of the pier lay in darkness, and the entire shore looked deserted. We again took off running, down the esplanade, past the closed-up tourist stalls, the empty shops and *tavernas,* the shuttered Orestês Café. Up ahead, Basri's yacht, luminous under the moonlight, seemed to be just waiting to whisk us all away.

The sound of the Furies grew louder. Suddenly, up ahead, they began pouring out onto the esplanade. The four of us slowed to a stop. The great horde was rushing like a river toward the sea. As they reached the pier, they spotted us, and all at once a cry rose up—a shrill, ecstatic shriek. The noise was electric, and strangely paralyzing. We stood in stunned amazement. Furies seemed to be pouring out from every street and alley. Their numbers appeared to have multiplied; in seconds, they were filling up the broad expanse of the quay.

We backed away, then turned to run, following Damiana. All of us knew we were fleeing from our only chance to escape.

Ahead of us a pack of Furies spilled out onto the esplanade from behind the shuttered café. We slowed as they caught sight of us.

Still more poured out from another street.

"This way!" Damiana shouted, as she tore off into an alley.

The three of us hurried after her. Phoebe ran behind Dan and just in front of me. I noticed she was limping—she still had no shoe on her foot. The strip I'd wrapped around it was gone, along with most of the bandage. The sole of her foot was bare and bleeding.

Damiana turned up a rising street, a wider thoroughfare.

"Where are you going?" I asked her.

"The only place we'll be safe."

As we ran up the incline, I glanced back at the Furies. They were pouring out of the alleys and onto the open street. We passed another narrow lane where others streamed to join them. Their shrieks echoed off the stone walls, and it seemed you could almost hear them breathing, like the mad panting of a monstrous beast.

Phoebe suddenly stumbled in front of me. I tripped on her leg and went crashing down. I landed on the same shoulder that had been clubbed on the truck, and a bright light exploded in my head. As I struggled to my feet, I nearly fainted. Phoebe's voice sounded like an echo in a void, and I felt her taking hold of my arm.

"Jack!"

I turned. Furies were charging toward us.

They filled the width of the street and stretched back as far as one could see in the dark. A raging mass of wild hair and taut, gaping faces, half-naked bodies in ragged chitons, arms wielding *thyrses,* throats stretched, filling the air with their voices, a madhouse cacophony of lunatic ravings. Their hysteria seemed only to have increased with their numbers, as if the growing mob was feeding on itself, each new Fury adding fuel to the fire.

Phoebe and I turned to follow Dan and Damiana and saw that we had somehow lost them. They'd vanished into an alley or a side street. On the road up ahead, more Furies were streaming down toward us. I grabbed Phoebe's arm and we fled into an alley, a narrowly twisting lane that led us into darkness.

It quickly became near impossible to see. Phoebe limped ahead of me, panicked and in pain. We were forced eventually to feel our way along. The high walls seemed to rise up and merge with the sky. The Furies' cries echoed behind us.

"No!" Phoebe stopped, turned to me.

The alley had curled to a dead end. We faced a stucco wall with a door and a black window, the back of a house or a shop. I tried the door and found it was locked. The window, too, was fastened.

Phoebe ran to another door, farther back down the alley. When she reached it, I could barely see her. "It's locked," she cried. She looked off down the alley, listening to the shouts of the Furies. "They're coming!"

I turned and banged my fist on the door. "Open up! Please! Somebody help us!"

When no one answered, I pounded more.

Phoebe came up beside me. She shook her head. No one was going to come to the door; no one was going to help us.

The splintering sound of the Furies' voices coursed up the narrow lane.

I went to the window. Four panes of glass in a crossed-wood sash. I slid Phoebe's pack off my back and held it against the glass. Then I slammed my elbow into the pack. Once. Twice. Finally the frame snapped and the glass gave way. I shoved the pack in to break the pieces loose. When the opening was large enough, I climbed up and through the frame. Shards of glass tore at me, ripping my clothes and cutting a neat little slice in my calf as I fell to the floor inside.

Phoebe started in.

"Wait," I said. I fumbled in the dark for the doorknob. I found it, turned the latch, and opened the door.

As Phoebe entered, I saw them.

Two ghostly Furies, ahead of the pack, streaking out of the dark. They screamed as they spotted us.

I slammed the door and locked the latch, but the square of the window was open. As Phoebe and I moved into the darkness of the room, a blond-haired Fury thrust her face through the window. The woman had streaks of blood on her cheeks. She started climbing inside.

The room was some kind of storage cellar, filled with Greek god figurines and ceramic souvenirs—the back of a storefront. I tried a door on the inside wall, but it was locked tight.

"This way!" Phoebe said. She was climbing a stairwell that rose against the wall. I scrambled up after her, and we reached another door.

"It's locked!" Phoebe cried. She tried to force it open.

The blond Fury came screaming up the stairs at us. She'd been cut badly climbing through the window. I turned and kicked her, and she stumbled back, but she grabbed my ankle as she fell. Pulled off balance, I crashed to the stairs. She tumbled down below me.

The second Fury appeared, leaping over the first. She swung her *thyrsus* at me. I rolled off the stairs and plummeted to the floor. The woman dove on top of me, and her teeth locked on my hand. In a rage I threw her off me, and she crashed into the shelves. Greek god knickknacks shattered in a thousand pieces around her.

I grabbed her *thyrsus* off the floor and hustled up the stairs.

Phoebe was hurling herself against the door. I joined her and the two of us slammed ourselves against it. The door burst open.

We found ourselves in a dark apartment. Phoebe whipped the door shut as I raced across the cluttered room and popped the shutters open.

The street below was thick with Furies.

I turned. Near a disheveled bed, the shadowy figures of a man and woman stood cowering in the dark.

I shouted at them, "How do we get out of here?"

The old man barely shook his head: There was no way out.

Phoebe leaned against the door. The Furies were pounding on it. I aimed my *thyrsus* like a jousting stick. "Open it!" I shouted.

Phoebe let the door fly open, and I charged through with the stick. It rammed into the big woman's gut, knocking her back against the others, tumbling them back down the stairs.

"Here!" Phoebe had flung open another door. I raced after her as she scrambled up another set of stairs. It led to a trapdoor in the ceiling. She opened it, and we climbed out onto the roof. I closed the trapdoor behind us.

We could see again in the moonlight. Rooftops spread out around us—clotheslines, satellite dishes, chimneys. The dark mountain looming. We ran to the back of the roof and peered down into the alley. Furies were funneling into the house.

The trapdoor banged open. A frazzle-haired Fury began climbing out. I clubbed her with the *thyrsus* and knocked her down the stairs. Phoebe slammed the door shut again.

"Run!" I said.

"Where?"

The buildings butted up against one another all the way up the street. I ran across and climbed over onto the next roof. Phoebe, limping, climbed over after me. We continued moving from roof to roof.

The Furies emerged behind us.

We reached the gap of a narrow alley. A long jump, and Phoebe's foot was bleeding. I looked for a place to climb down. "Maybe we can—"

Phoebe suddenly leapt through the air. She landed, painfully, but got up and limped ahead.

I turned. Half a dozen Furies were racing toward us, flying across the rooftops. I jumped over the gap and ran to follow Phoebe.

We climbed onto a higher roof, then crossed two more before reaching another gap. This one worse than the last.

Phoebe hesitated, peering down into the alley.

I looked around for a way to get down. I spotted what looked like a trapdoor.

"This way," I said.

"Wait," Phoebe said. "Look."

She was pointing up the alley toward a steeply sloping street. Dan and Damiana were racing alone up the incline. Dan kept glancing behind him, as if looking for Furies, or for us.

"Where are they going?" I asked.

"There," Phoebe said, looking farther up the hill.

Over the rooftops, standing out boldly against the night sky, was the great gold dome with the Byzantine cross.

"The church," I said. "They're heading for the church."

25

WE RAN to the trapdoor. It turned out to be the glass pane of an old-fashioned skylight. I tried to force it open, but it wouldn't budge. Phoebe lent her muscle to it. Still it wouldn't give.

The Furies were heading across the roofs toward us.

I took my *thyrsus* and stood over the skylight. I wound up and brought it down hard on the glass. The skylight shattered, raining shards on the wood floor below.

Phoebe grabbed the stick from me. She could barely put weight on her bloody foot. "You first," she said. "You'll have to break my fall."

The Furies were racing toward us. I climbed through the sky-light, clinging to the rim while trying to avoid the remaining shards of glass. I dropped down and hung there, dangling in the dark. Then I let go and plummeted. I landed on glass, slipped, and crashed, my palms pressing into prickly shards.

The shadowy apartment appeared to be empty.

I looked up. No one could be seen through the skylight. I stood and called for Phoebe, but all I heard was the shuffle of feet and the screams and hollers of the Furies.

I looked around for a ladder, or a table, or something to allow me to climb back up on the roof. The cot in the corner looked too low, and the lamp table too flimsy. I went to grab the mattress to help me break her fall, but the second I stepped away, a naked Fury fell screaming through the air, landing with a horrible thud.

She lay facedown, perfectly still, a welt from the *thyrsus* bleeding on her back.

On the roof, the battle raged. I could hear Phoebe grunting while the prancing Furies raged.

How could I get up there and help her?

The woman on the floor started crawling to her knees. I took a step toward her, uncertain what to do. Suddenly, Phoebe plummeted from the skylight, crashing down on the woman's bare back. The woman crumpled beneath her, breaking Phoebe's fall.

I helped Phoebe to her feet. A triangular shard of glass was impaled in her thigh. She howled as she pulled it out.

The woman on the floor lay still. Above us, Furies peered through the skylight.

Phoebe glared up at them, angry and shaken. *"Fuck you!"* she screamed.

They cackled, laughing madly.

I grabbed the little table and tossed it upside down beside the woman on the floor. I turned the chair upside down next to it. When this happy band of Furies came after us—as I had no doubt they would—their landing would prove more painful than ours.

We hurried through a doorway and down a pitch-dark stairwell into another shadowy room. I ran to the window and threw open the shutter. Furies were heading down the street below. When I turned back into the room, I heard a tiny voice in the darkness, a squeaky, muffled cry. By a bassinet in the corner, a mother stood cradling her baby. We couldn't see the mother's face in the dark. She was wearing a bathrobe and appeared to be fairly young.

"Is there a way out through the back?" I asked.

The woman stared at me without answering, rocking the baby nervously.

Screams and painful yells erupted as Furies crashed to the floor above us.

"This way, Jack!"

I followed Phoebe down another set of stairs. We came out into a small restaurant kitchen at the back of a *taverna.* A cat on a counter whined. At a butcher-block table, an old man in bedclothes sat before an open bottle, sipping from a glass in the dark.

We looked at him, dumbfounded.

Another thundering crash upstairs was followed by shouts and laughter.

Phoebe ran limping to the back. Blood was running from the cut in her thigh. I followed her down a hall to a door that led into an alley. The two of us peeked out cautiously. The narrow lane was empty.

Outside, we could hear the cries of the Furies coming from the streets around us. They seemed to be everywhere. When we glimpsed a band of them passing by the alley, we took off in the opposite direction. We came out onto a broad, dark street, but were forced into another twisting alley when another pack of Furies appeared. This short alley led us to an empty, sloping street that somehow looked familiar. We started uphill, assuming that eventually we'd find our way to the church. Clinging to the shadows, we made our way up a steep sidewalk of stone steps. Near the top we came to a narrow alley.

I suddenly knew where we were.

"I've been here before," I told Phoebe. "This alley leads to the square." It was Damiana's shortcut, the one I'd followed her on the day before.

From above us on the hill came a frightening chorus of voices. We turned to see a white-winged flock of Furies madly swooping down the street.

We raced into the alley, Phoebe limping ahead of me. The high walls of the narrow lane left us in a murky darkness. We passed under the flying buttresses arching overhead. Soon the Furies' raving voices were echoing through the canyon. The twisting lane narrowed tightly, then turned inky black. We were moving beneath the arched top that covered it like a tunnel. As we emerged, the lane jogged, then turned sharply again. Phoebe's bare foot splashed through a puddle. Finally, we rounded the last bend and came out onto the street.

Across the way was the square with the bubbling fountain. At the end of it stood the great Byzantine church. As Phoebe and I rushed toward it, gazing up at the golden dome and the soaring belfry tower, I understood why Damiana would have chosen it as a refuge. With its rugged stone infirmary building, and its lack of ground-level windows, the church had the look of a medieval fortress. The only way in was through the heavy front doors or the side exits; no doubt they could be bolted. Locked inside, we might have a chance to hold the Furies at bay.

Seconds before we reached the entrance, the horde emerged from the alley. There were still at least twenty or thirty in the pack. Their voices shattered the silence, railing insanely as they streamed across the square. Phoebe and I pounded the locked double doors, calling for Dan and Damiana. No one came. *Could it be they've taken refuge somewhere else—Damiana's house, perhaps?* I turned in terror as the Furies advanced, racing madly toward us. *How can we possibly fight them off?* My limbs were turning to stone.

The door suddenly opened. Phoebe and I leapt inside. Damiana slammed it shut and dropped the massive bolt in place. Within seconds, Furies crashed against the doors. We stepped back as they tried to force them open.

The doors bulged as they rammed up against them, their shouts a muffled roar. We watched the lock and waited without a word; there was nothing we could do but pray.

Finally, the Furies ceased their banging. We heard them shout and laugh as they ran off around the church.

"How many other doors?" I asked.

"Three to the church," Damiana said. "Two to the infirmary. They're strong. I've locked them all."

"Where's Dan?" Phoebe asked. I hadn't even noticed he was gone.

Damiana glanced anxiously between us. "I tried to stop him," she explained. "He wouldn't listen. He insisted on going out to find you."

"Dan is *out there*?" Phoebe asked.

"I'm sorry," Damiana said. "He thought you would need his help."

Phoebe turned to me. She looked as if she were about to faint. When I stepped forward to hold her, I noticed blood running from her foot to the floor. It was draining down the side of her leg from the slash in her upper thigh.

"We need bandages," I told Damiana. "We have to stop her bleeding."

"There are some in the infirmary," she said. "The operating room has been kept as it was during the wars."

I walked Phoebe into the nave and sat her down on a pew. "I'll go look for the bandages," I said. "You stay here with Phoebe."

But Damiana was heading toward the other end of the church. "Just give me a moment," she said. "I told your brother if you showed up, I'd ring the bell in the tower. I must let him know you're back."

"Okay," I said. "But hurry."

Damiana scurried off. I knelt down beside Phoebe. She seemed increasingly drowsy and numb. I feared she'd fall unconscious. "Stay with me, Phoebe. Okay?"

She nodded vaguely.

I placed her hand over the gash in her thigh. "Try to stem the bleeding," I said. When I looked at her foot, I cringed. The pain should have been unbearable. Mercifully, she was still under the residual analgesic effect of the *kykeon.*

We listened to the cries of the Furies outside. The sound seemed to be coming from everywhere.

I peered up at the high, narrow windows in the dome. "Sooner or later," I said, "they're going to find a way in."

A sudden banging startled us. I rose to my feet, searching the shadows. The pounding resounded through the vastness of the nave.

"They're trying to force open a door," I said.

We listened for an endless minute. Finally, the pounding stopped.

In the silence that followed, the bell began to ring. One, two, three soft tolls.

We listened, hoping that Dan would hear. Praying he'd make it back.

"There's got to be something we can do," I said finally. "We can't just sit here waiting."

Phoebe lifted her drowsy eyes. "We're like them," she said. "When the Ottomans came for the slaughter, the townspeople hid in this church."

I found the parallel disturbing. "Lot of good it did them," I said. "It's their bones collecting dust in the tower."

Phoebe didn't hear me. She seemed caught in a descending spiral of thought. "Now it's the Ogygians doing the slaughtering," she said. "One atrocity leads to another. People carry grudges for centuries."

"It's absurd," I said. "Absurd that we got caught up in their bloody mad history."

Phoebe stared off vaguely. "*Eleutheria,*" she whispered.

"What?"

"People are afraid," she said cryptically. "People are afraid of freedom."

I wasn't sure who she meant. Ottoman Turks battling a rebellion? Pagan nuns locked up in a monastery? Ogygians chained to their tragic past?

Maybe she was thinking of all of them. She might have been thinking of me. After the experience I'd had on the yacht, *I* was ready to check into a monastery!

The harsh and splintering voices of the Furies seeped through the entrance doors. It sounded like the whole vast horde of the Bacchae was gathering together in the square.

"We've got to figure out how get out of here," I said. "They'll kill us if we don't get off this island."

I COULDN'T wait for Damiana to get back. I ran to go find Phoebe some bandages. We wouldn't be going anywhere if we didn't fix her first; she was losing too much blood.

I crossed the nave to the far apse and looked for the door to the infirmary. Only a few lamps were lit in the church; the walls fell off into shadow. In the darkness, I found the doorway Damiana had taken us through on the tour. A short corridor led directly into the main hall of the old infirmary building.

I found a switch on the wall and turned on the lights. The long, vaulted chamber was devoid of windows and built entirely of stone. Elaborate crisscrossing stone arches supported the broad expanse of the ceiling, and light from electrified chandeliers gleamed on the polished marble floor. The cots, which had once lined the length of the room, had long ago been removed, leaving a stretch of open space that looked like a mausoleum.

At the far end was a wooden double door, the entrance in from the square.

The operating room I'd seen on the tour was located down in the cellars. It had been adapted from a large, vaulted storage room at the start of the Greek revolution. I went down the zigzagging stone stairwell that led to a closed set of doors. These opened into a dark and dank subterranean corridor. The feeble illumination from the open doors allowed me to see only a few feet down the hall. I searched but couldn't find the light switch.

Moving off into the dark, I felt my way along the rough-hewn wall in the direction of the operating room. If I could find the door, I was sure I could find that room's light switch. I remembered how strange it was to see an O.R. lit with chandeliers, just like the ones in the infirmary.

The corridor was utterly silent. Even the clamor of the Furies had faded. I could hear the sound of my own breathing and the rapid pounding of my heart. Something was making me uneasy. Maybe nothing more than the silent dark, and the fact that the Furies were close. The doors were locked. Damiana had seemed fairly certain they would hold. The horde would probably need a battering ram to break the main doors open.

She had said the infirmary had two entry doors; I hadn't yet seen the second. I wondered now if it came in through the cellar. I wondered if it really was secure.

For a brief moment I considered turning back, but suddenly I came across a doorway. I felt my way inside the inky darkness of the room, searching the wall with my hand. After stumbling into a piece of furniture, I turned back to the other wall and finally found the light switch. It lit up a bare bulb that dangled from a wire to the ceiling.

This was a crowded storage room. It was stacked floor to ceiling with the metal frame cots collected from the infirmary. Bedpans, buckets, and an assortment of old medical gear were piled up over in a corner. I took a cursory look through the room and saw no gauze or bandage packs anywhere.

I left the light on and ventured back into the hall. The operating room was directly next door, and I found the light switch easily. This was the room we'd been shown on the tour. A large, high-ceilinged chamber with four electrified chandeliers, it featured two metal operating tables, a row of sinks against the wall, and a collection of antique medical equipment, arranged exactly as it once had been during the heat of the Second World War.

I went to the storage closets at the back of the room and began searching their shelves and boxes. I found a large glass bottle of alcohol disinfectant, a leather case of old surgical tools, a medicine chest filled with pharmaceuticals left from the 1970s, and—to my delight—a veritable treasure trove of bandages, compresses, plaster, and gauze.

Phoebe's wounds would be dressed in style.

Hurriedly, I packed a box with the alcohol and bandages. As I started for the door, I nearly tripped over a batch of steel tanks. One of them toppled over, clanging so loudly it frightened me. I bent to set it upright and was shocked at what I saw.

The tank was labeled "Ethylene."

For a moment I just stared at it. This was the same stuff Dan had used at Delphi, the vaporous earthly "soul" of Apollo turned into a surgical anesthetic. Two more tanks, one labeled "Ethylene," another labeled "Oxygen," stood beside the anesthesiology cart. These tanks were probably left over from the 1970s, when the O.R. had last been used during the Greek civil war.

Amazing, I thought. *The coincidence of that—*

A sudden noise in the corridor startled me. I froze, staring at the open door. My fears about the Furies came rushing back; for a moment I'd forgotten all about them. Now I was certain I had heard them in the hall. The noise had been quick and distinct, like the opening or closing of a door. Maybe from an outside entry to the cellar. There had to be an entry; I was sure of it; I'd seen only one set of doors upstairs.

I set the box down softly on the operating table and quietly crossed the room to the storage bins. On a shelf beside the pharmaceuticals sat the leather surgery case. I opened it and lifted out a scalpel. It had a long steel handle and a short, thin blade. I carried it back to the doorway and peered out into the hall.

The corridor lay in total darkness. In the storage room next door, the light had been turned off.

I pulled back inside. My heart was pounding like a fist in my chest. I felt a fluttering tingle in my gut. Impulsively, I flipped off the light in the room. Now the entire cellar lay in darkness.

Standing with my back up tight against the wall, I waited. I could feel my pulse throbbing in my upstretched throat. The Furies hadn't made a sound since the noise of the door; I figured there couldn't be very many. But even if it turned out there was only one, I knew she would try to kill me.

I listened. For a moment I thought I could hear her breathing. She seemed to be moving closer down the hall. My eyes were beginning to adjust to the dark. Now I heard footsteps, light as a feather, slowly creeping closer toward the door. Like an icicle, the steel scalpel burned in my hand. The sound of her breathing grew louder.

Suddenly a *thyrsus* pinecone struck my chest. My head flew back and cracked against the wall. I was stunned by the blow, but threw myself against the Fury, knocking her to the floor. I raised the scalpel and reached for the light switch.

The chandeliers burst into brightness.

I stopped. Lowered the knife.

Dan was sprawled on the floor half-naked. He had a look of terror in his eyes. His shorts and his shirt had been torn into shreds. His arms had been clawed, and his face was bleeding. He looked like some tortured phantom of Death.

"You could've killed me!" I shouted. "I almost killed you!" I flung away the scalpel; it clanged across the floor.

Dan was startled by the sound of it. He looked jittery and scared. There was blood all over his clothes.

"You look like *hell,*" I said. "Are you okay?"

Staring at me, he nodded.

I picked the *thyrsus* up off the floor. The pinecone seeds were razor-sharp. They'd ripped through my shirt, and my chest was bleeding. "These goddamn things are lethal," I said.

Dan's eyes darted nervously. "I thought you were them," he said. "I thought they must've gotten inside."

"How did *you* get in?" I asked.

"Damiana gave me the keys to the doors. The cellar was the only one I could reach without the Furies seeing." He looked around. "Is Phoebe here?"

"Yeah," I said. "Upstairs."

He heaved a huge sigh of relief. "Thank God," he said.

"She cut herself badly on a piece of glass," I said. "And her foot is all torn up from the climb off the mountain. I came down here to find her some bandages."

Dan looked utterly despondent. "I can't believe I dragged her into all this," he said.

I didn't remind him it was actually me that asked her to come to the island. I reached out to help him to his feet. He looked as if he'd barely escaped with his life. "What *happened* to you out there?"

He shook his head despairingly, as if in disbelief. "I'll tell you later," he said. "We've got to find a way to get out of here—now."

He seemed to feel a special urgency. "How many are out there?" I asked.

"There must be at least two hundred. I saw them all gathering together in the square. They were passing the sacrament again."

"The *kykeon*?"

"Yeah," he said. "They're tanking up to take another run at us. They're not going to quit until all of us are dead."

I knew he was right. If we'd learned anything at all this night, it was that these goddamned Furies were relentless. One way or another, they'd find a way into the church. Damiana, Phoebe—we'd all be torn to pieces, our bones stashed away with the others in the cave. Nobody in the outside world would ever know what happened, and the Furies' yearly harvest of blood would continue to go on forever.

Unless . . .

I scanned the room. The ethylene tanks. The two standing upright by the anesthesia cart.

"Dan," I said. "I think it's time to ask for a little help from Apollo."

26

DAMIANA WAS washing Phoebe's bloody foot in a bucket. When we set down the tanks, it startled them.

"Dan—thank God!" Phoebe stepped out of the water and hugged him.

"He almost killed me down there," I said. I leaned his *thyrsus* against a pew.

Phoebe stepped back from Dan's embrace. "You look *horrible.* What hap—?"

"I'm okay," he said. He pulled out the bandages. "You'd better wrap that leg."

I turned to Damiana. "I'm going to need a long, sturdy rope. Have you got anything?"

"There's a rope in the janitor's closet," she said, running off to get it.

"What are those?" Phoebe asked, eyeing the tanks.

"There're filled with ethylene," Dan said. "Same as I gave you at Delphi."

"We're going to knock the Furies out with it," I said. "All of them, all at once."

"Isn't it too dangerous?" she asked. She had lifted her foot up onto a pew and was wrapping her bloody thigh with the gauze. "It can take the oxygen out of the air. And you said it was explosive."

"The volume of air in here is huge," Dan said. "It shouldn't be a problem if we don't release too much."

Outside, the Furies were stirring. We could hear their voices growing louder.

"Everyone should hide down in the infirmary," I said. "I'll stay up here and—"

"I'll stay here," Dan said. "You go down with—"

"No, I'll do it," I said. "It was my idea. I'll open the door and lure the Furies up into the tower while you guys sneak out the back."

"The tower?" Phoebe said. "How will you get down?"

Dan answered. "I'll climb down," he said.

Phoebe stopped wrapping. "You're going to climb down the tower from a rope?"

"I'll do it," I said.

Damiana raced up, out of breath, holding a massive coil of rope in her hands. "They're coming," she said.

A violent pounding resounded from the doors. Shouts and shrieks arose from everywhere at once. The Furies were surrounding the church.

A chill rippled through me. I recalled the panic I'd seen in Dan's face when I'd turned on the light in the cellar. *What the hell had happened to him out there?*

"Dan?" I said. "That door you came in. Do you remember locking it?"

My brother slowly turned to me. His face was ashen white.

I grabbed the coil of rope from Damiana. "Hurry," I said. "I'll let them in the front. Hide until they all follow me in, then everybody exit out the back. I'll meet you at the boat."

Dan hefted his ethylene tank. "I'm going with you, Jack."

"Looks like we're all going with you," Phoebe said. She was staring across the nave toward the passage to the infirmary. Furies were pouring into the church. They carried *thyrses* and glinting axes. Their cries rose up to the dome.

"Run," I said. I laid down my ethylene tank and opened up the valve.

"Jack—" Dan shouted. "It'll be too much!"

"We don't have time," I said.

Phoebe stuffed the bandages into her pack. Dan threw the second tank over his shoulder. Damiana grabbed the pinecone *thyrsus.* I hefted the coil of rope, and we all ran off toward the tower.

We fled down the aisle out of the nave and through the entrance hall. In the room at the base of the tower, Dan ripped aside the velvet rope, and we started up the stairs. I glanced back and saw our pursuers open the double doors to the square. A huge, clamoring mass of Furies surged like a fire into the hall.

I followed the others up the narrow steps. Damiana led the way. The steeply twisting staircase passed the doorway to the ossuary. As Damiana and Phoebe continued climbing to the belfry, I stopped at the bone room and called to Dan.

"Bring the tank!" I told him. He followed me into the dark chamber. A shaft of moonlight from one of the oculus windows fell to the center of the floor. We laid the cylinder down in a corner and opened up the valve. With a hiss the sweet odor began to permeate the air.

"We'll have to get down fast," Dan said. "If anyone causes a spark, this place is going to blow." As we crossed the room to the door, for the first time Dan noticed the walls were lined with glass cases filled with bones and skulls. He paused to gape in amazement.

Shouts from the Furies echoed up the hall.

"Hurry!" I said.

A line of women was streaming up the steps. The first one held an ax in her hand—an ax with the bronze double blade. As I started out the door, she swung the weapon at me. I dove back inside, crashing into Dan. The women came pouring in after us.

The Fury with the ax attacked me, swinging the blade through the air. I backed away with my coil of rope, trying to avoid her slashes. When I backed up against a glass case, the woman came lunging at me. I rolled aside and her ax swept past me, shattering the glass and embedding itself in the wall. She pulled it out and swung at me again, her forearms now running with blood.

I took a swipe at the ax with my rope. The looped coils caught the blade, and I flung her body into the shelves. The glass imploded as she crashed to the floor. Skulls came tumbling out.

The chamber was filling with Furies. Dan had grabbed a thigh bone and was using it like a club, smashing back the women attacking him. The odor of the gas grew stronger. I tried to hold my breath and fight my way out, but I felt a whack on the side of my head, and the next thing I knew I was lying on my back, staring up at a wild-eyed Fury beating me with her *thyrsus*. Dan tackled her, and they tumbled into the shelves. Broken glass showered them, and the woman picked up a jagged shard and slashed it across his side.

Feeling dizzy, I struggled up through a chaotic sea of grimacing faces and grasping hands, trying to stand on my feet again. Women were pulling my limbs and fingers, and tearing my flesh with their teeth.

Dan had pulled his shirt up and was holding it across his mouth, clubbing back the Furies with his free right hand. I realized it wasn't the blow to my head but the gas in the room that had weakened me. Tearing my way through the wall of flesh, I found the shred of a chiton in my hand and used it to cover my mouth.

The women began gradually falling off around us, succumbing to the power of the fumes. Some collapsed, some crawled on the floor. Several just stood there, vacantly staring, their fury fading away.

Dan had been cut. Blood dripped from his side as he staggered over the fallen Furies strewn across the floor. I grabbed the coil of rope and, taking his arm over my shoulder, helped him out the door.

Damiana and Phoebe had come back down and were fighting off the women charging up the steps. With a vigorous thrust of her *thyrsus,* Damiana sent them tumbling. We climbed up ahead of her, Dan staggering between Phoebe and me, dripping blood on the stairs. I threw open the trapdoor, and we scrabbled up into the belfry. After reaching down to help Damiana up, we slammed the door shut on the Furies.

Damiana bolted the lock.

In seconds, they were beating at the door. We stood there, watching it, hoping it would hold. The door shook, rattling the bolt. The Furies screamed in rage.

"We've got to get off this tower," Dan said. He was holding the bleeding cut in his side. "With all that gas it could blow."

We went to the balustrade and peered out between the pillars that held up the overarching dome. The square below looked empty.

"They must all be inside," I said.

"They won't last long down there," Dan said.

Phoebe eyed the rattling bolt, Furies beating at the door. "I hope you're right."

"It'll take a minute for the fumes to reach them," Dan said. He slouched against the balustrade and slid down to the floor.

"Dan—" Phoebe crouched beside him and examined his wound. I peered over her shoulder. He had a deep, open slice in his side at the top of his hip. Blood was oozing from it.

Phoebe pulled a roll of gauze out of her pack. Damiana came over to help her as she started to wrap the cut. "I'll do this," Damiana said. "You'd better take care of your foot."

"Hurry," Dan said groggily. "The ethylene . . ."

I walked around the perimeter of the huge bell, looking for the best side from which to climb down the tower. It appeared to be a fifty-foot drop to the ground. I noticed the back side of the tower abutted the peaked roof of the narthex some twenty feet below. From there you could slide down the slope of red clay tiles and make another twenty-five-foot drop to the ground. It would be safer to make this two-stage descent in case anything happened to the rope.

While Damiana wrapped gauze around Dan's hip, and Phoebe bandaged her shoeless foot, I set up for the descent. I fastened the rope securely to a pillar, wound it around another pillar for resistance, and tied the other end into a loop. My plan was to lower each person down as they held to the rope while "standing" in the loop.

The Furies had stopped pounding at the trapdoor. I walked over and looked down on it, wondering if they had all finally fallen unconscious.

A loud crack startled me. The corner of an ax blade had pierced the door from below. The blade retreated, then chopped through again.

We all stared down at the trapdoor, watching as the ax struck again and again.

"Hurry," I said. "Dan, you're first."

"No," he began. "Phoebe, Damiana—"

"You're the heaviest," I said. "And you're bleeding. You won't be any help to us up here. It's going to take all three of us to lower you down. So please just shut up and do it."

Half a minute later he was climbing over the side of the balustrade, inserting his foot into the loop of the rope.

"When you get down," I said, "go directly to the harbor. Get the yacht fired up and ready to fly. We'll join you there as soon as we can." I looked to Phoebe and Damiana. "If anyone gets separated, rendezvous at the yacht."

Everyone nodded in agreement.

I pulled up the slack around the pillar, and the girls and I took a solid grip on the rope.

"Whenever you're ready," I said.

Dan let go of the balustrade and clutched the line at his chest. The rope cinched tight around the pillar and tugged at our grip. We could feel it stretching under Dan's full weight.

"Slowly," I said. "Hand over hand."

The three of us gradually let out the rope, lowering Dan to the roof. We could feel him gently bouncing against the wall of the tower. None of us could look over and see how he was doing. We could only watch the rope slide out around the pillar, its fibers scraping the stone.

The ax continued chopping at the trapdoor. I eyed the splintering wood, praying the fumes would take hold.

The rope went slack as Dan reached the roof of the church. Then it pulled at us lightly. "Careful," I said.

Suddenly we heard a shout, and the rope jerked, pulling hard.

"He's sliding down the tiles!" Phoebe said.

We held tight to stop his slide, then let the rope out slowly. When he reached the bottom edge of the roof, we once again felt his full weight on the line.

"Almost there," I said.

We let out more rope until, moments later, the rope went slack as he finally reached the ground.

I ran to the balustrade. Far below, Dan emerged from the shadow of the church, slipping away toward the town. "He made it!" I exclaimed.

The girls were pulling up the rope. I looked at the trapdoor.

The chopping from below had stopped.

I moved closer, listening. A narrow slot had been splintered through the wood. I peered down through it into darkness.

"Jack." Phoebe was helping Damiana climb over the side. "Damiana's going next," she said.

Damiana slid her foot into the loop and clung to the balustrade. She looked frightened by the sight of the roof so far below, but was trying her best to be brave. When Phoebe asked her if she was ready to go, she nodded to her quickly.

Phoebe and I took up our positions, holding the rope at the pillar.

"Okay, Damiana," I said. "Just take it nice and slow. We'll meet you down below."

She waited for a long moment. I glanced down at the slot in the trapdoor, wondering what had happened to the Furies. Smelling a whiff of the sweet ethylene, I thought they must all be unconscious. Then I worried how long it would take before air pouring down through the hole woke them up.

Suddenly, there was a great tug on the rope as Damiana let go of the balustrade. We heard her gasp out loud, and I could feel her dangling against the wall.

"Damiana?" Phoebe called.

We didn't hear her answer; she was too petrified to speak.

"Let it out slowly," I said.

Hand over hand, we released the line. Again the rope scraped around the pillar. Damiana was nearly half the weight of Dan, so even without the third pair of hands, letting her down was much easier. In a minute she had landed on the roof.

"Okay," I said. "Here she goes . . ."

We felt intermittent tugging as she moved down the slope. Then we heard a scream, and the line went slack.

Phoebe let go and ran to the balustrade. I continued holding the rope. "What happened?" I asked.

"Look!"

I hurried over to the rail. Damiana lay sprawled at the bottom edge of the roof, clinging to the red clay tiles. Apparently her foot had slipped free of the loop, and reaching out to stop her slide, she'd let go of the rope. The end now lay several yards beyond her reach. She clung to the slope in terror.

"Hold on, Damiana!" I tried to throw the rope out to her, but I couldn't get it close enough, and she was clearly too petrified to move.

Phoebe started hauling up the rope. "I've got to go down there and help her, Jack. You'll have to lower me down."

"You've only one good foot," I said. "How are you going to reach her?"

"I'll crawl along the peak and lower the rope to her. You can let her down to the ground, then pull the rope up to me."

We didn't have a lot of good choices. And if we didn't do something quickly, Damiana could very well fall to her death—not to mention that the tower could explode, or the Furies suddenly awaken. "All right," I said. "Let's do it."

Phoebe climbed over the balustrade and slipped her good foot into the loop. She looked at me and nodded. "I'll see you down below."

"Definitely," I said. I held firmly to the rope as she stepped off and grabbed a hold of the line. Slowly, I lowered her. Even though it was only me letting her down, Phoebe was the lightest of any of us, and I controlled her descent with relative ease.

Still, I watched the rope with increasing apprehension. It had begun to fray as it scraped yet again around the upright pillar and down over the edge of the balustrade. Tiny fibers were chafing loose, and in some places ragged little tufts had appeared. I wondered how many more drops it could take. Would it last for Damiana? For Phoebe? For me?

The rope went slack as Phoebe reached the roof. Still holding the line, I moved to look over the balustrade. Phoebe had straddled the peak of the titles and was crawling into position above Damiana. When she got there, she gathered up a few yards of the rope and tossed the looped end down. With some coaxing from Phoebe, Damiana managed to reach up and grab hold of the loop.

She looked completely terrified.

Phoebe glanced up at me and shook her head. Damiana was not going to be able to put it around her foot. The only way to get her down at this point was with her holding on to the loop with her hands.

I don't know how she did it, but Phoebe somehow talked her into giving it a try. I moved back into position by the pillar and slowly pulled up on the line. I kept it taut until Damiana slid off the edge, and suddenly I felt her full weight stretch the rope. My eyes were glued to the frayed fibers passing around the column. The rope held, and Damiana was now hanging on some twenty-five feet above the ground.

I began slowly lowering her down. Hand over hand, letting it out steadily, watching the rope scrape and fray around the pillar. My arms were growing weak, and my blistering palms were wet with sweat. The sweet perfume of the ethylene gas drifted through the air. I wondered if it was beginning to affect me, and I shot a glance at the trapdoor.

My heart leapt into my throat. A slender, bloody hand was emerging from the slot. Reaching for the bolt to the door.

"No!"

With the shock of it, I relaxed my grip, and the rope flew off, burning through my hands. Damiana screamed as she plummeted. I clamped down, and the frayed fibers tore my palms. The rope stretched to the breaking point. It held.

The hand slid the bolt aside, opening the lock.

I continued to let out the rope as quickly as I dared, fearing I would lose Damiana. My heart pounded like a caged maniac. My hands were ablaze with pain.

The battered trapdoor opened. Fumes filled the air. I stared in fear at the opening, still unable to release the rope.

A tall, white-draped figure emerged. She climbed the stairs until she loomed above me, a towering Fury in a grisly chiton, long locks of scraggly hair dangling down like snakes.

As she turned to face me, I shuddered. Her teeth were bared in a bloody grin, her fierce eyes were dark and gleaming. Her thin breasts dangled in the rags of her chiton, and her woolly cunt was in view. She'd been cut with a blade across the middle of her belly, and all the way down she was blood-soaked.

It was Phoebe who had cut her. She'd swiped her with the ax blade back in the cave.

This bloody hag was Thalia. Abbess of the monastery. Mother Capetanos. Unholy queen of the Furies.

She must have been the one hacking the door with the ax. Having breathed in the fumes, she had fallen into a trance, but air from the slot had awakened her.

Words now poured from her mouth in Greek, spoken in an Oracle's monotone. But these were not words of wisdom or counsel, but of bitterness, anger, spite. The malevolent spewing of a Fury.

She came toward me head-on with the ax. She swung it horizontally, aiming at the pillar. As the blade struck the stone, sparks flew and the line was severed. The rope tailed off through the balustrade. I tumbled back to the floor.

From below came Damiana's terrified scream.

I rolled aside as Thalia brought down the ax, missing my neck by inches. I jumped to my feet and backed to the rail. The hag came at me, slashing. I whipped her with the end of the rope in my hand, striking her shoulders and chest. The pain seemed to feed her ferocity. With a grin, she let out bright shrieks of excitement.

The double ax crisscrossed before my face. Falling back, I crashed onto the bell. The ax came down and careened off the bronze, sending off sparks and a piercing clang. I scrambled backwards across the floor as she carved the air in front of me. I rose to my feet at the balustrade and whipped at her face with the rope. When she raised the ax, I grabbed her wrist. We struggled for control of the weapon. Her eyes glared fiercely from behind her stringy locks. Her mouth was a blood red gash.

The Fury let out a hideous screech.

With her free hand, she grabbed hold of my crotch and squeezed with all her might. I doubled forward and the ax came down, slicing the back of my shoulder. A razor of pain shot through me. I whirled around dizzily and crashed into the rail.

With a shriek, Thalia rushed at me, raising her ax in the air.

I whipped the rope at her ankle. As it looped around it, I yanked. Her foot was pulled from under her. She spun and struck the balustrade, and her legs went into the air. Arms flailing, ax in hand, she tumbled over the rail.

As she fell, her shrieking stopped, and a frightening stretch of silence followed. Then came a sharp clatter as she smacked into the tiles.

I rose unsteadily to my feet and looked over the rail. On the broad slope of the angled roof, Thalia lay in a splattered heap, the ax still oddly clutched in her hand.

Several yards away, directly below me, stood Phoebe. She was staring at Thalia's inert body.

"Phoebe!"

She looked up. Her face was taut with fear. She was standing precariously on the peak of the roof with her back against the wall of the tower.

The rope had vanished over the side.

I called down to her. "Is Damiana okay?" My eyes searched the shadowy ground.

"I don't know," she said. "And Jack? I don't know how to get down."

Phoebe was stranded. Damiana had fallen and may have been killed. I was bleeding like a sacrificial ox. The church was filled with zonked-out Furies and suffused with explosive fumes.

"Jack!"

And now Thalia was moving.

27

THE AX had sliced open the flesh on the back of my left shoulder. I couldn't see the wound, and couldn't reach it, either, but I knew it was serious. The blood didn't stop running, and the pain produced a disorienting shock. It seemed as if a part of me had splintered off, or my mind in some way had detached from my body.

The fumes from below increased the sensation. I felt the same creeping numbness, the tingly strangeness I'd experienced at Delphi. Once again my body seemed to move too slowly, as if I were wading through water. My anxiety was similarly subdued: I noticed a surprising loss of fear, a dreamlike disengagement that bordered on euphoria, even in the midst of chaos.

Thalia was slowly creeping up the slope of the angled roof. With her arms and legs reaching out in the moonlight, she looked like a white-limbed spider, dragging the bloody rag of her body over the web of tiles. Phoebe stood only yards away. She was searching the architecture, desperately seeking a route to the ground or some way into the church. She kept glancing anxiously back at Thalia, who still held the ax in her hand.

Peering down from overhead, I discovered what looked to be our only chance. Down the wall, roughly halfway between us, was a large round window into the chamber of bones. It was too high up for Phoebe to reach, but with a little help, I thought she might just make it.

I told her to stay right where she was. Then I pulled off my blood-soaked T-shirt and wrapped it around my face, covering my nose and mouth the same way I had done at Delphi. If I was being affected by the fumes in the belfry, the level of gas below would be sure to knock me out.

I inhaled a last full breath of fresh air and pulled the mask over my face. Then I stepped down through the doorway into the dark. Bodies were strewn on the stairwell, and those that had fallen back down the steps had piled up at the floor. Trapped below when the door was locked, they all now lay unconscious.

The sweet odor of ethylene penetrated my mask. I closed the trapdoor to keep the fumes from escaping. As I stepped over the bodies on my way down the stairs, tiny hints of movement revealed they were alive: fluttering eyelids, twitching fingers, spontaneous moans and sighs. It seemed at any moment any one of them could awaken, just as Thalia had done. If the air from the slot in the door had aroused her, how long before these others would awaken now that the door had been open?

I endered the ossuary. The entire room was littered with Furies, heaped on the floor like corpses. With the collection of bones lining the walls and skulls scattered over the floor, it looked like a chamber of Hades. I tried to breathe as little as I could, but still the fumes were infecting me, making the strange even stranger. Stepping over skulls, broken glass, and sleeping, half-robed females, it felt like I was walking through the remnants of a dream.

In the center of each of the four walls, a deep oculus was carved through the thick stone and set with a large round window. I snatched a *thyrsus* from the hand of a sleeping Fury and carried it to the window that overlooked the roof. Phoebe was too far below to be seen, but Thalia was visible, crawling onto the peak. I gently broke the glass with the *thyrsus,* careful to keep the shards from falling down on Phoebe. Fresh air poured into the room. I swept the broken glass inside and leaned out through the oculus.

Phoebe stood below me with her back against the wall. A few yards away on the peak of the roof, Thalia rose to her feet. Blood covered most of her body. Through the hair that snaked down her face, her white eyes shone bright as the moon.

When I called out, Phoebe glanced up at me with a look of desperation.

"Take my hand!" I told her, reaching down as far as I could. She turned and reached up, but our fingers barely met.

Behind me, the Furies were stirring. I heard them humming faintly, their voices rising in a strange moaning rhythm.

Thalia staggered toward Phoebe, raising the ax in her hand.

I shimmied farther out while gripping the rim of the oculus. Reaching down, I grabbed ahold of Phoebe's outstretched hand. I pulled her up toward the opening. The eerie humming grew louder. Suddenly, hands took hold of my leg, and teeth clamped down on my thigh. I cried out in pain. More hands grabbed my ankles and feet. They twisted and yanked the joints.

Sparagmos!

While holding on to Phoebe, I tried to kick them back. Mad shrieks erupted.

On the roof, Thalia howled and swung her ax at Phoebe. Phoebe swerved to avoid the blade, then kicked back at Thalia. Thalia staggered and dropped to her knees. Then rose again to attack.

My legs were being wrenched apart. I hollered out in pain. Phoebe hung several feet off the roof but still had not reached the window; I couldn't let her go. Hanging helpless, she called my name. I pulled with all my strength.

Behind me the Furies released their grip. Other hands took hold of my waist and pulled me back into the room. Phoebe was hauled right up with me and grabbed the oculus rim. From there she dragged herself up the wall.

Thalia shrieked and swung her double ax. It clanged against the stone as Phoebe crawled in through the oculus.

Thwarted, Thalia wailed.

I helped Phoebe into the chamber. It was Damiana who'd saved us. She had a cloth wrapped around her face and a bloody *thyrsus* in her hand. The Furies who'd been after me lay moaning on the floor.

Air was flowing into the room. Again we heard the ax crack on stone and turned to see the blade hooked on the rim of the oculus. A a bloody hand reached up and grabbed ahold of the rim. Thalia was hauling herself up to the window.

Women continued awakening around us. Humming their unearthly tune.

"Hurry!" I shouted. We fled through the rising Furies and down into the stairwell.

The fumes were even stronger there, and the steps were covered with bodies. We scrambled over them, stumbling down in the darkness, Phoebe limping painfully. She was trying to breathe through her sleeve, but the gas was clearly affecting her, and to keep from falling she clung to me. Damiana led the way, probing the dark with her *thyrsus.* We heard the pursuing Furies' voices echo down the stairwell behind us.

There were still more bodies at the bottom of the tower. We scuttled over them as we left the stairs. Women lay sprawled on the floor of the narthex and down the vast aisles of the nave. All of them appeared to be awakening. The weird moaning infected them, an eerie, rising chorus.

Across the colonnaded narthex, the entry doors were open. The three of us went charging toward them.

Phoebe stumbled and fell to the floor. The fumes had overwhelmed her. I called to Damiana, and we helped her to her feet.

Furies were slowly rising around us. Their hum resounding louder.

Damiana glanced back at the tower. "*Run!*" she cried.

Thalia had emerged from the stairwell, followed by an army of ghosts. The shrieking women were streaming toward us across the marble floor. Thalia raised her ax. Their cries rose into the dome.

We dragged limping Phoebe past the columns of the narthex toward the open entry doors. Furies rising from the floor reached out to claw and grab us. I tried to kick them away. Damiana let loose with her stick. We battled our way through the forest of pillars until finally we reached the doors.

As we passed over the threshold, I glanced back at Thalia. She saw me and flung her double ax through the air. It soared across the narthex, tumbling like a tomahawk. As it came down at me, it glanced off a pillar, igniting a spark off the stone.

Flash!

A thunderous explosion blew me out the door. The ax came flying out with me. Windows shattered, doors blew out. I crawled away in terror. Phoebe and Damiana stumbled off ahead of me. The ground beneath us trembled. I turned to look as the growing blast rumbled its way up the tower, bursting out the oculi and exploding the belfry dome. Glass and debris rained down from the sky. The great bronze bell came tumbling through the collapsing tower and smashed through the roof of the narthex. It landed inside with a hideous clang, a sound like a human scream.

Then everything grew strangely quiet. Great, billowing plumes of smoke rose up out of the church.

Furies staggered out, gasping.

I dragged myself up and stood there, trying to catch my breath. Phoebe and Damiana were waiting behind me, hiding at the edge of the square. I picked the double ax up off the ground and looked at its glistening blades. The corner of an edge had broken off, but otherwise it was perfect. The ax was ancient, expertly made, and had a kind of magic about it.

According to Phoebe, the *labrys* was used in spiritual ceremonies by Minoan priestesses on ancient Crete. Clearly, it could be used for other things, too. Murder. Dismemberment. Revenge. This storied blade had even brought down a church.

Dual blade, dual purpose. Everything always came down to a choice.

I carried it away and ran off with my friends.

28

People were stepping out of their doors as the three of us fled to the harbor. Shaken from sleep, they emerged half-dressed in their nightshirts or pulling on their robes, padding dumbly out onto the street and gaping up at the sky. They stared in confusion at the plume of glowing smoke, wondering if they had actually awakened or were still in the grip of a dream.

These were the "ordinary" citizens of Ogygia, merchants and hoteliers, cooks and fishermen. They had lived their normal lives like any normal person, struggling to earn an honest living and trying to get along. But these seemingly innocent burghers had carried a terrible burden, a grievance buried inside them, like the shard of a broken blade.

An eye for an eye. Blood for blood. The law of retribution. There are painful memories that never seem to die, grave sins that can never be forgiven. They give birth to a mindless, fanatical rage. They spawn the untamable Furies.

The glow these Ogygians stared at now was the dawn of a realization—that their dark dreams and wishes could no longer be concealed. They watched us hurriedly limping past, torn, bloodied, tired, wondering why their avenging daughters had failed to seal our fate. Soon enough their shock, we knew, would turn to indignation. They'd come after us in an angry mob, another horde of Furies. If the tippling Sheriff ever made it down the mountain, he surely wouldn't bother to stop them. Even Damiana would be a victim of their rage.

This fear spurned us on toward the harbor and sent us racing out to the yacht. We found Dan waiting at the foot of the dock. He was greatly relieved to see us. "When I heard the explosion," he said, "I couldn't help thinking the worst."

I told him he'd better get us out of there fast.

From the dock, the glow over the square shone brightly. Black smoke drifted past the face of the moon.

Dan already had the engines idling and had pulled up most of the ropes. The girls followed him up to the pilothouse, while I cut the last two lines with my ax. In less than a minute we were pulling away from the dock and heading out into the bay.

I joined them all in the pilothouse.

"We've got to stop that bleeding," Phoebe said. I'd thrown away my blood-soaked shirt; the cut on my shoulder was open, and blood had run down my back. The ethylene had cleared from my system, but the loss of blood was making me faint.

Phoebe started wrapping me with a bandage from her pack. "My turn to take care of you," she whispered.

Dan stood at the wheel, busily steering the massive yacht and working the throttles on the console. Although he looked a little boggled by the complexity of it all, he seemed to be handling it okay. At least he got us heading in the right direction.

He glanced at the ax I had set against the wall. "Souvenir?" he asked.

I nodded, musing on the "double" thoughts I'd had outside the church. "That is my intention," I said.

Damiana stood behind us, staring back at the island. "There they are," she said.

Just as we'd expected, the citizens of Ogygia had begun spilling out of the streets, and were now self-righteously marching up the wharf. They didn't look happy to see the yacht speeding off, and several men ran out onto the dock. We watching them shout curses at us. Then they started piling into the police boat.

"They're going to try to come after us!" Phoebe said.

"Not to worry," Dan assured her, pushing up the throttle. "This yacht can outrun any boat in that harbor. And besides . . ." He emptied his pants pocket onto the console. Among the various items were three blackened spark plugs. "They'll have a little trouble getting that cop cruiser started."

Phoebe stepped over to stare at the plugs, then gave Dan a peck on the cheek. "You really *are* brilliant," she said.

He gave her a kiss in return. "Inspired by my Muse," he said.

The yacht was now out of the bay and cruising swiftly over open water. The pale, pinkish light of dawn appeared on the horizon.

"Where are we going?" Damiana asked.

An air of gloom hung about her. She clearly was heartbroken by all that had occurred, but I noticed what I thought might be a glint of hope in her eyes.

"I don't know," Dan said, trying to cheer her up. "But you can't go too far in the Cyclades without running into another island."

She nodded, then turned away to once again stare out the window.

Phoebe went to her side. "Try not to worry," I heard her say. "I'm sure your family will be all right. We'll take you back to them as soon as we can."

In the pile of coins, euros, and spark plugs removed from Dan's pocket, I now recognized something else: a small, carved, painted wooden bird, set within a round brass ring. It was another toy version of the wryneck birds we'd seen hanging in the monastery chapel.

I picked it up. "Where did you get this?" I asked.

Dan glanced over, and when he saw what I was holding, quickly looked away. I noticed his Adam's apple nervously bob.

"Dan?"

He looked at me a moment. Again he looked away. "I found it," he said. "On the street."

"When?"

"When I was out looking for you and Phoebe. Before I came back to the church."

I remembered the fear I'd seen in his face. He'd been so paranoid, he'd attacked me. Never had I seen him look so stricken.

I moved closer, studying his face. "What the hell happened out there?"

Again he swallowed. He glanced furtively at Phoebe and Damiana. "It's too horrible," he said.

"Tell us," I said.

Phoebe stood beside me. "Dan? What happened?"

He stared ahead out the black window. He couldn't seem to keep the memory away; you could see it tugging at his face. Finally he began to tell us.

"On a street . . . near the square. The Furies, there was . . . a mob of them. Thirty, maybe. Fifty. They were attacking someone. There was . . . a lot of blood. Everywhere. I heard screams. Horrible screams." He looked at us. "They were tearing him apart."

"*Sparagmos,*" Phoebe said solemnly.

"Who was it?" I asked. "Could you see?"

He stared ahead, a blank look on his face. "Yes," he said. "I saw. I tried to stop them. I tried to fight them back but . . . there were too many."

No wonder he looked such a bloody mess. How could he have possibly survived?

"What happened?" I asked.

He hesitated. "I . . . I ran away," he said. He couldn't bring himself to look at us.

Phoebe reached out tenderly. "Dan, they would have killed you. You didn't have any choice."

He looked at her. Unbearable pain and guilt in his eyes. "He was just a boy," he said. "He was just a little boy."

We stared at him in horror.

Damiana pushed between us, peering anxiously into his eyes. Then she turned to me. She looked down at my hand.

A cold dread came over me. I opened my palm and revealed the painted bird.

Damiana, tentatively, reached out and took it. Then she slowly turned to Dan. I saw her body trembling. She could hardly bring herself to speak. She held the bird out to him. "Where? Where did you find this?" she asked.

Dan looked frightened by the terror in her eyes. "On the street" he said. "After they left, I went back and"—he hesitated, remembering the bloody scene—"that was all I found—"

Damiana turned away. Her head rolled gently and her eyes glazed over. I jumped forward as she fainted and caught her in my arms.

"Over there," I said. Phoebe helped me carry her over to the bench, and we gently laid her down. Dan pulled the throttle and slowed the boat to a crawl. I grabbed an orange life vest off a hook on the wall and placed it under Damiana's ankles. Phoebe fanned the girl's face with her hand.

Dan stood over us, looking confused.

"I saw her buy that bird," I said. "In the outdoor market the morning I got here." I looked up at Dan. "She gave it as a gift to her little brother."

Dan shook his head in disbelief. "No."

"The boy must have been on his way to the church to find her," Phoebe said.

"Yes," I said. "And he was the brother of the Fury who betrayed them."

For a moment we stood silent, waiting for Damiana to awaken. Fearing it, too.

"Another tragedy."

We turned. The voice had come from behind us. A dark figure stepped from the doorway into the light.

The Sheriff.

The three of us stared at him, stunned. He had a bloody bandage around his neck.

"We Greeks are accustom to tragedy," he said.

Andreas Vassilos looked bone-tired and drunk. The impression came primarily from the bottle in his hand, and the way he held it, dangling at his side. But he also looked even more slovenly than usual. He had taken off his shoes and unbuckled his belt, and the dusty cuffs of his pants were dragging on the floor. His uniform shirt was unbuttoned and untucked, revealing a sweat-stained T-shirt, and several loops of fine gold chain dangling from his neck. The cop hat was gone, and his gray hair, curled from drying perspiration, flowed to his shoulders in soft, wavy, almost feminine locks. His clothes gave off the spicy odor of clove cigarettes, and the booze on his breath was so sharp I thought it might awaken Damiana.

He shuffled toward us in his socks, and he spoke in a weary voice. "Tender girl . . . new to grief. A bit of wine, perhaps. Medicine for misery. Dull the pain, ease the burden. Put a little sting of madness in her."

We eyed him warily. With the wrinkled tail of his shirt hanging out, I couldn't tell if he was wearing his gun.

He paused and raised his wine bottle, wagging his finger at us. "I am not a man who goes to drinking by himself. No, comrades. I prefer the company—the companionship—of women. But the mountain makes me thirsty. Someone took my car. I have to walk . . . many miles . . . before I find another."

He gestured toward the floor above. "This bar of yours. A thing like this should not be wasted. Long time I am waiting . . ."

The three of us backed away as he padded over and stood before the unconscious Damiana.

"Poor heart." He gazed on her despondently. "I taught your feet my dances. Why did you not share them?"

We were all too aware of his unabashed mendacity, but the regret in his voice sounded genuine. He lifted his gaze to the window behind her and pondered the island's fiery glow. "You are not the only one who suffers tonight."

He swigged at his bottle, then turned to us. His eyes wandered from Dan to me, then settled finally on Phoebe.

"I was badly treated by you. Very badly treated." He stepped closer to her, peering into her eyes. "Do you think I am just a man who wears the mask of a god?"

"I think you are a liar and a murderer," Phoebe said.

I swallowed, and glanced at Dan. The two of us looked at Phoebe.

Vassilos tugged the chafing bandage at his throat. "Then you do not know who I am."

Phoebe stood defiant. "Yeah, I do. You're a sick old drunk with delusions of—"

"Phoebe!" I said. "Easy."

I turned to Vassilos. He had noticed Phoebe's backpack laying on the bench and was peeking inside the top.

"What do you want?" I asked. "Why are you here?"

He set down his bottle and poked around inside the bag. "I fell asleep on your boat. I need for you to turn it around and please to take me back."

Dan and I exchanged a glance.

"We can't do that," I said.

Vassilos lifted out the shriveled orchid we'd taken from the monastery. He delicately laid it out on a ledge.

Dan eyed it curiously.

"I'm afraid you have no choice," he said. He was poking inside the bag again.

I furtively searched his waist with my eyes, looking for his gun. "Why?" I asked.

Now he pulled out the plastic bottle containing the purple *kykeon*. He held it up to the light. "Because you have seen things—things not meant to be seen."

Dan hadn't known about the *kykeon* sample; as Vassilos gently unscrewed the cap, he gaped at the precious elixir.

"We can't go back," I said. "They'll kill us if we do."

Vassilos took a whiff of the *kykeon*'s bouquet. "Yes. Is true. Our Mysteries will not tolerate those who cannot believe."

He turned the bottle to spill out the contents.

"No!" Dan shouted. "Please—"

Vassilos paused. "But you *must* make a libation," he said. "The god has been offended." He began to pour the *kykeon* out.

"No!" Dan leapt forward, grasping the bottle. The two of them struggled with it. I started toward them. Vassilos grabbed his wine bottle and clobbered Dan on the head.

Dan fell back, staggering.

Phoebe and I took hold of him. He was gripping the precious bottle of *kykeon* upright in his hands.

"So be it," Vassilos said angrily. "There are things more precious to be offered." He reached beneath his shirttail and drew out his gun.

The three of us backed off. The critical question had finally been answered.

I glanced at the wall behind him. The ax lay propped by the bench.

Vassilos continued: "When Agamemnon set sail for Troy with his armies, the gods stopped the winds and his ships were stalled. When he asked the Oracle how to appease them, he was told he must sacrifice his daughter. This he did, and the winds returned. The fleet sailed on into history."

Vassilos raised his gun, aiming it straight at Phoebe. "Let us see if your sacrifice will help to change our course."

"Wait!" Dan shouted, stepping in front of her. "Please. Wait. I'll take you—"

"He's going to kill us all anyway," Phoebe said. She glared at the Sheriff with loathing.

Behind Vassilos, Damiana was awakening.

Dan noticed it, too, and immediately tried to stall. "Killing us won't end anything," he said. "Tell them what happened to Agamemnon."

Vassilos scoffed. "In America, Homer is cartoon."

Behind him, Damiana quietly sat up. She saw him holding his gun on Phoebe.

"I'm not talking about the *Iliad,*" Dan said. "I'm talking about *after* the fall of Troy. When your victorious Greek heroes made their long journey home."

Damiana's gaze drifted toward the ax.

"You are speaking of the *Odyssey,*" Vassilos said.

"No," Dan said. "I'm talking about Agamemnon. Remember how he was welcomed home?"

"Of course," he said. "His wife, Clytemnestra, murdered him."

"In revenge for his killing their daughter," Dan said.

"Yes."

Silently, Damiana rose to her feet.

Dan continued trying to keep the drunken cop distracted. "Then their son, Orestes, avenged his father by murdering his mother."

"Yes," he said. "He had no choice. This was his duty as a son."

Damiana reached toward the wall for the ax.

"And for killing his mother," Dan said, "Orestes was hounded and attacked by the Furies."

Dan and I started toward him. Vassilos swiveled the gun from Phoebe to us. We froze.

Damiana rose up behind him.

Vassilos lifted his gun to our faces. "Is like I told you," he said. "Greeks are accustom to trag—"

The double ax flashed. Dan and I dove to the floor. The gun fired—shattering a window.

I looked up. Vassilos stood stunned. He turned to Damiana. The ax was buried in his back.

Damiana stared at him, in shock at what she'd done. The Sheriff raised his gun to her.

Phoebe screamed, "*No!*"

I leapt at his arm as he fired off a shot—knocking the gun from his hand. The pistol skidded across the floor, and I went scrambling after it. I quickly grabbed it and turned, aiming the gun at the Sheriff.

Vassilos, staggering, fell against the console, the ax still sticking out from his back.

Damiana stood perfectly still. She reached up curiously and touched a spot of blood on her chest. The spot dilated like a blooming rose. She raised her gaze to us.

Phoebe cried out and ran to her as Damiana collapsed.

I held the gun on Vassilos. His back was soaked in blood. He looked at me, grimacing, and shoved himself up off the console. Straightening precariously, he staggered toward the door.

I kept the gun trained on him. As he went out, I followed.

Dan came out after me. We walked behind him as he lurched along, stumbling his way toward the stern. The ax stuck out from his back like a limb. He struggled and strained to grab it. His socks smeared the deck with blood. His lungs sucked in air.

At the stern he paused, breathing heavily. Clutching the rail to steady himself, he gazed out over the sea. In the distance the glow from the island was fading, the fire burning out.

Dan and I stood there watching Vassilos, watching the blood run down his back, waiting for him to die.

He turned, floundering, to face us. His mouth was filling with blood, and he sputtered as he spoke.

"I am a god . . . disguised as a man."

I looked at him, then glanced at Dan. Finally, I lowered my pistol.

"Then you're a god who's dead," I said.

He turned his faltering gaze to me. The words he spoke brought a shudder." "*You do not know what life is. You do not know who you are.*"

He tumbled back—and vanished. Dan and I rushed to the rail.

Below, there was nothing but the inky sea. We had not even heard the splash.

We turned as Phoebe approached behind us.

"Damiana is dead," she declared.

29

When the great Greek playwright Aeschylus wrote the revenge trilogy of Orestes—father kills daughter, mother kills father, son kills mother—he managed to end the lugubrious tale on a surprisingly positive note. After killing Clytemnestra, Orestes is pursued by the Furies to Athens, where the goddess Athena takes pity on him, declaring that his fate should be decided in a trial. His defender in court is the god Apollo, his prosecutor the Chorus of Furies. When the ten-member jury ends in a split, Athena herself casts the deciding vote, and Orestes is spared. Compassion and the rule of law replace the barbarous tyranny of blood-for-blood. Athena persuades the Furies to tame their vengeful ways. They are transformed into the Eumenides, "the Kindly Ones," and are given a temple at the base of the Acropolis where they're worshipped as loving protectors of the Athenians.

The Furies in our tragedy, I regret to report, came to a far more grievous end. When the tower of the church collapsed, Thalia and twelve other women lost their lives. Twenty-three more suffered serious burns. Forty were hospitalized for smoke inhalation, and many more were injured or traumatized.

Considering the extent of damage to the church, it's a wonder there weren't more casualties. Most of the terra-cotta roof had collapsed, taking with it two of the narthex domes. The walls were badly charred and the famous frescoes ruined, but the majority of mosaics unaccountably survived, along with the principal dome, a fact proclaimed by the Orthodox bishop as nothing short of a miracle.

The three of us had landed on the island of Naxos, where we immediately turned Damiana's body over to the local police. Our wounds were attended to and interrogations performed. The police subsequently invaded Ogygia. Investigators at the monastery discovered a *kykeon* "distillery," and the following day we led them up to have a look at the bones in the cave. Working in concert with the Turkish police, they began an investigation of missing Turkish travelers and uncovered applicable records that went back at least forty years. Forensic specialists were called in and DNA testing began. Finally, the Hellenic Coast Guard started a search for the Sheriff's corpse.

When word got out, the press descended like another horde of Furies. They pursued the three of us everywhere we went and swooped down on the island of Ogygia. On the morning we emerged from a legal deposition at a courthouse back in Athens, the crush of the reporters' feeding frenzy felt like a media *sparagmos.*

The story blazed across Greece and Turkey, and then went totally global. My mother first saw it as a line on the Drudge Report: "*American archeologists in Greece uncover deadly ancient sex cult.*" From this minor misstatement, it grew into a kind of media myth, eventually devolving into a tabloid staple known as the "Night of the Furies."

The Greeks seemed to take the whole thing with a shrug, but the people of Turkey were appalled. The two countries had always had a knife at each other's throats, and now, with a couple of Americans involved, the Turks went into a frenzy. Conspiracy theories filled every fez. The CIA was to blame. The female secretary of state was a Fury. In the streets of Istanbul, enraged mobs burned effigies of the bewildered American president.

We watched it one night on the TV news in a bar near the Plaka in Athens. I couldn't understand the Greek reporter's words, but the faces and the crowds looked familiar. There was something Dionysian in their mad display of rage. Mouths drawn, fists clenched, shouting chants in unison, they seemed to lose themselves in their fury, merging in a mindless hysteria. It appeared as if they all had been invaded by the god.

Maybe Dionysus wasn't dead after all. Despite a search that lasted weeks, the Coast Guard never found the body of Andreas Vassilos. Rumors arose of various sightings. Dan actually wondered if the guy was immortal, but Phoebe insisted the clown had simply drowned. I liked to think he'd been devoured by sharks in a frenzy of pelagic *omophagia.*

A Greek genealogist traced the Vassilos name back to the seventeenth century, but no one could prove a relation to the ancient and esteemed Eumolpidae. A search of his house on Ogygia, however, did uncover this: a sixth-century BC black-figure amphora, in astoundingly good condition, picturing a scene from Eleusis. Demeter holds stalks of grain while, beside her, Persephone pours a libation into the proffered cup of a young, beardless man. The ancient amphora—easily worth millions—went far beyond the pay grade of a lowly island cop. Most assumed it was a family heirloom passed down through generations.

As for the mysterious elixir, it turned out that the "sacred objects" had a sacred purpose. Dan figured out that the ashes from the bone fires provided potassium carbonate, a key ingredient of the *kykeon.* At this point he had absolutely everything he needed to finally write his dissertation. But with court dates and legalities and all the media attention, he found it impossible to work. The news had brought a flood of requests from pharmaceutical companies that hounded him with offers to develop the secret formula. Scores of potheads descended on Athens, seeking out the famous elixir and its legendary discoverer. Even the Greek government got into the act, and Dan's graduate school became mired in a controversy: should an individual or academic institution have proprietary control of a religious sacrament? Shouldn't the key ingredient of the Eleusinian Mysteries be the birthright of every living Greek?

In the midst of this perfect Dionysian storm of reporters, TV crews, cops, lawyers, executives, druggies, politicians, and protestors, Dan asked Phoebe to marry him. It came as something of a shock to her, particularly given the timing. Phoebe told me about the proposal a few days after he'd asked.

"What did you tell him?"

"I haven't made up my mind," she said.

I thought I knew what was holding her back. "If you need some space to think about it," I said, "you could come stay with me in Rome." I had to get back to renew my lease.

"Sure," she said with a wry grin. "And what would I tell Dan?"

"You don't have to tell him anything. You're free to do as you like."

"He loves me, Jack."

"I know," I said. "But that's no longer the question."

We looked at each other in silence.

Two more days passed. Dan continued pressing her, but Phoebe couldn't decide. When it finally came time for me to head to Rome, Dan had a sudden inspiration.

"Dodona!" he said. "The Oracle of Zeus!"

Phoebe and I exchanged wary glances.

"I'll rent a car, and we'll drive you to Igoumenitsa," he said. "You can take the ferry to Brindisi from there, then a train on to Rome." He turned to Phoebe. "On the drive up we can stop at the ruins of Dodona. Who better than Zeus to help you decide?"

"Another oracle?" Phoebe whined.

"The oldest in Greece," he said. "Older even than Delphi."

"Don't tell me we have to use the gas again,' I said.

"No," he said. "All you need to do up there is listen to the wind."

In a tiny, four-cylinder Opel, we drove with some considerable strain across the magnificent crest of the Pindus range in the northwest corner of Greece. It was the same mountain route, according to Dan, the ancient Romans had journeyed across to reach Byzantium—modern-day Istanbul. In the opposite direction, a short hop across the Adriatic, it linked up with the Appian Way, the ancient road to Rome. Caesar's legions had marched this route to battle the forces of Pompey. Centuries later, Crusader columns snaked across it to take back the Holy Land. Now two American brothers and a pretty Dutch blonde were sputtering their way up the mountain road, with only the poor girl's heart to be conquered.

In the old days, a trip to consult the Oracle of Zeus was a long and arduous journey. Over the course of that journey, pilgrims would have a good deal of time to mull over their problem or dilemma, so that by the time they arrived and put their question to the god, they'd have worked it over, consciously and unconsciously, and be primed to hear the answer that they really *needed* to hear. In a way, deep down, they would already know the answer.

I thought about this with Phoebe. She'd grown quiet in the last few hours of the drive, staring out the window at the passing scenery. We were all exhausted from the punishing pressures of the past several weeks, but I couldn't help wondering if her silence reflected some final decision about Dan.

We arrived near the end of the day at the ancient site of Dodona. It lay over a ridge in a broad, green valley, surrounded by spectacular mountains. We parked the car and stretched our legs. A breeze was blowing; the air was cool and fresh. Rugged blue peaks reached up into the clouds. The sun was setting behind them.

"It's beautiful," Phoebe said. The serenity of the place seemed to please her.

We paid the entry fee at the gate, and Phoebe used the bathroom.

On the way back she consulted with the park official, an older woman with a badge on her blouse.

"Closes in an hour," she said as she rejoined us. "Last bus leaves in twenty-five minutes, so most of the tourists should be gone."

"Perfect," Dan said.

We followed him into the ruins. The main feature was a large and impressive ancient theatre carved into the side of a hill. Tourists were having their pictures taken while their children checked out the acoustics. We continued down a path along a flat, grassy plain littered with gray foundation stones. Dan led us past a complex series of low walls and stacked blocks to what he said was the ancient Temple of Zeus.

Inside the square outline of stone stood a large, solitary oak tree.

"The tree," he said, "is the Oracle."

The original oak had died long ago, but the archeologists who had unearthed the site had planted this marvel in its place. The tree was tall and wide, a great spreading mass of black branches and flickering green and golden leaves. Although it wasn't ancient, it gave off the tranquil aura of age and had a kind of gravity about it.

Like the sacred crevice at Delphi, the original tree had been consecrated to a mother goddess of the earth. Zeus had taken over early on. He communicated to his inquirers through the sound of the wind in the leaves. This rustling was interpreted by priests, called *Selloi,* the devoted prophets of Zeus. When Homer spoke of "wintry Dodona," he said the *Selloi* slept on the ground and refused to wash their feet. Dan claimed they did this in order to stay in contact with the earth, from which they drew the power of prophecy.

Following this inspiration, Dan had the three of us sit on the ground and write out our individual questions. We were each handed a scrap of paper and a pencil. Only one question could be asked, he said. "So, make sure you get it right." He glanced at Phoebe as he said this.

Phoebe looked luminous in the dusky light. I tried to read her thoughts, but her face was a blank. Her eyes seemed fixed on nothing. She bowed her blond head and scribbled out her question.

I wrote down mine as well.

"Now lie back and relax," Dan said. "Close your eyes and listen. It's okay to let your mind wander, just keep coming back to the sound of the wind." Dan fiddled with his digital watch. "We'll lay out here for half an hour," he said. "I'll take care of the timing. If you drift off and fall asleep, try to remember your dreams."

"Good luck," he said finally, and with that he lay back and closed his eyes.

Just before I did the same, I looked again at Phoebe. She was heart-stoppingly beautiful. I longed to tell her so. Yet she seemed completely lost in herself, much like she had been at Delphi. I could see no trace of her thoughts on her face.

Gently, she lay back on the grass.

There are no observers, only participants. I leaned back and closed my eyes.

LOSE YOUR skepticism. Suspend your disbelief.

Whose voice is that? Mine? It sounds a lot like Dan's. One thing I'm fairly certain of—it's not the voice of Zeus.

Why do I find this so hard to do? Why do I resist it?

Blame it on the ancient Greeks. It was they who invented logic and prized the power of reason. They doubted, questioned everything. The original skeptic was Socrates, and we are all his heirs.

Why then Dionysus? Where did he *come from?*

If the Greeks invented reason, they must first have discovered unreason: the instinctive, the impulsive, the emotional, the chaotic. When they tried to repress this part of themselves, it came back as a god to bite them

Listen to the wind. Just listen.

It sounds like the scales of a slithering snake. It sounds like surf on sand. It sounds like rain; it sounds like fire; it sounds like shattering glass.

Do you hear any voices?

No. I should have gone to the bathroom when Phoebe did, damn it.

Listen. Harder.

It sounds like the whisper of a girl. Or the crushing of grapes in her hand. Or the blowing of a thousand kisses.

Aphrodite leads the way to Dionysus.

You can say that again.

Aphrodite—

Okay. Shut up. Listen. What was the question again?

Is Phoebe my true love?

I think so. But how do I know? Because a voice inside me says so?

Just listen.

The wind sounds like the leaves. *The leaves sound like the wind.*

The whisper of the tree reminds me of a story. A story Phoebe told me. How the laurel became the tree of Apollo.

Apollo was the greatest archer, the god of the silver bow. When he saw Eros struggling to string his little bow, Apollo made fun of him, and Eros took revenge. The cherub pulled out two arrows from his quiver: one that kindles love and one that dispels it. The one that kindles was sharp and glistening, with a gold point; the one that dispels was blunt and heavy, with a lead tip. From the top of Mount Parnassus, Eros shot Apollo through the heart with the gold point. The leaden one he shot at a nymph named Daphne, the beautiful daughter of a river god.

Apollo fell immediately in love with Daphne, but Daphne spurned him and fled. He chased her through the woods. She ran like the wind. The further he pursued her, the more he fell in love, but Daphne grew more fearful the closer he came. As Apollo was about to overtake her, she cried out to her father for help, and the river god used his magic. A numbness seized Daphne's limbs, bark closed over her body, her hair turned into leaves, her arms into branches, her feet into penetrating roots.

She had turned into a laurel tree. Only her beauty was left.

Why did Phoebe tell me this story? Why has it come to me now?

Leaves. Wind. Matter in motion. *If you're in there somewhere, talk to me.*

Over in the theatre a boy shouts, "I'm coming!" A bus in the parking lot hisses. Far away, a hawk shrieks. It sounds like the cry of a Fury.

Who knows why people do what they do, why they love who they love?

Aphrodite? Serotonin? DNA? Fate?

Listen to the wind. *The leaves.* The wind.

I *listen.* The fluttering leaves swirl through my head, sweeping away all thought. I lose myself in a reverie, a windy, airy nothingness. Finally, the wind itself fades away, and I'm left in a tenuous silence.

Then . . . a presence, a shadow, a specter, as if someone is looking down on me.

I resist opening my eyes. I wait to hear a voice.

I wait. *I listen.* I wait.

She whispers, "*Eleutheria.*"

I open my eyes. No one is there. Only the branches and the leaves of the tree, perfectly still in the twilight.

Beep—beep—beep—beep—beep—beep

I WOKE up suddenly. I'd fallen asleep. Dan's wristwatch alarm was beeping. The wind was blowing hard, the massive tree tossing violently.

Dan finally shut off his alarm. He glanced around groggily. "Where's Phoebe?"

We stood up and scanned the ruins, squinting into the wind. Leaves skittered over the graveyard of stones. Phoebe was nowhere to be seen.

"Where did she go?" Dan asked.

"I don't know," I said.

We walked back over the ruins and up the path to the theatre. Wind howled through the empty shell. The tourists had all departed.

Back at the office, we asked the woman official to please check out the ladies' room. She said it was already locked; the park was closed. We asked her if she'd seen the girl, the blonde with whom we'd arrived.

The woman shrugged, shook her head.

"Are you sure?" Dan asked. He gave her a quick description. "She was here with us an hour ago. She spoke to you, remember?"

Again the woman shrugged. "No see her," she said.

I scanned the lot. The wind was whirling a cloud of dust. "Where are the buses?" I asked.

"Gone," she said.

We walked out into the parking lot. Our car was the last one left. Dan found Phoebe's scrap of paper flapping under the windshield wiper.

He read her scribbled question out loud: *"What do I want?"* He turned the paper over and read the answer. Frowning, he showed it to me.

Phoebe had written a single word:

"Eleutheria."

I looked at Dan in amazement. "What does it mean?" I asked.

"Freedom."

As he climbed crestfallen into the car, he tossed the paper to the wind.

I went chasing after it.